# ATTUNED FUTURE

## THE METIER APOCALYPSE
## BOOK 3

## FRANK G. ALBELO

MOUNTAINDALE
PRESS

# ACKNOWLEDGMENTS

I want to thank everyone who's made it this far into the story with me. Your presence here is what is letting me continue to live the dream of getting the tales living in my head out into the world. Thank *you*.

And, I hope all of you have a wonderful time delving deeper into the world of Metier!

# PROLOGUE

"How can they keep us here?" Marcus yelled, doing his best to reel in his voice as he realized his mother was but two feet from him. Instead, he slammed his heel into the door detaining the two remaining Metiers. The impact reverberated off the concrete walls. Marcus gripped his head, fingers digging into his skull as he took deep breaths. Ingrid watched him as tears silently fell from her face.

"It's going to be okay, Marcus. Your father wouldn't have done this if he had any other choice," she eked out.

"After all you two have sacrificed, the least those government D-bags could have done is saved him a spot! But noooo!" Marcus pantomimed with his hands and marched to an uneven beat. "They just had to get their little military men all lined up in a row!"

"That's enough!" Ingrid's voice cut through Marcus' tirade like a knife. The man was reeling, tears streaming from his own face as he looked at his mother, wounded. "Those people you are talking about had lives before the crystals fell. They probably lost just as much if not more. You cannot think one life is more valuable than another."

Ingrid was still crying, but her expression hardened. It hardened more than the cancer, more than the sky falling, had ever hardened it. The person who'd pulled her through both of those things was gone, and it was up to her to make it count. She embraced Marcus, holding him as he sobbed and cooled his anger. Unfortunately, she knew it only lay simmering. She just hoped it would be cold enough for them to make it through any other engagements with General Starden.

— + —

Elias led the two Metiers down to the bottom floor of the Bunker. They passed the greenhouse floor, which looked more like the *dirt* house floor to Marcus, and the medical level. The water treatment plant and the primary generator sputtered in the center of the room. A man with jet black hair and a strained smile worked the console, reading out pressures and filtration rates while a woman attempted to rein him in. Marcus did a double take as the brunette looked over her shoulder to the approaching trio.

"Ah! Mr. Elias. Please, I'm trying to get my brother to take a break but he appears to have duct taped himself to this machine!" the woman said gently, while still nudging her brother.

"Clara, you don't get it. The tape is for those pipes over there!" He gestured to one of the test drip pipes that was doing a *little* more than just dripping. "They turned this damn thing on without even checking the welds!"

"As you can see, we are having some issues. Mr. Elias, unfortunately I wouldn't recommend utilizing the kitchen or even seventy percent of the restrooms. The top floor has already been providing a greater volume than we anticipated," Clara said.

"I understand. Please, no need to be so formal. This is Ingrid and Marcus. Ingrid, Marcus, these two siblings are Dale and Clara Terrigan. I am hoping you all will get us sorted out here," Elias said, barely keeping the frown from his face. The man was practically glaring at the machinery.

"I will look at the field around the generator. The radiation might be stronger than predicted against the electromagnetic shielding," Ingrid said after shaking Clara's hand. Dale was thoroughly covered in gunk, shooting a meek smile her way instead.

"I know a thing or two about duct tape," Marcus added awkwardly.

"Snag a roll!" Dale said, already turned back to the control panel. Clara tossed Marcus some tape and he couldn't keep the corners of his mouth from twitching up slightly. It was the first hint of a smile that had crossed the man's face since he'd woken up in the Bunker over a week ago.

— + —

"Absolutely not." Ingrid crossed her arms. The scowl she kept out of her expression in front of Marcus returned in full force.

"We understand that you have an…apprentice of sorts. A protégé, if you will. It would be such a shame if something were to happen to him," Starden said evenly.

Ingrid Metier snorted, then full on laughed as Starden's face soured. The privates at the door looked between each other, shifting uncomfortably. Eventually the woman was able to get herself together. She ran her hand across the short hairs on her head, feeling the prickly sensation and remembering Raphael. Her expression darkened as she looked at Starden.

"I will work on the power issues for when we return to the surface, but my 'protégé' will continue to work on human adaptation to the growing radiation. Elias and that Ava woman have been working hard to pull him out of his shell, and I won't have you messing that up." Without further preamble, Ingrid stood and walked past the privates. Before shutting the door behind her, she peeked her head through the door.

"I'm glad you understand that threatening Marcus will only cause you problems. However, if you threaten someone I love again, the Fall will be the last thing on your mind." The door shut with a quiet click.

Starden let out a breath he and the privates didn't realize they were holding. "Monsters, all of them..." he mumbled under his breath. The privates could only silently agree as they remembered Ingrid's face.

# CHAPTER ONE

## The Weight of Corruption

The light of morning glinted through the newly uncovered windows. I blinked the swimmers out of my eyes as I spotted the drool staining the report I had been reading through. My mind started to boot up. The few blissful seconds of confusion didn't last long as the fight to rescue the trainees flashed to the very front of my mind. Pain, uncertainty, fear. All the emotions muddled my mind until I firmed my grip on my thoughts.

With a deep breath, I focused on my surroundings, taking in the details of the office around me. It was still bleak, but most of the strange experimental paraphernalia had been moved to another storage area. Samuel was slumped in a beat up couch, similarly half-asleep. At the very center of the room, bound by chains and plates of thick metal was the corrupted Metier Crystal. The Dreg Entity.

>Earth fleshbag is conscious.<

"That thing is the worst alarm clock!" Sam complained, turning over and pulling a blanket to block out the sun.

>Life fleshbag is weak. Should harden body if they seek to survive.<

"We've been over this. If you aren't going to say anything

useful, we don't want to hear it," I said, cracking my neck and back as I worked out the kinks of falling asleep at a desk.

>Fleshbag has all the information he needs. He merely lacks the conviction to force his will upon others.<

"That's it. Night-night, Charcoal." Samuel's hand rose out of the blankets. A spell chain formed around the metal, surging with life mana as the bush hidden by the metal surged with vital energy. The crystal squealed, a high-pitched whine that set me grinding my teeth. Just as quickly as it had started, the sound quieted. The malevolent purple glow from within the crystal dimmed.

"Man, I'm glad you and the healers figured that out. I was ready to pull my hair out if I had to listen to that pessimistic, conniving piece of rock," I said, rubbing the last of the sleep from my eyes.

"Yeah, we've gotten our fair share of practice. Unfortunately…" Sam drifted off. Snoozing answered after a few minutes of silence.

"Sleep in, big guy," I said, adjusting the blanket over Samuel as I headed toward the living area on the other side of the floor.

A makeshift fire stove had been installed against the wall, a hole punched straight through the building giving the exhaust a way out. I could see some of the previous owner's clothes and knick-knacks still scattered around the room, but I pushed past them to the tray set out on the counter. Roasted tomatoes with some cut slices of mystery meat. "Thanks, Danny."

My whispered thanks went unheard, the woman already out on her rounds. I split the meal in half, leaving the rest for Samuel when he woke up. I gulped down some water and walked up to the armor stands against the staircase. One set of armor, one empty stand, and a final one where a tactical vest and an H-shaped shield hung stood watch over the stairs. With practiced, mechanical movements, I donned my vest, adjusting the rip tape and pulling it snug. I pulled the side strap on my backpack, attaching my shield like a turtle shell and slid the infused pickaxe under it.

*I really need to work on some better gear.* Plans floated through my head as I went down the stairs, past the practice dojo of the Wild Guard and out onto the training fields. One tall figure already stood in front of a bunch of trainees. With my increased Perception, I could hear the words carrying across the open space.

"—ppen again? We all need to pull our weight through difficult times. The Guard needs its trainees now, more than ever. I will be instituting some changes to the squads to accommodate for missing members." The voice paused for a moment, looking over her shoulder to see me approaching before continuing. "In addition, I will be initiating an infusion course. This will be a mix of free time and research that I hope you all can assist with. More to follow at the evening meal. Now, break and start on your laps. I want even the slowest Geo doing laps on the Flappers. Got it?"

"Yes, ma'am!"the trainees called back, the strength of their voices shaking the ground before they scrambled for the starting point of the track around the field. Thanks to Devon's and Daniela's instructions, the group had actually started to utilize their skills to help them increase their movement abilities in a number of ways. I watched an elf zip left and right around a downed mermaid. An orc blasted fire out of her feet to leap clear to the front of the column before overcompensating and stumbling. None of her peers jeered at her, all focused on getting faster and using their friends to practice their own skills.

"Should have done this years ago," the orc woman who'd been instructing the trainees said, sighing. With all of them distracted by the laps, I was able to see the weight of responsibility she held flawlessly take its toll. The deep green bruises under her eyes, and the slight slouch in her posture that hadn't been there when I'd met her.

"You did always strike me as the drill sergeant type," I said, trying to lift the mood a bit.

"Ha! I've seen you and Daniela running them through accuracy training." The large orc shivered. "My methods are relaxing in comparison."

"You should meet Danny's mom!" We let out a chuckle, relieving some of the constant stress of the last week. The two of us lapsed into silence as we watched the trainees. Many were now starting to flag in their use of their skills. The aftereffects of their magic was taking its pound of flesh. Metaphorically speaking.

"That rock tell you anything new?" Sarah asked, still looking at the trainees.

"Nothing but annoying us. Nothing new from Kirby's notes other than being able to trace just who he was giving to the Dreg. Your father has taken it upon himself to contact any of the surviving family personally."

"I saw." Sarah sighed, breaking eye contact with the trainees and moving to a tent that had been set up on the edge of the field. A scattered array of weapons and infusions laid on a large, rough-made table. Scorch marks and deep scratches marked the whole length of it. "Sorry about the mess."

"You should have seen my workspace back home," I said, pulling over one of the nearby chairs and adjusting my gear. "Are we ready to talk about the elephant in the room?"

Sarah stiffened. I could almost hear the internal debate going on in her head, but eventually she relaxed. "The one about turning everyone into Dreg Warriors?"

"That's the one. I still need to run it by Tec—not sure if he's got the juice now that he's our acting prison. Hopefully it can, at the very least, give implants to all the Fallen old enough to fight. Gift or no Gift."

"Why still call it Gift? We know the crystals call them skills," Sarah said, deflecting the conversation.

She got one of my eyebrow raises, but she ignored it. I let out a sigh. "As far as I understand, it's still a Gift. Self-developed skills are more flexible than the ones we acquire from the Entity Clusters, at least at the start. Now can we bring it up to your father?"

"He's already brought it up himself," she said with a sigh. "As soon as you told him it was an option, he was practically begging me and the other squads to talk to the crystal for them. But I just don't…"

"Feel comfortable signing them up for a goal this danger-ous?" I finished for her.

"Something like that."

"The Entities aren't forcing anything. All they want to do is stabilize the planet, and if we want to *thrive* on the planet more than just survive, we will need their help. I don't know how the other larger cities are doing, but it sure looks like this one got the short end of the stick."

"You're right. It's just…this is the first time we've even considered pushing back against everything. The creatures, our own growth, and *others*. Clara's been arguing to support the other towns where possible for as long as she's been a squad leader. Looking back on it now, I'm fairly sure the councilman was not happy with the success she was having."

"Ex-councilman, Sarah." I added. "Kirby is a criminal. He's probably one of the biggest ones that didn't actually run a country pre-Fall. I know it's recent and I know you'll want to question every interaction you had with him, but it's not worth your time. We are making decisions for the *now* and for the *tomorrow*."

The orc woman nodded, falling back into silence. When I spotted a groggy Samuel stumble out of the training building we'd taken over, I stood and said my goodbyes to Sarah. "I'll be there for the lesson tomorrow. Were the scouts able to snag all the loot?"

"Yeah. Oliver is still working on separating everything. Dodge the center of town if you can. They were riled up this morning."

A grimace crossed my face, but I walked forward. Samuel spotted me and moved to intercept. "I thought those tomatoes were not that sour," he said lightly.

"No, they were great. The current situation? Not so much," I said.

"What do you mean?" the blond asked, rubbing his eyes to clear the last bit of sleep upon hearing my serious tone.

"There's just so much going on, and so many questions about what we might encounter that I don't know if I'm doing enough. The fight—"

"Ronan," he practically growled. "Do I need to get Daniela over here for another intervention? You are just one man. Part of the reason we joined up with the Guard and the town was because we realized that we would never get far without support."

"You are right, b—"

"But nothing. To quote our eloquent Latina companion, 'Don't be such a rock-brain.' We take care of our foundations, and then we reach out and crush all the crazy crap we can get our hands on."

*Man. If Samuel is the one hitting me with the inspirational speech, I must have been really far up my behind.* "Thanks, Sam."

"You are welcome. Now, what's the—"

A light flared from down the road, getting brighter as it streaked right towards us.

"Duck!" I yelled, calling on my mana and sprouting an <Earthen Barrier> for us to take cover behind. A spray of stone showered us and I interposed my shielded back over Samuel. Heat picked up around us as the rocks activated the kinetic-force-to-heat conversion innate to my shield. It also didn't help that the rocks looked like they were *on fire* as they impacted us.

"Sorry!" someone called out from the other side of my barrier.

When Sam and I extracted ourselves from our impromptu huddle, Daniela was jogging up. Considering the extent of her mobility, her jog looked more like one of my sprints. When she realized who it was that she'd rained fire hell on, her expression turned sour. My perception helped me catch the end of her whispered curse.

"—gonna hear the end of this."

Godfrey pulled up behind her, dirty shovel-hammer mix in hand and a guilty expression plastered on his face.

"Oy! I thought you were on patrol!" I yelled, slapping a fire down on my shoulder. Samuel slapped another I missed on my pant leg.

"I did my morning round already. Only Devon can keep up with me on that front. I thought you'd be at the meeting already." *Deflecting, huh?*

"I might have been, except the weatherman didn't say anything about percent chance of fire rock rain in the morning," I said.

"I forgot my steel umbrella back at the Bunker!" Sam complained from beside me.

"I'm so sorry. I thought I had the angle right, but Daniela's blast had too much power," Godfrey said, hanging his head.

"They are just giving me crap, Goddy, you can ignore them. If they are well enough to complain, then they are just fine." Daniela groaned. "On a more relevant note, I managed what you did, Samuel!"

"No you didn't. Tell me all about it! You'll be good for that meeting without me, right Ron?" Sam said.

The blond was already half-turned away from the center of town. He didn't even wait for my response. My best friends devolved into hushed and gibberish conversations as they discussed something they had access to: their freeform skills. I wanted to listen in, but the pair of them rushed out of sight without a care in the world. Godfrey looked at me, let out an awkward laugh, then powerwalked over to the training grounds. "Hey Sarah, you need any help!"

I rubbed the bridge of my nose, trying to relieve the headache that always seemed to linger when my friends got up to their own shenanigans. Part of me wanted to just rush after them and listen in on their breakthroughs, but I knew that I needed to keep my leadership hat on. *It's not like I have my freeform skill yet, either…*

What survived of the town of Wildwood passed me by. It wasn't actually the main portion of the city, but a community that had been bordered by several lakes and wetlands. The terrain, plus the tenacity of the residents, allowed them to survive through the changes Earth experienced as its species were attuned to mana. A few of the residents waved, a few stared at me in fear, and many simply directed curious expressions in my direction.

Something within me wanted to reach out to them, to connect, but having been born in a Bunker left me a bit apprehensive about large gatherings. Each time one of us Bunkerites tried to engage someone that wasn't a trainee or a member of the Wild Guard, a crowd gathered around. Daniela had somehow acquired a fan club, Samuel was looked at as a divine entity of healing, while I was more of an… attraction.

'The Vanguard' they called me. Pretty much everyone thought that I was some degree of crazy. Not even the more dwarfish-looking earth-attuned worked to take as much punishment as I did. It didn't help that the Wild Guard and the trainees had waxed poetic about my headlong charge into Kirby's madhouse— where we now were living—or his warehouse of horrors.

My musing was cut short as I bumped into Oliver and Rommel. The pre-Fall human and the fire-attuned orc were as contrasting as one might see outside of some of the neon-colored life-attuned fae. Both of them stood watch over the councilmen's office.

"Ronan," Oliver said simply. Rommel grunted.

"Considering you two are here, then both the councilmen are in?" It was a rhetorical question, of course, since Rommel was assigned to assist Dylan, and Oliver, Irwin.

"They've been waiting for your meeting," Oliver replied. The man opened the door, sending candles to flicker.

With a nod to each, I went into the room. The blacked-out big panel windows on the front allowed for vision out. The hulking form of Rommel took up almost all of one window.

Towards the back of the room were two desks where two men sat across from each other. A third lay empty a few feet from the entrance. Irwin, the head of the House of Commerce, and Dylan, the leader of the Council of Wildwood, sat facing each other as they rifled through numerous papers. When the door opened, both rose and rushed over to greet me.

"Please, I would have hoped we would be over these nonsense formalities by now," I said, pulling out Kirby's old chair for the head of the Council of New Earth and sitting.

Dylan could only scratch the back of his flame hair awkwardly. Both men looked ragged, the stress of the last week clearly taking its toll. The revelation that their fellow councilman had actually been trading their people to the Dreg for protection had been enough of a shock. When some of the trainees returned changed, and the secret of the Crystal's awareness was revealed, it was almost too much for them.

"Force of habit, sorry," Dylan said, slumping in his chair. Irwin responded with a weak wave, relaxing into his own chair. "Trying to fill in Kirby's old job has been tough. I don't think Irwin or I realized just how much subtle control he had over the town."

"The interior couldn't operate without the Guard or what they gathered," Irwin said, matter-of-factly.

"Understandable. I did think you were grooming Sarah for that," I said, gesturing to Dylan. The man's hair immediately dimmed, hanging down like a close-cropped haircut instead of the usual mane.

"I… think we may dissolve the council as it stands. Too many people are displeased, and neither Irwin nor I feel up to fighting the change. Kirby poisoned the well in that way. Sarah taking over…Well, if she did, I think it would be best if she did it differently."

I scratched at my growing beard as I thought over the man's words. While the Bunker provided a broad education, the intricacies of political systems wasn't something we covered. It was in part why our arrival to the town, and the way I subsequently crashed straight through the authority of the council, went less than optimally. The benefit was that it highlighted the corruption lurking around the corner.

"If I have some suggestions, I will pass them along. I would say not to change the infrastructure you have set up for now. If we agree in the main discussion of today, there will be more than enough change to go around. Some stability will do the people of Wildwood good, I think."

The two men zeroed in on my words. Some of the energy that had been weaned away by the aftermath of Kirby's betrayal returned in full force. Dylan's hair flared, falling down his shoulders and forming a fiery pair of mutton chops. Irwin was deathly silent except for the feline pupils being hidden by a second set of eyelids, revealing the predatory reptile traits he was most famous for. Had I been the true target of their energy, I might have been truly intimidated.

"Please. You know our stance. If you brought it up, then you have come to a concession," Dylan said after a few seconds, always the politician.

"Indeed. If my conversation with Tec—this town's Entity Cluster—goes well, I think that giving all of the Guard implants will be the first step. Then the trainees. Finally, the leaders of the various groups in the town, including you two, followed by the general population. While I know Tec looks like a big crystal, the energy of the crystals works differently to our own. I will push as far as it is willing to give. It would be foolish to break our current agreement for it to take Gifted prisoners and watch over the still-unconscious trainees."

Irwin's armchair creaked under the pressure he was putting on it. Deep grooves already marked where his permanent claws had done irreparable damage to the piece of furniture. "How soon?"

"That's my next stop for the day," I said. The two councilmen nodded, each moving to shake my hand. It was somewhat standing on tradition, something I wasn't a fan of, but they both met my eyes with conviction.

Irwin gripped my forearm, moving close enough that I could smell the hints of alcohol on his breath. Even as sharp as the man looked, it made sense that people had to cope with stress somehow. "You keep them safe. You give these children a *future*, and you'll have all the support these old bones can give you."

My voice caught in my throat for the first time in the conversation. "You know I can't promise that," I said quietly.

"Good. Then you are the right man to trust."

# CHAPTER TWO

## Dreg Legion

"No pressure, right? It's not like he wants me to single-handedly lead people to their potential deaths, or worse..." I mumbled. After that line from Irwin, I made my way to Tec. Regardless of how many times I laid eyes on the Entity Cluster, it impressed me every time. The several-story-tall crystal embedded in the shore of the lake was definitely an accent for the town of Wildwood.

My complaints and worries washed away as I crossed the threshold for Tec's inner area of influence. The 'Blessing of Magic,' as the locals called it. Wisps and currents of the elements flowed all around. My eyes traced the twirling dance of azure and beige that came off the mud at the bank, and the gold and blue that hung right around the wooden dock structure. Not long after entering the Blessing did a crystal limb sprout from the bulk of it and snag me by the torso. The wash of the Entity's whitespace flowed in around me, leaving a hovering orb of shimmering light above me.

"You really know how to greet people, Tec," I said, blinking my eyes to adjust them to the sudden change in setting.

—Dreg Warrior Leader Ronan judges social conventions.—

—Is action required for improved success against Dreg threat?—

"No, you are fine, honestly, but you could do with gaining a bit of a sense of humor."

—Human sensory organs do not include 'humor' organs. Biological scans do not reveal mutational trait structures that might fit the criteria.—

"Never mind. Just know that people will 'joke' from time to time. Maybe talk to Bec about it. And speaking of Bec, do we have any updates from it?"

—Connection remains steady. Current status appears to be 'unavailable.' Possible causes range from direct effect on surroundings to physical attack.—

"What!?" I said, focusing on the crystal.

—Agitation detected. Clarification on likelihood of latter cause will be provided. Low chance of direct hostile confrontation.—

*Deep breaths, Ronan. Different personality template, remember? Tec is still learning.* "Alright. So Bec is busy, but nothing else is out of the ordinary?"

—Affirmative.—

"Alright, let's just leave that there for now. Can you give me the full update for today?"

—Acknowledged.—

—Status of afflicted trainees is stable, and several of the less affected individuals appear to be recovering enough for conscious action. Dreg Warriors Daniela and Samuel's biological tending has been supported by Dreg Warrior Timothy.—

"Do you know how soon they might wake up? Getting things coordinated with any surviving family in the town would be key for helping them deal with the changes to their bodies."

—Sleep activity patterns suggest some will wake within two days, majority post a three day rest period.—

"That's great! What's the status as far as…dealing with their changes?"

—Prognosis is less than optimal. Permanence of changes cannot be reverted. Extensive recovery time is suggested.—

Once again Tec sounded genuinely sorry about the situation. I wasn't sure if that was because it wasn't able to heal them, protect them, or even save some other person that had suffered almost directly. Nevertheless, it was a clear demonstration that there was still more to learn about the Entities.

—Final 'update' concerning intrusive Dreg presence is unchanged.—

"Are the prisoners causing any issues?" I wasn't ready to argue about solitary confinement or what effects that might have on the traitors of the town, but if they were released for the Wildwoodians to deal with, they wouldn't get far past the 'door.'

—Negative. Low grade displeasure remains consistent. Dreg Liaison Kirby remains silent despite the nearby presence of his cohort.—

"How's the containment on their abilities? Has that been taxing for you?" *It was time to talk about the real crux of the problem.*

—Power constrained to no less than 80% current output. Cluster mass growth estimated to convert to 85% within the next month as a result of the increasing Dreg purification of the residents within area of influence.—

"That's wonderful…"

—Dreg Warrior Leader appears hesitant to speak.—

"As I understand, the Entity Clusters lose and gain strength based on their size, yes?" I said, probing.

—Affirmative. That has been a point of our previous discussion approximately two minutes, forty-three seconds ago.—

*At least this time it didn't—*

—Forty-four seconds… Forty-five seconds.—

"Right. Got it. I guess getting your feelings on this is the wrong way to go about it. Tec, what are your capacities as far as providing implants for the people of Wildwood, as well as access to the skill spell chains?" I blurted out.

The Entity Cluster quieted. I could see its orb shimmer and

bob slightly as if it were a loading screen indicator in one of Samuel's favorite RPGs. I'd always been more of a real time strategy man myself. My drifting aside, a ding like a baked good called my attention back to the Entity.

—Current category can be maintained at an implantation of sixty-seven-point-three-two residents.—

"Let's just round that down to sixty-seven. Okay, would that impact your current defensive capabilities, both at dealing with the prisoners and keeping the town safe?"

—Minor reduction of area of influence would occur. Power constrained would decrease to sixty-two-point-four of maximum.—

A chair of crystal materialized below me as I worked the figure in my head. I knew that the repulsion field around the crystals worked to keep high-quotient creatures from approaching the town. I didn't know the specifics of how they accomplished that, but it was a blanket effect. If that was reduced, then there would be stronger creatures closer to town, which wouldn't necessarily be a bad thing. There were two things Wildwood, and by extension our home Bunker, needed: fighters and materials.

—After review of my power consumption, I have identified two possible avenues for reducing the impact of the implanting.—

"I'm all ears," I said, turning to the orb.

—The primary way would be to limit skill gains regardless of quotient.—

"That could work for the non-fighters in town. I would like to adhere to Bec's recommendation that people not gain skills they didn't gain themselves too quickly. I don't want people to just drop dead from a brain hemorrhage thanks to stuffing too much information in their heads."

—Recalculating.—

"You didn't take that into account!?" I said, my eyes widening.

—Recalculating.—

*It's not Bec you are talking to. It's basically a big alien computer baby with more power than you could ever hope to hold in your body.* That thought drew me up short. *On second thought, that wasn't comforting at all.*

—Recalculated maximum constrained power at approximately seventy-four-point-five-six percent if rate of spell chain knowledge transplant is tempered to match Dreg purification.—

"Okay, I definitely don't think that will be an issue. I'll talk to the council and get them situated for having people get the implant as soon as possible. What was the second way of offsetting?"

—Mana donations from the captives.—

"Come again?"

—Mana donations from the captives.—

"Yes, I got that. The expression means more to clarify. I don't know how comfortable I feel with taking mana from them." While I held no love for the scumbags that betrayed Wildwood, I didn't know if I had the stomach to hook them up like batteries in the magical version of the Matrix. That analogy already brought way too many comparisons that made me uncomfortable with the whole situation.

—Mana cannot be forcefully extracted. Only willing channeling and release of mana in an enclosed room can allow it to be harnessed.—

"I'll run it by the council." I let my words hang as I tried to put my thoughts back in order. "I'm going to try to bring any parent of the afflicted with the first group. I think Eric is the only one actually in the Wild Guard."

—Access to blood relatives will be provided.—

"Thanks, Tec," I said softly. A pang of loss for those families that had been broken apart settled in my stomach. When I thought about how much I wanted to have met my own mother and father, regardless of my uncle's efforts to raise me, the need to protect people surged within me.

Without saying anything else, I stood. "Thanks for all the help. You and Bec have given us a fighting chance."

—If current recruitment plan is successful, as per my current information bank, it would be yet another unprecedented achievement.—

—Dreg Warrior Leader Ronan designation would be insufficient for level of responsibility displayed.—

—Ronan has initiated procedures to acquire a Legion of Dreg Warriors.—

While Tec's words should have been flattering, it only brought yet another wave of anxiety over me. Being even remotely responsible for the lives of that many people left me distinctly uncomfortable. *I didn't even want to be called 'Dreg Warrior Leader'!* My thoughts started to spiral as I got ready to nudge my conscious mind out of the whitespace.

—Tec reminds Ronan of available skill point.—

That, thankfully, brought my thoughts back to the present and not the innumerable *negative* futures I was imagining.

"As tempting as that is, I think I need a good ol' Ava training montage first. After that last fight, I feel like I need to tune up my current skills instead of adding more to the mix."

—Understood.—

"Thanks. We'll kick the Dreg out of Earth just yet, don't worry." With the reminder that there was strength to be gained still, I phased out of the white space.

— + —

"Hey Ronan!" Timothy called from the wall. The pink-colored fae waved down from his perch.

"Sarah stick you with the work today?" I asked, leaning against the set of rough-cut stairs that led to the top of the palisade.

"Just trying to give her a hand. We've already got so few healers that having one on the wall is rare. Ever since she took on training, the twins and I barely see her," he said, gesturing in the direction of the training fields.

"Understandable, if unfortunate. At the very least, you all should get some extra oomph within the next few days," I said.

"Oh?"

"The Guard will be getting the implants from Tec," I said, gesturing to the base of my skull. While the Tec-given implants were all made entirely of Entity Cluster crystals, the ones the Bunkerites had were mostly titanium with a tiny Metier Crystal within. It felt both exclusive and inferior, since our implants were still partly visible, unlike the ones given by Tec.

"That's great! After what happened to the trainees and then the state that George is in…"

"I think we'll be able to patch George up," I said, thinking of the brazen orc dude who practically threw himself into danger to keep me from getting death-rayed right in the chest. A subsequent attack removed his arm almost completely, but I believed that as the healers got stronger, they'd be able to restore the limb.

Not that I understood the intricacies of how life mana, or even regular healing, worked; I was just a glorified bulldozer. As such, I was back to my original reason for coming to the wall.

"There any squads out there?" I asked.

"We've got two. One is still working on grabbing loot from the fight and the other is trying to cull the horde of spiders that has been pushing out of their territory. We've never seen so many before," Tim said, concern clear in his voice.

"I'll lend a hand to the second group. Are they based out of the forward base or did they make it to our temporary dungeon farm spot?"

"Forward base. I don't think anyone's been able to make it back into spider territory without getting swarmed."

*That's both good and truly concerning. More materials is always good, but something has to be stirring up the spiders. This time, it wasn't us.* "I'll head out from there then."

"Don't you want some backup? The council said to never go out without a buddy!"

"I have a buddy, and it's a Blobby," I said, pointing to the wall section right beside Tim.

My slime companion dropped its camouflage, causing the fae to almost leap clear off the wall. His roughspun shirt flapped in the wind as he tried to pull breath. I felt a little bad, but Tim let out a nervous laugh. "I need to be better aware. If Blobby wasn't the neighborhood friendly slime, that could have been less than optimal."

"I still haven't figured out if the camo is an earth slime thing or not," I said. "And don't worry, it's hard even for *me* to know where he is."

"That's not nearly as reassuring as you think it is," Tim said with a shiver.

The walk from the town out to the reinforced building was short. Increased attributes and a now mostly restored road made the travel easier. The bounties of infusions and materials, or meals, that the town had been reaping from the spider dungeon farm had put their food rationing problem down.

While trudging past the western field, I spotted several air squirrels flitting about the treetops as well as dozens of normal-sized insects doing their business amidst the weeds. The whole thing made me pause. It was almost peaceful, which surprised me. Since returning to the surface, every moment had been jumping from one threat to the next. With the captured Dreg crystal and Kirby out of commission, we could take a breath and really consolidate our gains.

Getting to that point had taken a lot of sacrifice, and the repercussions were still being felt, but growth didn't happen without strife.

"Something interesting up in the trees?" Devon air-whispered in my ear.

I pivoted slowly to try to spot the man amidst the trees or the few ruined buildings flanking the road. My perception screamed that I was being watched now that it wasn't focused on philosophical quandaries.

"Gah! Dang slime ball!" A groan from right in front of me went up.

The elf stalker, plus two small Blobbys attached to his legs, trudged out onto the road. His smooth, elven features were twisted in a frown as he glared at the two thirds of Blobby slowing down as the last third rolled out of the trees, jiggling as if laughing.

I high-fived the slime, palm meeting gelatinous appendage. "Good catch. Dealing with all the pesky elves in the forest was really getting to me."

"Truly the height of comedy, Ronan. Now can you take your oversized muck off of me?" Devon said.

Blobby, like the independent amorphous traitor of the Dreg that it was, prodded Devon with a jelly limb before melting back into one whole. The slime rolled over to puddle beside me. I marveled at its size, having grown taller than my hip when all of its bulk was combined.

"What are you doing this way? I thought they had you pushing paper, rock boy," Devon sneered, as if my companion hadn't just disabled his sneaky advantage.

"Needed to hit something. I've been cooped up for the last week. As someone who lived their life underground, any kind of 'stuck' feels thirty times worse. Nothing like freedom right outside but you are forced to be still."

The elf nodded as if he agreed completely. Other than prodding Blobby for catching him, Devon parted from us. He was on scout duty while the others were out and he'd already had a few encounters with frisky squirrels. They weren't a threat alone, but their mobility while amassed made everything more troublesome.

I walked the last few blocks to the forward base and did a double take. The defensive measures had almost doubled from when it was quickly fortified. The ankle tripping wall of wood stumps was still around most of the place, but huge, sheer walls of soil rose up around most of the building. I could see rubble from the nearby structures blended in, reinforcing the berm-wall.

I let out a soft whistle that made Blobby shiver and actually called somebody from within the structure. A familiar demoness smirked down at me from what I assumed was an observation post. "Fancy seeing you here."

"Don't act like Devon didn't tell you I was coming. That elf would lick your boots if they got smeared a little." While a bit of an exaggeration, everyone in Clara's team trusted her completely. The fact that Devon acted as their information center even before they had gotten access to the communication features of the implant meant that he was constantly keeping tabs on as many of their squad mates as he could.

"You are not wrong. Come on in, we are just getting situated."

I moved around the building towards the front of it and ran into even more ankle-breaking stumps. The entrance had been fashioned from huge logs bound together, but they didn't look quite like the ones I'd worked into a sliding door at our Bunker. These were completely uniform, as were the vines running through the whole thing. With a tug, the gate opened outward just enough to fit a person.

Sure enough, the inside of the forward base had also been upgraded. I could see slatherings of mud hardening in the gaps on the walls and a small garden being worked in the corners of the fortification.

Milling about just in front of the doors to the building was a group of five individuals. Two of them I recognized as the trainees we had rescued, the others were one of the healers from the Guard, Clara, and Lilly. Other Wild Guard members were posted around the perimeter on raised log platforms. A few waved as they saw me enter.

"Meet the team," Clara said, pointing to the group. "After the success of our split squads, we've restructured some and tried to make the squads more flexible. This will be the trainees' first time out as a squad. Lilly will be testing them for field readiness."

"Hello Mr. Ronan." The female demoness waved. "My name is Merry. This is Nick. We just wanted to thank you again for all you did to save us."

She waved to the hulking orc beside her. He probably didn't reach chin high on Rommel but, then again, Rommel was a size in and of his own. The Wild Guard fae healer, Ophelia, smiled and shook my hand.

"Really, don't mention it. Without everyone there, the whole thing would have failed. I'm just a guy that's good at getting hit. Speaking of." I turned to Clara. "I was hoping to head out and help out. Do you all mind if I tag along and tank for you?"

Clara got the gist and said yes, but asked what I meant by 'tank.'

"Oh, I suppose Sarah hasn't told you some of what I hope to pass to you all. Its terms from before the Fall. It's a certain specialty that someone has. For instance, you already call most life-attuned that can repair wounds and illnesses 'healers.' Well, people like Rommel and Godfrey, built to take more damage and get right up in the face of enemies are 'tanks.' That's what I am, in addition to 'support.'

"Support is the category which healers fall under, and really, anyone capable of controlling the flow for the battle or providing 'support,' whether defensive or offensive. You are offensive support, Clara."

"Makes sense, keeping the group in the fight longer by weakening creatures," she said.

"That's right," I said, snapping my fingers and pointing at the demoness.

The *other* demoness had a curious expression on her face. "What about those that focus on killing things as fast as possible?"

"Ah, well we call those DPS, or 'damage per second.' Just like you said, you focus on getting as much damage downrange as possible. That would be something like my friend Daniela or

Devon. Though each of them goes about the damage differently, and different types of DPS have different names. Rangers, pure mages, rogues, etc. I'll try to give a better rundown, and it will hopefully improve the squad compositions going forward. I will say, chemistry and teamwork can make up for optimal parties any day of the week," I finished, wagging a finger.

Ophelia and Clara looked like they wanted to take notes, Nick was nodding along like he knew what I was talking about, and Merry had a smirk wide enough to show the enlarged canines of her Attunement.

"I look forward to seeing which I fit best," the demoness droned. For some odd reason, the hairs on the back of my neck stood up on end.

# CHAPTER THREE

## Tangled Assessment

Before heading out, with the addition of myself to the group, they all ran through the focus of their power. Instead of providing a total breakdown, they laid it out in general terms of the class system I'd brought up. Merry said that she was a DPS through and through, corrosion being her strongest Gift. Nick grumbled something along the lines of DPS and support, making parts of the territory inhospitable with his fire. Lilly's ice abilities I was familiar with, and Ophelia said she had something similar to Sam's vine ability, but focused on pollen.

The brief snippet of the team sent a thrill of excitement through me. The world had *magic* now. With it being a part of my life and such a relevant pillar for humans to return to the surface, I'd forgotten. *Magic.* On top of that, everyone had variations to it, since their bodies processed the mana of the world differently, even within the same Attunements. I couldn't help myself as I focused on the group; my implant highlighted each of them in gold before their information populated in my peripheral vision.

<Merry (Human)>

\<Attunement: Death\>
\<Refinement: Corrosion\>
\<Perceived Metier Quotient: 3\>

\<Nick (Human)\>
\<Attunement: Fire\>
\<Refinement: Smolder\>
\<Perceived Metier Quotient: 3\>

\<Ophelia (Human)\>
\<Attunement: Life\>
\<Refinement: Foliage\>
\<Perceived Metier Quotient: 4\>

"Nothing like practical work to get concepts to set in," I said, clapping my hands together and giving the group a smile. Without wasting any more time, the group shuffled out of the base. Clara waved us off before closing the gate behind us. I spared another look to take in what the Wildwoodians had accomplished in a week. *I really need to update the fortifications of the Bunker camp...* My mind worked through several plans as we followed the street to US 301.

While the path from the forward base to the town proper had been fairly cleared, and as uniform as a quarter century of asphalt decay could be expected to be, the old main street had seen better days. Whole sections of the asphalt had been lifted up by tree roots forcing their way towards the median; grass, ferns, and vines had filled in the rest. Thanks to the familiarity that everyone had with the pseudo-urban environment, progress across the road and slightly north went smoothly.

Lilly and I took point as soon as we entered the woods on the other side. Blobby did what Blobby does and vanished out of sight. I knew he would be close by. The trainees didn't utter a peep as we pushed deeper. A cursory glance at my Local Positioning System marked our location. A quick check with Lilly told me we were just at the edge of spider territory. The further we went, the stronger and more multitudinous the creatures would get. For the purposes of testing the trainees, they wanted to stay on the outskirts and around the territory towards where we'd found Kirby's secret warehouse.

"I'll stay in the lead, Lilly will take the rear. If we encounter something, I will set up a wall and if Lilly does, she will too. Ophelia in the center at all times. Even if you take some damage yourself, make sure she is as capable as she can of putting us back together. Understood?" I glanced between the trainees and Ophelia, who nodded. Lilly smiled at me, shooting me a hidden thumbs up. Right before we'd left the forward base, she'd asked if I was willing to take point. She could focus on watching the trainees *and* she hated the responsibility. Considering I'd been taking point since my friends and I dug out Bec, it didn't really bother me at all.

"Keep your eyes peeled and looking up. I'll keep a look at ground level, but pretty much all of these spider turds have tried to get the jump on us as opposed to rushing directly." The comment elicited a small chuckle from everyone before the tension returned. Since we weren't going deeper, I wasn't particularly worried, but it didn't hurt to keep an eye out. The elite spiders that Devon had mentioned certainly seemed like they could cause problems if caught unaware.

Things in the forest scurried away from our presence, but the webbing along the canopy told a different story. My perception strained to pick things out from the gloom, but a flit of light and shadow told me something was watching us. It wasn't long enough of a look for the implant to lock in, but I halted our advance. Nick stepped up behind me, a red glow hazing around his fists.

"They are watching," he said. "Should we attack?"

"Not if we want them to fight. Unless they initiate, the spiders will just escape. Daniela found that out the hard way," I said, my voice dropping as I recalled our first run at farming the spider territory.

"They best get to it fast," Merry said, shifting from foot to foot.

"They'll—" I cut myself off as a rain of silk came down from above. "Now, Nick!"

The organic form of Nick's skill manifested. Based on the transition into the ground, it was a materialize skill. It didn't take long to confirm my suspicion as the pulse of heat around us doubled, tripled, then sunk into everything *not* human. Everything grew red veins of fire, and our assailants were released by the hellish glow. The two closest trees were alive as a wave of spiders rained down on us.

<Orb Weaver>
<Attunement: Air>
<Refinement: Gossamer>
<Perceived Metier Quotient: 1>

<Orb Weaver>
<Attunement: Air>
<Refinement: Gossamer>
<Perceived Metier Quotient: 2>

"<Earth Shell>, <Mineral Strike>!" I called my Skills out loud, helping me center myself as the arachnid deluge landed on the smoldering earth. They were not happy, and quickly sought the closest, safest location: my body. Thankfully, I'd opted to defend *and* attack. An aquamarine stone started to form over my palm, but I didn't wait for it to completely materialize. It was already sailing into their midst, colliding with one of the larger spiders and spraying shards all over the place. The rush of spiders got pushed back for a moment, letting me see that more were pouring out from deeper within. *This is like when we were deeper in!*

That was all the time I had for deep thought before I got swept over with spiders. The rat-sized creatures were intent on getting their fangs on me, but my growing armor of stone protected most of my squishy bits. Mana flowed into my pickaxe and I reshaped the crystal into a scythe. The first sweep took down two spiders before the others leapt out of the way. Their attempt to shoot webs was thwarted by the building heat of Nick's skill. The man in question was drawing the attention of the second group of spiders that didn't have me in between them.

I thumped my shield with my pickaxe to let out a pulse of heat, drawing the spiders to me as I shrugged off the first offenders. Thankfully, I didn't have to keep all the creatures at bay as a whistling spray of green rained down on the second group that had been targeting Nick. Anywhere the green fluid touched, an acrid smoke rose up followed by chittered frustration. The attack didn't look lethal, but more than a few spiders lost control of their limbs as they fell prey to its persistent effect.

"Eat my acid!" Merry cackled. The shift in mannerism almost threw me off, but when you have spiders trying to jump on your face, that tends to take priority. The woman was jabbing out with a spear in hand, covering Nick as he focused on his skill. The heat grew once again.

"Rein in your fire, Nick!" Lilly called. The woman had erected a shield of ice around her and Ophelia. Her hook and one of the hatchets I'd infused flashed in her hands as she killed spider after spider. Almost like an afterimage of the blow, the insect's ichor froze in the air before flying into one of its compatriots. Unfortunately, I could already see that both her attacks and defensive wall were blunted; the daggers didn't retain their cohesion long, and the spell chain around the wall had to be kept up.

"Tighten up on Ophelia!" I called, body-checking Nick out of the way before a Q2 spider could get a hold of him. Said spider managed to punch through the armor on my forearm. A warning telling me I'd been afflicted with inflammation flashed in my vision as the burning sting cleared my mind enough to act *and* think. Four half-powered <Mineral Strikes> flopped to the ground. I was vaguely aware of my guts twisting in on themselves, but the adrenaline let me fight back against my mana side effects. It was the largest back to back casting of the skill I'd done to date.

Like timed grenades, the multicolored rocks shattered and pushed back the horde long enough for me to get swinging room. The pick-turned-scythe sucked up some more of my mana as I pushed it to increase in size and swung. Spider after spider fell with each swing. Nick retargeted his smolder zone to beyond where I was fighting, weakening and spacing out the spiders that tried to get to our group.

"Merry, target the larger ones!" I called, interposing my shield as webs shot out from the Q2 spiders in the mix. The strands were thicker than their smaller brethren, but visible enough for me to pick them out. With Nick's skill needing time to surge up and stop *that* attack, I was forced to fight against the strands attaching to me. When a half-dozen dog-sized spiders were tugging on my shield, my feet started to slip on the earth.

"<Earthen Barrier>!" I grit my teeth against the growing amount of strands attaching to my shield. My hardened earth barrier appeared low and thick, giving me the grip I was quickly losing. "Get ready for incoming!"

With a bicep-snapping tug, I hoisted the large spiders closer. The moment they were in the air, they released their webs. They hadn't been expecting to be pulled *towards* the enemy.

That was when Ophelia and Merry really joined in the mix. The demoness had been keeping the smaller spiders from overwhelming our group along with Nick, but now she switched from an area spell chain to targeted. Bolts of green-black energy fired into the general location of the falling spiders. Each took one in the thorax or leg, dying or being put out of the fight. Ophelia sent out a pulse of gold-green energy into the ground around us. The portions blackened and charred by Nick's skill were ignored as the pulse continued into the patches of hardy grass and ferns. They immediately turned on everything that wasn't vegetation. Whirling blades of turf and weeds cut all the downed spiders and halted the advance of the rest.

"Finally!" Lilly called. I glanced over my shoulder to see an icy version of Dai the lizardman's Flurry summon. The creature hovered in the air for a whole second before turning into an ice-javelin launcher. Each half-spin of its body lobbed an accurate spear of azure ice into the center mass of the larger spiders, completely removing them from the equation.

"Don't forget about me!" Nick roared as fire pulsed from him into the ground. Everywhere fire had smoldered, spurts of fire rose up like miniature impromptu volcanos.

I swiped my pick once through the air, killing the rush of spiders that had survived the onslaught. A pesky survivor rounded my left to get at Nick. My injured arm didn't respond fast enough to interpose my shield, but I didn't have to worry. A spear thrust out, pinning the creature to the ground as Merry swayed. She was looking green around the gills, but there was a savage grin on her face. The whole terror look was completed by the spray of ichor matting her hair and horns.

"Sweep the area!" I said, extracting my feet from the hole I'd dug resisting the pull of the spiders.

"Ronan, please come here," Ophelia said gently. When I gave her a confused look, she pointed at my left arm which hung limp. *Right. Adrenaline is a hell of a drug!*

My eyes roved over the small clearing we'd created with our fight as Ophelia pulsed healing energy into my shoulder and then down to my fingers. Unlike Samuel's refreshing heal, this was a warm embrace. Comfort eased the muscle that had been snapped and coiled before reattaching it. Minor scrapes and the bite on my arm faded away as the mana washed through me. Ophelia slumped as I watched her eyes dilate. "Don't push it. You cast that big skill during the fight."

"Just need… a moment," she slurred.

"Nick, keep an eye on Ophelia. Merry, stick with her until your side effects pass," I said, rising to my feet from the knee Ophelia had me take.

"I'm—Ugh." When Merry tried to respond, the woman

had to stop herself. Having seen it on Clara, I knew she was about ready to show us what she'd had for breakfast.

"Sit. Recovering as quickly as possible is more important than loot or anything else," I said, putting a bit of steel into my voice. The woman gave a small, meek nod before grabbing her head. Apparently shaking her head in any way was a bad idea.

Lilly still had her summon hovering a circle around the group, her eyes locked on the woods around her. Her legs and arms were shivering as the coldness of her side effects took its toll and she made a concerted effort to ignore it. "They *are* reacting much more."

"This was almost as bad as when we set up that temporary base," I agreed.

"At least they were all the same element," Lilly said, pointing to one of the flanking spiders she'd killed. They were gray in color, with shocks of iridescent lines where they'd been tangled in their own webs. Over half of them on her side had been cleaved by axe or ice blades.

"You are right, different Attunements would have complicated things," I said. "Is anyone reporting these large numbers?"

"Nothing quite this large, but yes. I'm not sure if we upset some kind of balance by taking out the Tendrils, but the woods are *angry* now."

"Good and bad. I just hope we can adapt fast enough," I said quietly.

The two of us lapsed into silence, taking opposing positions around our group. A quickly approaching shadow almost had me call the others into combat readiness. Thankfully, it was only my helpfully absent gelatinous companion. Except, what it held within its body once again gave me pause. Long legs that could only belong to one of the female banana spiders stuck out of its body at odd angles, at least three of them visible in the lime green bulk. Blobby didn't even try to comment on anything, instead it slumped into a camouflaged puddle beside a pile of the smaller spiders. A lazy appendage pulled two of the Q1 spiders into its body, each getting obscured quickly as the slime started to dissolve them.

"I'll be damned." I chuckled to myself. One of those bad boys had to be at least Q3, and it seemed like Blobby had at least scared it off. My thoughts flashed back to when I'd first seen my companion fight the other slimes. For something without a face, I couldn't help but think it had been snarling at the other Tendril creatures. "I'd believe it."

"Believe what?" Nick asked as he approached me. He'd been cut deeper by the spiders I'd missed. However, unlike my own Limestone Skin-<Earth Shell> combo, his skin was mundane by comparison. Only a few hazy scar lines were left now that Ophelia had been able to heal him.

"Blobby kept one of the stronger spiders from engaging us," I said, pointing to the almost indistinguishable mass if not for the spider legs sticking out of it.

Nick looked between me and the slime, shaking his head before returning to Merry. "He *is* a monster," I heard them whisper to each other.

I pushed past the strange blend of feelings that comment caused, starting the looting process. With each boot nudge, the spider bodies would crystalize before crumbling in on themselves. Iridescent gold sprays of Pith rose up into the air, hovering before spider-webbing into all of us except Blobby. The surge of warmth of the Pith eased my body. I almost braced for the nauseating feeling of the Dreg contained within, but the spiders were just attuned beasts. The ratio of Dreg to Pith absorbed was laughable compared to Tendrils.

Ophelia unfolded two large duffels from her gear, passing them to the trainees. They went about collecting the massive influx of infusions and spider bits. *The benefits of seniority.* I chuckled as the two teens groaned almost every time they bent over to pick the loot up. *I wonder if this is what kids cleaning up their room was like?* The thought of some slight normalcy compared to pre-Fall Earth brought a smile to my face.

While they worked to gather the sizable pile of loot, the rest of us kept watch. I used my pickaxe-turned-axe-axe to clear some of the low hanging branches, reducing the ambush spots and opening up our view. It was while clearing one of these that I caught a glimpse of the sky. Pinprick dots of black drifted in a tight cluster, shifting and swirling within each other. My head tilted in confusion as I watched the spectacle for several seconds until my brain slotted the image with one of Alexis' biology lessons from years ago. "Murmuration…"

The general cloud of birds swept further and further out of view, heading in a particular direction despite their ambling coordinated motion. "East… The town!" I screamed as I realized what the birds had to be.

"Ronan?" Lilly asked.

"Grab whatever we have already, we need to go back!" I yelled. Matching action to word, I hauled one of the duffels and threw it over my shoulder. "Blobby, make sure our path is clear!"

The slime jiggled, spitting out one of the half-digested spiders before mitosing into three. Each took one of the Metier Crystals in its center with it, but the smaller Blobbys were much faster as they sped eastward into the woods. The rest of the others adjusted their gear and followed a step behind me.

# CHAPTER FOUR

## Complications

"Ronan… Explain please!" Lilly called as she caught up to me. The others were lagging behind, but I made sure to keep my pace to something manageable.

"Those dots up there, it's gotta be those crows again!" I called as soon as we made it to the road. The others glanced up at the sky, seeing the swirling mass already far ahead of them and growing in size by the second. I could see the confusion and concern on the merwoman's face. While she hadn't been present in the town when we'd first been attacked, I was sure she'd heard about it.

The trip back to the forward base was short by comparison to our trip out, yet it was still painfully slow. When we were rushing past the base, Clara poked her head out over the barrier. "Me and one other are left! The rest rushed back to the town!" she called from the embanked wall.

The duffels got unceremoniously dumped as we upped our jog into a run. The cleared stretch of road let us pick up speed, passing the first external field minutes later and then sighting the walls a few more after that. Unfortunately, we were already too late. Droves of crows plunged from the sky like rain. At least a hundred of the creatures swept towards the ground at a time, but their coordinated chaos made it impossible to get a good count.

Of course, the gates were unmanned. With a roar of frustration, I picked up speed, leaving the others behind as they struggled to catch their breath. The brown glow of my mana flared along my arms as I put my memory to the test. *Two cross bars. One two feet up, another four feet up.* I fed even more mana to my left arm as the spell chain accepted the empowered cost of my skill. Less than twenty feet from the gate, I released.

A double-charged <Stone Spike> bloomed, impacting roughly where the first crossbar was. My second <Stone Spike> triggered a half-second after the first, sprouting from the initial spike to fork-strike into the second crossbar. The gate shook, metal groaning, as the supports on the other side ripped out of the wood. The doors fell inward, one half-cocked as my attack ripped part of it clear off the hinge. Blobby slipped through the gap without hesitation, and I was forced to stop and lean against my created spikes.

When the others arrived, they stared wide-eyed at what I'd done. Ophelia moved closer, as if to heal me, but I waved her off. "Go! I'll be fine in a minute!"

The whole group hesitated, but set their shoulders. Nick shoved the unhinged door aside and the four others slipped inside. On my part, I did my best not to curl up into a sorry ball of pain. While Samuel was the one that had learned knots, my intestines were showing they'd taken a crash course. The twisting pain had me doubled over, but I managed to shuffle through the broken gate.

Nauseating gusts of bile did not help the abdominal distress. The same disgusting regurgitations of the crows from the first encounter riddled the town again. Once habitable buildings were decaying visibly as the carrion corroded the shingles, metal, or wood without care. Somehow, the fact that those buildings wouldn't have been as affected if they had been constructed with mana manipulated materials flowed through my mind.

Shaking my head to concentrate, I tried to watch the cloud of crows for where they were concentrating their plummeting attacks. The LPS map sprouted in the corner of my vision, and I could almost picture the swarm on the map, tracking it in a general southeast direction. My feet were already taking me, cutting through pre-Fall backyards that had been turned into personal subsistence farms and relaxation spots for the people of Wildwood. When I skirted the wetlands, the main cluster of the birds showed their clear target. The training building.

Suddenly the puzzle pieces slotted together. Regardless, I rushed through tall grass, around several crayfish traps and back on the road. The team I'd led earlier had joined up to push back the birds from the center of town. I could see Nick hauling people to an igloo summoned by Lilly. The other civilians had picked up rocks and sticks to fend for themselves, clustering around the other Wild Guard members battling the crows. Zaps of electricity flew from a nearby rooftop, arcing between several of the diving birds, preventing them from flaring their wings to bank. The civilians then proceeded to end their lives.

With the majority of the town in good hands, I pushed towards the training grounds. A few carrion regurgitations flopped to the ground around me, one close enough that I had to use my shield to prevent the wet splash from reaching me. Nonetheless, I charged. When the basaltic stone spike I'd made a while back came into view, my steps slowed. A giant hand of flame was keeping most of the crows away from the trainees, while they contributed spurts of their own Gifts into the defense. Two of the dwarves were spreading a stone roof off my spike to cover them from the rain of bile.

As I watched, a clump dropped like a tactical missile towards the group, angling perfectly to hit Sarah's exposed form. A vine sprouted from the barren earth of the training yard, catching the clump even as the verdant tentacle disintegrated. *Samuel!* The vine curled in on itself before sprouting back to slap another offending blob from the air. My feet turned in that direction until my eyes spotted something that chilled my blood.

The cloud above us swirled. Crows circled, making a gap like a school of fish around a predator. The thing in the sky was definitely a predator. A school-bus-sized crow pulsed down from the sky like a comet. Wisps of purple mist trailed its path, and I watched as several of the crows that got within range of the smoke simply slumped out of the sky.

The creature landed on the training building, shaking the ground through the foundations with its landing. Its arrival put it just in range of my implant and perception, eliciting yet another chill.

<Dreg Appendage (Crow)>

<Attunement: Death>

<Refinement: Death>

<Perceived Metier Quotient: 6>

"What is that!?" Sarah yelled as she saw me approach.

"Something big and mean!"my brain managed. The beast touched down almost gently on the roof of the building, shredding the top like one of our insta-meals. A purple-pulsing orb flickered within its grasp. A metal-encased, purple-pulsing orb of black crystal.

"It came to get the Dreg Entity," I whispered. Sarah didn't hear me, focused on drawing back her fire hand to conserve mana. The diving attacks had halted with the arrival of the Dreg Appendage. As the last skills of the trainees fizzled in the air, an eerie silence permeated the town. Even the crows crispy fried by swats from Sarah died without uttering a peep.

>The Aberrant do not forget, fleshbags.<

>Opposing the Dreg was the last mistake of your insignificant existences.<

The swell of crows escorted the behemoth out of the town, several more dying just in the smoky trails of death around it. Wet splats were the only sound for several minutes as the trainees and everyone else tried to process what had happened.

— + —

"Anybody have any idea what in the fresh Metier hell just happened?" Dylan asked, not at all calmly.

The councilman was more than a bit agitated, which wasn't a surprise. Thankfully, while a large swath of the town had been injured in the strange raid, most had actually managed to gain a Quotient from the whole ordeal. The reduced need to heal people thanks to the boost of breaking into a new level had helped settle some of the panic.

Several hours later, however, the leadership of the town was trying to figure out what happened and what it meant for the future of Wildwood. Dylan, Sarah, Irwin, Sam, Clara, a lizardman named Trey, who was in charge of the fishermen, a rotund dwarf named Arnold, who was in charge of the crafters, and an older regular human named William, who was in charge of the farms, sat around a bonfire just outside of where the Blessing of Magic began. It was really quite the audience and they all turned towards me, my childhood friend included.

"Okay, well, before we really get going. Do we know where Daniela is?" I asked, locking eyes with Samuel.

"She sent me a message saying she was fine before dropping out of contact. I haven't been able to get a hold of Devon either, so I'm hoping they are together," Clara answered. That both comforted me and brought a whole new set of concerns I didn't feel quite equipped to handle right then, so I pushed through to the meeting.

"Right. Well, let's keep tabs on that. As for what happened, well, we got raided and robbed is the short of it. My best guess is that the Dreg Entity was somehow able to call for help even through Tec's distortion field," I said, putting my hypothesis out there.

"But why now? What changed?" Irwin asked.

"It's possible that it was because I wasn't around," I said. When the group gave me quizzical looks, I explained that since we'd captured and restrained the crystal, either Samuel or myself had been nearby. It was just a sheer coincidence of trying to move into the now-derelict training building and deal with researching the massive amount of stuff Kirby had accumulated.

"But you went out with the trainees today, and I was working with Danny before meeting up with Sarah," Samuel added.

"Okay, assuming that the crystal had some proper alone time, how was it able to call a giant flock of creatures, *and* what the hell was that thing at the end?" Dylan asked, throwing up his hands.

*The normally composed politician was definitely not in the house today.*

"I was able to get a look at it before it got out of range. Apparently, it was something called a Dreg Appendage, Quotient Level 6, so it's one of the strongest creatures we've encountered since coming to the surface," I said.

"I'm sorry, Mr. Terrigan, but we aren't quite familiar with your 'level' system. What exactly does that mean?" old man Williams asked.

"Hopefully, the implant program will be able to change that, but we'll talk about that next. Each level is roughly three times as strong as the previous one, qualitatively speaking. Physically speaking, its growth is a tenth of the average strength of the creature. For something like that giant crow, I have no idea what that would be, but it is at least one-point-six times stronger than the average… Whatever it is.

"Most of the town is actually Level 2, which I suspect has something to do with surviving and being in the area of influence of Tec, while the Wild Guard and trainees are in the 3 and 4 range. It's somewhat speculative numbers, but it would take three Level 5 people to contend with that thing."

"This is an evaluation in a vacuum. You can't quantify experience and tactics," Arnold the dwarf complained.

"Precisely, which means we are probably at even *more* of a disadvantage. As far as I know, only Devon can fly and that's more of a 'sort-of' than a 'for sure,'" I said, laying out the situation. It wasn't pretty. The implication that the Dreg had a concerted force and a communication network of some kind bumped the threat even higher.

"What can we do? That attack was already enough to destroy a huge swath of what we've worked on," said William. The lines on the man's face were accented by his growing frown.

"We rebuild, like we've always done," Dylan said. He stabbed the air with his finger, pointing at each of the people present. "This isn't the first time nature has slapped us in the face."

"It is the first time it's done it on purpose," Trey added. It was somewhat hard to read expressions on reptilian features, but he looked defeated.

"There isn't much we can do right now other than hunker down. I hoped to make the announcement under a more hopeful atmosphere, but this might be just what we all need.I've spoken with Tec and it should be able to start providing the Guard with implants. Based on the power that it is using to keep the stronger creatures away from the town proper, it might only be able to give everyone access to one skill at this time."

"Skill?" Arnold asked.

"Gifts. That's what you call them. I'm also going to be working with Rommel to churn out gear, *real* gear, for the Guard. Hopefully by the time that has happened, we can give the trainees more practical exams, leave them in charge of defense, and use the squads to grind the spider dungeon or any other we can find. I think that each creature territory probably has a dungeon, otherwise how would they be able to push so many creatures out?" I explained, putting my plan on the table. Even with the faster rate of reproduction of certain species pre-Fall, it didn't make sense otherwise.

Everyone around the fire looked hesitant to comment. I had already discussed the implant portion of the plan with Dylan and Irwin, but it was the first time that the other heads of the town had heard of it. It wasn't a secret anymore that we were interacting with the Crystal directly, as much displeasure as that caused, but the results spoke for themselves. Without the communication abilities the implant had allowed us, we would have lost all of the trainees during the fight with Kirby.

"Take the night to sort through your thoughts and give me any comments in the morning. I have suggestions for each of your areas to benefit from, but I can't be everywhere," I said, putting an impromptu close to our meeting. The group didn't scatter but instead fell into contemplative silence. Sarah and Clara looked at me with questions in their eyes, so I walked away from the bonfire. The two women and Samuel followed me towards the Crystal and through the Blessing of Magic.

The wisps of colored mana floating around us cast an ethereal glow over the wooden planks. Propping my back against the railing and crossing my arms, I turned to face the others.

"Who died and put you in charge?" Sarah asked, mimicking me and crossing her own sizable arms.

"Sarah, we both know he's too far in the clouds to even notice us small folk," Clara said, half-turned so as to not even look at me.

"Well, that's why it's our job to keep him *grounded*," Samuel added with a huff. The two women groaned at the terrible word play.

"Not entirely sure what's going on right now, but I just want it to be clear I don't *want* to lead anything. I'm all for someone else implementing ideas, or doing *something*, but there doesn't seem to be anyone interested," I said, shrugging.

"We aren't here to berate you for taking the lead, Ronan. We just want to make sure you don't try to hold up the town alone," Sarah said, tilting her head to the side. "To be honest, we were kind of surprised we had that meeting at all."

"I was going to have the meeting to let everyone know about the implants anyhow," I said, somewhat defensively.

"Good. Everyone is on the same page now. I'll be busy helping the farmers and the healers," Samuel said.

"While I will be getting the trainees turned into proper defending Wild Guards," Sarah added.

"While she's doing *that*, I will be keeping the patrols in order, and expanding on our forward base," Clara continued.

"Wait a minute…" I squinted my eyes as I watched their serious expressions twitch. "That sure sounds like you are leaving the crafting and research for me to handle."

—Dreg Warriors present outstanding delegating abilities. Dreg Warrior Ronan's expertise lay in that field.—

"Oy! I don't wanna hear from you," I said, turning to point an accusing finger at the Metier Crystal as their words scrolled by my eyes. The others couldn't hold back anymore, laughing at the situation. I found myself chuckling along, having been led by the nose and read like a book by even a giant sapient rock.

The invisible, self-imposed weight of responsibility that I chained myself to lightened ever so slightly. *And here I was, being all serious, while they had everything planned out without me…* My worries faded for just a little while as we discussed the future without letting the looming threat dictate our actions.

# CHAPTER FIVE

## Memory Movie Reel

"You said meet you in the morning," Arnold said, cracking his neck and stroking his waist-long beard.

"Can't deny what I said…" I mumbled through a yawn. Light was spilling down into the training building through the leafy ceiling Samuel had constructed to patch where the Appendage had pecked. The man in question was already gone, surely to deal with farming shenanigans.

"Well, I've got a question."

"Can I get some time to wake up?" I said, almost flopping to the ground when I tried to stand from the couch. *Did the people on the surface lose their sense of personal space?* I wasn't entirely bothered about Arnold entering the house since there wasn't anything secretive going on, but pseudo-acquaintances didn't normally shake you awake while you were doing your best to sleep in.

The dwarf waited a whole two seconds. "That good enough?"

"Fine, whatever. Walk and talk. I need some breakfast," I said, rubbing the sleep from my eyes and heading towards the living area of the training building.

"I done did speak with Rommel. He told me about your infusing. We need to get everyone going on that."

"That sounds more like a command than a question, Arnold," I said, wagging my finger in his direction. A bowl with strawberries and oranges laid completely unprotected on the counter as I slunk closer.

"Fine. Please?"

"Better, but that isn't the main problem. Perhaps when the Crystal has given more people implants, it will feel so inclined as to tell us what the requirements are for what I do, but I'm the only one able to pass the miscellaneous skills. Something about needing a boatload of mana. If all goes well, then maybe you can take over the job." Arnold didn't seem to appreciate me gesturing with fruit, but it was too early for me to really care about his opinion. *I wonder if anyone might have some coffee beans around. No doubt Sam could grow some and save everyone's mornings...*

The frown on Arnold's face could have split rocks. For all I knew, that *was* part of his job, even if there weren't very many large rocks in Florida. He fumbled about with his thoughts until he finally asked what I planned to do.

"Why, thank you for your consideration, Arnold! I was going to check in with the councilmembers, figure out when they were going to start running people to Tec. Then, I was going to look for you, maybe try to set up a few <Infusion> transfers before lunch time, followed by that lesson I mentioned. That sound good to you?" You could have drowned in the amount of sarcasm I was putting out.

The dwarf grumbled, but just nodded in turn. He snagged an orange from the table before he vanished down the stairs.

"It's going to be a long day..."

— + —

As it turned out, Dylan already had everything coordinated. Somehow, the councilman had woken up, visited Tec, gotten an implant, and then returned to speak with Sarah. "When opportunity comes knocking, you answer the door even if you are in your underwear," he said, as if it was some sage saying. Sarah, on the other hand, was running the trainees through a new set of cardio exercises. Whenever she saw a group return, she would single out people for them to head to the Blessing of Magic. The ones that returned were pretty much out for the day as they tried to get acclimated to the status and to new skills acquired thanks to the Entity Cluster.

With the implantation process ongoing, I headed out to meet Arnold near the center of town. Several crews of people, including a redheaded merwoman from the Guard, worked to clear away the bile regurgitations of the carrion crows. The rest of the crafters, lacking facilities for them to ply their crafts, assisted transporting goods to and from the recovery efforts. The whole thing was controlled chaos, as the pavilions that had once stood proudly in the center of town were so much firewood. Rotted firewood, which was probably worse.

"Ah! He finally shows up!" Arnold called out.

*He's less than five years older than me, why does he feel the need to prod for authority?* It was entirely possible that I'd woken up in a less-than-stellar mood thanks to the way things progressed the day before.

"Yes! And he can't stand the mess that he's seeing!" I called back in reply. The dwarven department head seemed a bit taken aback, but I didn't give him enough time to recover. "You aren't using people to the best of their abilities."

"What could you possibly mean? We are still working on the problems from yesterday," he said, frowning.

"Not that, I mean the way you have things set up. You've got people walking through the bile washout just to get to the destroyed stuff. Use the environment to your advantage. Are you going to use this stuff for anything?" I pointed to the pile of half-decayed, half-usable wood the townsfolk were collecting.

"Errm... Maybe?" The man backpedaled slightly. "What would you suggest we do instead?"

"We are going to have to restructure this whole area if we

are going to move from just standard crafting to infusion crafting. A lot of what I will be teaching you is just how to dip your feet in; I haven't had the time to explore the limits of using infusions. What I *do* know is that infusions are highly dangerous if not handled carefully, and that the aftereffects can be... unpredictable.

"My suggestion? Dump anything that isn't completely clear *onto* the carrion piles to erode, *then* wash it out into some kind of basin using the Guard's help. We are talking magic here, there is no sense in using normal physical logic. The rest of the stuff we set aside, and I get the other earth-attuned to help. You included, if you get an earth manipulating skill with your implant."

Arnold really had nothing to say to that. He repeated my instructions out loud, getting confused looks from almost everyone working under him. Except for the merwoman. She gave me a knowing smirk before releasing her spell chain. She'd been fire-hosing down the asphalt parking lot and cleared home foundations where the pavilions had been erected. Instead of staying with the others while they worked to mound up the damaged materials, she strode up to me.

"We haven't been introduced. My name is Jolene." The woman held her chest and I watched her gills flutter before my eyes locked with hers. Emerald green ringing a deep black hole, framed by auburn locks and a dazzling smile.

I took a step back, reaching out with my hand just to break the unwanted details of my perception. *Why did I want to start counting her freckles?* "Ronan."

"Of course. I don't think there is anyone here who hasn't heard of the *Vanguard,* mighty hero of stone," Jolene said, swooning dramatically before straightening and shaking my hand. "What brings such a celebrity of the new world to this corner of swamp land?"

"Uh... what?"

"What are you doing here, silly? Sarah told me to help out

Arnold since the squads are dissolved while we integrate the trainees. Since it looks like you just told Arnold what to do, I'm now helping *you* out. Make sense?" Her gills fluttered again, and I was only just able to get my thoughts in order.

"Just trying to help the town get moving. If we want to make enough gear to make a difference against Dreg or otherwise, then I'm going to need some serious help," I said.

"Ah. A scrapper, a leader, and a craftsman. Tell me, *Ronan*, is there something you *don't* do?"

*Why is she making my skin crawl when she says my name? Why do I want her to say it again? Magic, it has to be some kind of skill.* Unfortunately, there weren't any visible spell chains about her person, and when my eyes zeroed in on her, her information in my status didn't lend itself to someone capable of affecting the mind.

<Jolene (Human)>

<Attunement: Water>

<Refinement: Pressure>

<Perceived Metier Quotient: 4>

"Is there something on my face?" Jolene said, stepping back from where she'd most certainly been inside my personal space bubble.

*Not that I minded...*

"No, sorry. The implants, if you are close enough and attentive enough to someone, bring up their information. If all goes well, you'll have one too by the end of the day," I said, quickly switching topics. The instincts I'd honed for beasts was flying off the handle with the woman, and I wasn't sure why. She wasn't even wearing armor or weapons.

"Right, of course. My apologies." *Dazzling smile number three.* "So, what do you need, Ronan?"

"Well... I don't want to bother you too much, but I need Sarah to send any earth-attuned—you guys call them Geos—to help make the infusion area. Maybe she can send you to get your implant while I work on this stuff?"

My voice dropped slowly as I saw her smile slip slightly. However, instead of slipping all the way, she nodded with a serious expression. "You got it. If I overheard you right, I won't need to wash all that muck off until later! I will see you later, *Ronan.*"

I wasn't sure how long I stood around, but it was enough that Arnold came back. The man snapped his fingers in my face, drawing me out of my thoughts. "We're done pushing stuff back. Did you want to do your magic mumbo jumbo now or later?"

"I'm going to pass <Infusion>to each of the people in charge of different trades first. Well, as many as I can take with my mana. Might as well start with you, that way people will be less hesitant to approach," I said, glancing at the workers who worked to stack up the last of the rotting materials. The rest were piling up the salvageable stuff inside one of the houses-turned-warehouse within Wildwood.

"Gah. Fine. Just don't do anything strange, will you?" I reached down and placed my palm on his forehead. "Like that..."

He didn't get to finish the thought as my own mind pushed the concept of <Infusion> into him. My mana dropped at a steady trickle. Thankfully, unlike in previous times, <Memory Canal> didn't trigger. However, snippets of memory did spill through the brief connection. The joy of hammering metal. The companionship between me and my father, working the bellows. Then the coldness of the forge when the beasts of the Wild took him. Hammering that metal to protect and grow the people of the town was what kept me going. Even if I had to hammer it alone, the goal was still the same.

The image cut out with Arnold staring daggers at an earth infusion that I knew belonged to his father. The one I knew was tucked away safely in a necklace hidden behind his prominent beard.

"Gah, that's a headache not even some 'shine will give you!" the dwarf said, groaning and stepping back from my palm.

"That's what's coming for those who will work with infusions. Don't worry, it will pass. For now, I want you to start separating out what stock of them we have into the different quotients. People without the implants will be able to infuse, but they won't be able to check which Quotient Level they have." When the dwarf scrunched up his face in confusion, I waved him off. "That will come in the lecture! Just go get your implant and separate out the stock we have. If one of the implanted Wild Guards are around, have them help you."

The still somewhat dazed Dwarf stumbled off towards the Blessing of Magic. It only took a few seconds for me to realize that neither him nor Jolene were there to introduce me to the leaders of the different trades. "Wait, Arnold!"

— + —

Even with my trickle of mana regeneration, my sizable mana pool let me transfer <Infusion> to five people before needing a break. *Yet another thing to ask the Entities.* After giving <Infusion> to the seamstress, carpenter, farmer, blacksmith, and boatwright leaders, the general workers funneled through where I was marking out the crafting area.

It was my most ambitious project yet, and having the help of the other earth-attuned Wild Guards made it the first construction project I'd directed. I was more than a little bit excited, despite the entire lead up to my expedited efforts.

Godfrey and his shovel-hammer were exceptional at moving large quantities of material from one place to another. The Karl-Carl twins were excellent at consolidating and hardening with the massive spell chain they could cast together. Group skills were something I hadn't even touched as an offensive possibility, but I did my best to keep my mind from wandering.

The twins I directed to consolidate the worn and cracked parking lot area. They would use their <Rock Hammers> to break any stubborn portions of asphalt before leveling the whole area. Godfrey essentially dug a trench around the entire space, throwing the magically formed and mundanely excavated dirt into person-tall berms. The idle crafters watched the process somewhat flabbergasted until I had them start to mark out their work locations. Other than a central hallway and the location of supporting, reinforced walls I marked, they were free to organize the space as they wanted.

Jolene returned, somewhat dazed, a few hours later. Right away, the woman utilized the skill she'd acquired, pushing a finger thin stream of water out of her palm. The runic symbols spun slower or faster as she cut through the ground ahead of Godfrey, softening it and letting him rip larger chunks with each of his dirt tosses.

The day went by in a flash. *Well, more like a nonstop strobe party of unwanted memories.* At some point Arnold called an end to the work day, the sun starting its dip out of sight. While it didn't look like much, a roughly rectangular mud wall with piles of dirt arranged in rows down the middle, it was the foundation of a proper building. I sat on one of the walls, leaning into the sun-warmed soil, letting my muscles relax as I sank into the uncon-solidated earth.

I'd mostly been marking and digging the trench outlines, but my mind spun hundreds of different ways. Over thirty snips of life, of living memory, bounced around my head. One for each of the people that I'd imparted <Infusion>. Childhood, youth, adulthood, old age. Childbirth, sorrow at the death of loved ones, uncertainties of the future. Entire personality molding events for the people I'd touched, cramped into first-person picture frames that muddled my own thoughts. It was nowhere as intense as when I'd forcibly extracted information from Charles in order to find the trainees, but the volume was some-thing my mind would not let me ignore. I'd become more inti-mately familiar with the crafters of Wildwood in the span of a day than I had any right to be.

The demon night-shift crew piddled around, getting ready for the day ahead as the rest of the others wound down. A few were crafters like the day workers, and so Arnold directed them to my slumped form. I cracked my neck, rising out of the warm earth to do one final round of people for the day.

"You folks can snag Ronan tomorrow. I'm sure we'll all be plenty busy, and as you can see, we've done a whole lot already, yes?" A voice like that first surface summer rain rolled over me.

To much grumbled consent, the approaching group of demons wandered back to Arnold for other tasks. The dwarf frowned in Jolene's general direction before pointing them to the scattered materials and different equipment that needed to be relocated.

"Thanks," I said, sinking back into my dirt pile. *Man, maybe I should just sleep outside?*

"You are most welcome, Ronan. You are a busy man for someone that just joined our little town," the redhead said, pulling a stray bucket over so she could sit across from me.

"One does what he can," I said, slowly drifting deeper into the mound.

"Did you forget you promised to pass on the skill? The one I got from the crystal has been immensely helpful, so I can only imagine what the one you have been giving out will do," she said softly.

Propping myself on my elbows, I met her gaze. Her emerald eyes were staring intently at me and for some reason I couldn't put it off. She didn't strike me as a crafter or anything of the sort, but she was determined. Who was I to deny that?

I wiped my hand as clean as possible on my pants once I stood. She was almost a foot shorter than me, something that I had neglected to notice thanks to just how much bigger her presence made her. She kept her eyes on me as I placed my palm on her forehead. The scales were almost indistinguishable from her skin at a glance, unlike with the lizard variants of water-attuned, however they stood out against my hand. Letting out a soft breath, I pictured wrapping my mind around <Infusion> and passing it through to her. My mana trickled, then jerked into a torrent out of me as <Memory Canal> triggered as well.

"Ah, sh—" was all I was able to get out before my consciousness was swept up into a whirlpool of memories. Flashes of Jolene's life appeared through my mind as barely more than wisps until I landed square onto the wall of Wildwood.

"Donovan?" I called out, voice as soft as ever. A flowing spell chain like a babbling brook orbited my hand as I swept the area right around my post. Donovan was supposed to return almost an hour ago after bringing the farmers back. Now, I stood guard alone for him to return.

Just outside of view, I could see something lurking in the shadows of the destroyed buildings. The people of Wildwood had opted to work the farm as opposed to clearing the area around the wall as much as possible. Sarah had told them they should, and Sarah always seemed to have a hunch for those things, yet they hadn't listened. A strangled cry cut through the silence I hadn't noticed falling around me. My spell chain wavered, my hands shaking as fear wrapped tighter around my heart.

"Donovan!?" My voice cracked. The shadows tensed in the trees and I knew there was something there, lurking.

"Sarah! We have something outside!"My voice wavered, but I passed the warning down the line. Another of the too-young guards, Karl or Carl—I could never tell them apart—took up the call.

When the message was repeated the third time, Donovan appeared. The part goat man hobbled into the open, picking up speed when his hooved feet touched worn asphalt. My heart nearly stopped in my chest as I watched him bleeding from numerous wounds, a spell chain of his own wrapped around his leg. I knew he didn't have healing abilities, only something to boost strength, but if he was already injured…

A yip cut all rational thought. My hands gripped the edge of the battlement. Fear and the desire to rush out there battled inside me, the spell chain rotating faster and thinner than ever before. "Just a little closer, Donovan!"

The satyr didn't have time to make it just a little closer. Just into the range of my water bubbles. A hound, or a coyote, or something vaguely dog-like cut through the field with ease, pouncing on Donovan. Another creature pushed out of the bush towards my love and I hesitated. The hesitation broke a few seconds later, but it was too late.

My spell chain broke as I poured all of my heat, all of the warmth I lost with my magic, into a punch of water. The spray knocked one beast into the other just as a gun cracked. The second beast yipped, running off into the woods and out of sight. Before I knew what happened, I had pulled open the gates and hovered over Donovan. There was just so much blood. Everywhere. The scruff goatee on his face quivered as his own heat was drawn out of his body.

"Oh... Donny..." I whispered. He knew better than to use his strengthening magic. He bled out faster!

"J-Jolly," he chittered. "I-I made it." The man's eyes fluttered one last time as I felt his skin go as cold as my own. The cold of the dead and lost.

The memory cut out midway through Jolene's strangled cry and the emotion flowing through the memory caused me to falter. Jolene held me up, slightly dazed herself but giving me a quizzical look. "Are you alright, Ronan?"

"Y-yes. I'm alright. Might just be too many transfers for the day," I said. My voice was somewhat choked up as I shook my head, trying to clear the image of Donovan dying right before me. The first death I'd seen—human death—even if not through my own eyes, carried through emotions I couldn't even begin to comprehend.

"Of course. I'm so sorry, I shouldn't have pushed. You wouldn't have been laying down if you hadn't been spent," Jolene said, frowning as she led me out of the work area. "Let me make sure you are at least on your way."

Her eyes and mine met for the briefest of seconds. I was

somehow able to pierce through and understand what I'd witnessed just from the passing glance. The moment when she'd gained her Refinement, and the weight of the loss it carried. My thoughts were a turbulent mess as I climbed the stairs and barely made it to my designated couch. *Should have just stayed in the dirt pile…*

# CHAPTER SIX

## Work Where Possible

"Ronan!"

"Gah!" A <Mineral Strike> exploded out of my hand, nearly taking Samuel's head off as he stepped back. The quartz shard I'd manifested punched a hole through the vines he'd used to fix the ceiling before exploding into a twinkling mess of shards. I blinked against the sudden beam of sunlight cauterizing my eyeballs. "Sam! What the hell, dude!?"

"Sorry. I heard from Danny and Devon. Figured you would want to know," the blond said, sitting atop the shredded metal that had once contained the Dreg Entity. His tone was the farthest thing from apologetic. *If only he was as shy with me as he tends to be with others...*

"Well, don't leave me hanging, man. Who needs coffee when you have fight or flight, am I right?"

Samuel produced a rolled up bundle of paper and... leaves? "I didn't *hear* from the two of them, more like I heard from Anthony. He had this tied around his neck when he showed up at the wall. Clara helped him find me since I was out at the farms."

"Okay, well, what's it say?" I pushed back all the nightmares and strange dreams I'd had haunting me in favor of informa-tion on just what the heck the two had been doing.

Samuel cleared his throat before reading. "'Hey twerps. Daniela here. Devon, the speedy fart, followed me on the way out of town. Said something about 'bold and stupid' but I just assumed he was talking about himself. I digress. We've been chasing the big bastard that took the evil rock. Spotting him has been near impossible after the first few hours, but there are signs of the crow's passing as far as the eye can see. I think it's keeping most critters off our backs, but we are feeling the pres-sure of cutting straight through the woods.'"

He switched through the papers until he got to the ones scratched onto leaves. "'Balance of creatures off. Terrain is changing, like with ants. Will continue for another day. If we do not return by the end of the week… Send help?'"

I wanted to blast another hole in the ceiling. My breath came unevenly as I fought to keep myself from just rushing off into the woods. The last time Daniela had been separated from us, she'd been taken by spiders, and now she was going head first against one of the strongest creatures we'd encountered. Incomprehensible curses tore out of me as I lobbed a small end table straight at the wall.

"Calm down, Ronan," Samuel said, using his magic to catch the table midair. The vines grew to patch in the hole in the ceiling and lower the table down. "She knows what she is doing."

"She's alone, Sam!" I yelled. The blond didn't so much as flinch. "How can I be calm when I don't know what she is facing?"

"She isn't, and you know that. Devon is as much a fighter as you are, and you saw how he was when she was taken the last time. We can count on him," Sam said evenly. My perception picked up his frown, but I could almost feel the confidence he had in those words. The hope that they would prove true was written on his face.

"What do we do then?" I asked, wringing my hands and forcing my voice to a more reasonable decibel.

"Same thing we are doing, just faster, if possible. If there is a stir up of creatures, we may need to head back to the Bunker and up their defenses. Bec isn't even close to Tec's strength level," Sam said, switching gears.

"Right. We don't even know where she is; it would be a waste to try to find her when she could be on her way back already," I said, convincing myself. *Wildwood hasn't recovered enough. Leaving now would leave them crippled even with their larger population.*

"I'll see if I can get Anthony to head back home. I'll feel a bit better if they had him for reinforcement while we are over here. After all the fights recently, I don't even know what to expect," Sam said. Even with his confident front, I could see Samuel crinkling the papers in his hands.

"Me either... Hey." The blond stopped pacing, blinking his eyes at the realization that he'd been moving. "Try to set up some Q0-infused plants near the training ground. No life Attunement, just in case, but try the others. If we have some of those boosting meals, they could make all the difference. At the very least, we can work on learning more about them."

The blond nodded, set the bundle of messages down, and headed for the stairs. "Some jerky in the kitchen, plus the usual fruits," Sam added on the way out.

My blood was more of a gentle rush than the roaring torrent it had been a few minutes prior. Speaking with Sam always helped sort my thoughts out even if the man always left more anxious than when he arrived. *Get yourself together, Ronan. You may not want to lead, but that's what you are doing. That means you suck it up and make the best decisions.*

The swirling mass of memories from before chose that moment to resurface. Emotions sought to both rile me up and calm me down, leaving me with a sense of crippling confusion until I was able to get my thoughts in order. The rumble of my stomach helped sharpen my concentration and get my emotions under control. As distinctly uncomfortable as the strange surge was, I felt much calmer about everything afterwards. Suspiciously calm.

"No time to worry about that now. Later. When something isn't trying to kill people I love," I said. The bitter laughter that followed came unbidden from my lips.

Breakfast went by in a flurry as I got dressed and armored. Considering what I was going to be doing during the day, it would have been easier to just wear my undershirt and cargos, but with the potential of raining corruption at any time, I felt better being prepared. By the time I made my way out of the training building, Sarah was already running the trainees through drills. While none of us were 'militant' in nature, we recognized the importance of structure when working towards a goal. It was how the implants had even come about in the first place; each of the specialties of the Bunker kept it running and building the parts.

What Sarah was doing was something along those lines. There was a clear separation between the trainees who had received the implants and those waiting their turn. One group was working on strength conditioning, another was running sprints around the makeshift track, and the last one worked on making defensive structures. The other group yet to receive implants did their best to demolish said structures. It was a veritable mosh pit of magic, each intermingling and fighting for supremacy. Rock sprayed all over the place picked up by sharp winds, fire scorched vines, and sprays of ice and water diluted toxic-looking clouds of sludge. All the while, Sarah was yelling comments and pointing out ways in which they could improve their efforts. I had a sneaking suspicion that the trainees were being trained for more than protecting the town.

Most of the trainees that spotted me waved in greeting and Sarah gave me a nod in acknowledgment as I headed toward the center of town. What I saw there surprised me yet again.

The industriousness of the people of Wildwood was on full display. Crates of rough-cut wood had been set out at the edge of the construction area. Each had an attunement and a level carved into the lip. Inside were the assorted masses of the loot the town had collected over the years, as well as what we had managed to get from farming the dungeon and fighting the Dregs. It was...a sizable stock.

"You did tell me to get this here done, didn't you?" Arnold said, slapping me on the back.

"That I did. Did you have people working through the night?" I asked, running my hands through the tops of the crates. Even with how different each of the infusions looked, they always felt the same: squishy blobs of gelatin. *Kind of like Blobby...*

"Them night horn folk are nimble, lemme tell you!" Arnold laughed awkwardly. His sudden blush at the mention of the demon Fallen derailed my train of thought and then dropped it straight into a chasm. Not only did a blush look strange on a dwarf, but the meek eye shift that fit more on an anime character was too much.

"Riiiiight. Well, this is great!" I said as energetically as I could, moving down the crates until we got to the ones set up for Quotient Level 4. There were only four: death, fire, water, and air. I was pretty interested in finding out the story behind those, but opted to leave it for another time. Instead, I selected a handful of Q0 air infusions, as that was the most abundant, and a few Q0 fire infusions.

<Quotient 0 Infusion>
<Air - N/A>
<Integrity: 14%>

<Quotient 0 Infusion>
<Fire - N/A>
<Integrity: 7%>

The percent on each of them varied wildly from ninety to the single digits. I hadn't spent any time researching that rate of decay, or what that implied, but it did tell me that those infu-sions were at least older than our arrival at Wildwood.

I picked out the lowest percent ones and threw the rest back in the bin. No sense in using more complete infusions if the rest would suffice for a demonstration.

"Any last people that need the skill?" I checked with Arnold.

"Some of the night crew, but I think that's about it," Arnold said, looking off in the distance as if he were working through a list in his head.

"Awesome. Let's get this party going then. I can give the lecture right here, if you want," I said.

"I'll get everyone wrangled up," Arnold said, already shuf-fling off on his shorter legs.

"Oh, and tell the other Geos they can keep working on the building in the meantime!" I called out. He waved his hand dismissively without turning around.

"It's fun to see Arnold get bossed around so easily," a soft voice said behind me.

Had it been any other pitch, I think I would have run them through with magic, but Jolene was stealthy *and* smooth.

"Not trying to, just getting everyone on the same page. Once this is done, I'll be back out there." I gestured vaguely towards the walls.

Jolene didn't reply, instead leaning back on one of the crates as we waited. Of course, I couldn't just stand there enjoying the company and had to do *something*.

"You think you can cut my rock?" I asked.

"That a challenge?" Jolene said, her smile turning into a wide smirk.

"Just a question. Should give people somewhere to sit, you know?" Instead of explaining, I reached into my mana pool.

Since getting to Q4, my <Stone Spike> at base cost had gotten almost three feet thick at the base. A half-cost cast could give me half that, and so on. So I worked five <Stone Spikes> at once. It was the largest multicast I'd done and I immediately felt the strain. A nonstop gut punch that wanted to hitch my breath and drop me to my knees, but instead I grit my teeth.

The sensation peaked as the brown spell chains completed and five perfectly in line spikes sprouted from the ground. They were just shy of my height, but the bases were thick enough for stools, which was the goal.

"Cut them at hip height for me? Please?" I asked, turning to Jolene. I'd expected her to still be smirking at me, but she looked genuinely impressed by my display of magic. She wasn't even looking at me anymore, but between the spikes and her hand.

Right away, she walked up to the first, calling forth her azure spell chain, the one acquired from Tec, and set to cutting my spike. Even with her full concentration, it still took her several minutes to grind through enough rock to snap the top off. She shivered as her magic side effects ran through her body, but her eyes were glued to the next spike. The subsequent one was just a bit faster.

Once my mana was recovered, I repeated the process a few more times, as well as using <Earthen Barrier> to raise benches along the back and sides of the open air classroom. Jolene didn't stop even as people arrived and complained about the muddy mess she was making with the runoff of her skill. A quick use of my passive mana effect, and the water was pushed out of the soil, streaming downhill towards the wetland to the southwest and leaving a smooth surface.

People milled around until I gestured to the different seats. They looked hesitant, seeing the sharp edges Jolene had cut in the rock, but they sat nonetheless. Once everyone that was around got situated, roughly thirty people plus a few watchers off in the distance, I used <Earthen Barrier> to raise myself a work table. Also, with a swing of my pick, I chipped a few pieces of rock to use.

"Hello everyone. While some of you may know my background as a person born in one of the survival bunkers, I just want to put it into perspective. This group gathered here is almost as large as all the people I've known most of my life. If I fumble through some of my explanations or anything, please let me know and I'll do my best to address it. This is my first, uhhh...lecture, shall we call it."

The intensity of the people was a bit unnerving. My hands got a bit clammy just from watching them watch me. Their eyes pierced me with their attention and my legs felt a tad unsteady when I noticed that no one refused eye-contact; they were *ready* for a speech from the Vanguard. *I can fight mutated humans and ants the size of cars but a captive audience bothers me?* Instead of denying my own nervousness, I leaned into it. This lecture was just another creature to be slain... So to speak.

"Before we start, I want to preface this by saying I myself am still learning. There is untapped potential in using the infusions, and it's going to take all of us innovating to get there. With that said, we are going to start simple.

"What is an infusion? Can anybody *not* in the Guard tell me?" I asked.

An elf near the back raised their hand until I pointed. *I didn't even consider that Wildwood must have a basic education program of some sort! I just assumed, which I suppose is a good sign for how well their system is working.* "Is it like an organ that comes out of killed creatures?"

"Close. It is part of their energy, solidified. As far as our understanding goes, and this comes from the conversations I've been able to have with the Metier Crystals, killed creatures can do one of..." I counted in my head quickly. "Three things.If they are unattuned, like most of the plant life is, they simply die and leave a body. You can harvest materials and anything else you can get from a corpse. However, if the creature is Attuned, it can either dissociate or have its mana locked. A mana locked creature would act just like a dead unattuned creature, except for the fact that it is already stronger than its unattuned counterpart."

"Is that why things have gotten so much bigger?"one of the pre-Fall people in the crowd asked.

"Yes and no. Size is more of like a selective trait for the

creatures, even if it does affect how strong they are. However, the biggest contributor to that size and strength is their Quotient Level. The higher that is, the stronger they are. My *own* study into this reveals they are roughly three times as strong as before for each level."

That tidbit of information caused a stir in the crowd. Questions were shot and the overall drone of the people made it hard to think. A shrill whistle cut through the space.

"You lot best get your heads on straight. Since when are we prone to this nonsense? Let the man speak!" Arnold called out, his voice a rumble from where he stood on one of my benches just to be seen.

There were low mumbles amongst the people listening, but I was able to keep talking at the least.

"I didn't realize that would cause a stir. I want to add that this is also the case for humans. Pre-Fall humans are also affected, but I'm not clear on the specifics. When I was Quotient 0, this was all I could muster." I cast a <Stone Spike> at roughly a tenth of my power. The three foot tall protrusion even *looked* weaker than the spikes the people were sitting on. As part of the demonstration, I tripled the power until I did a full cast of the skill. The eight foot pointed rock towered beside me, causing people to finally quiet completely.

"There is a qualitative change in power, in addition to a baseline quantitative increase to your body. The things leading to these changes are Pith and Dreg." The group tensed at the mention of the Dreg. I raised my hands, trying to placate them so I continued quickly. "The Dreg, like anything in excess, is bad. The Crystals are here to purge it, but every living thing produces it. Best as I can tell, it's like the magical version of the water or nitrogen cycle."

"The what cycle?"one of the lizardfolk in the group asked.

"The water cycle. You know, water evaporates, condensates in clouds, then precipitates down. Rinse and repeat?"

There was mumbled discussion amidst the group. Some of the old humans in the group explained it to the Fallen, getting nods of understanding. *Good education, but probably don't have the resources to sit back and have youths just learn.*

"Sorry, I wasn't trying to make any assumptions. The water cycle analogy isn't exactly pertinent to our *crafting* discussion, so I'll keep moving forward."*I am bungling this up something fierce...* "So, creatures not mana locked. They break down into three things. The Pith-Dreg cloud, a condensed material that was part of the creature, and an infusion. The cloud you've all seen, as well as the looted materials, and these crates are full of infusions collected from all the things Wildwood and my group have killed and absorbed. That make sense so far?"

"Why do we care about any of this? I can make tools and weapons just fine without any magic nonsense," said a regular human near the back. He had his arms crossed and was practically looking down his nose at me. "All you need is a fire and some metal."

From the strange metallic sheen to his skin, he had to be earth-or fire-attuned. Instead of wasting time glancing at his information via the implant, I unslung my pickaxe. A slight flex of my arm brought the weapon crashing down onto my presentation table. The group jumped like an uneven wave. The people I knew for a fact were higher Quotient jumped before the others, a funny side effect of the increased attributes and their enhanced senses.

"This here is a Quotient 1 infused pickaxe. I suppose it looks fairly standard, other than the crystal right through the eye. You might very well be able to make something like this, even with the need to use more primitive forging techniques. What your mundane crafting isn't going to make is this." I pulsed my mana into the weapon, going for the most impractical thing I could think of, which just so happened to be a five foot blade of crystal that almost reached the people sitting in the front row. Every eye was on the weapon that had manifested before them. With a mental switch flipped, the mana flow cut off and the crystal disintegrated slowly. "Magical weapons and armor. Utilizing this weapon gives me a corresponding boost to my strength. Others I've made increase speed, and I hope we can figure out how to boost any of the attributes you will need to learn about."

My little display caused an even bigger stir than when I told them about the Quotient strengths. Questions flew in left and right, but I put up a halting hand. "The basics, first. This is an infusion…"

# CHAPTER SEVEN

## You Get an Infusion, and You Get Infusion, and You...

For the next hour I worked through the steps of infusing. I'd learned the hard way. I described the basics of 'directing' the Pith as the infusion unwound. With how many of the magical blobs I'd manipulated, it was a piece of cake to put on a demonstration. The mostly spent infusions practically disintegrated the moment I unspooled them. There wasn't a single set of eyes not mesmerized as I swirled the Pith thread in the air, describing the sensation of grabbing it with my mind.

When I was sure I had their attention, I slammed the thread into the rock chip I'd made earlier. The air infusion winked out within seconds; considering it was the shortest thread I'd used, it didn't surprise me. Immediately, the chip started shaking, going from a small wobble into a vibratory dance that I distinctly recognized. With a smooth motion, I used my pick—which was still impaled on the table sans giant crystal blade—to form a dome over the chip. The pinging of rock on glass was all that the group heard as the piece of rock blasted itself apart. A gasp went up from the crowd, suddenly looking uncertainly between the crystal dome and me.

"And this, folks, is why we are working on *that*," I said,

pointing to the slowly growing mounds of soil the dwarves of the Wild Guard were churning. "I want to make it clear that everything I tell you in this class is based on my own experiences. I have not experimented with all the attunements. I have not experimented with all the materials you could possibly acquire in nature and as drops from creatures. I have not even experimented with a tenth of the combinations of effects you can get from infusing a material with a certain innate Attunement with a different one. Is that clear?"

I worried very briefly that some heads were going to fall off shoulders with how rigorously they nodded their agreement. Even the skeptical ones amongst the group had nothing to say after that.

As another example, I repeated the infusion process with the fire infusion. While not as explosive as the air one, the rock visibly changed color from mud-brown to a dull red before crumbling into a small pile of sand. My explanation included warnings that each of the infusions caused different effects during the infusion process. From the ones I'd worked with: air vibrated the material, fire heated it up, water froze the material, earth compressed it. Unfortunately, I hadn't been able to work with life and death infusions other than the live experiment on Samuel's plants. A glance behind me at the crates brought a smile to my face as I considered the opportunity to learn that was present not only for the people of Wildwood, but also for me.

Once the basics of the process were complete, I explained a bit about how Quotients scaled. Just like a creature's level, the infused items would grow in power the more infusions were applied. I shared my theory about crafting materials with the group; the level of the material provided a sort of cap for the crafter to meet. Something could only hold so much Pith before it failed, just as the rocks had done even with the trickle of Pith in the decayed infusions.

The blacksmiths volunteered their surplus mundane materials to practice their skill before actually using up the stock of loot dropped materials the Guard had acquired over time. Many of said pieces were already incorporated in a 'mundane' capacity in the armor and gear of the Wild Guard, so getting it upgraded to actual infused equipment was a priority for the town. The crafters seemed to agree when I brought it up.

Instead of jumping into the actual creation of an item or any of the 'tweaking' techniques Bec had taught me to improve the final product, I started to pass out the decayed infusions. The group was distinctly confused until I explained that it was time to put what I'd shown into practice before we discussed anything else. The reactions were... varied. Many looked apprehensive to even be holding the air or fire infusions, some looked eager to mess with the elemental forces, and others looked at the blobs in hand like they were going to explode and kill them on the spot. Rommel, the only one I'd given a rough primer to before my lecture, had actually joined the group at some point. He grunted as he took the infusion in my hand.

I sat back, giving the internal discussions a listen as people compared the fire and air infusions, others talked about their fears, and some just twitched to do something with them. *Man, I bet my uncle would be all over teaching this stuff.* The thought of our families back at the Bunker made me distinctly homesick. Instead of dwelling on it, I continued to pass out pebbles and promised that we would go and reinforce our home as soon as possible.

"Now, everyone, I want you to do your best to pull the Pith thread *out* of the infusion, and *into* the rock. Yes? If you feel your rock is shaking too much or getting too hot to hold, drop it in this hole." I pointed and enlarged the gap in my makeshift work station. "Two at a time please," I said. *Just in case I need to cover someone with my pickaxe shield...*

A lizardwoman and a human were the first up. Both had air infusions and both succeeded in getting them into the rock. Unsurprisingly, they started getting ready to blow up. They dropped them in the hole, and I covered it with my shield. The impacts pinged gently off of the chitin, releasing a gust of heat around. The effect gave the human pause. "Is it supposed to do that?"

"Innate property of infused material drops. Yet another thing I don't know everything about. However, this takes force and turns it into heat, reducing the impact," I explained. The human's frown was deep, and he tugged on his graying beard as the pair walked away. The lizardwoman smiled with too many teeth, bowed her head, and followed after the man.

And so it went for almost another hour. Several people failed on the first pass and had to get another infusion from me before passing on the second try. Something I noticed as the testing wore on was a pattern between the different Attunements. The fae and satyrs could pull the string with ease, but struggled to control it, for instance. The fire-, air-and water-attuned could slam the threads much more easily. The few diurnal demons that joined us seemed perfectly capable at pulling and control, but no better than any others. For the earth-attuned, the same was the case, except they didn't look nearly as drained as everyone else did handling the infusions. *Maybe a correlation towards attributes?* While I wondered absently, Jolene strode up to my table.

"Does the professor have time for more lessons?" she said, smiling. I could see that it wasn't a perfect smile now, more of a mask. Her flash of memory was too recent, too vivid, for me not to overlap the memory each time we spoke.

"I can answer questions, but I think everyone needs to digest what I taught today. After working on the building, I plan to make some items, so you are free to watch," I said, gesturing at one of the crates that had assorted materials piled high. It was practically begging me to craft to my heart's content.

"The thing you did with Clara's weapon... What was that?"

The question brought me up short. I hadn't expected a simple question, but not a question about the augmenting trait item either. "To be honest with you, it's still a mystery to me. My best guess is that it had something to do with the main material I used, the stinger. While using it... well, it acted like a focusing point for the mana. Except it was fire-attuned to my earth and Clara's death. Haven't had much more time to mess around with it either," I said, shrugging. "Yet another thing I don't have time for."

"Hmmm…" Jolene went silent, as if she were weighing something in her mind. "Do you think you could try to make something like that again?"

"Uh… Sure. I can't guarantee anything, since I am still working on the specifics of the whole thing. Just having the tools infused, however, makes a difference," I said, pointing to my equipment. "This is actually some of the worst stuff I've made. Except for that tricked out gardening shovel," I said, smiling at my first test project.

"I'll drop it off at the training center. Let me see if those builders of yours need help before I hop back into the watch rotation," Jolene said. She hesitated, shot a more subdued smile my way, and disappeared through the crowd of crafters.

I stared after her for several seconds before a barrage of questions landed on me. Two hours of the time I'd intended to work on construction turned into a Q and A session with the crafters as they left to work on their tasks, but came back with burning questions. While it made me happy to have ignited so much drive to learn infusing in the people of Wildwood, and many of their questions were things I hoped to test and work through, I watched the sun climb and couldn't help but feel like time was slipping through my fingers. Arnold once again came to my rescue.

"Let the man take a breath! You'd think he was an elf with how much wind he's been throwing at yah," the dwarf yelled, shooing away the crowd with less-than-gentle shoves. Everyone grumbled, but before long, the makeshift classroom was clear but for Arnold and myself. "You alright there, friend?"

I considered plowing through as I had, but he'd been straight with me so far. *Too* straight sometimes, but not really rude. "I'm alright, just… drained. This *is* literally the most people I've interacted with at once. Well, not if we count fights, but the situation is different."

The dwarf huffed. "Understood. Do what you need. You've given us a huge leg up already. I don't want to see you answering questions during the day; I'll take care of that." Arnold paused, and I saw him chew on his beard.

"Go ahead, I appreciate the consideration," I said, patting the man on the shoulder. Considering his height, it wasn't hard.

"How… How long for the building? The work orders are piling up and I know it's not your fault, but working space is at a premium," Arnold said with a sigh.

"If I can churn the rest of the day, you'll have walls done today and the first portion of the ceiling. That work for you?"

Arnold stammered for a second. "Y-yes, of course. You just let me know what you need!"

"What skill did you get?" The dwarf tilted his head in confusion. "With your implant."

"Oh! It's called <Stone Anvil>, but I haven't tested it yet…" Arnold looked around, as if talking about having magic would make it vanish.

"Let her rip. If you want to help, then I need to know what you can do," I said, smiling encouragingly.

The dwarf set his shoulders and nodded before turning towards the ruins of one of the nearby houses. He yelled out his skill with his chest, a spell chain forming a wide circle of runes. The soil around immediately heaved down, only to rise up in the center as a perfect square block roughly two feet cubed. Arnold staggered from the aftereffects, but I kept a solid grip on him to keep him from falling. When he was well enough to stand, we both walked over to examine the result.

It looked like a modified version of my own <Stone Spike> mixed with <Earthen Barrier>. The soil had concentrated many times more than with my spike, and formed a solid block of smooth, beige-black rock. As a test, I swung my pick onto it only for it to be deflected. There was only a slight dent where the point had struck.

"Damn Arnold. How much mana did this cost?" I asked, slapping the block.

"Eh… Says I have thirty percent left here in my implant…" Arnold swiped at the air, obviously trying to touch his mana bar.

*Damn, that's costly…* "Alright, here's what you can do for me. I want you to work on the smithy and on one of the empty rooms. Your goal is to make many of those blocks there," I gestured to the stone anvil, "and make them part of the walls. The second room can be our testing and higher Quotient crafting room. That sound good?"

"Of course it does! Just… what should I do in the meantime?"

"For the head of the crafters, you sure do seem to be hesitating a lot, Arnold," I said, crossing my arms and smiling at him.

"Ha! You try getting dropped in the deep end of mag—" He saw my slowly rising eyebrow and opted to clear his throat. "Right. Well, we are still quite inexperienced."

"Use the passive form of your mana when you don't have enough for <Stone Anvil>. It works the same, just hold back on releasing the skill and the spell chain, the floating symbols and stuff, will materialize. It will help consolidate and harden the ground or walls. Got it?"

The man didn't even reply. Instead, he devolved into fiddling with his newfound power.

My eyes drifted from Arnold, to the lingering crowd of crafters, to the half-built structure next to us, and finally to the crate with materials. A long, whistling sigh escaped my lips as I realized that my hope of actually crafting was unlikely to happen soon. Instead of dwelling on that too much, I focused on the fact that I was leading the construction of a building created almost solely with magic. That single thought brought a smile to my face and I climbed the growing mounds of dirt.

The twins were hammering away at the ground, smoothing it out with their oversized rock hammers. I ducked out of the way just as Godfrey propelled more dirt from around the parking lot into a nearby pile. There was rubble intermixed in it as the man worked to clear the cracked foundations of nearby buildings with a trio of others he'd somehow roped into helping. Already, the moist earth and ground stone dust lingered in the air. Even as it settled on my skin, I couldn't help but feel energized to be knee deep in it.

The surface had so much space to grow, to build, and there was no way I was going to waste the opportunity.

"Godfrey! Spread it out some, or that mound is going to collapse!" I yelled, sliding down into the marked building as my mana thrummed through me.

# CHAPTER EIGHT

## The First Hall of Crafters

The rest of the day's hours vanished in a blur of mud, rock, and dirt of unprecedented proportions. Samuel came by with some jerky and potatoes for lunch, but that was only the briefest of breaks from the work. While the twins worked on consolidating the base of the building and Godfrey provided support, me and Arnold went *up*. Overcharged <Stone Spikes>spaced every ten feet rose up as pillars for the building and the many walls. The rest of my mana, I burned using <Earthen Barrier> to consolidate the soil between spikes. The abundant earth mound meant that the solid rock surface didn't take soil from the base to consolidate, letting the wall climb higher and higher.

While much slower than my own skill, Arnold didn't let the side effects of his skill stop him. The dwarf was a block producing monster, which translated to the entire outer wall of the 'test' room being completed. Seeing how their efforts were being rewarded, the other dwarves kicked their efforts into high gear. While the twins complained about heartburn and Godfrey huffed with each breath, they had soon joined me on working the exterior walls. The twins didn't have a compacting skill like me or Arnold, but they figured out that if they used the passive form on either side of a mound, it would compress towards the center. Much less efficient, but no less effective. Godfrey resorted to slapping the mound with his shommer, packing it down where we had yet to arrive.

When the golden rays of the sun bleached orange, the outer walls and internal supports were complete.

The four of us practically slumped to the ground, a twitching mass of groans and complaints due to our overzealous use of mana. So, naturally, someone had to rain on our commiserating parade. Literally. A deluge of water rinsed a thick layer of dirt I hadn't even noticed covering me and the others. We sputtered and wobbled to our feet to see a smirking Jolene, frowning Samuel, and a laughing Irwin.

"You boys sure know how to get carried away," the councilman said, wagging his finger in mock admonishment. "Here I thought you were slacking off when you were building a building all alone!"

"Ron, what have I told you about pushing your body like this? Ava is going to have your hide when I tell her about this," Sam said, crossing his arms.

"There's no need for that!" I jumped to my feet in an instant. "It was just a little maxing out. I never emptied my mana pool!"

"You *did* keep people out of the loop. The other crafters have been trying to check in and ask questions all day after your lecture. They came to *me* with questions when they saw me working on the infused plants! To *me*, Ronan!"

I winced internally. As much as he cared about people, Samuel wasn't the best with talking even with others in the Bunker. It always seemed to take a lot out of him. "Sorry, Sam. That should be the bulk of the work on the building though…" I added by way of defense.

As if looking at what we'd accomplished for the first time, he glanced at the structure behind us. From the outside it looked… less than beautiful. Since we were looking for material strength and speed, the walls looked like a hodgepodge mess of grays and browns where the soil, rock and rubble had been compressed. The walls rose up eight feet all around the perimeter, with the <Stone Spike> pillars rising almost ten. A central hallway connected the main street of Buena Vista Boulevard that ran through the middle of the town to the building.

The east wing was dedicated almost entirely to the more physical trades. The forge had already been moved and materials were being carried by the night crew to fill it with its normal accouterments. Many looked like torture implements to me, but I wasn't a blacksmith, so who was I to judge? The bottom corner of the east wing also shared a strong wall with the testing room, the one Arnold feverishly worked to build. Archless doorways led to both rooms from the main path, the ceiling still missing in its entirety. On the western wing was… everything else. A half-dozen rooms separated into tailoring, carpentry, masonry, and tanners. The corresponding crafters had already started moving some of the materials they'd salvaged from their destroyed pavilions in order to secure one room or another. I'd ignored most of the squabble over the 'best' rooms or their positioning, focused on just getting the walls done.

Having finished the outside, I really felt like we'd made progress. Knowing what I did about my barriers, and having tested Arnold's <Stone Anvil>'s durability, the infrastructural future of Wildwood was in good hands once a few of the other dwarves gained implants and skills.

"Damn," Irwin said, nodding his head in appreciation. "Color me impressed as hell."

"Thanks. It was a group effort," I said, gesturing to the other dwarves slumped on the ground around me. I was the only one half-seated; the Wild Guards were paying attention to the exchange but not bothering to engage other than an initial greeting. Arnold was already snoring his butt off.

"You got a plan for people to *breathe* in this building?" Jolene asked, cutting right to the building's flaw. For all our construction speed and strength, minor modifications were still outside of our arcane expertise. Or even our mundane expertise, considering the Guards were primarily fighters and Arnold was a blacksmith.

"I was hoping you'd be able to help with that, actually," I said, flipping the script on her and rising to my feet. I included Samuel in my sweeping arm gesture. "Both of you actually."

"I'm listening," Jolene said, raising an immaculate eyebrow up in question.

"I need you to cut windows and vents into the building, as well as drainage paths. Sam, I need you and probably a few of the more vegetatively inclined healers to weave a ceiling after I build the truss supports."

"What, like some kind of thatch roof?" Sam asked in confusion.

*He didn't outright say no, that's a positive.* "Whatever you think will keep water out of the building when it rains. We *are* in Florida right? What you did for the training building inspired the idea. Why get caught up in a heavy ceiling or roof, when magically reinforced plants are lighter and can do the job just as well for now? You know, since sturdy buildings are somewhat in demand, thanks to the puke air raids we've suffered."

"That's unfortunately not one of the craziest things you've ever devised." Sam let out a suffering sigh, practically wincing with the words. "I'll talk to them about doing the ceiling. Worst case, you know I'll be your construction lackey."

"Heck yeah!" I high-fived him, and he couldn't keep the frown on his face anymore.

"And I suppose you just expect me to be your construction lackey too, no?" Jolene said, somewhat disbelieving.

"Hmm, yes? *But* I *am* making that weapon for you," I said, pointing at her. She grumbled something that sounded mightily like 'snake' under her breath before agreeing.

"Great! I'll catch you both after lunch tomorrow then. I'll get together with the crafters and see if they have any special needs for drainage or ventilation before giving you directions, Jolene. I hope to have the truss system done by lunch, Sam." I

glanced over my shoulder at the slumped pile of dwarven workers. "Well, if that lot wake up tomorrow."

"Wouldn't really exclude yourself from the late morning
bunch, Ron," Sam said with a smirk. "Come on. Let's get you
some grub before you turn into a fossil."

"I can wake up early when I want to!" I complained.

"Sure you can!" Sam said, throwing an arm over my
shoulder and patting my back condescendingly as he led me
towards the cooking areas near the center of town.

"Why I ought to…"

The next morning came all too soon. Breakfast passed as I
dragged my feet back to work. *Never thought I would have a 'job.'
Even if Dale was grooming me to take over the water system, without new
people in the Bunker, what was the point? Now I suppose I could get a job.*
With thoughts of the future swirling around in my head, I
walked up on the construction site of the crafting hall. It was
*much* livelier than the day before, as crafters and non-crafters
really took the opportunity to see what we'd accomplished. I
spotted Arnold arguing loudly with some of the non-crafters
and approached.

"—we don't have!" I heard him say.

"It doesn't have to be now, Arny, we just want in on this
construction action," one of the women talking with him said.

"Bah! You think I work for free, do you!?" he yelled back.

"Actually, you know Irwin lifted the pay scale. We are
working on communal income right now, so it's the only time
we can afford to talk to you," the man, an orc unlike the other
non-Fallen, said.

The grumble under his beard was hardly a mumble. "Dang
council with their dang rules and their dang profit-cutting initia-
tives and their—"

"You know, *Arny*, no one at the Bunker had any kind of
currency. Not that I care, since I think bringing back capitalism

will take a while. Fiefdoms are more likely before the ol'democratic system rolls around," I said by way of greeting. Not surprising me at all, the small group looked at me like I'd grown a second *and* third head.

"Don't rightfully know what in the great crystals you are saying," Arnold was finally able to get out.

"Not a problem for now. What *is* a problem for now is what these folks are talking about."

As if sensing an opening, the orc pounced. "We are asking Arnold and his workers to improve some of the houses. The attack of those birds didn't destroy just the crafting area, but a lot of good crops and homes that we'd cared for."

"Reasonable," I said, turning to Arnold, who felt like working on his beard braid right then was the right choice. "I'll have a talk and he'll get back to you."

"Thank you, Vanguard," the orc said, followed by a bow from the group before they scurried off to their tasks. The last bit of the exchange gave me a significant amount of pause.

"What in the heck was that?" I asked, stunned.

"Oh, that? Well, you've got a reputation, Ronan. Mostly around doing crazy things and getting in trouble, but also for getting things done. I assume they took you at your word that you'd 'have a talk' with me." Arnold scoffed. He didn't even look my way as he gathered some of the tools he'd been arranging before he'd been mobbed.

"Okay, maybe that makes sense. What's the deal with the bow there?" It made me distinctly uncomfortable.

"Most of the town does that for the Wild Guard, Clara and her misfits in particular. They see it as respectful, considering all the contributions those with Gifts give to the town. Me? I know better. You lot are just a bunch of adrenaline junkies."

Mechanically following Arnold into the roofless building, I let my thoughts really tumble. Of course the Wildwoodians hadn't gotten my joke about fiefdom and capitalism, and the council was already a step beyond just having a sovereign king, but it was entirely possible that an Attuned Earth would have returned to something akin to the Middle Ages. Unfortunately, my knowledge was sorely lacking, as were pretty much all the STEM-focused members of the Bunker, in the field of historical politics. *How are the other small towns organized? What about the other towns or cities beyond that? If Wildwood survived, then surely there are others.*

My train of thought only snapped back into reality because a toe-tapping Jolene stood waiting inside the crafting hall. Her usual calm demeanor and otherworldly smile was replaced with a deep frown that even my socially inexperienced eyes could read as frustration and borderline anger. Her tone quickly confirmed it.

"You make it a habit of keeping people waiting, oh great Vanguard?"

"This here is your problem," Arnold whispered before he shuffled off towards the smith room.

"Sorry, Jolene. I wasn't trying to get caught up, just lending a helping hand."

"Right. Sure. Now, what do you want me to do?" she snapped.

I scratched the back of my head awkwardly for a second before opting not to comment on the conversation. I explained the breakdown of what I'd gathered from talking to the crafters during the dinner meal the previous day. The smiths wanted as much ventilation as physically possible, while keeping the heat concentrated on the corner with their forge and bellows. Barrels for water and various oils they used were their only drainage concerns. The carpenters, tailors, and masons only needed some ventilation and windows in their space, while the tanners wanted *targeted* ventilation and drainage. They explained that they had several vats they ran the hides through before they were ready to use, and each one produced a number of byprod-ucts. So, to accommodate what I understood of the process, I marked out three basins, each with individual drains, into larger basins outside and away from the building.

While she seemed annoyed with me, Jolene paid attention to

my whole explanation. She even went so far as to make suggestions to my markings that would simplify the use of her high-speed water skill. Once she was set to the task, I looked up into the cloudy sky overhead and got to work on my own goal.

It didn't take long to find the dwarven group milling about, waiting for me to finish my talk with Jolene. "She take your head off?" Godfrey asked.

"No?" I asked, uncertainly.

"Good!"

"Dagnammit!" Karl and Carl called.

When I turned back to Godfrey, he shrugged. "They had money on whether she was going to blow up on you."

"Worthless money," Arnold mumbled. He grumbled to himself before turning back to me. "What's the plan, then? I've been eager to fire up the forge after so long rolling in the dirt!"

"You might just get the chance, then. Here's my plan…"

The four of us worked in tandem. While Arnold recovered mana to create more hardened stone blocks, the others chipped the tips off the columns and extracted the blocks from the dip in soil it created while forming. Using some of the fire infusions, I soldered the block to my pillars before casting <Stone Spike> on it. The super compressed rock provided more than sufficient material to stretch out over half the distance of a room without compromising the vertical portion of the structure. When we placed the next stone anvil block, I was able to match both ends of the spike into a triangle truss. It wasn't the best design, since the spikes made everything nonuniform, but I was confident in their strength.

We got into a rhythm, even taking a break to help Arnold set up the forge and push out the compressed blocks Jolene cut out as windows. Our rhythm was so good, in fact, that we had completed the trusses before the sun was even at its zenith. Jolene was still working with the help of the twins, but Godfrey was able to return to guard duty and Arnold to churn magic blocks and stoke his fires.

Ahead of schedule, I ambled the town in search of Samuel. The first person I spotted was old farmer William, poised atop the southern wall with a look of concentration plastered on his face. Instead of calling out like a rude individual, I watched with curiosity. The logs directly around him seemed to pulse with green energy for a brief second before the man slumped.

I hurried to his side. "You alright there, William?"

"Oh, Ronan. I'm alright, my boy. Just getting a little feel of how the crops are doing. I've just never been felt *back* by said crops," the man said, shuddering slightly.

Considering all the magical nonsense I'd experienced up to that point, it wouldn't surprise me if he could invite plants over for tea. When I looked down at where he'd been looking, I spotted what he'd been talking about.

A field easily five times the size of the western ones stretched out before me. Some distance away was an old brick building that had been turned into a similar structure as the forward base toward US 301. In the space between the palisade and the building, Samuel and a few other life-attuned worked. Sections of soil had been cordoned off and marked with stakes of various colors, clearly identifying the Attunement my childhood friend had forced on the plants.

At a glance, you'd think they were just odd-colored tomatoes. Upon further inspection, the changes became more noticeable. A lingering ash cloud, or a misty fog that had no business existing in full sun. A thorn briar where gentle stems should have been. I stood flabbergasted at the extent of testing my friend had done because, sure enough, when my eyes focused on the individual plants, all but Life Attunements were represented.

"Ronan!" Sam called, waving from the field.

"Go on, son. I'll be just fine. I have a sneaking suspicion I've got life left to live just to see what crazy you lot bring into my life," William said, shuffling off the wall and down the steps. I watched the man for a few seconds before meeting up with Sam.

As much as I wanted to ask him what exactly was going on with the extent of his vegetation, I focused on finishing the building. Sam was all gung ho to do a little bit of his own construction. He spaced out as he communicated with someone via the comm-plant before the two of us returned to the standing walls. He let out an appreciative whistle.

"Gave us a good frame to work with," Sam said, glancing over his shoulder as Ophelia joined them. "I've been thinking of some fun features we might be able to implement thanks to Ophelia. I'd bet the two of us can get this done soon. You just take a little break and work on that gift for Jolene."

"What are you—" I asked before he cut me off.

"You didn't even notice the sack she dropped off yesterday?"

*Ah crap. I told her I was going to make that today but I got too caught up with building…*

Patting Sam on the shoulder, I rushed back to retrieve the bag of materials without even looking inside. By the time I returned, the first crafter's hall was utterly changed.

Thick vines wound around the entire truss system while palm fronds the size of people sprouted from their length. The giant leaves overlapped slowly, taking on a shingle pattern until they drooped over the side of the wall. Sam and Ophelia were nowhere to be seen outside, but I stood and watched the organic marvel unfolding before me. As the frond shingles reached the tips of the trusses, a white flower bloomed at the top. If I wasn't wrong, there was a gentle glow coming from each of the half dozen flowers.

"Sam!?" I called out. Shaking myself out of my surprise, I watched the human and fae stumble out of the crafter's hall like a pair of drunks trying to support each other instead of biological architects.

"Heyyya, Ron!" Sam slurred.

"Are you two alright?" I asked, rushing forward to catch them as they stumbled.

"Pfffttt, we are just fine!"he said, yelling right in my ear.

"Just a wee bit of gardening," Ophelia added just as loudly.

"Right, you two need to sit." I raised an <Earthen Barrier> just to the side of the building and propped both of them as they devolved into a pile of giggles. By this point, a crowd had gathered to stare at the strange direction the magical-yet-some-what-orthodox building had taken.

Arnold came stomping over from where lunch was usually served in the town, gasping in abject horror. "My beautiful building!"

I smiled back at him and the chittering mob behind him. "Welcome to Wildwood's first crafting hall!" I said. It was hard to keep the crooked smile off my face.

"Whoopie!"the life-attuned roofers cheered from behind me.

# CHAPTER NINE

## Crafting and Drafting

The rest of the day devolved into a pseudo party in Wildwood. Apparently, making their first magically constructed building was a milestone they didn't know they wanted to meet. Of course, Sam and Ophelia got sucked into the festivities while still dealing with the side effects of their magic. This in turn led to much partying on their part, which was distinctly out of character for my blond friend.

Casks of some sweet beer were dredged up from reserve, and food was brought out of storage. The bonfires sizzled as they grilled a number of fresh vegetables. Wildwood wasn't well off in the food department, but even a few weeks of concerted effort from the life-attuned had turned their harvest into something impossible before the Fall.

On my part, I skedaddled out of the mass of people as soon as possible. While a break would have been nice, there was still too much to do. If Daniela didn't return within two days, it was up to us to find her. Once she *did* return, we would have to go back to the Bunker.

I let my concerns percolate through my mind just until I made it back into the brand new crafting hall. I gave it another look over and noticed that the vines were reaching down into the soil right around the pillars. *Keeping itself alive?*

As I walked through the central threshold, I looked up at the roof. The vine pattern was a fairly loose weave that left the waterproofing to the fronds while also giving it structural support. Sure enough, where the flowers were, sunlight filtered through unimpeded, somehow reflecting off the petals to spread it around the inside space. *Dang, Sam. You guys built in lighting!* The longer I spent looking at the roof, the more impressed I got with how quickly and how well they'd crafted it. The plans I had for the Bunker camp shifted drastically as I took in my friend's growing magical capabilities.

"Later, Ron. Get your head out of the clouds," I said to myself.

I entered the test-room-to-be. The wall it shared with the forge was Arnold's impressive piece of stonework and I felt confident that I wouldn't accidentally blast someone to death fiddling with infusions while they worked the forge.

The space was bare bones, just a few of those rough wood crates stacked on the far wall. Gauging the space, I formed an L-shaped workstation up against the strong wall using <Earthen Barrier>. With my pick, I carved out a few cubbies to hold infusions while I worked. Finally, using the chisel head of my pick, I broke the top off a <Stone Spike> to give myself a seat.

While my mana regenerated, I dumped out the contents of the sack gently. It wasn't at all what I expected. A gator skull roughly two feet long by six inches wide tumbled out, along with a fine golden chain, and a water infusion.

My eyes drifted over the materials, frown pulling deeper. The chain was mundane enough, but it was gold; the first bit of gold I'd seen since the lab in the Bunker. The gator and the infusion populated my implant.

<Quotient 3 Infusion>
<Water - N/A>
<Integrity: 18%>

&lt;Alligator Skull&gt;
&lt;Attunement: Water&gt;
&lt;Quotient 3 Density&gt;

"Must be from the same creature…" Based on the fact that it was highlighted as a material, the reptile in question had been dissociated instead of harvested. The decay also suggested it happened a fair bit ago. I didn't want to pry as to the source of the components, so instead I tried to figure out just what the heck I could possibly build with a gator skull.

Ideas ranging from clubs to pauldrons floated by me, but nothing felt quite right. An hour or two went by before my stomach complained about its lack of sustenance. I'd sacrificed food for a clean escape from the party in town.

After recreating a Mission: Impossible stealth scene to snag some food from the still raging party, I decided I needed some inspiration. So, I did the equivalent of dumpster diving in the crate of assorted materials the town had collected. Unlike the other crates with infusions which had been neatly separated into attunement and Quotient, the material one was thrice the size and had absolutely no organization. I could see various bones that surely came from humanoid Tendrils, fangs and teeth of a few different creatures, beaks and feathers from a number of birds, spider and ant bits galore, random slabs of fur, as well as sections of other gators sans skulls just on the surface.

Hoping to narrow down what exactly to build, I snagged several of the water-attuned materials, as well as assorted slabs of chitin and fur. *No one said I can't work on some armor while I'm here.* With my plunder secured in one of my trusty duffle bags, I returned to the test room.

Food absently made its way into my mouth as I used a piece of rock to sketch out several designs directly onto the strong wall like a chalkboard. The whole experience made me feel vaguely like a fashion designer as I used my body to get rough dimensions for things as well as marking them on the wall-drawn sketches. I never thought I would want a ruler or tape measure more, but I opted to use a vaguely-foot long ulna to compare sizes.

With the rough idea of the things I wanted to make, I set out to work on the creature pelts first. Since I was most familiar with fire infusions, that was what I led with. The sizzling thread unspooled out of one of the worn infusions before twanging stiff in my hands. With my thoughts focused on a cutting torch, I worked the thread like a hot knife through butter. Before long, a handful of infusions were disintegrating, but I had strips of earth-attuned leather binding ready to use.

Just because I couldn't help myself, I experimented with using water, earth, and death infusions to try to cut up some of the pelts available. For the sake of the scientific method, I used an identical pelt to the one I'd made into strips. In order to keep in line with what Bec had told me, I did my best to picture what each element did best that related to cutting. Targeted freeze-thaw or razor sharp icicles for water, diamond edges for earth, and just localized rot for death. All served to cut the material, but had slight variations on how it reacted. For instance, the water infusion edge left jagged, uneven flaps while the earth cutting edge left extremely clean, almost machine-made, cuts in the pelt. The death edge… Well, it cut, but seemed to leave the edges weakened somehow, as the leather there was splotchy and softer.

Having allowed myself that tiny bit of experimentation and extensive expenditure of materials that were technically not mine, it was time to give back to the war on Dreg efforts.

Focused funneling of near-full fire infusions into the ant chitin left them with my own shield's innate heat dispersion ability. With that portion of the construction done, I emptied my mana pool churning out four near-identical chitin buckler shields. They weren't made from stronger base materials like my own, but they were all of an equal Quotient once I completed the infusion.

<Quotient 1 Enhanced Shield>
<Attribute: Strength>

<Trait: Force Dispersal>

"Let's rename them to something more specific," I mumbled to myself. All it took was a mental prod for the text on the implant to shift. I wasn't sure if the name would make sense to some of the Fallen, but the blast of heat right to the face sure felt like a personalized sauna.

<Q1 Chitin Buckler of Impact Sauna (Shield)>
<Attribute: Strength>
<Trait: Force Dispersal>

<Muscle Memory and Material Breakdown Identified>
<Blueprint for [Chitin Buckler] has been compartmentalized>
<Knowledge of Blueprint transferrable to compatible Dreg Warrior>

"Huh," I said, tilting my head at the strange update. The moment I broke my workflow state, I started to feel the drain of a full day's work with my skills, plus several hours of infusing. There were still several prepped bundles of materials, plus Jolene's special commission to go through, but my body rebelled against moving any more magic muscles, or otherwise mundane ones, via a pair of flashing afflictions.

<Mana Exhaustion>
<Temporary Reduction of Refinement and Containment Attribute>

<Physical Exhaustion>
<Temporary Reduction of Strength and Mobility Attribute>

*Less regen if I push too much for too long, huh?* It made a certain level of sense. If repeated use of skills led to physically mani-fested side effects, then there had to be a breaking point where it detrimentally affected the body. *Just like how too much healing gave me the <Overhealed> affliction.*

It could have been ten minutes or an hour, but I sort of just spaced out while leaning against my work table. The only reason I didn't just slump and take a nap right in the test room was because Samuel came in hollering up a storm. He froze when he spotted the completed armor pieces and my general disheveled state. "Ron, how long have you been in here?" he asked slowly.

"I dunno... few hours?" I mumbled.

"You realize it's probably nine in the morning, yes?" Sam said, still stunned.

My brain tried to process that, but it wasn't running on all cylinders. Clearly, it shouldn't doubt the information coming from the blond healer, but it did for some reason. "No, it can't be."

Samuel reached his hand up in the air just as a spell chain formed around his wrist. The verdant roof parted, blasting an unfiltered ray of sunlight to scorch my eyeballs. *He's right. Damn.* "Okay, well, maybe I've been up a minute."

"Just... Go take a nap. Danny is back, she's fine, and she's got news," Sam said, most of his enthusiasm on arrival tempered by the frown creasing his face. "Jolene!"

I was even more confused by the random call when the woman in question showed up at the door to the test room. Her hair was pulled up in a tight bun, allowing the hellish morning light to illuminate her smooth features perfectly. "Samuel? Is something wrong?"

"If at all possible, can you hose down this thing I sometimes call my friend? I think he forgets that just because the world has magic now people still need to shower."

*Ouch.*

"Sure," she said, smiling easily.

"Now, wait a min—bluggehgegeg." A firehose of water rained down, pushing me back against the strong wall. The spray continued for several seconds, giving me the spot-free rinse treatment as the water drained out of the room through the well-sloped flooring I'd had the Karl-Carl twins shape and

Jolene carve. Once the hose was off, Samuel slapped my shields on the table to trigger the heat pulse to start drying me out.

"I'll let Danny know what's up. I better not see you before lunch, doctor's orders!" the blond called over his shoulder.

Jolene had a smirk plastered on her face until her eyes landed on the yet-to-be-constructed item components. She managed a weak nod in my direction before vanishing to… wherever she had been that was within earshot of Sam.

"Talk about tough love," I said as I looked over the table full of shields. I shrugged as I pulled some of the pelts I'd been working on and just laid them out on a dry spot. I pulled a pair of the shields with me, and thumped them as hard as my reduced strength allowed. The cool-warm contrast of my morning soak combined with the heat from the shields was more sleep-lulling than my exhausted body needed. I spared my status a look just as the darkness of unconsciousness overtook me.

**Subject:** Ronan Terrigan
**Health:** 92% (Mana Exhaustion/Physical Exhaustion)
**Mana:** 84%
**Metier Quotient:** 4 (65%)
**Dreg Accumulation:** 0%
**LPS:** Wildwood, FL
**Communications**
**Skills -** *(1) Selections Available*
**Traits -** *(13% Banked)*
**Attributes -** *Growth Quantified*
**Skills:**
Offensive - <Stone Spike> / Imbue / <Mineral Strike>
Defensive - Direct / <Earth Shell> / <Earthen Barrier>
Misc
- <Pith Mana Lock>
- <Infusion>
- <Memory Canal>
**Traits:**

Limestone Skin
Quake Osseum
Unformed (23%)
**Attributes:**
Strength: 1.59 >1.62
Mobility: 1.43
Perception: 1.72 > 1.74
Refinement: 1.30 > 1.32
Containment: 2.13 > 2.15
"And talk about *gains*…"

— + —

When I woke up, it was well into the afternoon, but I felt like a million pre-Fall bucks. Who would have thought that proper sleep and nutrition could affect your mood? Regardless of how my sleep was, I was up and at 'em the moment my memories of the previous day percolated into my mind.

I wasn't running, per se, but I was certainly moving quickly through the town in search of my *other* childhood friend. Thankfully, my hunch to check the council's office was correct.

Daniela, Samuel, Dylan, Irwin, Clara, and Devon were hunched over a map, talking quietly up until I burst in.

The group jumped into combat readiness immediately. Irwin brandished his claws, Dylan's hair flame flared as he unholstered a pistol, and the others had spell chains slowly circling their hands, wrists, or even the floor right around me.

"Tense, are we?" I asked, holding my hands up in the air as the mana and palpable hostility faded.

"Good to see you too, dust mop," Daniela said, shooting me a genuine, but tired, smile.

"Same here, hothead," I said, pulling the Latina into a tight hug. I whispered in her ear. "No more running off into the woods without warning, alright?"

The woman stiffened, but when she met my moist eyes and

saw they lacked admonishment her expression softened. "I can't promise, but I'll try to not make a habit of it."

"I understand we are all having a very emotional moment right now," Devon said. "But we have a massive threat just on the horiz—"

*Ah, thanks Clara.* The demoness in question had elbowed the elf in the gut, cutting him off from his tirade. I gave her a nod of thanks. "Everyone here knows what's at stake, Devon. Let's get Ron up to speed and move the discussion forward," she said.

Daniela patted me on the shoulder before walking over to the map. Samuel scooched over to give me room at the table.

"Daniela and Devon just finished their report. They also took a nap before ambling in. Short version: we are in a pickle. Longer version: we are in a pickle, said pickle is fifteen miles away, and has a death flavor topped with life icing," Irwin said.

"I don't even know if these kids know what a pickle is, Irwin," Dylan said, sighing while holding his head.

"We're familiar with the phrase, but can I get details and not an idiom?" I asked, my mind already trying to piece the information together with the changes that had been added to the map. For one, it was much larger than the one I'd seen before; three blue squares marked the Towns of Summerfield, Stonecrest, and Lake Weir. Each was further to the northeast than I'd ever traveled, but I could see a line had been drawn to probably mark a clear path between the towns and Wildwood.

The territories marked out for the different creatures on the surface, which likely correlated to dungeons and other non-Dreg affiliated Metier Crystals, were much more expansive. The true scale of the ant territory and the spider territory really hit home when our Bunker home and the neighboring towns were not even a tenth of the area *combined*.

"Wait, you marked the Bunker?" I asked, corroborating my own implant map with the paper one in front of me.

"Yeah, Dai already knew where it was and now that we got rid of the mole in Wildwood, we can fully collaborate with the town," Daniela said, not brokering an argument with her snappy tone. "Plus, the council has info on where some of the other bunkers are."

I snapped my gaze to Dylan and Irwin. Both stepped back awkwardly, clearly shaken by my sudden intensity. "General locations. The government before the Fall announced that there were five such bunkers north of Orlando. Some of the survivors in town talked about there being a bunker in Deland, one near Jacksonville, and one by Tallahassee. Assuming those locations are correct, it might at least narrow down your search," Dylan explained.

"That's a problem for another time," Devon said. "Can we focus on the thing that promised revenge and our eradication?"

"As much as it pains me to agree with our pointy-eared friend, that piece of information is more relevant right now. Just keep it on the back burner for us, all right?"

The two councilmen nodded before Dylan started to clarify what Irwin said. He pointed to the portion of the map outlined in black; it was never a good color to see when talking about land. There were no upper borders to the area, just a skirting perimeter that bordered something called the 'Predator's Playground' north of the spider territory.I saw our two scouts flinch as the councilman ran his hand down the map through the Playground and up to that black barrier.

"We believe that the giant creature and the crystal are operating out of this territory. Even the terraforming of the fire ants doesn't compare to the extent of changes in this area. Would you like to elaborate?" Dylan said, gesturing to the map.

"The flying bastard has a quick and easy shortcut over all the bruisers in the forest," Devon started.

"We followed it through the Playground. Thankfully it was daytime, otherwise we would have lost it right away. Scaling it off our Local Positioning Systems, the lower boundary is just shy of ten miles at a straight shot. The problem comes with getting there. A big enough group will just draw the attention of the predators and get smoked out," Daniela continued.

"Why not just go around? Take the long way by the towns to the east," I asked.

"It's not quite so easy," Clara interjected. "While the area north of Wildwood isn't marked as any *one* territory, it's become sort of a mediating ground for the different species in the area. The only safety is at the towns, and even then they often rely on being too big of pains in the butt to root out more than actual defensive forces like here. This is the main reason trips to the towns take a few weeks to do safely. Thanks to you guys, we know it's with the help of Tec that we've been able to keep a perimeter this large at all."

"Have you all checked through the state of the road? US 301 cuts straight north to the border of the death territory," I said, tracing the faint line marking the old highway.

"Not any worse than at the forward base," Danny said.

"You are thinking of just charging up through the roads, possibly ignoring the territories?" Irwin asked.

"It's an option. If at all possible, I think it would be best to hit the Dreg when they least expected it. Only a few days after their rescue extraction? That sounds like the best time," I said, frowning. It was certainly not the best plan, because…

"They would roll over us," Daniela said, cutting to the heart of the matter. "Each pack of the predators had Level 5s or 6s, just like that bird. On top of that, I'm fairly sure that bird is on some steroid feed. Just look at its cousins that dropped around town. They were all hanging out in the decayed forest."

"Not to mention that they still have some Tendrils in reserve, as well as Galloway," Dylan added. He stroked his chin for a moment before continuing. "I'm not sure how *it* compares to the Appendage bird, but anyone that interacted with the speaking Tendril ended up with the shakes."

"It'll probably be inside the marsh bloom, if I had to guess. Definitely screams 'evil lair headquarters' to me," Daniela said, pointing further west from the black border.

When I looked at her in confusion, Devon shrugged and elaborated. "It's some kind of megaflora thing. It's right in the middle of those rot fields, so I would say it has no business being there other than because of what Daniela suggested."

A headache unrelated to my poor sleep crept up on me. The situation was *not* good. There had to be a reason the Appendage hadn't just demolished us when it came to get the Dreg Crystal, but the pieces just weren't falling together. It didn't even attack as hard as it could have with the crows, just pestered the Guard and Wildwoodians long enough to extract the evil rock. If we tried to attack, but it came back, then the town would be vulnerable. If the terrain was unfavorable, not to mention that there was supposed to be a large number of flying enemies, then even if we attacked, we could easily get bogged down.

"We need to grow," Sam said, snapping me from my downward spiral of thoughts. The room turned to the member of the Bunker Busters who'd remained quiet during the whole ordeal. "Think about it. We attack in force now? Bad. We try to be sneaky? Bad. Stay here and consolidate our power? Maybe bad, but maybe what we need. Once the trainees are up to speed, they can cover the town while a higher level guard hits the Dreg."

The others around the map weren't hanging their jaws, but it was a close thing. A smirk crept up my face as I saw Samuel immediately retreat when he realized that every eye was on him. Daniela slapped him on the back, causing him to jump and relieve some of the tension in the room as the two bickered about the exchange.

"You're right. We need to remember, too, that we aren't the only ones invested in surviving. Maybe I can slap together a quick run to the towns. With our extra skills and equipment, it would be a good time to test the trainees, while also seeing if we can get a few more people for the fight. There's no way at least the people of Summerfield haven't been running into these death critters," Clara said.

"Why didn't we think of that?" Dylan mumbled. "Control the battlefield and gather allies. We've been working blind and alone for so long…"

"I think Rommel has a good idea for controlling the battle-field," Devon said, smiling widely. The councilmen gave the elf a look, but he shook his head. The surprise wasn't his to give, apparently.

"I'm two-thirds to Quotient 5," I said. "If we can zero in some more dungeon farming, get as many people matched up with the level of the Appendage, then the numbers advantage will be less of a problem. The air battle will still be a problem…"

"Let me take a crack at the trainees. I'm sure I can get a slapstick set of anti-flyers," Devon said, looking to Clara.

"I'll talk to Sarah, but no lightning. Some of the older trainees still flinch every time you walk by them," admonished Clara. The two excused themselves from the table, talking over just what the plan for training more anti-air mages would be. All I heard before focusing on the councilmen was something about 'mounting gusts.'

"Irwin and I will keep the town running. Like we mentioned, I think it would be best if we stepped back, but this isn't the time. He's already flipped our economy to 'total war' mode. No currency is passing hands for services, and the defensive efforts are taking priority. I'll have the healers double down on food production, just in case we get raided by those carrion crows again and lose some of our crop," Dylan said.

"What are you three planning to do?" Irwin asked.

Daniela paused mid-way to poking Sam to pay attention to the conversation.

"Need to shore up the Bunker." "We need to go home." "Our family could use some help." Daniela, Samuel, and I said at the same time.

We shared a look and a laugh. While Sam and I had discussed the need to reinforce the camp, Daniela had been off scouting. Knowing that my friends—no, *family*—were on the same page lifted my spirits more than any plan. It was time to mark our own territory on Earth, together.

# CHAPTER TEN

## Parting and Gifting

With a hunker down order passed through Wildwood, it was time for the Bunker Busters to return to their namesake. However, before we could leave the town of survivors to their own devices, our group had responsibilities to fulfill. Daniela worked with whatever mysterious project Rommel and Devon were tinkering away with, while Samuel pushed his skills to the maximum. The blond singlehandedly grew an acre of harvestable food during the morning, and spent the afternoon tending to his attuned plant experiment.

The people of Wildwood were bitten by the workaholic bug, seeing the trainees, Guard and even us, the outsiders, working to protect them every waking moment. Several of the kids, barely in their teens, exploded with newfound Gifts. Magic ran rampant through the town, and I wasn't sure if it was a result of the sheer volume of it now drifting through the air, or just how many people were displaying arcane inspiration to impressionable young minds. On the second day after the planning meeting, I watched a dwarf and elf playing chase when the earth-attuned *dove* into the ground like it was water to avoid a lunging touch. Immediately after, the chasing air-attuned *double jumped*, stepping on the air as if it was perfectly solid. As if they hadn't just unlocked their own skills, the two continued skirting the day's responsibilities.

All the while, I worked the test room like a man possessed. The amount of life and activity around me kept me grounded. Burning out would not do anyone any good. So, I worked with the various crafters and gave a very simplified lecture on item creation. As had become habit, I made an effort to become completely unavailable—to Samuel's complete chagrin. *Serves him right for being so approachable.* I laughed at the thought as I snapped the last infusion into my latest creation.

<Q1 Mandible Hatchet of Lasting Burns (Axe)>
<Attribute: Strength>
<Trait: Scorch Touch>

<Muscle Memory and Material Breakdown Identified>
<Blueprint for [Insect Hatchet] has been compartmentalized>
<Knowledge of Blueprint transferrable to compatible Dreg Warrior>

The flash of heat as the weapon stopped changing barely registered on my face as I stared at the sets of equipment I'd constructed. Three days of work, gone in a flash, but I had five bruiser sets of armor. My eyes roved over the other creations that had been added to my blueprints.

<Q1 Segmented Cowl (Chestplate)>
<Attribute: Strength>
<Trait: Haze Cloak>

<Q1 Tanker Armor (Chestplate)>
<Attribute: Strength>
<Trait: Force Dispersal>

Three tanker armors and two cowls. Enough to shift the strength of five squads noticeably or one significantly more. Arrayed with them were the six shields and four hatchets I'd created. Thanks to my efforts, the town of Wildwood was actually almost out of low Quotient fire infusions. With the bulk of the gear I planned to create completed, I turned to the three sets of items that had been haunting me throughout my work.

Jolene's alligator head, the femur from one of the life-attuned Tendrils we'd fought, and a set of Q3 earth deer antlers. While the alligator head had no outline, the font the implant marked the femur and antlers with was tinged slightly green. I wasn't sure if that was some kind of perception issue, but I doubted it. Bec had been very deliberate in what it copied from our memories to program the status into our implants. My best guess was that these were 'uncommon' materials. *If I recall correctly, that ice heart back home was also like this…*

Shaking my head, I focused back on the three components. Nothing directly was coming to mind for either the gator head or the set of antlers, but the more I stared at the femur, the more I realized that I didn't *need* to change it. The club was roughly twenty inches long, with the hip socket and knee joint thickening to about two inches. The ball joint was what gave me the final push to commit. Without delaying anymore, I cleared my workspace and went to fish out several earth infusions.

With deliberately smooth motions, I carved down around the ball joint, leaving three ridges that could have easily been confused for bone spurs. The actual head of the femur, I flattened slightly, goosebumps running up and down my arms at the grinding of diamond-visualized infusion edge and flaking bone. Nonetheless, I kept going. It was a rough chiseling job, but the club head was the best it was going to get. With the last of the Q1 infusions in my hand, I roughened the surface of the femur while picturing a low grit to improve the grip of the weapon from the smooth bone surface. My hands flew along the surface, working the thread all along the length and stopping at the knee joint. I then took some of the fire hound leather bindings I had, wrapping them around the bottom half of the femur and welding them in place with a fire infusion.

I contemplated adding more to the rough weapon, but I didn't want to accidentally compromise its structure or spend many more resources when I didn't even know what infusing a weapon with a life infusion would do. So without delay, I grabbed the Q3 life infusion from the cubby on my workstation and unspooled its Pith thread. Gold blazed between my fingers as the thread manifested. I didn't even wait to have the full length extracted, and pushed it into the club. Just like one of the many healing skills I'd seen the Guard and Samuel use, the bone glowed with an internal light. The shadows in my workspace vanished as I watched the material go from bleached white to an aged yellow tone. The red of the fire bindings faded to a pale pink and the edges curled up into themselves.

When the last of the Pith entered the weapon, a pulse of physical exhaustion flowed through me unlike any other infusion. For a brief second, under the glow of the still-changing weapon, I could see the bones in my own hands muted against my Limestone Skin. At that point, the weapon started to *grow*. The femur itself stretched by about five inches, somehow maintaining its thickness. The club head I'd carved grew to the size of a fist, elongating the head back to more of a hammer even as the spurs I made condensed with newly-grown osseous material. The leather bindings *regrew* fur, joining together as if they were a whole, perfectly circular pelt.

The light dimmed before my eyes focused on the first life attuned item I'd created.

<Quotient 3 Femur Club>
<Attribute: Refinement>
<Trait: Genesis Amplitude>

Synapsis fired in my mind as I held the weapon. The word 'amplitude' got me fairly excited, since it was the same type of trait that the stinger staff had. If there was a pattern, then the genesis was life to the singe's fire.

"No sense waiting to test it!" I shouted to myself. Before I knew it, I was facing the wetland not far from the road. <Stone Spike>'s spell chain formed around my hands until it touched the club. It got sucked up into the head of the weapon, spinning gently there as the brown mana was tinged with gold and green flecks. A mad grin split my face as I focused on a tree in the distance. The earth condensed, leaving a sizable divot in the muck, before the point struck the tree. The impact sunk into the wood as I expected, but the point of contact immediately bloomed with vines lined with thorns. They snapped around the target without direction from me, but did a fairly good job of keeping the target stuck in place—if it had been mobile. I glanced to the corner of my vision.

<Stone Spike>

<Infusion Augmentation: Life>

<Rock Thorns>

"Yes!" I cheered, pumping my fist as I twirled the club in hand. I wasn't sure if the 'uncommon' categorization was necessary to make an amplitude trait happen, but two for two was a good start. Getting up to four for four would be the best way to confirm that particular hypothesis. Giggling like a madman, I returned to the test room. The few Wildwoodians and the crafters I spotted on the way scurried out of the way as soon as they saw me, but I was in a world of my own. *Creating was so much fun!*

My wheels spun slightly slower once I laid eyes on the materials, but I decided that hesitation would only stop me from making *something*. Humanity was in dire need of *any* gear they could get their hands on. Deliberately leaving Jolene's materials for last, I focused on the set of antlers. I wasn't sure how pre-Fall hunters used to identify different bucks, but I had to warrant a guess that the rack was from a four-point. The top of the deer's skull, and a pair of antlers that grew up and out into four points, were what had condensed from the drop. Just thinking of how many obstructions the earth deer had caused, both offensively and to cover the escape of the Tendrils, brought me a headache. "Headache, huh…"

Muse fiddling away in my mind, I knew just what to do with the antlers. First, I scrounged the material crate for any more chitin plates I could get my hands on. Unfortunately, only two of the head-sized sections had made it through my armor crafting extravaganza. Instead of letting that take the wind from my sails, I dug deeper until I came upon a water gator skin. There were a few rips and tears from what I assumed were wounds on the creature, but it would work. *No, it will improve it!*

My hands were a blur as I used earth infusions to slice through the tough scales of the alligator, manipulated a Q2 fire infusion to weld the flesh back, and formed a skullcap of sorts. The inside was terribly rough, so I used some of the leather bindings I had left to cushion the inside. Making a deliberate effort to leave the rough, spine scales of the gator long along the back of the skullcap, I secured the deer skull to the top before using more leather bindings to strap it in place. It wasn't pretty, but it looked properly attached. To finish it off, I used yet another Q2 fire infusion to weld the two chitin plates to the skull and to the cap, forming stiff sides for the helm. A test fitting of putting on the thing proved it was snug, but I didn't feel confident it wouldn't fly off at the first hit, considering how top heavy the antlers made the armor. So, I used one of the many <Vine Whip> sections I'd forced Sam to provide me with for the armor to make a chin strap. With the construction complete, I thumbed the earth infusion in hand. It was one of the ugliest pieces of gear I'd made, *but* if it worked, it could boost my abilities to unknown heights. The thread snapped between my fingers before <Infusion> pushed it into the helm.

A sound like wood ready to buckle under pressure echoed inside the test room. Brown light flowed over the surface of the helm. I took several steps back, interposing my shield between me and the piece of armor. Peeking between the top legs of my H-shield let me see as the whole helm seemed to *shrink* visibly. The scaly skullcap flowed up from the back, encasing the base of the antlers, while the maroon chitin flowed up to cover the upper jaw in a thin layer of chitin. The chin strap compressed, going from a fleshy, dried length of plant matter to something more akin to pinky-thin fibrous cordage. As an encore, all the shades of the helm toned down, going from maroons to a deep mahogany.

Before I knew what I was doing, I had the helm in hand. Somehow, it wasn't top heavy anymore, and instead was balanced right along the bottom of the chitin plates, helping itself to stay on my face. Even if the outside had shrunk, it was more like going from a regular t-shirt to the sport fits we wore for exercise in the Bunker. Before I slid it on my head, its information flicked by my implant.

<Quotient 2 Antler Helm>

<Attribute: Strength>

<Trait: Accretion Amplitude>

I wasn't sure why the Quotient had dropped from 3 to 2, but it was also the most radical change in design I'd seen out of the items I'd created. The first shovel I made was a close second, with the way its metal edge changed, but the helm had had its *matter* redistributed to make it easier to wear. Yet another mystery to try to uncover about the whole infusion process. Regardless of how silly I might have looked, I was back outside to test *my* new piece of armor.

I moved away from where I'd tested the life club and focused on getting another poor tree. The spell chain snapped from my hands straight to the antlers as soon as I funneled magic into the item. The helm vibrated, but didn't release anything. I tried to cast my skill normally and, sure enough, it manifested the spike, piercing the tree. When I tried to cast the skill again via my helm, the vibration kicked up a notch and I saw the spell chain that had been circling the antler's trigger.

<Stone Spike>

<Infusion Augmentation: Earth>

<Tectonic Rise>

The first spike got swallowed as a sedimentary rock monstrosity punched clear through the tree, severing it at the base. My usual skill was a conical spike that condensed the nearby soil in addition to that formed from mana. The Tectonic Rise formed a blade of rock that reminded me more of a rock-made axe head than a spike. The attack took double casts of the skill to trigger, effectively halving my mana in addition to the drain of the item itself. The results, though, were undeniable as I watched the tree topple onto the <Tectonic Rise> and barely shake under the weighty impact. *I really need to try this with all my skills!* As much as I wanted to burn the rest of the day testing my new gadget, I still had a promise to fulfill before returning to the Bunker. *Plus I'm almost out of mana, even if it didn't feel like I almost emptied my mana pool. Was it because I went through the item?*

Thoughts still ambling, I returned the dead-eyed glare of the alligator skull. Really nothing came to mind, so I played with the skull for a few minutes, pretending it was talking to me, telling me what it wanted to become.

I wasn't *at all* worried that I was going to bottom out my mana; a benefit of my containment being so high. Even after spending a ton for testing the antler helm, there was still plenty that I could use to infuse.

When I slipped my hand in the gap where the gator's throat would have been to marionette the bones, I realized I was over-thinking it. I could have made a pauldron easily with the skull, but it wouldn't fit Jolene's general fight style. But a gauntlet made of a gator skull? She definitely struck me as a knock out type of gal.

As soon as the fire was lit, there was no stopping. How would I keep her from getting her hand hurt by the fangs? Suspend a rough glove inside the jaws. Link the upper and lower jaws with...something. I scurried over to the material crates, spooking the soul out of a poor satyr on the way, and plucked the first water attuned bone material I could find.

Remembering how the life infusion had changed the femur, I snagged a handful of them from the Q1 crate. Before long, the bone I'd taken was fused partway down the inside of the jaw like the grip on my shield. I used the last fire infusion I had to torch cut what looked like an ulna in half. It gave a roughly four inch gap between the deadly teeth, but Jolene's smaller hand would have plenty of space. With the last of the earth infusions I'd snagged earlier, I worked gator skin into a tube before binding it with the life infusion into the throat gap. The scales glowed as they crept up the back of the skull to the eye cavities before the infusion ran out.

The fit was uncomfortable for myself, but the whole thing had a considerable *heft* to it. Getting smacked by even the incomplete item would leave a bit more than a bruise. Excited to finish the item, I snapped several water infusions into the gauntlet. Unlike the femur and the helm, the degraded infusion wasn't enough to meet the item's requirements.

With each bit of Pith I flicked into the weapon, the faster the temperature in the test room plummeted. With a frosty pulse, the weapon was complete. Ice crystals formed from my sweat as I let out a misty breath of satisfaction.

<Quotient 3 Snap Jaw Gauntlet>
<Attribute: Mobility>
<Trait: Deluge Amplitude>

I let myself lean back against the strong wall, looking over the weapon on my workstation. The scales had crept a bit further, deepening to an almost black navy blue. The teeth within the jaws had turned to point forward. Each had gained a blue hue that reminded me of the countless videos I'd seen of the ocean while in the Bunker. *I really want to see the coast now for some reason...*

With that thought, I sagged deeper against the strong wall. I thumped my shield, sighing in satisfaction as the magical warmth conversion pushed back the chill. *Just a little nap...*

— + —

Several hours, and one panicked discovery by a message girl later, I was resting in the training building. Samuel had rushed over, only to discover that I had done a repeat of my over-exhaustion the day Danny had returned. The man didn't even acknowledge the equipment I'd worked on and instead hauled me off to put me in time out until the next day.

I did manage to tell him that I was done crafting for the time being. My meaning came across easily, the blond letting me recover as he prepared for our departure the following day.

That night was plagued by more flashes of memory from the transfer of skills. They were disjointed and intermingled amidst my regular dreams but there nonetheless. When I finally woke up, unable to get back to sleep after the death of someone named Dana, I ruminated on what my <Memory Canal> meant for me. Not only that, the blueprint system would be invaluable in shortening the time it took to train people to make passable gear. If transferring blueprint knowledge also forced more memory flashes into my mind, I didn't think I would be able to endure it. Thankfully, most had just settled into my subconscious, but they still resurfaced whenever I tried to rest.

Breakfast passed quietly and I barely noticed the presence of my friends until they spoke up.

"He alright, Sammy?" Daniela asked.

"You know I'm sitting right here, right?" I replied, almost biting into my hand before realizing that there was no more jerky there.

"Yes, but *are you* though?" Sam asked, quirking an eyebrow in my direction.

"I am, really. It's just…"

"Spit it out, mud stomp. None of us have time to be your mood dentist. Those self-reliance roots are too deep even for us," Daniela quipped.

I felt the urge to snap at her, but it didn't come from me. It was lingering frustrations from the last memory flash. Instead of trying to brush them off, I explained how transferring <Infusion> had affected me. How I planned to try to transfer the blueprints I had, so Wildwood could prepare better while we were gone. My two best friends listened raptly, their frowns deepening as I described some of the memories, even Jolene's more vivid one.

"No more plundering people's brains until we figure this out. No, don't argue with me. You can do your experiment with the blueprints, but no more skill transfers. If they want the skill, they'll have to learn it the hard way, just like with a Gift or our Freeforms. Got it?" Samuel said, pointing a finger in my direction.

I almost argued until I realized I *didn't* want to experience any more flashes. Should the situation require it, like with Charles and his ilk, I would do it in a heartbeat. For something less life threatening? Big pass.

After getting the heavy part of the discussion out of the way, the two of them updated me on what they'd worked on. We discussed how much the town had improved, how food was already becoming less of a concern for the Wildwoodians, their defenses were stronger with the trainees pitching in to use their skills for the town as opposed to being fed into Kirby's bottom-less pit of Dreg tributes. When we were all talked out, the sun was already filtering through the yellowing vines of Sam's roof patch job. He told us he was going to replace it, so Danny and I went ahead.

The two of us grabbed the crate we'd brought from the town and loaded up with the gear I'd crafted. There wasn't enough space, so my brunette friend threaded all the shields onto her naginata like a deadly bindle.

If the sun was shining, I knew where to find Sarah. Sure enough, the orc woman was already hollering to the trainees as they finished breakfast together. She turned toward us when one of the trainees pointed us out.

"Oh! This must be that Christmas thing all the old folks talk about." She laughed, smiling wide through her tusks.

"Something like that. If Santa gave deadly weapons out like candy," I said, laughing at her visible enjoyment.

I pulled out everything but the amplitude items. The trainees practically salivated when I showcased the haze cloak, force dispersal and scorch touch. I made a note to myself that I would explain the visual distortions of the cloak trait and the extra burn damage courtesy of scorch touch during the next lecture I gave on crafting. At the same time, I was somewhat excited for my 'students' to discover some new ones without me mucking about. With the extent of my responsibilities, crafting time had been somewhat limited, much less for experimental projects.

As for the leader of the Wild Guard trying to stand stoically next to the trainees, Sarah was ecstatic about being able to outfit so many people; it was clear as day that the trainees were even more excited to test run the equipment.

Jolene was nowhere to be found, so I asked Sarah to pass on the gauntlet and the gold necklace back to her. The orc woman nodded like it was a serious mission before waving us off. We left the new councilwoman of New Earth to her antics to meet up with the other councilmen. Irwin was off somewhere, but we found Dylan in their office, working through stacks of paper. *Even in the apocalypse there is still paperwork. Astounding.*

"So, time for you to go, is it?" Dylan said, barely glancing our way as he stamped one last paper. "Since I know why you are going back, and that you've come back in our *hours* of need, I won't try to persuade you to stay. Just take care of yourself, alright?"

"You got it, torchlight. I'll be making some message runs between the Bunker and here, so you don't have to worry your pretty little head overmuch," Danny said. I was pretty sure I saw Dylan's eye twitch, but the rest of his expression was politician stiff and locked into a genuine-ish smile. While we didn't get along the best, I was fairly confident that Dylan and Irwin were just doing their best to keep the town running. That was something I could definitely respect.

"I left a little present with your daughter, and hopefully the crafters will have a few more goodies for you once they get the hang of their skills. Keep the lights on," I said.

"Ain't going anywhere," Dylan said, the flame on his head flaring with his determination.

We left the office and started heading for the gate. Early risers and late morning demons lingered about, giving Wildwood a definite lived-in feel, even with its sparse population. We waved and exchanged some pleasantries with the townspeople that we met along the way. Many asked when we planned to return, but since we weren't sure, we just told them 'soon.' Thankfully, no one made a big fuss about the whole situation.

Until we met up with Sam at the west gate.

"Wild Guard, attention!" Sarah called out from atop the palisade. The two dozen members of the Guard, sans Clara and Oliver, stood flanking the open gate. Roughly lined up behind them were the many trainees and recently inducted Guards.

"Uhh... Sarah?" I asked, confused by the pseudo military parade.

"The Wild Guard wishes to demonstrate their thanks to the Bunker Busters for their efforts in protecting them and the town of Wildwood!" she yelled out, not meeting any of our eyes. "Present spells!"

Almost sixty spell chains manifested in the air around us. A palpable thrum of energy hit everyone as their passives overlapped. Something akin to the Blessing of Magic gathered around the Wild Guard as they sustained their mana. Wisps of brown energy snaked around people's feet, gold and green wove between all grass, and the gray of the breeze stirred up all the rest of the elemental colors represented around us.

While the people of Wildwood were serious about this show of faith, they couldn't stop themselves from letting their eyes drift onto the spectacle they'd created. From the many looks of surprise, I didn't think they'd practiced the actual spell chain performance. If they had, they hadn't seen *this* effect before.

Sarah was finally able to snap herself back to her original goal. "Go with the blessing of friends made." Of course, she had to add a cheeky line that left me and my friends smirking. "And stronger, otherwise we'll surpass you."

We waved to the group as we exited the gate. It was hard to describe the feeling in my chest, but I knew then that it was something that was worth repeating. The will to thrive, not just survive, was something we came to the surface with and it was time we spread it far and wide. Threats or no threats, it was time to look to the future.

# CHAPTER ELEVEN

## Camp Busy Bunker

Traveling beyond the town was much less exciting after the number of times we'd done it. It was funny to think that going further than we ever had in a single stretch of our lives could become rote or *mundane* regardless of how much an Attuned Earth had tilted towards a wilderness. While we stayed mildly on our toes, the section of road between the forward base and the town proper was as safe as could be expected.

We stopped briefly at the forward base, but didn't linger long. Sarah had already let Clara and Oliver know we were headed out that way. She did mention that the New Hopers would be striking out towards the town within a few days, taking the trainees close to being accepted with them. The biggest surprise, although not really a surprise, was Clara herself.

<Clara (Human)>

<Attunement: Death>

<Refinement: Crippling>

<Perceived Metier Quotient: 5>

She was the first of the Guard, and our group, to make it to Quotient 5. The woman waved away the compliments we gave her, instead echoing Sarah's sentiment. It was about time for us to push forward and *really* stake a claim on Earth. With yet another fire burning in our soul, we barely noticed the distance as we cut south on US 301, swerved at the Geode Palm and crossed the southernmost portion of the spider territory.

My perception highlighted a few spiders off in the woods, and their webs were present pretty much everywhere, but none attacked us. As a matter of fact, Blobby finally showed its rotund, gelatinous self and with two, still dissolving, spiders within its bulk to boot. I'd been so focused I'd forgotten about the camouflaging slime the entire time I worked. *Good thing it is both self-sufficient and apparently incredibly sturdy.*

We heard the click of a firearm before we saw anyone. However, the three of us had been honed by all the nonsense Earth had thrown our way. My shield came around first, Sam sliding behind me with two quick steps, while Daniela blurred into the trees. Her fire wisp hovered right where she'd been, pointing its miniature flame body in the direction of the sound.

"Good to see my kids haven't gotten too rusty without me to beat discipline into them," a familiar female voice called out from further in the woods.

"Mama!" Daniela yelled, dissipating her skill and rushing at the voice. A grunt followed by a series of giggles revealed Ava working to pry Daniela off of her. It was the weakest show of force I'd ever seen the fierce trainer put out.

"You three have no idea how glad I am to see you," Ava said when she finally committed to extracting herself from her daughter. Her tone had more than just relief at seeing us built into it.

"Let's get back. You can fill us in," I said, picking up the crate singlehandedly. Samuel had been helping me lug it, so he quirked an eyebrow at me. I sent him a quick, "Keep your hands clear. Something is going on back at the camp," through the comm-plant. The blond didn't question anything, but I saw him pull his hands off where he'd been holding his armor.

Only a few minutes later, and we saw the 'problem' immediately. The Bunker was having a day visit. Almost the *whole*

Bunker. The instant that the previously ground dwelling pre-Fall humans saw us, they lost their absolute minds. My uncle was already making his way towards us, vague snips of his attempted platitudes audible even across the clearing. "Yes, I'm sorry, please. Urgent business, of course. Have to just make sure they aren't in need of any assistance." *How does he manage so many words without a breath?*

Soon enough, *I* was the one worried about breath as he enclosed all three of us in a rib-breaking hug. Very nearly so, as his information populated thanks to his utter proximity.

<Dale (Human)>

<Attunement: Water>

<Refinement: N/A>

<Perceived Metier Quotient: 4>

The radical jump in level sent worrying signals up. However, my uncle was focused on unloading as much of the physical contact he'd missed out on with our absence.

"Dale, let those kids breathe. And you lot, back it up. Back I say, shoo, shoo." Ben rolled in like a bald savior. Our old teacher huffed and puffed enough to pass for a train, but did manage to corral the other Bunkerites to the edges of my vestibule. He then clapped each of us in the back, forcing Dale to release us. "You kids look alright."

"Thanks, Teach!" the three of us echoed, widening his and my uncle's smiles.

"Come on, we've got a lot to catch up on, and I don't know how long the others will be able to keep from burying you in questions," Ava said, sobering the mood a touch. She placed a gentle hand on our shoulders as she guided us to a rough cut... feasting table was the only word I could use to describe such an unnecessarily long log table.

— + —

Catching up took the rest of the day. I'd hoped to get some work in, but my uncle had some very choice words about not relaxing and just working headlong into something. Ava quickly agreed when she realized he was revving up to go off into one of his overly positive rants.

Retelling the escalating conflict with Kirby's hidden machinations, the search and interrogation, as well as the eventual rescue of the trainees really put our efforts into perspective. Most of the praise I still dismissed out of hand, but it made me realize just how much we'd been scraping by since coming to the surface. While we'd cleared the immediate threat, the source wasn't dealt with. The issue was more covert than overt and it drove me nuts.

Somehow, just when me and Sam started talking about the success of our infusion research, Alan materialized amidst the group. He didn't say anything, but the tablet in his hand didn't stop clicking the whole time we spoke about the amplitude items, attuned vegetables, and the manifestation of the Blessing of Magic under the Guard's concerted efforts.

Daniela talked about her progress with her and Sam's Freeform skill. They finally let spill the breakthrough: temporarily combined skills. Similar to how the amplitude items added an attunement to a skill, Freeform could allow you to combine the nature of two skills together, albeit at the cost of both. It was how Samuel had used his <Health Bump> through his <Vine Whip> to bring my butt back into the fight to rescue the trainees. Daniela had also used it to great effect against the beast Tendrils by using her wisp to release <Flame Bursts>'All over their stupid faces,' she said. Neither of them thought that they'd reached full control of their Freeforms, but it already made me want to unlock it.

After all the theoretical knowledge and practical notes we had to provide, the discussion turned to the future. Unfortunately, by the time Alan managed to squeeze into the conversation, others collected themselves enough to crowd the three of us.

After the fifth elated response from people we'd known our whole lives—Peggy the grower, Alexia the doc, and the weaver trio we called the plant fiber menders of the Bunker—Ben called our meeting to an end before heading inside my vestibule. When he returned, he brought more than just a well-cooked meal.

"Papa!" Daniela cried, running to hug her father. Juan, ever warm but unmovable, raised an eyebrow in her direction. She halted in place, the look on her body remembered more than she actually wanted to comply to, before her whole body sagged in disappointment. It was no secret how much Danny loved her parents and the cold reaction left even us reeling.

To Juan's credit, he passed off the tray of food to pile onto Ben's before *he* rushed his daughter down.

"Ah, mi corazón," he whispered, muffled by her brunette curls as the two let out a joyous sob.

Juan wasn't the only one, as Samuel's father poked his timid head around a gnarled elder it took me a second to recognize as Elias. Jerome Fallon, as adverse to physical contact as he was, gripped his lanky son who towered almost a foot over him. Elias placed a gentle hand on Sam and Danny as he passed, cutting a path straight to me.

The closer he got, the more I realized how he'd aged. He was probably old even by the standards of Wildwoods population. Elias sat across from me, smiling the same knowing smile he always had when the three of us got into trouble. It was a stark reminder that while my mother was gone, and my 'father' had been my uncle, these people were my family.

"Welcome home, Ronan. I've been told you three have been causing a stir. You even somehow managed to drag all these bags of bones to the surface again," Elias said.

"Boy did they ever!" Ben called out, slapping an insta-meal in front of me. The instinctual recoil caused everyone present to roar with laughter as Teach swapped it for some tofu slabs braised with tomatoes and potatoes. A rough salad bowl was slapped onto the table along with several others along its length.

A quick count of those gathered told me something amazing. The entirety of the Bunker was present, and there were just enough stump-seats to accommodate everyone. It was a small detail that didn't escape my notice, but sent another flush of warmth through me.

Parental figures close at hand, Samuel and Daniela sat to either side of me. She had a smile so relaxed I could have sworn she'd just played the best prank on me or Sam, while the blond was practically giddy seeing his father after so long. In fact, seeing the mood of the gathering, he excused himself before returning to the crate we'd been lugging all day.

"Jerky, anyone?" he said. As if he'd sounded a call for war, the somewhat-composed residents of the Bunker scrambled on hands and knees to get close to a real piece of meat after almost three decades without—insta-meals didn't count.

The official-unofficial mayor of the Bunker cleared his throat loudly, halting everyone before the madness really kicked off and gestured to Ben and Juan to distribute the jerky evenly. Samuel's confused and scared grin set Daniela giggling. Elias gave everyone a few moments to sidle over to the table before calling out loudly, "Let the first Bunker feast begin!"

— + —

"And I said, 'No, you can't use a potato for that!'" Sam said, laughing so hard he fell over backwards from his stump. The crowd of old men listening to his farming tale roared in time with the joke. It didn't take perception to see the red flushes on their faces. *Apparently someone's been making booze in the Bunker again!*

I was stone cold sober, but I could see the signs as clear as day in several of the residents even outside of Sam's little group. A few had even slunk off into the vestibule, either to return below ground or just pass out for the night in one of the cots Ben had set up. I caught more than one staring wistfully up at the firmament.

As the party died down, Elias and Ava took their turn updating me and Daniela. As he'd mentioned, this had been the first time that the entirety of the Bunker had actually come to the surface. However, ever since the last time we left for Wild-wood, Elias had applied pressure to rotate people to spend time above ground. Not only did it let Ben, Ava, and Alan take a brief break, it got those hesitant to risk their safety to dip their toes, so to speak.

After the first few rotations, they'd started to come in *droves*, using their numbers to push through their hesitance of being on the surface. When Ava sent word that we'd arrived, Elias had pulled out all the stops. The old man grinned deviously as Juan and Dale helped clean up the mess of meals and Alexia checked on those less than sober. Unfortunately, not everything was good news.

Ava stepped in to tell us about the side effect of having more people on the surface: overwhelming Bec's defensive area of influence. The crystal hadn't communicated with any of them for quite a while and even while feeling regular pulses radiating off of it, the ants and spiders had been stirred up. Ben and Dale took the physical brunt of the new attacks, while Ava consoli-dated their firearm usage. Even with their trickle of Dreg being purged for energy, the Entity struggled against sheer numbers. The woman even walked us over to where she'd been working on a rudimentary bow for the older Bunkerites, as well as a whole wall of wooden spears she'd taken to use in order to conserve ammunition.

While the three had taken on the defense of the camp, the other Bunker residents had taken over the more 'mundane' tasks. Alexia and June studied my uncle and Ben each time they were injured, watching how healing had changed, fundamen-tally, for them. Juan ran around like a chicken with his head cut off as he singlehandedly ran the mess hall below ground and the kitchen for those on the surface. Jerome didn't spend much time on the surface. Without as much support from Ben and Dale, he'd taken over maintenance of the Bunker as well as running the logistical nightmare that was the Bunker's ration system getting an injection of 'the surface needs a little bit of everything.'

As I quickly realized that the Bunker had been no less active than we'd been—sans conspiracy and corruption—I knew we needed to get working. Improving the defenses of the Bunker and feeding Bec more Dreg were the first steps. While I wanted to get as much training as possible, making sure that the Bunker was safe in our absence was a priority. Armed with the knowledge of what the town was working on, and how much they'd started to get comfortable on the surface, my long term plans suddenly became very much short term. The thirst for freedom was something the Bunkerites had forgotten, but with the first drop, the burning desire had been rekindled.

"I need to do some research," I said, excusing myself from the group. Daniela called after me, but my mind was spinning in too many ways already. All she got was a thumbs up from me, and a promise that there would be work in the morning. I smiled absently at all the people I passed, who greeted me or provided a quick side hug. As politely as I could, I plunged past my vestibule, past the old world lobby, and down into the depths where I'd been born. It was time to learn from the past.

# CHAPTER TWELVE

## Keep-ing Up

The blare of an electronic alarm snapped me from sleep's sweet embrace. A considerable amount of drool had pooled around my head from some unknown source, and I wiped it away lest people got the wrong idea that it had been me somehow. With the mess cleaned up, I blinked my eyes against the light of the terminal in front of me. The clock in the bottom right of the terminal marked it as *early*. I hadn't remembered setting up an alarm, or even staying down in the Bunker, but apparently sleep-deprived Ronan had more awareness than conscious Ronan did.

I took a blurry look at the lab, spotting several cluttered tables and buzzing equipment that I had not the slightest clue about. Beyond, I could see Mr. Cantero wiping down the gym area. Everyone took a turn as janitor, doing their best to keep our hole-in-the-ground home as hygienic as possible while varying the tasks each worked on. His perpetual frown was plastered there as always, and his milky white mustache wiggled as he worked. My still-sluggish mind took the tranquility of the Bunker to really draw out its boot-up sequence. Mr. Cantero ambled over to the lab, having spotted me staring off into space.

He didn't say anything, but he did look over the chaotic sketches and notes I'd scribbled while doing research the night before.

He huffed once before pointing to one of the top sheets. "Don't need crossbeams if it's all made of rock." Having said his piece, the man went on with his turn as the Bunker janitor.

I looked over the papers, pieces of *why* I'd spent the night at the terminal finally clicking into place. Not only that, with Mr. Cantero's comment, the design I'd been working on finally made a whole lot more sense. Lugging and placing stone horizontally would have been a really tough job. *Note to self, maybe don't pull all-nighters when designing defensive structures.* Shrugging off the last of sleep, I gathered my notes and headed for the surface. I passed by a few Bunkerites on the way up, notably June as she manned the infirmary, before I was back through the three stone doors to the surface. Getting the pieces of rock to move was a cinch with my increased attributes, once again highlighting how much we'd changed since being Attuned.

Ben was already wolfing down something that looked like hashbrowns for breakfast, Ava and Juan sitting across from him. Sam and Danny were nowhere to be seen. "Ah! The *Vanguard* makes his appearance!" my old teacher mumbled through his meal.

"Uno espera recibir decencia cuando está en la mesa, Benjamín," Juan said, turning from his wife to the bald man.

"Mi amor, you know he never took the time to learn Spanish in the Bunker. He can't know how you insult him that way," Ava said, making a mockery of chastising her husband.

"Better that he doesn't. Otherwise I'd have nothing left to one up him and Dale," Juan joked, smiling.

"Case in point, Ronan," Ben said after swallowing his mouthful. "You weren't the only one that had to put up with *particular* people."

"I think it keeps things interesting," I said, chuckling at the antics of the old group. Seems one was never too old to rag on friends. "Where are *my* intrepid companions?"

"Sam couldn't keep himself away from the farm. Said

something about 'tending to his worms' and 'petting his cows.' I warned him that Raymond has been *pretty* pissy as of late," Ben said, taking a swig from his canteen.

"Daniela took a shift with your fa—uncle," Ava said, catching herself before powering forward. "We had another small attack last night."

My eyes drifted to the weak pulsing light of Bec built into the wall of my vestibule. Even with the added rooms covering part of its surface, the Metier crystal had been the only source of light needed. However, it seemed that the crystal might need some support if it wanted to remain our glorified nightlight.

"Then I'll get to work right away. Can you tell me who and what I have to work with?" I asked. Instead of the usual dismissive jokes the older members of the Bunker used, they were dead serious from that point in the conversation.

"Depends on what you need. I planned to work on the farm today, but Sam can do my work *and then some.* I'm sure Juan could lure some off-duty folk with some of his culinary concoctions," Ben said, gesturing to the Latino puffing his chest out.

"We are going to be raising the roof on this place. Figuratively and literally," I said, pulling out the papers and scattering them on the inner benches of the vestibule. The trio leaned over, eyes widening as they took in my plan.

"How long is it going to take to make this?" Ben asked, his doubt clear in his voice.

"Hopefully no more than a week, depending on how much time I actually get to work. I don't want to leave you all exposed anymore than I have to while we are away. Danny is going to be running messages between us and Wildwood, so if something major happens, we should know fairly soon."

"This is...ambicioso, Ron. Are you sure you don't think your time would be better spent somewhere else? The things attacking us *can* climb you know," Juan added, gesturing to the walls of my vestibule.

"Oh, I planned for it, but there is no sense letting out *all* the surprises now. Is there?"

The three fell into contemplative silence before nodding in agreement. Ben headed off to gather tools while Juan made a beeline back down to the Bunker, hopefully coming back with a few overly qualified grunts. Ava pulled me aside before I could charge outside and start construction.

"I talked with Danny and Sammy before they left. I've been working on a regimen to train your skills and tactics. It's going to take me a few days to incorporate what you three have learned since the last time, but hopefully I can roll *your* training into your construction work. Don't overdo it. Your friends already told me what you've been doing, pushing to collapse with your crafting. The first time I see that, you are banned from work for the next day. You do it again and I'll make it two, got it?" Ava had the sweetest of smiles on her face, but her words didn't broach any argument.

At some point I'd started nodding, so she just smiled wider. She patted my cheek gently before heading off to... whatever she needed to do. One really didn't question Ava, and her results spoke for themselves.

"Suppose it's time to get to work then. I wonder how my helm can help out..." I couldn't keep the wild grin off my face.

Coordinating a fairly willing crowd of people was easier having known them your whole life. The main goal for them was to cut an extensive ditch around the whole Bunker mound. Said soil would then be the source for most of the wall I intended to build tight around the Bunker.

Before I wasted their efforts with untested magic, I headed out to the outer perimeter of the clearing. Just because it stood out, I walked to the northwest where all my early wall-creating testing still stood. It was very much an eyesore, especially with how much I'd refined my skills, but it did divert attacks from that direction. It also gave me one additional modification to my wall, but it wasn't something for me to think about while working my skills.

I eyed the space before channeling mana into my helm. The antlers glowed with umber light but nothing happened like the last time. However, as I formed the second <Earthen Barrier> spell chain, it got sucked up into the item.

<Earthen Barrier>

<Infusion Augmentation: Earth>

<Earth Wall>

The earth groaned in protest as it was *pinched* by invisible fingers of mana. I held my breath, but the magic didn't take longer than a second to manifest a true wall. While less wide than the earthen embankment the skill formed, it was thrice as tall and had gone through an initial bit of condensing. Still awestruck with the magical manifestation, I walked around the nine foot wall. It had to be some eight inches thick, which was significantly thicker than I had expected to make the wall. *The ones of the Wildwood crafters hall were just shy of six inches!* While casting via the item would still take almost half my mana pool, I wouldn't need to do much with the wall after that.

"What if...?"

I took *many* steps back before my final test. Upon further consideration, I took several more. <Mineral Strike> flew into my helm, once again causing the antlers to glow. When I prepared the skill again, a head-sized chunk of fluorite formed in the air. It hovered gently before dropping like a brick. Somehow I had the presence of mind to shove it while it was still weightless. The slope of the clearing had it rolling forward before long, and me running backwards. A quick check showed that I was alone, so I cast <Earthen Barrier> ahead of me. Hurtling over the mound, I started to tuck myself behind the raised earth. Unfortunately, I wasn't fast enough.

"Gahh!" I screamed as a shard launched toward my face, taking a piece of my shoulder with it before embedding in the ground. To add insult to injury, the shard was apparently still large enough to explode again. Smaller shards peppered me from the front. Thankfully, none of those were strong enough to penetrate my Limestone Skin, but I was very quickly covered in bruises. Stemming the bleeding, I looked at the notification that had warned me less than a second before the augmented skill triggered.

<Mineral Strike>

<Infusion Augmentation: Earth>

<Crystal Cascade>

"Note to self, better testing facilities," I muttered through grit teeth. *I need to figure out how to make my own strong walls like Arnold...*

"Ronan?" Ava came running down the slope to see me curled up on the ground. The blood splatter and churned up earth from the exploding mineral must have been a shocking scene, because the usually even keeled woman freaked out as she put on the speed to reach me.

"Hey, uh, Sammy. I might need a little bump, my man," I sent through the comm-plant.

"Coming," he replied. Instead of coming in person, I saw him hoist himself way up in the air on one of his <Vine Whips>. A small, finger-thin tendril of grass sprouted in front of my face, turning in the air like a dog sniffing. "Where's the boo boo?"

"Uh... shoulder?" I said, staring at the tip of the vine, mesmerized, as it followed my movements. It shot forward like a snake, striking not far from where I was missing part of my trapezius. Even with the warming relief, the muscle fibers pulling together hurt—a lot—like snapping rubber engine belts over and over on the same spot. That hadn't been a pleasant experience the first time in the Bunker, and the healing hadn't gone any better.

Understandably, when I started to squirm under the heal, Ava continued to freak out and look around as if something had attacked me. She even shot the vine healing me.

"I'm... okay... Sam is... healing," I managed. The woman didn't look convinced, but she *did* put the gun away. Apparently having seen and heard the encounter, Samuel regrew the vine and resumed healing me until I could actually lift my arm and I didn't feel like I'd been run through a meat tenderizer. So, very much in character as Daniela's mother, she started to whack me and berate me for not being careful. I was just glad she didn't have a sandal in range.

It took several minutes of explaining to get her to release me from her tirade, but she huffed and returned to whatever she'd been doing in the vestibule. She mumbled a number of questionable things under her breath as she walked.

"Thanks, Sam," I sent through the comm-plant. The blond waved off in the distance before lowering himself with his vine.

*I really need that Freeform. Could I combine that ability with the amplitude items?* I shook my head. *Not now, later. Stay on task, Ronan!*

With the knowledge of what my abilities could do, it was about time that our Bunker got some proper defenses to help her defenders. I went over my plans once again while I waited for the Bunkerites to arrive. A wide smile crossed my face as I spotted Ben with a half-dozen shovels on his shoulders. "Alright, everyone. Thank you for volunteering, I just hope you know what you are getting into. First, we'll…"

By the end of the week, a third of the inner wall was done and the trench was complete.

It wasn't as far as I'd wanted, but things on the Wildwood front had been silent. According to Daniela, *too* silent. The Wildwoodians were digging in wherever they could and the training continued to ramp up. With Gifts popping up left and right, the Wild Guard had taken on a minor teaching role as they demonstrated the dangers of magic as a type of public service announcement. With the threat of the Corrupted Entity a big question mark, there wasn't a reason to produce more problems for themselves.

With the other survivors in order and semi-daily updates

from Danny, I stayed the course. Getting additional defenses done meant that my focus wouldn't be as deviated between home and the town. So, I dove into my construction efforts with renewed vigor; just because things were holding steady didn't mean I wouldn't be having to drop things part way.

The process was hell on the decently-in-shape, but older, population of the Bunker. Taking note of how quickly they tired, I set up a rotation system for them to take a break and do lighter tasks as opposed to the main project. Said project was digging the trench around the perimeter of the Bunker mound as a *whole*. One would think that digging a five foot deep hole was easy, but when it was almost three feet wide and the roughly four hundred foot circumference around the Bunker, it was more of an issue. The backside of the Bunker was just over-grown grass and tough weeds, but we dug there too. My idea was to build the housing and further facilities *above* the existing mound and concrete foundation, giving them the highest vantage out of the camp. An inner wall built around the inside side of the trench would force anything climbing to go through the muddy moat I planned to put in there.

Whenever I wasn't making an <Earth Wall>, or putting a <Stone Spike> support between the wall sections, I was down in the trenches with the other Bunkerites. The chisel head of my pickaxe was like an excavator bucket, dragging soil behind me as I dragged it out of the trench towards the Bunker. The revelation that had come to me as a result of my first wall-making attempts was that we didn't need to construct the whole wall at once in order to benefit from it. So, I marked out where my spikes would go, and created the wall by skipping sections. The gaps would provide an opening for any defenders to funnel attackers through instead of having entirely unprotected sections. Implementing this particular construction technique wasn't a priority on the inner wall, since we weren't likely to be attacked without warning inside Bec's area of influence, but it would be key for the outer wall.

Throughout this whole process, Ava watched me like a

hawk. I wasn't sure if she was trying to make sure I didn't overdo it with my magic again, but the long cooldown between casting my augmented skill gave my body plenty of chances to avoid both mana and physical exhaustion afflictions. Whenever she wasn't watching me, Ava was perched atop one of the built sections of wall. She'd roped Sam into making her a vine ladder and hanging chair to keep watch over the camp without having to move. While I was in charge of the construction effort, it certainly felt like I had a task master.

Apparently, her observing hadn't been for naught. On the eighth day of working on the scarp for the Bunker, she pulled the Bunker Busters aside after breakfast.

"I have your training regimen set up now," she said.

"Mama, we need to finish working on the town. We'd agreed that training would come afterwards," Daniela complained, crossing her arms and frowning at her mother.

"Yes, you are quite right. *But*, stagnating risks getting you all killed and that can't stand. Which is precisely why I rolled your training into your building, growing, and scout jobs. When I said I would choose to see you all as adults, it also came with the caveat that you are all still my children. As such, you will not go unprepared into the wild, and I can see that you've all built up some bad habits while out in the world."

"Not to question your training, Ms. Vega, but how could you know if we've built bad habits?" Samuel asked.

Instead of answering Sam, she thwacked him with the butt of her spear. The strike went right on his brow before she spun the weapon to hit me with the pointy end and Daniela with the butt. My brunette friend had just enough time to shift and take the blow on her armor, while I blocked the blow with my forearm. It barely registered thanks to the combined effort of Limestone Skin andQuake Osseum. Not to mention Ava didn't seem to be actually trying to hurt us. Except maybe Sam, because he groaned while channeling his <Health Bump>.

"Samuel, I have seen the massive utility of your skills, however your situational awareness is much worse than

Daniela's or Ronan's. Ronan, while you may be able to take a blow, it does not mean that you *should*. Danny, I know you are fast enough to dodge that; holding back your abilities can have its uses, but it will only cause you to hesitate when you need them," Ava said, pulling back her spear and planting it on the ground. She produced three pieces of precious paper from the Bunker. "These are your regimens. Expect to be tested at the end of the week."

With that, the woman walked away and settled back into her perch, tablet already in hand and tapping away.

"Daniela, I can't decide if you took more after your dad or your mom. Because your mom sure is intimidating," Sam said, absently rubbing his temple.

"Hey! I can be intimidating, leaf boy!" she complained.

"Not if you are going to use weak insults like that," I mumbled. After being put on alert by Ava, I was just barely able to dodge the fireball Danny released my way. Sam and I scurried away after that, not wanting to deal with the brunette's *fiery* temper. My inner wall got an impromptu fire test as Daniela washed it over with flames. "I'm workin''ere!"

"Just finish your little castle already, Ron! We've got ants to kill and another town to tend to," she yelled back, stomping off into the treeline. Ava just shook her head up on her perch. She hadn't even been shaken by the flames crashing down a few feet from her.

"Yeah, yeah, yeah. Everyone's a critic when you are trying to build a proper medieval keep with magic," I grumbled.

# CHAPTER THIRTEEN

## Why Are You Hitting Yourself

Opting to keep Ava happy, I had the rest of the Bunkerites take the day off. I didn't miss the huge wave of relieved sighs that escaped them as many ambled off towards the farm or back down to the Bunker. *Maybe I was still working them too hard,* I thought. Dismissing that particular managerial problem for later, I found myself back in my crafting room adjacent to Bec. His glow was still weak, but I could tell there was a marked improvement from our arrival. *Probably Daniela chunking ants and spiders.* The thought of Danny fighting spiders solo or with Anthony gave me pause, but I knew she wouldn't take risks without sending out a warning. She *had* scouted out the Dreg's territory with just airhead Devon…

"Focus, Ronan. Don't waste so much time. When you aren't being threatened on all sides, you can deal with your sprawling trains of thought," I told myself, making a concerted effort to set the paper down and read.

Most of it outlined what I'd already been doing: controlling the output of my skills, pushing and withdrawing to have better control of each spell chain. There were a few suggestions for how my enhanced attacks could be used to hem in creatures, while also punishing them. Walls didn't have to just defend, they could also be used offensively.

Shelving those for the moment, I saw the bulk of the exercise Ava wanted me to work on. The short version was that she wanted me to 'roll with the punches.' Adjusting my movements to lessen the blow by moving *with* the hit instead of receiving it fully. She added a note stating that she understood there were instances where there *wasn't* an option to do this, but the practice would be key to avoid mounting damage in prolonged fights or in quick, intense fights. The final piece of her training was her suggestion on *how* I could train said ability while also building.

"'Attack yourself'?" I asked out loud. I could have sworn I saw Bec's light twitch, but I couldn't be sure. I wanted to go and ask Ava just how she thought that was a good idea, but I opted against it. Better try, and possibly fail, than just go to her for the direct answer. One doesn't gain as much that way.

Having given everyone the day off, I decided to take one myself and focus on getting the hang of the training. The training yard to the east of camp was still very much empty and sandy, especially after we removed all the trees. I spent several minutes warming up with some simple exercises, making sure I was comfortable with my gear. Even with the redistributed weight after infusing my helm, it still stuck out almost a foot on either side of my head. After thirty minutes of light cardio and mock dodges that made me feel silly, I decided that trying to hit myself with <Stone Spike> was just the best option for training. Possibly work <Mineral Strike> explosions into the mix. *I feel like Sam is going to be getting a real good bit of training himself...*

"<Stone Spike>," I called, somewhat hesitantly. It was half-powered, so that an eight foot pillar didn't just skewer me outright, and to conserve mana. I'd aimed the spike *back* right at my chest from where I was standing. While I'd seen at least a hundred of my spikes manifest, I hadn't really been on the receiving end. If I hadn't interposed my shield in anticipation, I would have been kabobbed. As it was, I grunted and fell back as the force dispersal trait of my shield activated and washed me with a significant amount of heat.

The ground was as comfortable a place as any to groan as I gathered myself up for another attempt. *Fast, but it seems it didn't pierce my shield, which is good...* I found my feet, set them and decided not to do anything fancy other than to take the brunt of the impact and see how it worked its way through me. So, I released the spell chain and a spike struck my shield. Almost immediately, my feet left the ground, removing any strength advantage I might have had against the blow. However, right before my feet left the ground, I felt *something*.

The sensation didn't have anything to do with Ava's training, but somehow I knew it had to do with my own traits. *Am I feeling the force dissipation of my Limestone Skin? Is it working in concert with my Osseum?*

For the next two hours, I proceeded to bruise myself blue. Even regulating the mana expenditure of my <Stone Spikes>, each blow still took its pound of flesh. Subconsciously, I started to angle my shield better to deflect the blow up, instead of getting knocked off my feet each time. Once I managed to *really* feel the blow through my body, the ripple of force became almost obvious. It certainly felt like I'd been working on a 'see the forest for the trees' way when it came to my Limestone Skin, instead of managing each blow individually. The more hits I took, the more I got a hang of directing the force. It wasn't anything refined enough to actually use, but when I forced the impact to travel away from my weapon arm, the blow barely affected my grip before it transferred into the soil beneath me.

I almost didn't want to break for lunch, throbbing muscles notwithstanding, but a throat clear sent via the comm-plant from Ava sent me shuffling over to the vestibule. While I hadn't really been working out, or moving for that matter, tensing with the blows was much more of a strain than I realized. By the time I slumped onto the feasting table, my legs were jelly and I'd let my helm thud onto the table. My face missed the porridge Juan had cooked up by mere inches...

"Ron?" Sam asked, nudging me with his bowl.

"Say, who the what?" I said, jerking up and summoning a spell chain on hand. My eyes focused on Sam's frown and I dismissed the skill. "Sorry, I must have snoozed," I said, yawning.

"Must have been a good one," Samuel said, pointing to the dark stain on the wood from where I'd drooled. *Did I use to drool this much? Maybe I am pushing my body a bit too much.*

"Sorry, trying to get a hang on how to train for Ava's comments," I said, spooning the now-cold porridge into my mouth. As soon as the salty goodness touched my tongue, the rate of consumption tripled.

"Same. I don't know how I am supposed to get my plants to try to attack me while I'm working," he sighed.

"Wait a minute, that's your training?" I asked, pausing lunch just long enough to gawk at my friend.

"Yeah, what about you?"

"I'm supposed to attack myself too. Well, more like learn to roll with the attacks, but it's the same thing really."

The blond scratched at his stubble, frown deepening comically. "How have you been doing?"

"Just aiming my <Stone Spike> at my chest," I said, shrugging and immediately regretting it as my shoulders protested. "Don't you control your vines with your mind?"

Samuel waved his hand side to side. "Somewhat? It's hard to explain, but they listen the best when I am pantomiming an action."

"Pantomime them hitting you, then try to do that enough that it's reflex," I said. "That's how I've been able to improve my shield positioning."

"That… could work…" Sam's strange nervous system tentacle hairs bristled out of his palms as he ran them over the wood. It was clear from his expression he was running his own skills through his mind.

Instead of disturbing him, I went back to my meal and cleaned up. I wasn't sure if it was a result of the increased healing of having an Attunement, or my increases in the strength attribute, but I could almost *feel* my body recovering. The two of us sat in silence as we worked through our bottle-necks. When the other Bunkerites stopped by for lunch, we spent a few minutes talking, once again regaling them with our adventures at their behest. However, not long after that, we headed our separate ways. If I wanted to implement my block training into my building efforts, I needed to get as much direct practice as possible. *Back to the grind.*

— + —

"I don't think she was including her own training in the exceptions for exhaustion," I said, muscles twitching even as I laid on the grass.

"Agreed," Sam groaned from beside me. The life-attuned had stumbled back to the camp from the farm thoroughly whacked. Literally. He hadn't been able to get his plants to attack him subconsciously, but they moved unpredictably enough when given general commands. For my part, I'd been basically throwing myself at my vertical spikes and walls to practice minimizing damage and moving with my gear over dynamic obstacles. The afternoons were when I beat myself silly with targeted skills to the chest.

Ava had been pleased with our progress, taking thorough notes on our individual training and urging us to push ourselves further while 'testing.' I was fairly sure she was doing *that* and driving in the point that there was always something to improve.

She'd made me dodge *rocks* she threw without a hint of mercy while not being able to move my feet. It hadn't gone as terribly as I'd expected, even deflecting a few of the projectiles purposely rather than by chance. Sam had a similar test, except with cut up chunks of leaves that were much lighter but were thrown by a half-dozen people. Danny had taken her test else-where, but she'd been smug when we'd seen her so we assumed it went well.

The rest of the week after we got Ava's tests had been a whirlwind of pain, learning, and construction for me. The inner wall was complete, and the trench on the border of the clearing was well on its way. While the bulk of my helpers worked on digging the outer trench, I helped to remove any trees in the way as well as work on the two removable half-log bridges I'd created in order to access the Bunker complex.

When *that* was finished, I started to work on the actual 'keep' portion of the camp, opting to save the outer wall project for when I had a higher Quotient and more time. I focused on building some basic rooms as well as a hardened earth slope to reach the second level. I expanded on the shower area, adding a small reservoir next to the actual rigged system on the second floor.

Without the help of Jolene, or precise building tools, I had to improvise how I built windows into the second floor. Instead of building every wall with my <Earth Wall> augmented skill, I left one of the outer walls open on each of the four rooms I made. Using half-powered <Stone Spikes> and then cutting off the pointed bit, I added some gothic-looking windows to the budding building. I didn't have any specific goal for the rooms, but they could at least serve as housing as the Bunkerites spent more time on the surface. Only so many people could sleep in the vestibule and lobby before they had to really rough it.

All in all, I was content with how it turned out. Not only would each person have a room with a window and door, the second floor's roof gave a perfect vantage point *over* the inner wall. With the spiral ramp on the perimeter, the tiered first and second floors in the middle had been vaguely inspired by the Tower of Pisa. Much shorter, but I also had plans to have the Bunker's Keep reach much higher. *Wonder if that monument survived the end of the world?*

Structure complete, training passable, and body thoroughly ragged, I took two days to recover. Really recover. I returned to the Bunker to rest on my familiar bed. I spent an unknowable amount of time fiddling with the infusions that belonged to my mother and grandmother. The information from the implant was cold, devoid of just what the blobs meant to me.

<Quotient 0 Infusion>
<Water - Tranquil>
<Integrity: 99%>

<Quotient 0 Infusion>
<Fire - Fervent>
<Integrity: 99%>

The most curious thing about them was the fact that the infusions hadn't degraded like all the others on the surface. I wasn't sure if that was a result of their passing before being Attuned properly, or what had caused Daniela, Samuel, and I not to change like the other Fallen from Wildwood.

Regardless of the reason for their permanence, the perfect icy marble that had been my mother and the still-smoldering coal of my grandmother kept me company as I relived a day in the Bunker life. An hour of physical training in the gym, almost laughable with my strengthened body. Tofu meal snagged from Juan before he'd finished the larger batch of breakfast. Several hours of browsing the archive terminals for just about anything on construction and materials. Lunch. Rotating tasks between the greenhouse floor and the water treatment facility. Dinner. A round or four of 3D pinball at the terminal. Shower and sleep.

The whole thing almost felt alien. While it hadn't been six months since we'd returned to the surface, things had already changed and progressed more than our entire lives. Nothing on the surface was stagnant, because if it was, it was liable to get trampled by its neighbors. The lives of the other Bunkerites hadn't been nearly as hectic without magic in the mix, but what would a fully populated Earth have looked like? What would the overgrown and ruined buildings flanking the streets have looked like in their prime? Crowds so big that individuals were unrecognizable from one another? The scale of that still escaped me.

While philosophizing, a brunette blur did a three-quarter somersault right onto my chest. I had just enough presence of mind to flare mana into <Earth Shell> around my abdomen. The hardening rock plate was thin at best, but it took the blow easily before dissipating back into mana.

"Hey bum," Daniela said, feet still propped on my chest as she balanced herself on one hand. Her other hand was holding a small plastic bag, which was unusual in and of itself. Not many of those were still around compared to studier storage alternatives.

"Is there a time where you *don't* try to bother me when I am just resting?"

"Heard from your uncle that you've been moping around the Bunker. Figured I'd bring you something to remind you that the future isn't stuck in the past." To mark her words, she plopped the bag on my chest before curling her legs back to stand.

I huffed at her esoteric wording before looking in the bag. A small spread of the meats of Wildwood, as well as several of the fruits they grew in the town, were a welcome sight. The meaning, of course, wasn't lost on me. "Time to head back?"

"Soon. I'm going to need help, though. Bunker Buster help," she said, sighing and leaning against the wall. When all I did was pluck an apple out and quirk an eyebrow at her, she continued. "The ants. They've been getting bolder and bolder with their probing attacks. I'm worried if we don't push them back *hard* before we leave, they will hit the camp with a surprise attack."

"Well, we were going to try to bump our levels anyway. Have you confirmed that they are sensitive to levels?" I asked, remembering one of the theories I'd heard for why territories formed, not simply as a result of the presence of a Metier Crystal.

"Oh yeah," she said, smiling deviously. She tapped her eye before pointing at herself, clearly indicating our implants.

<Daniela (Human)>

\<Attunement: Fire>
\<Refinement: Flames>
\<Perceived Metier Quotient: 5>

"Hot damn!" I said, jumping to my feet.

"*Hot* damn is right," she said, forming a spell chain in her hand. The temperature in the room immediately climbed. It was like an open stove concentrated on her palm.

"Does Sam know?" I said, pulling her into a congratulatory hug before remembering our third musketeer.

"Told him just this morning. Been running around getting used to the power gain when I heard what you'd been up to," she said.

"He's not Q5 yet, is he?" I said, suddenly aware of how detached I'd been from pretty much everyone while building and training. Even if people needed their space to work, I should have at least been checking in on Danny and Sam.

"No, but he said he's close. Something about having to deal with pesky worms not listening to his commands."

"Then we need to head out. If at all possible, I would like to confirm whether the ants have a Metier Crystal or not," I said, mind already drifting as I formed a mental list of what we would need if we wanted to head out the following day. "If not, then clearing some waves should throw their scent off the camp. Maybe sending one of the Wild Guard squads here instead of the spider dungeon might be the better long term solution."

"Considering the trend, I'd say it's unlikely we spot it by chance. It's probably with the queen, somewhere underground in their territory."

"Yes... Makes sense..." I absently placed my mother and grandmother's infusions back amongst my minerals. *My gear is here, but we would need to gather some food and water before leaving. Also, making sure we have at least some backup firearms would be a good idea. Definitely a few duffels for loot. Sam might be able to rig something so Anthony could carry—*

"I'm the fire-attuned, so why is smoke coming out of your ears?" Daniela said, poking me in the ribs before heading out of my room. "Dress me slowly because I am in a hurry!" she called from down the hall.

"You know I don't understand when you translate Spanish idioms, Daniela!" I shouted back.

"If you know it's an idiom, then you *do* understand!" She giggled. "Just get moving, rock boy! I know you don't want to get left behind."

She wasn't wrong. The prospect of more magical power was a draw in and of itself, but it was merely a stepping stone to what it would let us achieve. I piled up my gear and a change of clothes on my shield before following up the stairs.

# CHAPTER FOURTEEN

## Ashlands

"You made a wagon!?" I said, slack-jawed.

"You don't have the market on crafting cornered, Ron. Plus, if I didn't help you with my vines, I don't think you'd even be able to make even passable armors," Sam said.

"When did you make this?" I asked, still amazed. He'd cut slices out of the thickest logs we'd harvested, then carved a hole in the middle to make a wheel where he pushed a thinner log to act as an axle before mounting the axle to the sled we'd once used. *I didn't even realize we still had that thing.*

"Just yesterday when Danny stopped by. Knowing you two, I knew we would be heading out to fight *something,* so I just put my own plan into effect. I also made a hitch for Anthony. Since he's been patrolling with Danny, he's gotten a lot bigger. This bad boy has more cart than any cart could cart." The blond slapped the side of the wagon proudly.

"Hilarious…" It was still an impressive accomplishment, and sent my mind spinning with possibilities of vehicles and mounts for travel. I felt a bit like a cartoon character waving my hands in the air to dismiss the thought bubble before I could get too caught up.

"You get supplies and stuff already then?" I asked, getting back on track.

"I've got the food and the empty crate we've been lugging around," he said, pointing at the back of the wagon. "Two days' worth."

"We'll get with Teach before we leave. Getting new magazines for our pistols will be a smart idea. No sense going in half-cocked."

"You did that on purpose," Sam said, narrowing his eyes at my word choice.

"Maybe…" I smirked, leaving him to put some final touches on his wagon before calling out to Daniela through the comm-plant.

"Finishing a conversation with my mom. Meet you by your crappy wall bits," she said before cutting the connection. She didn't get to hear me grumble about her comment.

Nevertheless, sometime before ten o'clock, we were ready. The ant territory wasn't far from the Bunker, so it was entirely possible we would need to retreat all the way back, but there was no sense in wasting the day. The bulk of the Bunkerites showed up to wave us off that time. We headed off to cheers and calls for our safe return.

The mood set for the trip, we made quick time through the woods, Danny in the lead, with me and Sam flanking Anthony and the cart. Blobby finally decided to show up, as I knew it would, the moment we crossed the tree line. Even Daniela was surprised when it appeared. We had to stop a few times to repair the wagon as it still struggled through the root-infested forest floor, but the now human-sized Anthony did a commendable job pulling it. The little Formicidae critter was larger each time I laid eyes on him, and stronger to boot.

About an hour later, Daniela called a halt through the comm-plant. "I'm in sight of a patrol. Go ahead and set up the defense."

Sam and Anthony kept watch while I focused on the area around us. Trees were practically a detriment when it came to fighting our fiery neighbors. In order to combat this, I spent another good hour forming a hexagonal room in a small clearing, leaving the north and south facing walls missing to give access to the incoming enemies. The two sections of wall facing towards the ants I made with <Earth Wall>, while the rest I used stacked <Earthen Barrier> to make.

While I worked on a secondary <Stone Spike> perimeter to funnel the creatures towards the hex, Sam used his vines to physically clear away the tree canopy. The blond tore branches off at the base, setting them up far from our clearing. Just to give us the best option to retreat, I consolidated the ground out of the back opening for about a hundred feet so we could at least have a clean exit. Whether we would be able to hitch Anthony throughout a fighting retreat was up in the air.

At some point during our work, Daniela checked in to tell us to stop as a group of ants scurried by. After gauging their power, she suggested we go ahead and engage. We attacked them on two sides. The six sub-Q3 ants didn't stand a chance as vines tangled them, crystal stunned them, and Daniela cleaved them with her naginata before the shards of my attack had even dropped to the ground. The Pith they provided was something like six percent for Sam and I. It was even less for Danny. Regardless of those gains, we snagged the loot and headed back to the defensive hex.

Daniela nodded appreciatively as we adjusted our gear and had a quick snack. Anthony shrugged off his hitch, probing us with his antenna and getting some pats from everyone. It said something about our time on the surface that the slime hanging out and the giant ant asking for pets barely seemed strange at all. Danny latched her naginata to Anthony's back before giving us a thumbs up. "We don't have long before they notice that the patrol didn't arrive; they are quite prompt for insects."

"Let's go over the plan one more time. We skirt, cull as much as we can, then head into their territories. Once we've got them coming our way, we retreat here and clean up. Anything at Q4 we skedaddle and come back tomorrow or the day after.

Loot is important, but not a priority," I said, pointing to the structure around us and at the cart stored within it.

"Isn't this like the third time we are going to a dungeon territory?" Daniela asked, lifting her brows as if to say 'duh.'

"Yes, but we don't want to talk about what happened the other times, do we?" I said, meeting her eyes sternly. She obviously knew what I was alluding to, so she nodded instead of throwing another complaint into the mix. Sam just shook his head.

Without fanfare, we pushed north. The closer we got to the fire ant's territory, the more scorched and sparse the trees became, the grassy undergrowth quickly replaced by tough shrubs covered in ash. A few oaks had just been turned into ashy husks where new trees were attempting to grow. A rustle was all the warning we got as another patrol appeared.

A quarter-power <Stone Spike> was enough to deal with the dog-sized ant at the lead. Just like with the previous patrol, Sam provided crowd control while Danny and I cleaned up. Instead of focusing on the loot, we absorbed the Pith and just stacked it up next to the closest ashen tree. My spike was marker enough if we made it back.

We went the rest of our scouting patrol free of ants, which made us tense even more. The ashlands that marked the core of the ant's territory was not far through the trees, but we didn't want to be spotted just yet as we retraced our steps. When we were roughly in line with the hex, we plowed into the ashlands. A valley of ash and a few hunks of petrified charcoal stretched out before us. There weren't any ants within sight, but we knew they were fairly quick on open ground, and if there was an underground access, we would have to find it or follow a patrol back.

After only a minute into the ashlands, I was ready to fight something. The stuff was so thick and fluffy on the ground that we all sank up to our ankles. Out of frustration, I channeled mana into the passive form of <Earthen Barrier> to compress a path through the ash. Even if it got swept back into the consolidated space, it wasn't nearly as thick. I continued forward until I hit the ninety percent mark on my mana pool.

"How much noise do we want to make?" I asked as I put up two <Earthen Barriers>, ash-edition, on our flanks.

"I'm feeling quick today. Sammy?" Daniela asked.

"One moment." The blond closed his eyes, green and gold circles forming in his palms before transferring into the ground. Grass pushed through the ash, its blades taking on a strange blue tinge the more it grew. Sam stayed with his hands on the ground for several seconds as the circle of grass expanded, even managing to grow on the mounds of my <Earthen Barrier>. When he removed his hands, there was ash-covered grass in a ten foot circle around us. "That should let me get vines out faster. Give me a minute to regen my mana and you can be as loud as Daniela chewing."

I stifled a chortle even as I watched Daniela's face turn redder than her flames. While she attempted to strangle Samuel as quietly as possible, I kept a look out over the ashlands and our two non-human companions. Anthony moved through the ash with the same ease others of his species did, while Blobby swelled with ash before spurting it out of its body. Knowing as little as I did about my gelatinous companion as it was liable to either *have* to do that, or it was its way of passing the time.

"Topped off," Sam said. Daniela echoed the sentiment.

As the melee fighter, I pulled my gun and fired it twice into the distance. The crack of the gunshot echoed in the empty space and I could have sworn that the wind decided at that moment to stop blowing just to remove the gentle whistle of its passing. Our group flexed fingers, rolled shoulders, and twitched eyes. Just as I was about to try for the shot again, small plumes of ash shot out of the ground around us. *Maybe we went a little too deep...* Ants surged out of the very ground.

<Fire Ant>
<Attunement: Fire>
<Refinement: N/A>

&lt;Perceived Metier Quotient: 0&gt;

&lt;Fire Ant&gt;
&lt;Attunement: Fire&gt;
&lt;Refinement: N/A&gt;
&lt;Perceived Metier Quotient: 1&gt;

At least two dozen of the creatures scurried our way in a panic. I wasn't sure what had triggered them to that extent, but I didn't think it had just been the gunshot.

Instead of letting the numbers overwhelm us, I decided to put some obstacles in the way. Two &lt;Earthen Barriers&gt; redirected the ants coming from the north and southeast, while I lobbed three &lt;Mineral Strikes&gt; into the closest grouped ones.

Daniela wasn't idle either. Her wisp took to the air and started unleashing fiery hell on the creatures. While not as directly effective as my crystal shards, it did concuss the creatures enough to put them out of the fight. Sam made sure that any creature that got too close got tangled, so I halved my mana pool unleashing &lt;Mineral Strikes&gt; and then focused on finishing the closest ants with my pick.

Anthony and Blobby remained on standby, harassing the creatures on either side of Samuel.

"Ron, give me some height," Daniela said.

Complying, I cast &lt;Stone Spike&gt; on top of my ash barriers. A swing from my pick gave her a flat-ish perch, which she quickly used to balance. We remained tense, unwilling to approach the many bodies around us in case more ants were on their way. Sure enough there were, however they didn't do what I expected.

The plumes of ash rose up under each of the bodies scattered around. That was when Daniela yelled, "Tap the bodies close to us! They are eating the dead!"

Me and Sam surged forward, kicking and slapping ant corpses wherever we could get to them. Unfortunately, after a few seconds, we were out of corpses in reach that wouldn't leave us totally exposed. I was also beginning to think my hardened circle had something to do with why the creatures weren't swarming from right underneath us.

I kept a wary eye on my mana as it ticked up. Already a slight amount of discomfort was clawing its way through my abdomen, but I squashed it quickly. Even without mana, I had to hold the line for the others.

"Q2s incoming!" Daniela called out, summoning her wisp once again.

I spent the ten percent of my mana pool I'd been able to recover to coat myself in <Earth Shell>. Making a silent promise not to use mana until it was up to forty percent, I stepped out into the soft ash. Daniela's heat picked up as she cast her wisp, and three leg-thick vines sprouted from the ground. The moment a fireball flew out of the wisp, the battle started in earnest.

Doing my best not to breathe in the ash was hard, but I spun in half-circles to bat ants away with my unchanged pick-axe. I roared right in the insects' faces, taunting them and drawing them towards me instead of past me to my friends. Anthony and Blobby worked with each other to cover the rear guard while Samuel was a human slap machine. Instead of going for the restraints, he struck the creatures back when they got too close. The impact rattled them, and gave more than enough time for either me or Daniela to skip over and snuff the creature out.

Time quickly lost meaning as I took blow after blow on my shield or on my <Earth Shell>. What I quickly realized had been missing from my training was a *true* threat. People say that practical experience is key, so long as you have a strong foundation; out in the ashlands was where I really felt the two start to click. When the fire ants got into close range, not only would they try to clamp with their mandibles or stab with their stingers, but some also had *gifts* of their own in the form of flamethrowers, not unlike Anthony's.Instead of taking the brunt of those attacks, I did my best to angle my shield to redirect the flames while also moving into the small blind spot the smoke created.

It was in that frame of mind that we rolled. I was fairly sure we could have kept that dance of death going for several more minutes, but a plume of ash erupted from the middle of my fortifications. Hardened ash turf rained down on our defensive point. Unlike the smaller plumes in the fields around us, this one was a pressurized geyser. A car-sized ant started crawling out of the sinkhole, glaring at Sam and Daniela. Daniela had nearly fallen off her perch thanks to the surprise, but Sam had been quick enough on the vine draw to catch her before she fell amidst the ants.

Risking a blow, I concentrated on the hole that the ant was crawling out of before releasing three half-powered <Stone Spikes> radially around the hole. Like a bone in an external cast, my spikes pinned the Q3 fire ant around the thorax. Flames escaped its mouth, attempting to spray my friends, but Samuel put an end to that. His femur club burst one of the creature's compound eyes, which cut off its magical attack. My blond caveman companion then proceeded to turn the chitin around it into pulp even while his vines slapped away ants without his direct prompting.

The surprise attack stifled, Daniela and I focused on cutting down the rest of the ants. Instead of up on her perch, Daniela was now in the mix side by side with Anthony. The sleek ant had delivered his naginata payload and was wrestling any ants that tried to flank Daniela. Our fiery Latina was a human blender as she spun the weapon almost faster than I could keep track of. When Blobby knocked me out of the way of a fire ant bite, I knew it was time for me to focus on the fight.

"Start the retreat!" I called, glancing at my mana pool as Blobby encased the ant that had tried to attack me. <Mineral Strike> formed in my palm and I held the attack until Samuel started to cross the lithified path I'd created earlier. The shard plunked down into the hole where the Q3 ant had been, exploding and embedding into several offending ants that had the audacity to take advantage of the breach. "Daniela, touch some of the big ones!"

The woman didn't say anything, opting instead to channel her mana into the naginata so she could zip through my barriers with three Quotient's worth of mobility boosts, tapping the Q3 boy and several of the Q2 swarm. The Pith chased us as we retreated from the growing plumes of ash misting in the air.

"I'm doing the math, Ron, and I am not liking this calculus!" Sam called through his comm-plant. His focus was still on slapping ants, keeping them taunted while we retreated to the treeline.

"Never took you for a mathematician, Sammy!" Daniela panted through the implant. Her wisp let rip a burst of fire that obscured us further in a plume of ash and smoke.

"At least I paid attention at all! Ron, if it takes three of a Quotient to make the next, how many are we at now!?"

*The Q3 is dealt with, but a dozen dead Q2's makes roughly four of those car-sized Q3 bastards...*"Let's just focus on getting to the hex!"

As if to make themselves known, the *actively leveling* ants sent a wave of heat that flash dried the last remaining leaves on the border trees. The heat washed over Daniela with barely a tussle of her hair, but I felt my skin pull tight. Samuel stumbled, gasping for breath as it was robbed from him. Instead of stopping, I snagged him by the back of his armor and hauled him up. "Danny, slap some water on his face!"

The woman only glanced briefly, pulling her canteen off her belt and splashing liquid relief onto our blond friend even as he sputtered for breath. "Why couldn't we have something *cool* to deal with in Florida?" he asked as he finally got his breathing in order. He didn't get an answer, of course, because we were too focused on running for our lives as the less-charred woods enveloped us.

# CHAPTER FIFTEEN

## Q5

The glittering cloud of Pith was finally able to catch up to us, sending a rush of energy that cleared some of the exhaustion the previous fight had piled on. We ate up the ground, leaving the ants to crash through the forest as we followed the memorized path back to our second layer of defenses.

"There's too much smoke!" Sam called out as we made it to the hex. The blond clambered up the side of my wall to get a good view of the clearing. Unfortunately, the cloud of ash and smoke had followed us.

"Daniela, leave your wisp to do its thing! I need you to keep stragglers off me," I said, glancing at my half-full mana pool. The ticking of seconds and my fairly low refinement attribute had never bothered me as much right then.

The brunette was a red-trimmed blur as she climbed onto the set of walls opposite Sam. Blobby and Anthony took up the rear, with one of the slime's mitosed clones hovering by my leg defensively. *Think, Ronan. You need line of sight. Remember these are blaze ants!*

"Sam, can you grow leaves on your vines?" I called over my

shoulder, focusing on the growing vibrations that left my toes tingling.

"Eh... maybe?" The life-attuned didn't say anything else, but I watched the spell chains circling the base of his vines shifting and rib-like growths sprouted from the vines flanking our hex.

"That works! Try to get some of the debris out of the air!" No sooner was Sam's <Vine Whip> cutting through the smoke than an ant face chomped down on the vine. The verdant tentacle withered at a visible rate. "Contact!"

<Crystal Cascade>!My thoughts were thankfully enough to prompt my helm into activating the amplification trait. Half of my restored mana vanished in a flash, but in exchange, I had an explosive clump of cinnabar that promptly struck the ant in the face. The impact itself only staggered the ant, but the explosion planted chunks of crystal into its head. I just barely had enough time to block a hunk that flew towards the hex. Remembering what was coming next, I punted the chunk back into the ash and smoke. A satisfying chittered scream told me it had at least hit *something*.

"Using my club!" Sam called out as Daniela unleashed a truly massive fireball that removed the head off the second Q3 ant that showed its face. *Two more?*

Rumble. *Flanking!?* Another Q3 appeared behind us. Several of my <Stone Spikes> defenses had left cracks on its chitin underside, but it didn't appear to bother the ant overly much. I wasn't sure if the smoke and ash were messing with my perception, or if the growing pain in my abdomen was dulling my senses, but I'd only noticed the creature through my feet. Thankfully, Anthony and Blobby were there to meet the creature.

While Anthony wasn't up to the task of meeting the blaze ant bulk-for-bulk, there was a deceptive amount of power in our insect companion. It headbutted the blaze ant, causing it to crash into the hex wall. The impact reverberated off the wall, but it held. Not wasting time, two-thirds of Blobby locked down one of the ant's legs while Anthony blowtorched another right at the joint. The car-sized ant flexed its abdomen, hoping to strike Anthony with its stinger, but Blobby split just in time to coat the stinger. It didn't survive the strike. The blobite exploded in a spray of superheated slime that covered Anthony, but also sent the blaze ant reeling.

Sam finished his augmented skill.

The *trees* bent to his will. Branches as thick as my arm snapped down onto the blaze ant, locking it in place. The bark darkened under the aura of heat coming off the creature, but held. Anthony wobbled onto the creature's back, stabbing his own stinger right into the creature's eyeball. Its dying throes set my ears to ringing.

A blast of heat snapped me from my trance. *There's one more!* Not only was there probably one more blaze ant, but assorted numbers of Q1s and Q2s were rushing through the forest now that I paid attention. Thankfully, while I'd been drooling at the ant versus ant match up, Daniela had been acting as exterminator. Whichever strike didn't take a fire ant's life left it slowed as her naginata's trait entangled the creatures.

"There's one more!" I yelled, coalescing a Mineral Strike and sending it deeper into the rolling ash cloud still coming from the north. By that point, it had encompassed us, and I could hardly see deeper than ten feet into the woods. My feet took me to all the ants Danny hadn't finished off, ending their entrapment with a pickaxe to the forehead. Instead of leaving them for fodder, I grabbed a hold of them until they started to crystalize and dissociate. Pith trickled into me, fueling each step as I killed more of the stragglers.

"I don't have eyes on it!" Danny called, slicing a Q1 clean in half with her naginata five feet from me.

"Ugh." I spat ashen phlegm on the dirt around us. "Regroup on the hex!"

Daniela and I made it back into the hex just as Sam, Anthony, and Blobby rolled in. I kept a <Stone Spike> at the ready, and I could see Sam gripping a tuft of grass that hadn't been inside our hex before.

"Where is it?" Sam said before giving us a look over. He yelled in alarm as he pointed at my leg. "Ronan!"

"What?" Like a smart guy, I followed his finger to see the portion of Blobby that had stuck with me keeping my leg from buckling. The slime was encasing a section of my calf that had been burned clean off by one of the many attacks I hadn't been able to dodge. The lime green inside of the gelatinous creature was shot through with crimson blood as the slime acted like a giant external clot. When my brain had enough time to process the sight, the world was suddenly *very* unsteady.

"You adrenaline punching bag idiot!" Daniela said, holding herself back from punching me in the shoulder by bunching her fist up.

"Stay—"

The quiet roar of our fight shifted. I wasn't sure where the response came from but it was a primal place. I could practically feel my body harmonizing with my surroundings. The last of my adrenaline exploded through me as the world moved in slow motion. I shoved Sam and Daniela back towards the kink of the other two walls just in time for the one behind us to crack under a ton of force.

Hemming us in, and nearly crushing me, I managed to release my <Stone Spike> to keep the eight foot wall from turning me into a pancake. Instead of completing the cast, the pointed rock formation fused with my wall to leave a two foot gap. While I wasn't claustrophobic, the heat under the wall climbed unabated, quite literally baking us between the collapsed wall and the ground. I couldn't see the creature that had broken my <Earth Wall>, but when a torso-thick insect leg tried to scrape under the wall, information populated in my vision.

<Fire Ant>

<Attunement: Fire>

<Refinement: Inferno>

<Perceived Metier Quotient: 4>

"Ron!" Sam called. I glanced up at my friend to see blood staining his hair and leaving one of his eyes shut from where he'd hit his face against the wall. It didn't seem to impede him as a vine wrapped around my leg, essentially cocooning it and pushing Blobby out as healing energy vanished my dizziness. "We can't stay here!"

I had enough mana for two more <Stone Spikes>, but there was no way I could see the creature. My pickaxe was somewhere in the ground under the wall, but it would be futile to waste time trying to find it.

"Can you hold it in place above us!?" I asked, sweat streaming down my face as I crab-walked towards my friends. Blows shook the wall-turned-ceiling and I released a half-powered <Stone Spike> that fused with the wall for extra support. It brought my reserves down lower, but what use was mana when one of your own elemental attunement skills was your cause of death?

"I'm almost tapped out," Sam said, wincing as the ant continued to try to crush us. Another precious ten percent mana added yet another support when I heard a cracking sound I was distinctly not a fan of.

"Well, we need to do *something*! This thing is going to bake us and turn us into a pastry!" Daniela said, holding her hands out towards the open spaces of our makeshift defenses; I could practically see the shimmering heat waves being redirected by her passive skill. Each of her breaths was like a furnace bellows on our faces, but her concentration was unbroken.

"I just need a minute to get enough mana for an augmented skill. If you can lock it down, it should hopefully be enough!" I said, watching my mana tick to thirty-four percent. *Just another six...*It wasn't the time to test and see what a partially powered augmented skill would do. I berated myself the whole while for not training that facet of my abilities when Sam gave me a grim nod.

"I don't want to know what will happen if this doesn't work, do I?" Danny said. Her breath was coming hot from her fire gills as well as her mouth, and the shade of red on her skin told me she wasn't doing too hot.

A thud marked another strike by the ant and Samuel cast, "<Arboreal Grasp>!" The grass pushed through my consolidated soil as a spill off from his mana. The creature above us wailed as a waist-thick tree crashed down on it with purpose. The few visible legs sprawled and scrambled for grip on the ground as the tree pinned the creature to my broken wall. The heat inside our personal oven picked up once again.

"Rahhh!" Daniela cried out, her mana flaring to push the heated air away from us. I released my augmented skill as soon as my mana hit forty percent. This time, the fight had really taken a toll as it took everything I had not to coil in on myself. The iron taste of blood filled my mouth, a chunk of my tongue surely missing, as I grit my teeth against the rebellion in my abdomen. My palms touched the broken <Earth Wall> and folded to my will. The augmented skill ate up our rocky shield to produce a blade of stone that cleaved the trapped ant down the middle.

Boiling ichor rained down around us, but I did the best I could to interpose myself and my shield between it and my friends, especially Sam. Efforts aside, all of us screamed as the heat of the ant, the rock, and the blazing forest wrapped around us.

I wasn't sure how long that went on for, but eventually Blobby and Anthony, the least drained of our group, managed to drag us out of the fight's wreckage. The inferno ant was still twitching and most of the trees around us were on fire or already charcoal black.

One of my eyes was very much not cooperating, but through the other I could see the choking black smoke rising into the sky. Pieces of Sam's wagon were scattered and charred from where the inferno ant had stepped on it. Blobby rolled unevenly as it used its bulk to put out any fires that got closer to where Anthony had dragged us.

*Really wish Lilly or Dai were here... Devon works too...* My thoughts drifted until I spotted the inferno ant. As its front half started to rise, so did my panic. I dug my fingers into the ground, dragging myself forward towards my friends.

Sam was drunk as a skunk, but at least my touch was able to draw his attention. "Ronny Ron T! What cancha' do for ye?"

"He—" I coughed and licked my lips to try to get some moisture to my mouth and vocal chords. "Heal," I rasped.

"Sure!" Sam made to stand up only to slump back down. "Ouchy poo. Guess those ol' legs ain't kicking right meow," he said with a giggle.

*Oh no. He's tapped past his pool!* It was the only explanation for his extra, *extra* loopiness.

"Why are you two bugging me, I don't feel well!" Daniela complained. She didn't look totally conscious, but it would have to do.

"Danny, you need to finish off the ant!" I rasped, a bit more of my voice coming back.

"How's she gonna do that, silly?" Sam interjected. "You seen her hands?" He giggled like a madman. When I looked at Daniela, sure enough, her hands were a charbroiled mess of flesh pretty much down to the bone. There was barely a hint of the small, calloused kitchen hands I remembered. *She's in shock...*

A roar rumbled deep through me as I started to do the worm towards the inferno ant. My lower body wasn't working right, muscles spasmed out of my control and even my palms twitched while I tried to grab hold of the grass. I was on a ticking clock as the smoke thickened and the flames drew closer.

Anthony tried to stop me, but I met his bloodied compound eyes. "Kill. Ant." Instead of holding me back in safety, his mandibles closed around my upper arm and he helped drag my sorry body to Daniela's naginata. With it in hand, he dragged me the rest of the way to the Q4 ant.

Said ant was *not* happy about us still being alive. Its one remaining leg swung wildly, trying to crush me before I could get in range with my spider weapon. What was essentially napalm dribbled out of its mouth, but apparently the inferno ant needed its lower half to spew the attack properly. *Good to know.*

My mind took in all those details, slotting them in as a distraction from my pain and the growing heat the closer I got to the fire-attuned beast. Anthony dropped me, catching the flailing leg in his mandibles before it could slap me silly. He immediately started using his blowtorching flamethrower. Apparently, the inferno ant was tough enough not to be damaged by that level of heat because it kept flailing, taking my insectoid ride with it as Anthony kept his mandibles locked on the limb, weighing it down.

I fed mana into the air item, feeling the boost to my mobility turn my worm crawl into a shuddering spasm, but it was enough to plunge the blade into the creature's mouth. I twisted my whole body, turning the blade until finally the twitching stopped and Anthony dropped to the ground beside me like a sack of potatoes. Our ant companion was still alive, but it had lost two legs in the process and there was a nasty crack on its thorax.

Gasping as my breath was stolen by the intense heat, I slapped my hand to the once-living stove that was the inferno ant. Like a crystalline rash, smoky quartz exploded to encompass the creature regardless of its torso separation. When it dissociated, glorious Pith flowed out of it into me, before splitting into my friends.

Gasps of relief exited all of us. My bruising immediately vanished and the wound on my leg finished knitting together as the energy of rising in Quotient suffused me. My health climbed from a less than stellar thirty-one percent back to full in a matter of seconds. The most relevant change of the jump, however, was the relief it brought to my abdomen. As my muscles knit tighter, bones hardened, and lungs expanded, so did my ephemeral mana pool.

"Sweet apple crust!" Daniela howled as the damage from her hands got a massive healing boost. Her hands weren't totally healed, as evidenced by the flakes of black muscle hanging from her palm and the two places I was fairly sure were just skin-covered bone. *Gaining Pith also restores our bodies, not just a level up!* It was a significant piece of information, but I also stashed it away for later as I hobbled back to my friends.

Samuel was blinking away like the world was much too bright which, considering the encroaching fire, was entirely possible. He already looked ten times more sober, but I knew that he'd just dumped God knew how much Dreg into his body.

"Sam, can you help Daniela?" I asked, grabbing his chest plate as gently as I could to get his attention. It took his eyes a few seconds to focus, but he answered mostly coherently.

"Just a minute… There's too many of her for me to heal right now…" he said, glancing at Danny before snapping his eyes shut.

"Daniela, what's your status?" I asked, drawing her eyes to me from her still-mangled hands.

"*Pain.* Lots of it. So *much* of it." She was groaning, arms coiled close to her body defensibly, but at least she seemed uninjured everywhere else.

"Okay, that means we are alive. Cart's busted, so can't use that to carry—"

Something reverberated through the ground. Neither Daniela nor Sam reacted to the sensation, which was followed immediately by five more. It was subtle, but strong enough that even my addled companions should have picked up on it. Absently, I remembered the strange feelings I'd picked up while obscured in the ash cloud. My brain immediately made the connection, as much as I hated it for that. *Something is coming!* Whatever the thing, it was big enough for me to sense it when it wasn't even within sight.

My mind wheeled as I took stock of our surroundings. Anthony was up, but shaky. Blobby had rejoined its surviving blobs, but it was lacking quite a bit of mass. Smoke blocked out the sky, fire to the north, east, and south, as well as a plethora of afflictions still impairing us. Even with the bulk of my mana feedback alleviated and wounds restored, I didn't feel up to running a marathon. When the rumble crawled up my legs and registered in my brain, I corrected that to a sprint.

"Really need to fight something that doesn't catch everything on fire next," I grumbled as I helped my two friends up. Daniela seemed to snap out of it when I clapped my hands in her face. When I told her something was coming, she didn't argue, bit her lip against her ravaged hands, and started to help Samuel around the southern wall of fire. I saw her wince as she used a spell chain to ward off the embers and licking flames. Her face clenched as if she'd eaten something sour, but the next moment she was hidden by smoke.

*Rumble.* "Alright, Ant the ant. I need you to latch on to me. Blobby, please tell me you can roll?" I said, turning to my non-human companions.

For Anthony's sake, I took a knee, which allowed the ant to clamber onto my back. Even as strong as I knew the ant was, he was fairly light. Possibly a result of the missing limbs and the hot fluid that dripped down my back out of his wounds. Blobby jiggled weakly before taking a wide rolling path around the fire, following after Daniela. For the second time that day, we retreated. *I just hope it's enough.*

# CHAPTER SIXTEEN

## Ant-agony-stic

Even when I kept my jinxing thoughts to myself, the world felt it was necessary to rain on my parade. Not long after moving away from the fiery remains of our fight did the rumble pick up speed. Coincidentally, it was preceded by a chittering cry that seemed to make the trees come alive and set my feet to moving, exhaustion from the fights be damned.

Less than half a mile from getting into range of comm-plant to the Bunker, the source of the rumble made itself *very* well known. Particularly in the form of an uprooted tree that crashed off to my right. The attack in and of itself wasn't the concern, since I almost knew it was inevitable, but the explosion of *mundane fire ants* that surged out of it definitely put yet another pep in my step. *That's a new one.*

"Daniela! Please, answer!" I called mentally through the comm-plant. My mouth and other organic bits were too focused on running from the living blanket of ants that now chased after me.

"We're going as fast as I can! Samuel is less coordinated than a newborn right now!" she snapped back, her panting was audible through the connection.

"Contact the Bunker! We are still being followed!" Anthony yanked on my shirt, throwing me off balance to the left. Another log sailed right through the spot my body would have occupied. "It's throwing things!" The tide of ants surged out of the log. "With ants in it!"

I didn't bother to be very intelligible as I channeled mana into the naginata still in my possession. It'd served well as a pseudo walking stick, but it soon became the only thing keeping me from turning into lunch for the swarm of ants. A few calls pinged through my implant, but all I could do was describe what was raining down around me. I didn't even check who they were from exactly. When I started to spot cut down trees, then the edge of the clearing, I risked a look behind me. Instant regret.

<Fire Ant>

<Attunement: Life>

<Refinement: Reproductor>

<Perceived Metier Quotient: 5>

A flying ant the size of an eighteen-wheeler loomed in the distance. It plummeted to the ground just long enough to pluck sections of trees that it then launched. Once again, had it not been for the companion clinging to my backside, I probably would have died like a deer in headlights. Didn't help that I was actually wearing a deer rack on my head for that mental picture.

Anthony tugged me, letting the hunk of wood fly over my head, clipping through the treeline to reveal the Bunker camp in all its post-apocalyptic glory. Unfortunately, I didn't have time to feel relieved, because a swarm of unattuned fire ants stood between me and any semblance of safety.

Untested waters were better than ant-riddled ones. Half-powered <Earthen Barriers> sprouted out of the ground as I ran over the ants. Some died buried in the compressed soil of my skill, but they quickly scrambled up my makeshift stepping stones. A wave of heat sprayed down my back as Anthony used his flamethrower to cull the closest ants. While none of us

Fallen Bunkerites had ever had the pleasure of popcorn, I was fairly sure the popping crackle of the dying ants was a good auditory approximation.

Thanks to my <Earthen Barrier> steps, I completely bypassed the outer trench the other Bunkerites had been working on. Going to need to come up with a solution for that... I didn't have any more time for the train of thought as yet another tree flew in my direction. Without a forest around me, I was able to use a burst of speed to dodge before it struck. A wash of angry red flame cut off the new swarm and I looked up to see Daniela on the ramparts of the inner wall. She was most definitely not alone.

At least two dozen rifles tracked the ant as it made its way towards the Bunker. Daniela focused on setting as much of the ground behind and around me on fire as possible. When I approached the closed bridge path, instead of the people inside lowering it, a vine grabbed me around the torso and lifted me up onto the ramparts.

Anthony flopped beside me, and I just barely caught a glance of Blobby squeezing through the gaps in the sides of the bridge. If its crystal cores fit, then so did the slime.

Samuel was holding himself against my <Earth Wall> like a man to a piece of flotsam. His eyes were still swimming but he managed a crooked half smile my way.

"Wait for my shot!" I heard from down the line of people. It was strange to see such an aged and usually mild-mannered group armed to the teeth. There wasn't a single unfocused eye in the bunch, even Alan had his impressively flippant focus zeroed in on the beast rushing us down.

"Ready!"the same voice called out and I spotted Ava, flanked by Ben, as she held a rifle almost as long as she was tall. The two of them were standing far off on her perch that Sam had made, some fifty feet from the rest of the Bunkerites. A bipod had it affixed to the wall, which quickly removed itself when she fired.

I was sure Devon was around because a crack of thunder

reverberated through the trees and the massive ant howled in protest. A moment later, the world was a buzz of weapons fire as the various rifles and numerous handguns plinked onto the Reproductor.

The creature attempted to continue its aerial assault, but thunder-generating rounds had a different opinion. Ava locked onto the creature, several rounds snapping a wing in half. Like a stringless kite, the membrane lifted up and away while the rest of the ant struggled to keep itself aloft. More bullets struck the creature the closer it got, a few punching holes in its massive wings before it finally plummeted to the ground. The rumble I'd felt earlier flowed even more clearly through my wall, and I knew that ant was still coming.

Its main assault, however, was no longer in person. The swarms of ants had coalesced into mounds, and every few seconds, a Q0 ant would get spit out or consumed to generate two more.

Daniela and I focused on those creatures. Her <Flame Blasts> were no longer compressed for concussive power but let to release washes of flame that turned the ants into crisps. My <Mineral Strikes>, half-powered to conserve mana, crushed ants upon landing before explosively dispersing any clumps of mundane fire ants that tried to consume themselves to jump Quotients.

*That fifth level is already making a difference!* While I still felt like a used rag, the increase to my attributes helped me aim, toss further, and recuperate mana faster. Minutes slogged through as waves of ants mundane, Q0, and Q1 surged out of the treeline. It almost seemed like it would be endless, but I noticed that the trees between the Bunker and where the ant had crash landed were toppling one after the other, yet no more flew in our direction.

When I did the biological math from what I knew of leveling and how ants *should* replicate, I realized that the biomass had to be coming from *somewhere*. The forest was an obvious source.

"Ava! You need to kill it before we wear out!" I called through the comm-plant.

"I can't see!"she yelled, firing a blind shot towards where she thought the creature should be located. Other than the thunder, nothing responded but the chitterling of the incoming ants.

"I can help with that!" Daniela raised her burnt, but significantly more fleshy, hands up in the air. Her wisp manifested, except it was much larger than before. The living flame was closer to a beach ball than a fist. It hovered in the air for a second before shooting off into the trees. After lobbing another hunk of quartz at the attacking ants, I turned as Daniela illuminated the bulk of the Reproductor. The miniature sun outlined the creature for only a second before a giant leg slapped it down to the ground, but it was enough.

Ava emptied her high-powered magazine into the creature. I was tempted to ask Sam for a heal for the hearing damage, but the chaos that followed took all of my concentration.

The once orderly waves, clumps, and otherwise coordinated attack of the fire ants fell into disarray. They all still moved in our general direction, but their advance was almost squirrelly. Fire attacks from Daniela were less effective, and I was lucky to hit more than one of the higher Quotient insects with my <Mineral Strikes>.

Thankfully, we didn't have to deal with the minutiae of the disengage. A surge of static flowed through all of us on the wall before reaching the ants. The mundanes were not messing around with whatever the source of that was and they immediately turned tail and ran. The attuned insects hesitated for a second, but vines rose up out of the ground to crush them; the ones not in Sam's field of focus ran for the hills. Figuratively speaking, since we were still in Florida.

Everyone on the wall held their breath as we watched the creatures flee. I almost didn't believe that we'd made it.

"For the Bunker!"someone called out. It didn't take long for the chant to pick up. The sound flowed through my wall, amplified by whatever strange new sense I was developing.

"For...the Bunker." I sighed. The naginata I'd been death-gripping flipped once before embedding in the ground and I slumped against my wall. Congratulatory cheers continued, but I caught sight of a glowing light coming from the vestibule. It blinked twice in quick succession and I half-saluted Bec, certain the Entity Cluster could see me however it perceived the world.

"Thanks mate," I whispered before I took a much appreciated nap.

— + —

Of course, said nap was much too short lived as I woke up to screaming and shouting, followed by a pulsing line of text in my vision.

<The Bunker needs your help!>

I didn't need to be told twice as I jumped to my feet. Joints protested and my shirt-vest combo ripped clean off my chest as the final threads gave up on life. Slapping the armor away, I took in my surroundings. The problem was immediately obvious, even if it left me stumped: Attunements. Attunements everywhere.

I wasn't sure why I hadn't thought about it, but all but the implanted Bunkerites were still mundane humans. Since Ben, Ava, Dale, and Alan had taken on the brunt of the defensive fighting, no one else had been changed by the mana and Dreg permeating the surface.

Unsure of what I could do about the many and varied elemental manifestations happening around the clearing and near the Bunker entrance, I beelined for Bec.

The Metier Crystal was talking before I'd even made it inside the vestibule. "You need to help me with the earth-attuned!"

"I don't know what to do, just tell me!" I yelled, confused about what I could even do to help.

"Focus on your implant. I'll use it as a medium to funnel the Dreg accumulated in their bodies. My hands are already full handling the other Attunements so I need you, Daniela, and Samuel to handle yours respectively. Just touch them somewhere and I'll do the rest," the Crystal blurted out. I was already turning around as fast as my feet could carry me. "It won't be pleasant!"it warned.

*Doesn't matter.* That thought echoed in my head. All I needed to do was think of the Dreg-afflicted trainees back in Wildwood to know I wouldn't want my family to suffer that same fate.

My friends practically crashed into me. Without waiting, I turned them around and filled them in via the comm-plant. The closest Bunkerite was Belle, one of the older women that worked with Juan in the kitchen. From the gouts of fire flaring from her body, her Attunement was obvious. Daniela peeled off, placing her hands on her head to brace it. Some of the fire flowed directly through her palms into her body and Daniela grunted as her own body heated up. Sam and I didn't have the time to dawdle.

The life-attuned spotted Alexia and June amidst a pile of medical supplies and a stretcher. Without a moment of hesitation, he placed his palms on their now grass-growing bodies and part of the change redirected towards him.

There were a number of others around us struggling through the Attunements. Thankfully, Sam hadn't spotted his father slowly become encased in ice, or the blond would have dallied longer. Besides Jerome and a fiery Juan Vega, Elias laid folded like a piece of origami. His body did *not* look to be doing hot, and I could see what appeared to be stress fractures through his very skin.

Before I knew it, I was at his side. As soon as I pressed my palm to his forehead, the usual gut wrenching agony of casting magic too quickly funneled through me. My veins and muscles stiffened as I fought the surge of energy. Just as quickly as it arrived, it was gone and I slumped to my knees.

<More people!>

Bec's message blinked incessantly before me, drawing me out of my stupor and to the next person I saw take on a chalky, fractured exterior. Person after person, the pain got stronger with each passing, yet I continued. I was vaguely aware of Daniela's groans as she touched fire-attuning people, and Sam giggled as he hauled his increasingly drunk self around. Probably thanks to whatever Bec was doing to intervene, the frosty water-attuned, levitating air-attuned, and mushroom-covered death-attuned didn't appear to be suffering. Ava, Ben, Dale, and Alan were apparently unable to take our place. Instead, they worked to drag people of the corresponding Attunement closer, saving us a trip and improving their chances.

Time lost meaning, but at some point, we were the ones laid out next to the Bunkerites. My eyes fluttered as morning light cut through my eyelids to awaken me. Blankets and various sheets were strewn on those still unconscious around me as I pulled myself up to my elbows. I saw Ava up on her perch, rifle trained on the tree line while her mouth moved, probably using the comm-plant to communicate with someone.

My eyes continued to drift, spotting a few of the people that had been up on the wall the previous day. Other than the group of people still laid out, which was concerning but not alarming, the changes to my body were the most shocking thing. Spider-webbing lines of gray overlapped my circulatory system, blooming to cover my chest and visible even under my thickened Limestone Skin. For several seconds I just rested, frozen as I tried to come to terms with yet another strange physiological change. When I was finally able to focus beyond what I was seeing, I noticed the lines of text in my vision.

<Come see me when you wake up.>

**<Traits:>**
**<Slurry Ichor>**
<Your circulatory system has taken on some of the viscous properties of suspended particles.>
<*Trait overbanked.* When exposed to air, blood hardens to enhance clotting.>

"Well, that explains a few things…" I mumbled under my breath.

My body felt oddly limber for having slurry blood and getting thoroughly stretched to its limit, but I didn't question it too much. After all we'd gone through, it was just another thing added to the absurdity tray. I passed my blanket over to a still blue-frosted water-attuned, hoping it would provide a tad more comfort, before heading to my vestibule. The first thing that struck me was that Bec was quite visible, even before I made it into the building. A crystal covering had spread along the surface of my ceiling, smoothing out the imperfections I hadn't been able to address with my still-developing skills. The inside was no less covered in the stuff, reaching halfway between where the crystal had installed itself and the old lobby building that led to the Bunker proper.

My uncle, Ben, and Daniela were huddled over a meal, talking somberly with one another. Sam had either woken up and decided to go to bed, or just made it to his accommodations as the blond snored away in the corner of the room. Ben and Dale jumped to their feet the moment they spotted me, and Daniela gave me a weary wave. "Hey, rock brain."

There was not enough time to respond as my uncle wrapped me in a tight hug. He sobbed a few times into my shoulder, and I let myself relax in his embrace. Ben placed a reassuring hand on my shoulder, but left me to my uncle's death grip on me. For the duration of that hug, I forgot all about the biggest lie of my life and remembered all the moments when Dale had been my father. The admission still felt like a pit in my stomach, not just because of the lie but because of the fate it had told me about my family. Nonetheless, after the ordeal with the Dreg, the threat of the ants, the attuning Bunkerites, and everything else the surface had thrown at us, it felt good to have my father, adoptive or otherwise, there.

"I'm sure you all have questions," Bec started, clearing its throat as much as an artificial intelligence with a hunk of rock for a body could. Thankfully, while the Entity Cluster's crystal body radiated a soft white light, its central pulsing orb of iridescent colors that acted as the source of its voice didn't cause the whole room to turn into a strobe light mess.

Me and my uncle separated. His easy smile turned dazzling when I kept my arm thrown over his shoulder like we used to do down in the Bunker. Before everything got turned upsidedown.It was a natural pose since I was almost six inches taller than him.

"I think we do, Bec. Let's start at the beginning, shall we?" I said.

# CHAPTER SEVENTEEN

## Changes and Answers

Over the course of a few hours, our team—sans a sleeping Samuel— and Bec ran through everything that had happened since our last visit to the Bunker. Considering the fact that the Entity Cluster was still mostly in contact with Tec, it went fairly smoothly. I held off on most of my questions when Bec started to update the group on the increased ant activity. The crystal mentioned that it hadn't detected any other wildlife due to how much pressure the fire ants were putting towards the Bunker's territory. While not the best of news, dealing with the ants at least simplified the threat that the surface posed.

The not-so-smooth portion of the conversation was when the Metier Crystal tried to explain just what in tarnation had happened after the fight. Understandably, Daniela and I were pretty agitated while Ben and Dale were just plain confused.

"The simplest way to explain it is energy overload. As I know you have surmised, there is a rough triplicate scaling to the Pith accumulating in your bodies towards the next Quotient," Bec said.

"Yes, that's how I've been able to save on infusions. I hadn't been able to totally confirm it as far as our levels, but I figured it worked mostly the same," I said, making a 'go on' gesture with my hand.

"Well, if you think about how much Pith the Reproductor Fire Ant released when it dissociated, the predicament starts to make a bit more sense. If you take Quotient Level 0 to represent one 'unit' of Pith, then Quotient 1 is three, and so forth. The people of the Bunker, including those already attuned, received almost enough Pith to jump to Q3."

"Why would that be a problem?" Daniela asked, tilting her head. I could practically see her trying to run the numbers in her head. "We all know attuning is not the most pleasant experience, but you said they were in danger."

"That comes from unchecked traits," Bec said. Before he resumed, the cause clicked.

"The Dreg we get from creatures scales to whatever Quotient we are on," I said, snapping my fingers.

"Something like that. When I designed the status to work off your implants, it looks at currently mutating tissues and assigns it the accumulated Dreg value, since that is the most obvious sign of the Pith byproduct within your bodies. When you enter the area of influence of me or Tec, we can repress the active mutations by purifying the Dreg into mana. Hence your 'banking' percentage," Bec started, fully in lecture mode.

"The higher your Quotient, the more Dreg it takes to effect a change in your physiology. This is proportional to the Pith units absorbed, plus or minus resonance from the composition of the Pith you absorbed. If your Attunements align, then you receive more Pith and less Dreg. If they don't, the opposite. From our studies, Tendrils give a disproportionate amount of Dreg to their Quotient, but we aren't quite sure of why that is yet. None of my or Tec's memory banks have information on Dreg ever being... proactive, like we've witnessed here on Earth. Perhaps once we reach higher categories, but not as of yet."

"So, wait. That means the other residents got over two hundred percent Dreg accumulated..." Daniela whispered, her eyes widening with the realization. Ben and Dale still looked lost with this portion of the conversation, so I made a mental note to explain it later.

"That is correct. As you all well know, not converting those mutations can lead to—"

"The Dreg afflictions," I said, thinking of the trainees and their elementally transformed bodies.

"Yes. The variables that determine just *where* the overbanked traits become afflictions are still being worked on by the Entity Cluster, but overbanking by over fifty percent seems to be a guaranteed threshold if you aren't able to receive assistance," Bec said, its light dimming.

"That's what you used us for," Daniela said, turning from her burnt hands to the crystal. "To take over some of the Dreg from the others because it would be less of a concentrated mass for us."

"Yes, I apologize fo—"

"No, don't do that," Daniela snapped. "It's a simple situation, really. What would have happened to the people of the Bunker if we hadn't intervened?"

"Perhaps I would have been able to prevent a second order of afflictions from taking hold, but at my current size, the energy was too much for me to handle all at once," Bec replied shamefully.

"My dear crystal friend," my uncle said, releasing me and moving closer to Bec's core light. "What she is trying to say is that they would rather bear the pain than see their loved ones changed or injured forever."

"The timeline, well, if I had had more time, I might have—"

"Bec," I said, leveling my eyes on the Entity Cluster. "You are not to blame. Without your help, we would not have survived the surface. Without your help, we would not have data on the Quotients or on infusions. Without your help, we would be stumbling blind in a world that would eat us up or sacrifice us for just one more day of false freedom."

It was impossible for me not to think about the people of Wildwood. Just what would they have been able to accomplish if they'd had access to their status earlier. Would Kirby have even turned to the Dreg for safety, or would he have seen a true path forward for the town? I was fairly sure that question would haunt me. The drive I'd had to search out the remnants of humanity kindled anew. If what I had could give someone else the chance to seize their own future, then we needed to reach far and wide.

"Thank you. While we are not organic beings, your consideration for Tec and myself is a value we hope to internalize beyond our personality matrices. Perhaps... we might find a purpose beyond purging the Dreg." Bec was silent for a few seconds.

While the Entities had been a tad cold and inhuman when we first started interacting, we'd come to count them among us. Before I could utterly fumble the emotional moment, Bec got back to business. "While I wasn't able to ease everyone through their changes, we managed to prevent any afflictions from taking hold. You three each have new traits that I can only hope will assist you in your travels. In addition, with the majority of the population of the Bunker now attuned, I should be able to assist them with various illnesses and conditions they suffered from. It is my hope that, now that I have acquired such a large reservoir of energy, I should be almost always available. It is not sufficient to push me to the next category, but I am close."

"What will the next category bring for you?" Daniela asked.

"I will have access to most of Tec's abilities, restricted by the size of my reserves, of course. The most important one is what you have dubbed the 'Blessing of Magic.' That field is actually the area where our crystalline matrices can actively purge Dreg from our surroundings. It is the starting line, so to speak, from which we are meant to combat Dreg on a planet. Creatures, as they harness Pith, do this internally and boost the process along. This is why your assistance in actively purging Dreg is unprecedented and revolutionary to our imprinted memories," Bec said.

"That's good news then," Ben said, stroking his scruff beard. " I wonder if we can get some of the others to range out with us, maybe get you to that threshold."

"We need to wait for everyone to get acclimated, Benjamin. We don't know how the traits have changed them," Dale said, waving a finger at our old teacher.

"It is both Tec's and my own theory that the traits you acquire move you closer to the different Fallen attuned," Bec added.

"I've never bothered to ask the Wildwoodians what their traits are," I said, mostly to myself.

"While it might seem a bit of an invasion of privacy, we have access to all the information of each Dreg Warrior. The overall trend is for individuals of the same Attunement to develop traits of a certain type. Fire- and water-attuned have a significant propensity to develop temperature regulating traits, for instance."

"Is that why it says I can breathe fire now?" Daniela said evenly.

"The data suggests so, yes," Bec said.

Ben, Dale, and I shared a look as we turned to Daniela.

"Care to run that by us again, little Danny?" my uncle said.

Instead of replying with words, Daniela took a deep breath. My perception highlighted how her fire gills fluttered and I watched a spark ignite within her throat somewhere before a gout of flame about three feet long spewed out of her mouth. All three of us jumped back in alarm and I even saw Samuel jerk awake at the sound of a roaring flame indoors. The flames lasted for a solid second. Even if the little display left Daniela coughing and sputtering, she gave us a cheeky grin nonetheless.

"Wow. I thought my new trait was impressive," Sam yawned.

"She just likes to show off," I said, smirking as Daniela stuck a blackened tongue out at me.

"What did you get, Ronan?" Sam asked.

"Cement blood... I think. Haven't been hurt yet to check," I said, gesturing at my exposed chest. The moment I did, of course, I became somewhat self-conscious that I hadn't been wearing a shirt through the whole conversation. It wasn't a habit I wanted to start, even if my Limestone Skin and Slurry Ichor made it look like I was wearing a nude-color textured shirt or something. "And you?"

"I think it's kind of like temporary mind control?" Sam said. I almost wanted to be surprised, but I'd seen him work his mentalist magic on the cowherd and the other mundane farm-life in Wildwood.

"I don't know if my heart can take all this excitement, Dale," Ben said, laughing and patting his chest. "It's like the *Lord of the Rings* is happening in modern times."

"Can they be called modern times, or are they *post*modern?" my uncle asked, *very* seriously. Neither him nor Ben said anything for several seconds, meeting our eyes evenly.

Daniela broke first, and before long, all of us were laughing at the terrible joke. I wasn't sure if it was the stress of the situation or the actual joke, but we spent a solid five minutes cackling like madmen. It would have probably continued for a while longer, but a very ornery and unamused Ava appeared at the door to the vestibule.

"I am happy to see you all recuperated and ambling," she said by way of greeting. Dale and Ben immediately stopped laughing, and very conspicuously vacated the room.

"Hey, Mama. We were just getting Bec up to speed," Daniela replied weakly.

"That is correct, Mrs. Ve—" The Entity Cluster didn't get to finish.

"Magnificent. If that is finished, then there's work to be done, yes?" Ava said, not a single inflection in her voice. *If I didn't know any better, I would have said she was a fire-attuned with a laser refinement the way her eyes are piercing us.*

"O-of course," Bec stuttered.

"Good. Alan has a number of questions for you, Bec. Don't worry, I will take care of these three summarily and make sure they are using their new abilities to the utmost." Drill Sergeant Ava stomped off, and the single look over her shoulder was enough to tell us we needed to get a move on.

"Sorry, Bec, we'll finish this conversation later!" I said, quickly entering the lobby and snagging a shirt before heading out after my friends. I had a sneaking suspicion we were in for a talkin' to.

— + —

Ava stood perfectly still in the middle of the training area. Neither of my friends, nor I, wanted to ask just why the woman was eyeing us like glazed hunks of meat. After several minutes of the strange standoff, I broke the silence. "Is there something wrong?"

"I can't condone you three going out into the wilderness anymore," Ava said tersely. Before any of us were able to bring up any arguments against her statement, however, she held up her hand. The woman visibly deflated, her usually perfect posture cracking under some unseen stress as she leveled with us. "Being sure that you are as prepared as possible for what you face out there is simply impossible. We thought that the biggest threat were the Tendrils, but now you have this Appendage thing to fight? And Bec, don't get me started on the fact that there is an *evil* version of him out there. Probably more! The entire Bunker almost got rolled over by a single ant!" she yelled, her voice cracking at the end.

Perhaps we'd spent too much time under threat of death, but the slowly mounting situations didn't shake me as much as I thought they *should*. Ava was usually a very composed person, but I could clearly see the fear in her eyes as she looked at Daniela and the rest of us. It wasn't the same devotion I had to protect my friends, it was something greater. And yet, I could tell where she was going with her speech.

"It would be unjust and just plain idiotic for me to try to stop you all from going back out there. Danger doesn't always wait for you to find it, and in this case danger is a sentient piece of corrupt rock with magical powers. Of death, if I might add," Ava said. Unlike when she started talking, I could see her pulling herself together with each word. Her resolve hardened with each phrase. "I will do my best to adapt to the threats you all find, polishing you, and molding your abilities to best use what you are each blessed in. The lengths to which you all went to incorporate my suggestions did *not* go unnoticed."

"Hurt a fair bit," Samuel mumbled, scratching the back of his head.

"If it takes a little pain now to save your lives later, then I will take that trade one hundred times out of one hundred," Ava said evenly, her posture fully restored.

"Great, because it seems like we are too deep into our own heads to notice what we are doing wrong," I said, smiling. Daniela complained and Samuel tried to argue that the only one with his head buried in the sand was me. Ava smiled as she listened to us bicker and I knew that things would be alright.

"With that said, you three will have the day to relax and recover. Tomorrow, we are going to make sure the rest of the Bunker is operational before I run a battery of tests on your bodies and new abilities as Quotient 5 individuals."

The mention of abilities reminded me of something I'd been holding off on for a while. Now that Bec was online, I could only hope the Metier Crystal assessed that my mind was ready. Perhaps maybe even answer some of the questions that had been picking at me.

After that brief talk, Ava led us back to the vestibule. While most of the people in the Bunker were now up and about, they weren't all there. Some were adapting to various notable phys- ical feature changes like scales, horns, fins, gills, webbing, *bald- ness* in some cases. Others struggled with internal changes that Alexis and Ava had been working to categorize. Regardless of their state, they could use the experience and guiding hands of the higher Quotient members of the group.

We spent the rest of the day showcasing some of the

changes we'd undergone thanks to our traits, explaining that it didn't take long to get used to the features, but it did take a while to make the best use of them. Through this process, I finally realized that all of our immediate family *had* undergone changes while we were away, but never mentioned it. Ava, for instance, essentially had the same ocular trait that let her 'zoom in' that Oliver and his team of pre-Fallens had. My uncle had gained webbed feet and retractable fins along his calves. Ben actually had a crystal skull now, apparently. I'd thought his dome looked particularly shiny before, but once he pointed it out, it was hard to miss the slight glints under his bald head.

It was oddly refreshing, seeing just how much everyone had changed. In a sense, I started to realize that most of the traits and Attunements aligned with what I knew about each person. For instance, both Alexis and June had acquired Samuel's nervous system trait, but theirs allowed them to sense rather than connect with their target, making them better at diagnosing illness and injury. Ava's constant observation and her eye trait spoke for itself also.

All in all, even if the way most of the Bunkerites gained their Attunements was traumatic in more than one sense, it brought the group even closer together. Through all this, I couldn't help but think of my father, how he'd been ostracized and misunderstood until he lashed out. While the military group that had once inhabited the Wildwood Bunker didn't sound like stellar role models from Elias' recounting, they were still people.

*Hopefully everyone can keep pushing for our survival regardless of how much Attunements changed us.* Unfortunately, even as optimistic as I was, events in Wildwood had thrown a scoop of doubt as far as humanity leaving behind some of its pre-Fall selfishness.

# CHAPTER EIGHTEEN

## Modifications and Permutations

As it turned out, a 'rest and relaxation' day for Ava just meant vigorous running and organization within the Bunker and on the surface camp. Not only that, but the *day* turned into two as the marching orders became providing enough accommodations within the Bunker's keep for everyone.

With those orders, I donned my antler helm and built a pair of rooms overtop the vestibule. The rooms I built as a second floor above the lobby subsequently got <Earth Barrier> bunks that were given <Vine Whip> mattresses. Samuel's control over his vines had grown once again with his level, and providing a cushy but tight weave of the plant matter wasn't particularly difficult, if time consuming.

As for the two rooms above the vestibule, it became a sort of men and women's dormitory for our camp crew. Me, Dale, Ben, and Samuel snagged the eastern room, and Ava and Daniela took the other. Alexia planned to spend more time on the surface now that she had her Attunement, and so the woman set up a small physical exam area for her and Ava. Alan, surprising no one, still lived in his workspace attached to the vestibule. With a bit of help from me and Samuel, Juan was also able to set up a proper kitchenette at my old workstation. Thankfully, the man made a concerted effort *not* to use pond water for his culinary escapades, unlike me and my infusion testing. With all the Bunkerites up and on their feet by the second day, Ava finally sequestered us in her makeshift exam area above the vestibule.

"I'll start with you, my love," Ava said, patting one of the circular swivel chairs Ava had had Alexia bring from the Bunker.

The woman ran a physical on Daniela, followed by Alexia. Other than the obvious physical changes, Daniela seemed to run a full ten degrees hotter than a human should normally. Both the doctor and the trainer were perplexed by the fact that Daniela seemed to have gained some sort of cavity on the right side of her chest.

"If I had to guess, that would be the ignite organ that I got from my trait," Daniela said. "Good to know where it is, more or less."

Alexia and Ava were a flurry of notes as they sketched anatomical diagrams and wrote a number of hypotheses on the margin. After several minutes of this, they eventually opted to talk to Alan at some point in the future. While the man wasn't necessarily erudite in biology, no one other than the Entity Clusters knew the effects of mana the best.

Next they threw Samuel on the chopping block. They really weren't able to test anything as far as his feelers, but they did notice that they responded with all the muscle reflex tests they did. The blond also lost weight somehow, even if he looked more or less as gangly as he usually did. Ava made a note for him to increase his caloric intake, and maybe try to grow some beans to improve everyone's protein variety. Sam was instantly excited to put in a test bed of infused bean stalks, but somehow I imagined it wasn't going to turn out like he hoped. The last set of magic beans didn't turn out well for that Jack fellow.

Finally, I was put on the spot. Turns out that having skin that transfers vibrations makes it inherently difficult to use a stethoscope on me. Nonetheless, the two women ran the physical. Their biggest findings were that I'd grown two inches, gained about forty pounds, and had highly concerning heart readings. I was running a solid fifty beats a minute while my blood pressure was up in the hypertension range. By all mundane human accounts, I should be dead, but clearly that wasn't the case. When I mentioned my Slurry Ichor, Daniela actually joined the test and sliced open my palm with her dagger. After wincing in surprise, I watched one of the most noticeable changes to my physiology literally pump out of me.

Instead of vibrant red blood, something more akin to umber-colored stock poured out of me. The wound bled for only a few seconds before the fluid hardened. Right before our eyes, the wound clotted and scabbed.

"Good to see the trait does what it says on the tin," I said, an awkward smile on my face as I looked at the two women. If I didn't know for certain they were healthier than they had ever been, I would have said they were ready to keel over.

"Honestly, this data is way outside our expertise," Alexia said. "This kind of organic diversity might fit a veterinarian more than a standard doctor."

"Ouch, doc," Danny said, pressing her hands over her fire gills.

"Daniela, you know you are not that sensitive," Ava said flatly. Her daughter could only chuckle in turn as she released her neck. "We'll work with Alan and Bec to establish a baseline and try to come up with a catalog of the traits. While I know _you_ can heal almost all injuries, Samuel, and the crystal the rest, I think having this knowledge for us old timers will be invaluable."

"Thanks, Ava. Whatever you get together, we'll take with us to Wildwood. They have more healers than us, but more knowledge isn't going to hurt anything," I said, nodding at the woman's assessment. We were just getting the hang of our bodies and there was no sense in squandering information that could help in the future.

"So it's true. You guys are going back?" Alexia asked, hesitantly. I didn't need my enhanced perception to point out the death grip she had on her clipboard. Daniela also picked up on the woman's tone also and placed her hand on her shoulder.

"Yes, Miss Lexi. Unfortunately, this isn't the only place where we are needed," the brunette said gently.

"I know that, of course." Alexia sniffed. "I don't know how I feel about you kids going out there and getting hurt. Samuel can heal you, sure, but that doesn't take the pain of injury away, and… you could die."

"This is true. However, I know that it would be for something. That I didn't give up on the future of humanity just because it hurt or because it was uncomfortable," I said, meeting the woman's watery eyes. Ava was gritting her own teeth and I gave her a nod in acknowledgement. These two women and the Bunker as a whole had taken care of us. In a way, they were *all* our parents or grandparents. Their own families had almost certainly been wiped during the early days of the Fall.

"We have each other," I said, drawing an end to the conversation. Alexia had more to say, but she couldn't bring herself to say it. The old doctor nodded her head, pulling me and my friends in for a hug. *Has she always been this small?* It could have been the simple fact that I *had* grown, but I was fairly sure that after traveling the surface, our lives in the Bunker would always seem smaller. Lacking the luster and vitality that Earth threw at us in spades.

After the emotional moment, the two women chatted with us for a few minutes before splitting off to deal with their tasks. Daniela and Samuel looked lost, but we agreed that the following day or the next, we would head back to Wildwood. While we'd bitten off more than we could really chew as a solo group, it had turned out well in the end. Danny went to gather our gear and take stock while Samuel went to the farm to give some final boosts to the Bunker camp's resources with his magic. As for me, I had a meeting with a crystal rock.

I had a sneaking suspicion I could have just talked to Bec through the floor of the two dormitories, but I opted to enter my workshop. A few infusions were scattered in cubbies, and I saw several ant chitin plates piled up in the corner. The urge to craft something pulled at me, but I kept on task.

"Hello Bec," I said, sitting on my workstation facing the crystal growing in the corner.

"Ronan."

"I have some questions pertaining to a certain skill."

"Doesn't surprise me, based on what you've been mumbling in your sleep," the Entity Cluster said seriously.

"The flashbacks," I agreed.

"Before you think that I had something to do with the formation of your <Memory Canal>skill, I didn't. It was close to unthinkable that you would internalize the pathways via which we, as creatures of pure mana, access the internal mana of others."

"Wait, what do memories have to do with mana?" I asked in confusion.

"Boring you with a discussion about the immutable nature of the soul would get us nowhere. Suffice it to say, the source of your mana exists within you and without. When you link the two, you create a skill. The patterns I have helped imprint in the Dreg Warriors act as instructions which in turn manifest in reality after being filtered by your soul. Whatever form the patterns take, whether the shifty swirls of the Wildwood Gifts or the glyph script, your will is made manifest.

"Any action that a creature of mana does requires that to happen. It is why speaking with you uses up *my* mana. What your skill is doing is tapping into the internal patterns of the mind that contribute to their will. Eavesdropping on their thoughts with your own, so to speak."

"Can I...*not* do that?" I asked, a small hint of pleading in my voice.

"Mastering the skill would be the only manner in which you might do that. Unfortunately, my computational power has been otherwise engaged by constant threats to really analyze how you and your friends are developing. Since growing in size, I have already started devoting a large amount of those resources to coming up with a means of dealing with the Corrupted Entities. These...aberrant," Bec replied.

"I worried that was the case," I said, sighing and leaning my head against the warm stone wall. Thankfully Bec was a patient conversationalist, because I spent several minutes running the conversation over in my head. As it mentioned, the whole soul bit was a bit above my paygrade, but touching minds made sense since that was sort of how it felt anyhow.

"If transferring skills require us to 'touch souls,'" I said, making air quotes. "Are there going to be other people with this skill cropping up? How does doing that affect this blueprint system you created and the miscellaneous skills?"

"It is entirely possible other people will gain a skill similar to yours. The chances of it happening are low, increasing with how often they transfer skills. The actual transfer is more of an imprint than a skill, which is what miscellaneous skills are: a way of moving your mana to create a reaction. Locking Pith binds it to the flesh instead of drawing it towards you, infusion lets you manipulate the threads of Pith, etc.

"As for the blueprints, much like the fine aspects of the status, they are a work in progress. I've been using the implants to retain information and update the information as often as I dare spend the energy. With Tec's help, those updates have been coming faster and better refined."

"Is there a chance that <Memory Canal> will trigger if I try to pass on these blueprints?" I asked, almost scared of the answer.

"You should be fine, Ronan. You won't be connecting, more like stamping the information," Bec said, its core of light bobbing within the crystal. It was almost like it was trying to be reassuring.

"Nothing I can really do about it even if it did have a chance for it to trigger," I grumbled. While it wasn't optimal, I knew that Bec wasn't actively trying to sabotage me with the skill. It was possibly something I would have to deal with regularly in the future, but it was worth it to try to find a solution early. "Thanks Bec."

"As much strife as you three bring me, I would not have wanted to gain my personality from anyone else," Bec said evenly. *Danny's sarcasm, huh?* I couldn't help but laugh at the crystal.

"Not the news I was hoping for exactly, but I think I can live with them for now." If people could intuit skills of their own, then directly teaching people the flows for the miscellaneous skills should also be possible. There would be no complaints from me if it saved me from having to take multiple unwanted ganders through memory lanes. "You mentioned updates?"

"Optimization of how information is presented for the Warriors. I am working to see if I may be able to use your perception to acquire further information from enemies."

"That sounds incredibly useful!" I said, eyes widening as I considered how that might help us in the coming fights.

"Unfortunately, I do not believe your senses are honed towards mana enough. I remain optimistic that you will stop lacking eyes to see what is right before you." Bec practically sneered. An impressive feat considering I was talking to a rock.

"Hilarious. I did have a suggestion, if you think it's possible?" I said, thinking back to one of the biggest staples of the RPGs in the Bunker servers. "Can you give us more control over the map, and possibly a minimap option?"

"A minimap, you say?" The crystal practically hummed with the words. "I have the memories; do you have something specifically that you might benefit from?"

"The tactical view of where allies are. Oh, and of course being able to mark locations as we discover them. Now that I think about it, maybe being able to share revealed areas with others might also be important, even *necessary* for scouts," I said, drifting off into my thoughts. The hum from the crystal intensified, snapping me out of my reverie. "Uh, Bec?"

"One moment!" It sounded like the Entity was speaking through a megaphone.

Alexia popped her head in, frown marring her features. "What's going on here?"

"Not sure…" I said, backing up into the vestibule as the pitch of the vibrations started to change. A ringing started in my ears, scrambling any semblance of coherent thought I might have wanted to apply to the situation. Then, just as quickly as it manifested, the ringing vanished.

"Done. I believe you will like the changes I've actualized," Bec said.

"Ronan! What in the bork just happened!?" Daniela yelled through our comm-plant. The other implanted Bunkerites also echoed some form of expletive and complaint. Ben's were not as tame as Daniela's, to be sure. Bec beat me to the punch.

<Metier Implant Status Update Complete>

<Version 1.1 Active>

A mess of responses once again flowed through the comm-plant. My weird vibration sense warned me a second before Alan sprinted into the vestibule, tripped over one of the stone benches, then jumped to his feet all in one simultaneously astounding and clumsy display of dexterity. "The crystal modified my software directly while still implanted and wirelessly?"

"Uh…yes?" I said as Alan's eyes bore down on me.

"Magnificent. Propriety must take a back seat. I will be in my office. Bunker Entity Cluster, I surmise that you are now able to sustain multiple strings of conversation?"

"Uh… yes?" Bec replied hesitantly.

"Wonderful." Alan disappeared into his office and a slat of wood I hadn't noticed before slammed over the open space.

Alexia, the floating core of Bec, and I shared a look before silently opting not to mention the strange happening. I spent the next few minutes running everyone through what had happened via the comm-plant. When they were finally somewhat appeased, and busy looking at their own changes, I pulled up my full status. The most obvious change was underlined in gold in my vision.

**Subject:** Ronan Terrigan
**Health:** 100% (Unafflicted)
**Mana:** 100%
**Metier Quotient:** 5 (9%)
**Dreg Accumulation:** 0%
**LPS:** Wildwood Bunker, FL
**Communications**
**Party**
**Skills -** *(2) Selections Available*
**Traits -** *(5% Banked)*
**Attributes -** *Growth Quantified*
**Skills:**
Offensive
- <Stone Spike> / **Imbue** / <Mineral Strike>
Defensive
- **Direct** / <Earth Shell> / <Earthen Barrier>
Misc
- <Pith Mana Lock>
- <Infusion>
- <Memory Canal>
**Traits:**
Limestone Skin
Quake Osseum
Slurry Ichor
Unformed (47%)
**Attributes:**
Strength: 1.74 > 1.76
Mobility: 1.53
Perception: 1.89
Refinement: 1.42
Containment: 2.27 > 2.28

"A party system?" I asked aloud.

"Yes, it should function with anyone that has received the implant. The party will also benefit from overlapping enemy detection via the minimap. If they are in the field of awareness of anyone in your team, then the enemy will be highlighted on the map. Allies are also highlighted, for obvious reasons. As an afterthought, I also added instance scanning," Bec said, entering full Samuel lecture mode.

"Instance scanning?" While familiar with the words, I had no idea which iteration of the definitions the crystal was using.

"While actively engaged, your map will keep a marker on the last known location of an enemy. Beyond *that,* after the way your fights against the ants and spiders have gone, the instance scanning will highlight the highest pockets of energy as opposed to adding individual markers for each creature in a horde currently trying to murder you and your loved ones." I gave the Entity Cluster a flat look. "Am I wrong?"

"Dang glitter rock," I grumbled, but focused back on my status and the party section.

**Party**
<Current Link Limit: 1/10 Dreg Warriors>
<Ronan Terrigan>
<...>

"There's a limit to the party size?" I asked.

"Processing power and mental limitations. These permutations and bits of tracking aren't being done by me or Tec. It's all on you. If the data from the field becomes too overwhelming, you can break up the party. It goes without mention that getting outside of range of the communications system will remove that individual from the party," Bec said.

"I think this conversation is way out of my scope," Alexia said, backing up slowly. "Just wanted to make sure everything was okay, Ronny."

"We can take it from here, Miss Lexi. Thank you," I said, dismissing my status and smiling at the Bunker doctor. She gave a small smile in reply before heading to the spiral ramp up to the second floor.

The first thing I did with the party system was mentally send an invite to the implanted Bunkerites, minus Alan. Sure enough, the command triggered and five names populated in my party. The others acknowledged the addition before returning to their various tasks.

Before handling the final bit of business I had with Bec, I glanced at my LPS. An option to display a minimap prompted me to place the map in my peripheral vision, but I opted to leave it alone for the moment. The large square map of before took over my vision with a few large improvements. A faint distance grid had been overlaid on the explored areas, and six blue-colored dots marked the relative locations of my friends. One labeled Samuel was shifting back and forth to the south-west, Daniela was towards the north, while Ben's, Ava's, and my uncle moved around the camp and in what I assumed was the Bunker. When I zoomed out on the map, I saw a gold arrow had been added to mark 'Wildwood Bunker' and 'New Wild-wood.' Ominous red arrows marked the suspected location of the Corrupt Dreg Crystal, the central region of the fire ant territory, and the last known location of the spider dungeon's Metier Crystal.

"Bec, this is amazing!" I said, unable to even muster a drop of sarcasm for how quickly and effectively the Entity had implemented the changes.

"What can I say? I'm invested in your collective survival," Bec replied. While it was sometimes hard to tell the crystal's tone, the flutter of light was enough of a reaction to tell it was happy about the positive reception.

"Maybe a little warning before the next update though?" I said, smirking. Considering the amount of pain we'd endured since coming to the surface, the update had been nothing more than uncomfortable, but if it happened in an inopportune setting, it could be lethal.

"Noted."

"Just one more thing and I'll get out of your hair. I bet the discussion in there can't be going easily," I said, pointing with my thumb towards Alan's office.

"You have no idea, Ronan." The Entity let out a sound that I supposed was a sigh. "What else do you need?"

"I think it's about time I get access to my Freeform."

# CHAPTER NINETEEN

## Tag Along

"Especially considering your recent rise in Quotient, I would say this is an optimal time," Bec said. "As a matter of fact, if you wanted to forgo your Freeform, you could unlock your full suite of innate skills."

"The flexibility of blending my skills will be more important than having just one more skill," I said, having already contemplated the option. "Plus, I need practice with my new defensive skill before I can really implement it with my others effectively."

"Well said. It also seems like you've decided on which Freeform to focus on."

"If I don't take the hits, my friends do." The sight of Daniela's hands earlier in the day came to mind. Her vicious struggle to keep Sam and I safe while we dispatched the inferno ant was burned in my mind. My spoken and unspoken commitment to always stand at the front hardened each time something like that happened.

"So be it. At the very least, it will give me an excuse to put Alan on hold." I chuckled as the new crystal ceiling reached down and wrapped around my wrist. My consciousness snapped into Bec's whitespace.

"You really should decorate some in here," I said, looking up at the now larger orb of light representing Bec. The white-space easily melted away to show the training area at the camp.

"Better?"

"Oh, you know it." I opened my skill section and focused on the direct option of defensive skills. The familiar pressure of information flowing into my brain rose, except this time when it receded, it was followed by a much more intense one. I took a knee as the runes and glyphs floated through my mind's eye and concepts that overlapped with my other defensive skills linked with one another. The mental picture wasn't too dissimilar to me putting up my <Earth Wall> panels to create the Bunker's keep.

That mental picture felt relevant, holding something more than just a representation of the information in my head, but just like that it was gone, and I was sitting in the training field dirt. Bec hovered quietly next to me. A prompt formed out of the air.

<Mudpit>
<Radically agitate and moisten an area of soil>

<Defensive Freeform>
<Rudimentary control over Target, Intent, and Potency of mana manifestations>

With practiced ease, I called forth the spell chain for my new skill. After hundreds of times using my other skills, espe-cially my defensive ones while building up the Bunker and Wildwood, it was just a matter of thought. Instead of trig-gering it, I watched the runes and glyphs rotate gently around my wrist. The passive form of my skills started to affect the ground, packing it down and hardening it. The longer I stared at the runes, the more I felt like I could understand what they were saying. It was like looking at a partly solved sliding puzzle, just waiting for the pattern to jump out at you. Nonetheless, it remained out of reach after several minutes of concentration.

Sighing, I released the new skill and watched fifty percent of my mana get sucked out. Thanks to being in the whitespace, I didn't feel the painful mana side effect but I grimaced thinking about practicing with my new skill to get it to a manageable level.

The cost-to-effect ratio almost disappointed me as the spell chain flew from my wrist and plunged into the soil. The ground right around the impact point quivered before taking on a runny texture. Before I could complain to Bec about how much the skill had cost, the ground rippled like a wave. A first wave reached out a foot, liquifying the soil. Then a second reached out another two feet beyond that. A final wave extended almost five feet, stopping just shy of where I stood.

The ground quivered gently, keeping the soil from settling and hardening. This went on for almost a minute before whatever energy my skill was feeding the soil ran out and the ground mellowed out. The surface hardened at a visible rate until a thirty foot area stood clear of plants and debris, like a tranquil pond of dry mud.

"Well," I whistled. "Color me impressed."

"The skill affects what seems to be the top two feet of soil. Probably relevant," Bec added over my shoulder.

"Thanks Bec. Really. If we hadn't found you, we would have probably been killed by the ants, definitely that haze wolf, or the spiders, maybe even those tortoises."

"It has been my honor." The orb hovered lower, eye level with me. "You are not the only beneficiary of these interactions. Our time together and my growth beyond the initial personality formation… Well, it has to mean something. Maybe our creator never intended us to be zealots against the Dreg, but merely provided a worthy goal for us to formulate our own lives around. I hope you will allow me and Tec to continue this journey with you. Perhaps there are more of us out there that can benefit from a… friend."

The Entity and I spent a few minutes talking about how things had changed since me and my friends dug it up. Unfortunately, Alan's insistence to speak prompted Bec to release me from the whitespace in order to conserve some mana while speaking with our resident Metier Radiation expert. As I felt the Entity's attention shift into the next room, my mind settled back into my body.

I was well aware that the whitespace was a mental space, but the out-of-body transition still didn't feel entirely natural. It was less notable with Tec since the giant crystal encased us completely instead of just linking our nerves, but it was still jarring. Moments later, I was jumping up. The preparation for the trip to Wildwood wouldn't make itself.

— + —

"Let me tell you, I completely forgot about this," I said awkwardly.

"Not surprised at all, rock brain. I'm surprised you have enough rocks in that noggin to spark those devious ideas of yours," Daniela said, shaking her head as she laid down an assortment of items on the feast table.

Markedly amongst said items was my pickaxe in poor condition. *Who am I trying to convince?* The trusty crystal weapon was a stiff breeze away from shattering and the haft was bent in a ninety degree angle. What it meant was that I was essentially out of my main weapon without a ready replacement.

"You can hold on to the spider naginata for now, but I expect you to come up with something." Daniela pointed an accusing finger into my chest. "That thing is probably your best bit of craftsmanship."

"I beg to differ. It has to be Samuel's club, or maybe my helm, but to each their own," I said, smiling at her groan.

"Can we focus on what we've got?" Sam said, tapping the center pieces of the materials in front of us.

There was a pair of compound eyes highlighted in green by

my implant. Nestled next to them was the flawless marble infusion of a Quotient 5 life creature. I couldn't quite put my finger on it, but the infusion itself almost seemed to radiate its Attunement. All around it was another veritable mountain of chitin, mandibles, and even a few hooked claws from the fire ants. Unlike the first blaze ant, the others that attacked us only dropped a pair of large chitin plates.

The inferno ant *did*, however, drop another stinger. Now being familiar with the criteria of making amplitude items, I was fairly sure I could add another singe amplitude to our equipment somewhere. However, that was for another time.

"Are we all packed?" I asked, glancing at the new and improved cart that Samuel had put together. My life-attuned friend had apparently taken to vehicular engineering, because the new cart was the same as the last only in name. Not a bit of bark in sight. Now, smooth polished wood and vines wrapped around the whole thing evenly. He'd complained ad nauseum throughout the evening meal about how unhappy he was with it, but not a single person believed it was inferior.

"Crates loaded. Made a chest to separate out the more valuable goodies," Sam said, gesturing with his hand and controlling a vine from his cart to open a lid in the back.

"Once we get that cow herd more domesticated, we might even be able to start a mercantile business," I said, slapping Samuel on the back.

"We can call it S*amules* exports," Daniela added, getting a high five from me for the awful pun and a groan from Sam.

"The height of comedy. Can you two ever take anything seriously?" Sam said, leaning against his cart and looking down his nose at us.

"Sure, but then again, you are serious enough for the three of us," Daniela chuckled.

The three of us finished loading the materials into the cart. Samuel and Daniela hitched a mostly recovered Anthony to the front while Blobby finally made its appearance. The slime had been showing up only at meal times, vanishing out of sight almost as soon as it was spotted. While I wasn't concerned the gelatinous creature would abandon us, I just wished I could figure out what it was thinking. Or *how* it was thinking, to start at least. However, when the now double-core slime rolled up on our traveling group, it was business as usual.

We made appendage-to-eye contact and the mysterious creature had the audacity to jiggle at me before going up to Anthony. The two acted like pals who hadn't seen each other in a while and, just like that, the encounter was over.

"I don't know if I can let you go if you are going to be spacing out like this," Dale said, pulling my attention. My uncle had a strained smile on his face.

"Don't worry. Just have some things on my mind," I said, doing my best to reassure him.

"Remember to rely on your friends," he said, wagging his finger in my face. "Have some fun with Daniela, and make sure Samuel interacts with new people. I fear how so much time underground has affected your social skills. I don't think you can get those from Bec or some other over ambitious Metier Crystal."

Instead of bothering to come up with a reply for that, I pulled my uncle in for a hug. He was surprised, stiffening for a second before returning the gesture with fervor. Over his shoulder, I saw the entire Bunker together in one place for the first time in my life. Not even the feast had held everyone, but with our departure, the home that had helped us survive the end of the world was empty for the first time in twenty-seven years. Elias stood at the front, his skin the same rough tan that mine was and his back straighter than I could ever remember it. Improving attributes could really make a difference.

Jerome, Juan, Ava, and Ben stood together, waiting for my uncle. My friends closed the distance with their own parents. I drew back, holding the man who'd raised me at arm's length. "We'll make a difference. Don't worry about us," I said.

"Oh, you can bet your sweet Terrigan behind I will be worried." Dale couldn't hide the wetness in his eyes. "But I also know that your parents would be immensely proud of the man you've become. Who would have thought that the little chubby boy would be charging into danger like this?"

The chuckle that escaped me set my uncle off again. There was no use prolonging the goodbye; I had every intention to return whatever the cost.Many others waved and smiled and a few threw out whistles in order to draw attention to their own partings. Sam and Danny flanked me as we returned to the cart. Daniela hopped onto the back of it while Sam, Blobby, and I led the way down the cleared path to Wildwood. I watched the icons for Ben, Dale, and Ava wink out the moment we exited range. With the support of our families, we trudged forward to secure the futures of others.

— + —

"Hail!" a voice called from the forward base near US 301. We looked up to spot a youth with a red spell chain at the ready, aiming down at us. Another man ran up beside him, only to knock him on the back of the head.

"Them's the Bunker Busters. Are you blind? Do I need to send you back to council head Sarah?" the other man said, loud enough that my enhanced perception easily picked it up.

"I thought everyone in Wildwood knew us by now," Sam said, scratching his head.

"Might be one of the *new* trainees," Daniela said. "Sarah said she was ready to take on some fresh blood, maybe keep them on the straight and narrow with training earlier."

"Keeping watch out here is definitely one way to do that," I said with a laugh. The man who'd stopped the possible trainee opened the reinforced gates a few moments later. I recognized him from Oliver's squad of non-Fallen, even if his name eluded me.

"My apologies. The Guard has been running wild—pun not intended—since you left. We've had quite a few of the trainees and the hopefuls spending time here to deal with the spiders as they try to expand their territory," the man said, bowing his head lightly.

"No worries, we were just heading back. Hopefully we can help Wildwood really sink their teeth into the area," I said. I gestured over my shoulder at the ant-driven cart. "Plus brought some goodies. Hopefully we can put them to use."

"I haven't received my implant yet, but I hope to do so soon. Thank you for all your help!" The man hesitated for a moment, clearly wanting to say something more.

"Something the matter?" I asked, curious.

"It's Eric. If you could spare some time to speak with him, I think it would help. He's either listless next to the Crystal, or throwing himself at things until he's dead tired. His wife has tried to intervene, but it's like he doesn't listen. You helped him get his boy back, maybe he will listen to you?" the man pleaded.

"Don't worry. We'll talk to him," I said, adding that conversation to the growing list of things I needed to do. Since it lined up with checking on the afflicted trainees, I hoped it would be easy to find Eric.

The guard and the meek trainee hovered for a few minutes until Anthony very conveniently started to shuffle anxiously. Daniela shrugged when I looked her way. Another small group of Wildwoodians waved from inside the forward base as we headed east down the road.

While the little stretch from the Bunker to US 301 had overlaps between the spider and ant territories, which resulted in the creatures lurking in the shadows of the trees, the area right around Wildwood had been more or less secured. Not a single red blip showed up in our minimaps as we passed a significantly juiced up farm field. It was hard to think that not too long ago, it was where we'd met Sarah and the Big Guns squad. The field had been a mess then.

The vibrant life only grew denser the closer we got to Wildwood. The field just to the west of the palisade was magnificently tended and even Samuel let out a whistle of appreciation. My minimap blipped with a gray-colored circle off in the treeline. It was seconds between unslinging the naginata from my back and into my hand. Umber-tinged mana circled my hand as I zeroed in on the spot.

"A man can't even finish his patrol undetected. Remind me not to get on your bad side," a whisper of air passed my ear.

"Too late, Devon," I hissed, relaxing.

Daniela and Samuel had been prepared for a fight behind me. Their eyes roved uncertainly across the various vegetables, Sam in particular. After our tumble with a living plant in *his* farm, I figured he was hesitant to fight another. Nevertheless, I certainly felt good having my friends so ready to pounce just off my reaction.

"If that airhead is snooping again, I am going to torch him into next week," Daniela growled. Just like that, the elf rode a gust towards the wall, another to go vertical over it, and he was gone. "He was totally over there, wasn't he?"

"One hundred percent," I said. "You know, I don't think he was 'just patrolling.'"

"Oh, did our local brunette get herself a tall, handsome beau?" Sam said, fluttering his eyelashes at Daniela. Like a flipped switch, he turned to me and pounded his fist into his palm. "Where are we putting in the 'pain of death' warning?"

"*Did I hear that right!?*" All of us, blob creature and insectoid included, spun on our heels to see Ava fuming as she charged down the road. The surprise didn't end there as an extremely encumbered Alan followed up behind her. The man had four bags to the woman's one, minus the giant rifle slung over her back.

"Mama? What are you doing here?" Daniela asked, me and Sam still sputtering from the sudden appearance. She'd been even stealthier than Devon, and she had to have followed us all the way from the Bunker.

"Alan practically charged off into the woods after you kids. Said something about 'diametrically opposed attunements' before he packed up all the gadgets in his office. Ben and Dale were barely able to restrain him long enough for me to stick with him," the woman said as she got within a hundred feet of us. Alan was lagging behind, huffing under his load, but a glare from her sent the man a-running again. "So I come all this way, hoping to help him, and maybe you three, and then I hear about some '*beau*'!?"

"Really, Mrs. Vega, we were just jok—" Sam didn't even get to finish his statement as Ava picked up steam.

"Don't you give me excuses, Samuel H. Fallon. I want to know just what *exactly* is going on. As clever as you children think you are, you haven't lived *half* the life I have. Now, come on, git!" Ava gestured impassively towards the wall. "Alan, throw your bags in the cart."

With a huff, she was *off.* Alan shuffled over to us and I mechanically took his burden from him.

"It appears your mother is agitated," Alan huffed.

The three of us just stared at the man as he walked past towards the town gate without a care in the world. A small crowd had gathered at the wall after Devon left his patrol. Said crowd was now staring very confused at the two Bunkerites. Tim, the ever uncomfortable fae, was stealing glances at us as he tried to speak with Ava. Wildwood was not ready for the two, very different, human whirlwinds that had followed us.

# CHAPTER TWENTY

## Unorthodox Return

Much like our first time arriving at Wildwood, sans Tendrils attacking, we made a splash. Ava was still fuming about the potential fact that her daughter had a romantic admirer, but she couldn't keep that up in front of others. Not only that, but total strangers, something she hadn't dealt with for almost three decades. To top it all off, a number of them were Fallen children who came to snoop.

Conversely, Alan, the ever-inquisitive, shut down. As soon as she noticed our approach and Alan's reaction, Ava pivoted to let us make the introductions.

Other than Tim, there were a number of the Wild Guard present. From the lack of people I recognized, I was sure most of the New Hopers were still deployed to contact the other smaller towns. After several minutes of excited talking and murmured questions, we introduced the other Bunkerites, to their evident joy and dismay respectively. We were finally escorted past the gate.

As we passed the two foot thick timber wall, I was distinctly aware of how little protection it actually offered against creatures of higher Quotients. The Reproductorant practically laughed at ours with its ability to fly, but I was fairly sure that even if it wasn't flying, it could have plowed right through my defenses.

Thanks to two months of practice, I was able to keep my mental evaluation of how much we still had to improve Wildwood to myself while also providing a tour for Ava and Alan. Tim chirped in occasionally, adding in his own local spice to the tour. Unlike when he had first given it to us, the pink fae was much more confident and direct with his explanations.

Surprising no one, the highlight of the tour was Tec. The giant crystal still stood as the largest thing in the town and was visible the moment we followed the bend of the road.

"I saw images of the Metier Crystals in space, but seeing one now…just sitting there, well, it brings up a host of feelings I thought had long vanished," Ava said quietly. Daniela completely forgot about her mom's earlier outburst and moved to hold her hand. "Bec feels like some fancy quantum server but this… It is truly alien."

Alan didn't say anything, but all of us spotted the gentle quiver in his hands. He had often been praised by Alexia for his surgically precise abilities, but those were not on display this day. Instead of going physical like Daniela to her mother, me and Samuel flanked the quirky genius on either side. It seemed to do the trick as the quivering slowed slightly and Alan nodded once.

The tour proceeded at a much more somber pace after that. Regardless, it wasn't long before we had arrived at the training yard. The sheer mass of humanity in the town kept our two followers well engaged and the mood after seeing the crystal improved with each additional person they laid their eyes on. Even if Alan didn't seem excited to interact with others, the man became steadier with each group that passed and waved in their direction. He seemed particularly interested in the teams of fishermen and women.

When we arrived at the collective chaos orchestrated by

Sarah, Ava actually drew in a surprised breath. "It's beautiful," she whispered.

We knew that the place had been cleared of plant matter months ago, yet now I wasn't so sure that had ever happened. Patches of various obstacles had grown up in different areas. Trees with barely a foot of spacing between them, thick briars with thorns that glinted in the midday sun, and treacherous tangles of vines suspended from tall pillars of rock. Magic of all the attunements blasted all over the place as trainees, regardless of age, scurried around the perimeter of the training area. Like its conductor, Sarah stood on a raised platform just outside the training field. Two of the preteen hopefuls flanked her, taking furious notes of whatever she shouted at *them* whenever she took a break from hollering at the official trainees. If I hadn't known any better, I would have said the scene brought a tear to Ava's eye.

When Sarah spotted our group, ant-drawn cart included, she did a double take. After a brief word with her assistants, she called a break for the rest of the morning. When she saw the trainees visibly relax, she reminded them that she still expected them there for the afternoon session. A wall of groans that was practically a sound attack of its own emitted from the training field. Sarah walked over with her aides in tow.

"You can also take a break. Make sure you lean on your free time to master your Gifts. It will be a long while before you receive an implant to fight," the orc woman said, wagging her finger in the direction of her elven and demon assistants. The girl and boy nodded eagerly before scampering after the other trainees.

"Seems not even babies are going to get a break with you at the helm," I said, crossing my arms and smirking at the orc woman. Even with all I'd grown, she still towered over me.

"It's your fault entirely, rock brain." My smirk slipped as I heard Daniela's trademark insult coming from the orc. The two had been spending *way* too much time together. She clearly saw my face, and responded with a cheeky grin. "Not a bad thing to be guilty of."

"Sarah, this is my mother, Ava," Danny said, introducing our own personal hellish trainer.

"It is a pleasure, truly. My daughter has told me a lot about you and your squad. Daniela's description of your methods and thoroughness doesn't do it justice!" Ava said, giving the orc a firm handshake. Apparently the strength of the older woman's grip surprised Sarah, because her eyebrows shot up on her face.

"The pleasure is all mine. Your daughter and her friends are the remarkable ones. It also seems that each time they go back home, they get stronger instead of relaxing. Many people thought that your trips home were to relieve some of your stress in a cushy, safe Bunker," Sarah said with a serious expression.

"They said that?" Sam said, surprised.

"Vocal minority that has received all but zero traction. The fact that our healers now produce full harvests weekly and our number of defenders has swelled to twice our previous number almost overnight has earned you more than a bit of good will from the people of Wildwood. Even if you threw yourselves a debauchery of a party, however that would look in New Earth, they would still welcome you with open arms. The whole town has broken into motion thanks to you three," Sarah said, shrugging at the end.

"Seems your exploits weren't all made up," Ava said, glancing at the three of us with an even expression.

"*Anyway,*" I said, gesturing to the fifth member of our party hiding behind Ava. "This is Alan. He's our resident expert on the Metier energies. You probably want *him* to approach you; he gets uncomfortable around people, and I am sure it will take him some time to get acclimated to having new people around."

"Of course," Sarah nodded her head at Alan. When he didn't respond other than look away for a beat, the woman redirected back to me. "Did you accomplish your goal while you were away?"

"Take a look. I'm sure even your perception is strong

enough to pick up my status at this range," I taunted. The woman huffed, but I saw her eyes unfocus for a brief second before they rove over the three of us, even stopping over Ava and Alan.

"Damn. Devon isn't going to be happy," she said with a chuckle.

"Why *is* my favorite elf still in town? I thought the New Hopers were heading to the other towns," I asked.

"Clara took a large group of our near-pass trainees with her. She's hoping to feel comfortable passing them after seeing their performance. That blockhead Rommel and Devon have been working on some sort of secret project in the crafting hall, so I made sure I put him to work on patrol. They haven't told anyone what they are working on, but it sounds like a dang torture chamber in there. Tim or one of the other healers usually has to go in there at least once a day, but they are sworn to secrecy no matter how much we insist."

Both Alan and I perked up at her words. A dangerous project with dangerous propositions was just the thing I liked to work on. Alan probably wanted to get his hands in on any kind of tinkering going on in the town.

Samuel excused himself to talk to old man Williams, the head of the farmers, while Sarah, Daniela, and Ava had themselves a girl's day. They promised to meet back in the dojo space of the training building before the end of the day.

As much as I wanted to head over to the crafting hall, the group had left me with the still-hitched cart. Grumbling all the while, I pulled Anthony over next to the entrance and started the intense process of releasing him from the numerous hitches and knots Samuel had concocted for his cart.

"You can take a look around town, Alan. You don't have to stick to me," I said, smiling at the researcher.

"I wouldn't want to inconvenience you." For the first time, I heard a lack of confidence in the man's voice.

"You are free to do what you like. If you want to hang out with me, that's fine too. Actually, why *did* you follow us?" I said, finally releasing Anthony. The fire ant probed me with his antenna in what I'd come to recognize as affection before trudging off after Daniela. Blobby was already gone off somewhere.

"The Bunker Entity Cluster and I had a breakthrough," Alan said, plucking one of his bags from the back of the cart. His hesitation evaporated in seconds as soon as he focused on his work.

With lightning fast fingers, he pulled out a laptop terminal, accessed a series of documents, and pulled up some kind of spreadsheet. All of the cells with names were abbreviated, but I did recognize the one for Metier Radiation that had been used before we made contact with the Entity Clusters. A modified label seemed to identify various other values related to the first.

"Attunement resonance. The Bunker Entity Cluster didn't believe he had the processing power required to formulate this system in a way that was portable, but the Town Entity Cluster might be able to do so. Your own practical expertise with the concentrated energy nodules has opened up an avenue for me to progress my research. I believe Ingrid Metier would have cracked the code of mana already, but our efforts can build upon her astounding foundation." It was the most I'd ever heard Alan say in a single spurt. Not only that, but he'd been really easy to understand and had even thrown in some praise for my grandmother. I wasn't sure if Alan had willingly kept that secret, or if he'd just never needed to talk about his mentor before, but it brought a smile to my face nonetheless. Even after giving her life for the sake of protecting humanity, her efforts were still shining through.

After my brief nostalgic flash, I tried to parse what Alan said. The man didn't mince words, even if his words often left me wanting a degree in… whatever various fields he had them in before the Fall. The need for a larger Metier Crystal was something Bec had mentioned, but the Entity hadn't said anything about 'attunement resonance.' If my context clue skills were still passable, then the concentrated energy nodules were the infusions. "Alan, what about attunement resonance? And how does my infusing skill help you?"

"From my discussions with the Bunker Entity, I have developed a model to isolate and quantify the wavelength of Metier Radiation. Testing with the sensory features the Entity adapted from my monitoring implant showed that the status program was already discerning these wavelengths and providing that information. Each wavelength seems to correspond to one of the natural element manifestations, as correlated by my readings on the attuned members of our Bunker." Alan quickly tabbed over to highlight the six columns. With a few clicks, the researcher highlighted each of the frequencies with an easily recognized color code.

"If I can align the wavelengths, I may be able to cancel their energy, even briefly," Alan said.

My mind instantly went to the question of just how we were supposed to deal with the Corrupted Dreg Entity. The last time we'd trapped it, it had secretly been laughing in our face while dialing in for a pick up. I still wasn't sure how it had managed that range at its size, but the easiest answer was *magic*. Unfortunately, a level of magic Bec and Tec were still trying to parse. However, if we could cancel out its powers somehow, then that would be a win for everyone.

"What can I do to help?"

"This is just in the theoretical stage. I will need to discuss further with the Town Entity Cluster to see if the diametrically opposed attunement theory is practical," Alan said, flipping through a number of spreadsheets and entire drafted documents within a few minutes. Ninety-nine-point-nine percent went over my head, but I'd trusted Alan to stick a shard of magical rock into my spine. If someone could figure it out, it would be Alan.

Without delay, I escorted our resident researcher to the Blessing of Magic. The psychedelically wonderful side of the manifestation hardly registered in the man, but one of the devices he'd had me lug to meet Tec started beeping insistently.

That got his attention. While he sat cross-legged right on the wooden bridge, I walked over and reached a hand out to Tec.

—Dreg Warrior Leader returns stronger, and allied.—

"Family friend. I think you two will get along great. He's probably going to not stop talking until he has an answer. Alternatively, he might not say a word for several days. Either way, try to help him out where you can. I think he and Bec were closing in on something that will help us against the Dreg," I said, using the connection to speak with the giant crystal.

—Relative Bec informed of this development. Tec will assist.—

"Thanks," I said. I hesitated, and the Entity Cluster picked up on it.

—Concerns?—

"How are the afflicted doing? Bec explained a bit more about the process, but I know you two don't have the whole picture. Maybe this new method could help them."

—The afflicted appear to be stable. Their recovery is imminent. We suspect the manner in which they were afflicted by the Dreg lent itself to this coma state. Dreg Warrior Irwin has maintained their homeostasis as best as possible.—

I had been wondering who was taking care of the afflicted. While I was still concerned about what state they were going to be in when they woke up, I wasn't concerned about their physical health. If having parts of their bodies made up of elements could be considered physical. The fact that Tec had circumvented my comment about using the neutralizing wavelength thing Alan wanted to work on did not bode well. Of course my mind immediately went to said device destabilizing the afflicted's anatomy or some other such horror, but I pushed it out of mind for the moment.

Nevertheless, Alan seemed to be squared away with a new, bigger, living computer and it was the happiest I'd seen him as the Metier Crystal interned him into its whitespace. Before I left the giant crystal overseer, I checked that the 'update' hadn't actually gone through in Wildwood. In the hopes of preventing a blank-out throughout the whole town and having a huge pain in the rear explanation to deal with, I asked the Entity Cluster to run the updates while people slept. It said the update was liable to wake them up, but I still thought a grumpy sleep schedule would be better than interrupting them when they could potentially be hurt.

When I tried to return to the training field, I saw that Ava and Sarah were deep in discussion of something. Daniela stood over to the side, giving some of the elven and mer trainees instruction in high speed movement. Instead of interrupting what would likely lead me to become a test dummy generator, I cut a line towards the crafting hall. As the first, and only, magically created building, it stood out.

The most notable change was that the area around the structure had been cleared away completely, leaving the once-asphalt parking lot as a churned mess of blackened gravel. A partially built wall seemed to be sprouting from the side of the strong testing room, clearly the work of Arnold the dwarf. In addition to the new construction, a much larger number of people seemed to be flowing in and out of the building than I remembered there being crafters.

"I wouldn't enter there just yet if I was you," a voice called from above me. Dai, the isolated lizardman Guard, swung his legs over the side of the building's roof. His tail dangled beside him like a third leg.

"Oh?"

"Just give it a minute," he said by way of clarification while not actually clarifying anything. However, less than twenty seconds later, an earth shaking boom nearly threw the lizardman off the roof. I was sure that even without the strange vibratory sensing I'd been dealing with recently, I could have felt that from afar. The people I'd seen walking towards the building only hesitated slightly but kept going into the central hallway and scurried into the other wings of the building.

"What the hell was that?" I asked, checking my ears to make sure I hadn't popped them. They were ringing a bit.

"That would be Rommel. Devon went out for his patrol a little while ago, so I expect him to be back soon," Dai said, sliding down the wall with reptilian ease.

"I've got to see this," I said, picking up the pace as I entered the murky darkness of the test room to a choking smog of steam, cool mist, and rock dust.

# CHAPTER TWENTY-ONE

## Research and Destruction-ment

"Another bust," Rommel the orc grumbled as he pulled thick wads of cloth from his ears. He hadn't noticed my coughing form until he pulled the cloth. "Ronan!"

"What in the hell are you doing here, Rommel?" I coughed out. Surprising the usually mellow orc was almost worth the pound of debris accumulating in my lungs.

"Testing," he rumbled. "Weapons testing, as Devon called it."

He waved his hands to clear the air of some debris and the 'weapon' finally came into view. My first impression was how immensely ugly it was. A crude pillar of rock, several layers of what looked like charcoal-covered chitin plates, and a precariously balanced pendulum of wood and rock. Upon closer inspection, the pillar revealed that it was actually hollow and I just barely spotted embers flickering in its depths.

"*This* is a weapon? What am I looking at here?" I asked, somewhat incredulous.

"More like an exercise in futility," Dai said as he walked in the room. As he did, the air stilled and gentle whirls of water coalesced in the air. The temperature dropped noticeably and the dust in the air clung to the water beads in the air before he dropped his hands and they splattered to the ground. The gentle slope of the ground pulled the water towards the drain in the corner. *That was an impressive display of control.* It was clear that even if I hadn't seen the lizardman in a few weeks, he hadn't been idle.

"I can explain," Devon said, having materialized besides Dai thanks to one of his wind dashes.

"Hmmm, crowded," Rommel complained.

"Pay the large tusked individual no mind." Devon said, sweeping into the room to the eyeroll of all the others present. "As much as it pains me, I was actually hoping to get your thoughts on this, Ronan."

"Again, what *is* this?" I said, gesturing at the strange contraption.

"A cannon...Sorta," the elf said, turning on his best scientist voice. "This is one of your own personal spare <Stone Spikes> that we took the liberty of liberating for our use. The wonderful Jolene cut this here opening down the middle. Might I add, she seems to be quite peeved with you, so I would address that before you get cut to little ribbons. Next, we have Rommel infused fire plates slotted at the back and the triggering mechanics. A big ol' physical weight."

As the elf explained, I was starting to put the pieces together. "You are hoping to use the force dispersal trait to shoot a projectile?"

"Yes! Except, it's not working quite right. There is a whole lot of force, but never in the direction we want," Devon said, gangly shoulders dropping noticeably. Rommel's crossed arms also seemed to lose some of their stiffness. Really, that was about as expressive as the man got.

Instead of answering right away, I moved closer to the contraption. While I was no weapon connoisseur, I could see some immediate problems with their design. Mainly in the seal between the chitin plate and the 'barrel' of the cannon. Before making a comment, I prodded and knocked on the whole weapon. The <Stone Spike> section seemed to be holding out alright, if I could see that bits and pieces were missing from both ends where the force of the explosion had escaped. The plates also looked to be charred, if undamaged.

"What have you been using to test as a projectile?" I asked. Rommel gestured towards the corner where rough wooden spheres were piled up in a crate. The last thing I paid attention to was the fact that they had two Q1 plates facing in the same direction towards the barrel, which meant they were striking the backside of the chitin. "Why are you hitting the backside?"

"The force dispersal seems to only release the heat towards the exterior surface," Devon answered. *He must be desperate for a breakthrough, since he isn't actively trying to butt heads with me.*

That particular bit of information was not something I actually knew. Even with all my crafting and testing, I'd never bothered to hit the backside of the plates, since I always built with the curve in. I curled and uncurled my short beard as I tried to think of how to fix the problems I was seeing. The most obvious solution would be to just seal the backside, but I thought it was possible that the force would just blow out the back side. Without testing it, I wasn't sure we would really know the limits.

I shared my comments with the others, and they echoed the concern but weren't sure how to address it. Since I recalled that neither of them had actually been able to go to my Pith thread manipulations lecture, I gave them a short primer. Then, without delay, I retrieved some fire infusions from the crates outside. While most of the higher level Quotient infusions were now missing, used by myself, there were a bunch more of the Q0 and Q1s. My guess was that they were the spoils of the continued spider dungeon farming.

Regardless of where they came from, I channeled my mana and unwound the concentrated Pith. With mental gestures invisible to the others, I manipulated the fire thread and welded the chitin plates together, then to the backside of the stone tube. With a little bit of a flourish, I smoothed out the back edge of the tube, so that the weird pendulum contraption could strike more evenly. When that was done, I used the passive form of my skills to make sure that the spike was consolidated, and essentially seal any cracks that might be forming out of sight.

Rommel handed me one of the wooden spheres and I had to spend a few minutes shaving it down to better fit the opening. *Better make a note of that. If we want to use these, we will need a stock of uniform projectiles.* My thoughts drifted as I worked the wood with my utility knife. As a final precautionary measure, I used another infusion to melt a hole into the top of the cannon tube. It was smaller than my pinky, but would hopefully prevent the whole thing from exploding from built up pressure.

"Who's gonna hit it first?" I asked, straightening after my work and wiping my hands on my cargos.

"You aren't going to use the pendulum?" Devon asked in confusion.

"We need to get a gauge for how much force it needs. Your pendulum might be too much to start. If small hits don't do the trick, then we can use the pendulum and make notes of how the whole thing reacts at different drop heights," I said, arms on my hips.

"Is this that science thing Daniela keeps talking about?" Devon whispered to Rommel. I rolled my eyes at the poor attempt to keep the question to themselves, even without taking my perception into account. Dai was shaking his head side to side.

Testing methodology checked, I opted to be the guinea pig. Mostly because I was fairly sure I could almost take a cannon exploding to the face and at least survive. The rest of the group rushed out, and Dai left a lingering mist hanging in the air to help cool and reduce the effect of any potential explosion. As soon as they were out, I smacked the fused chitin plates. A puff of heat escaped through the hole I'd made, but I could tell it hadn't been enough to actually shoot anything. I used the back side of the spider naginata to push the wooden sphere back towards the plates.

This went on for a few minutes until I didn't feel comfortable striking the plates directly anymore. The puff of heat had grown larger and larger, even dispersing some of the mist in the air. I made a notch on the wooden frame to mark the first drop location before letting go of the pendulum and rushing to hunker behind my H-shield. The puff of heat was much more pronounced this time, and I felt the rumble through the ground. The sphere popped out of the cannon, but it dropped almost directly down.

"I heard the ball!" Devon flashed into the room, excited.

"Just the minimum threshold for it to come out. We've still got some work to do," I said, moving to observe the cannonball; it was scorched and cracked.

With each incremental increase, I rubbed on Devon's patience. Apparently, thorough testing wasn't his thing. On the fifth small increment of the hour, when I was rushing to take cover, he pulled it back up to the high setting he and Rommel had been using. His high mobility was on a whole other level and he was gone out of the room before I had time to stop him, or the falling pendulum. <Earth Shell> covered me, faster than ever before, just as the pendulum struck the fused chitin plates.

Not unlike a gun going off, but with much more unrestricted force, the wooden sphere blasted out of the cannon. With the modifications I'd made to the weapon, more of the force remained trapped inside and I was able to see the plume of heat flash out like a small gout of fire before the projectile struck the strong wall. The mundane wood was not up to the task of hitting the super compressed rock and exploded into a hail of splinters. Somehow a few of those found my shins, but my Limestone Skin and my <Earth Shell> kept the rest of my gooey bits protected.

It took a few seconds for the ringing to clear out of my ears and I watched as the mists repeated their dust gathering process before leaving the air clear. With the explosive threat gone, Devon rushed back inside.

My stone-encased fist connected cleanly with his jaw to

send him sprawling into unconsciousness. "Idiot," I growled. *I wonder if elves have glass jaws or if I am past caring what they are made of?*

I looked up to Rommel as he walked into the room. He checked that Devon was still alive, then hit me with a shrug. "Deserved."

"You alright, Ronan?" Dai asked, only giving the reckless elf a glance.

"I'm good. Some splinters, but Sam should be able to help with that. As for the cannon," I said, turning to the contraption.

While rushing to cover myself, I hadn't watched the aftermath after the wood cannonball splintered. Evident cracks ran down the length of the weapon and the backside of the pendulum had been sent reeling, dismounting it from the two A-frames holding it up.

One of the cracks ran the length of the infusion welds I'd created, highlighting them as obvious weak points for the weapon. Rommel asked a few questions about what I thought had gone wrong and I broke down my observations. The two of us worked through some possible permutations for testing that the orc actually looked excited about. As much as dealing with Devon could be infuriating, Rommel admitted that without his eagerness to push the bounds of their infused materials, the cannon wouldn't have come to be at all.

The most exciting part about the weapon was that it didn't need a Fallen to be operated. Nor did it need a high level non-Fallen either. The utility of it would be limited to a team manning the weapon, but the pendulum cannon could become a staple for defense while the powerhouses of the town were needed elsewhere.

While we worked, Dai also felt inclined to get involved. He mentioned that a few of the woodworkers and smiths were hoping to create bows as a stopgap to their practically non-existent ammunition reserves. Even with the limits restricting the use of firearms to certain members of the Guard, the constant scavenging for ammo and the growing strength of the Gifted

Fallen, the rest of the town still lacked a means of ranged defense.

I couldn't believe I hadn't even considered that as an option. I also hadn't even considered churning out the lowest quality, but biggest impact weapons known to history: spears. While it didn't directly give the town ranged defenses, it provided a low-training weapon that could be used by the makeshift militia that the entire town formed in a crisis. Also, it could be thrown in a pinch, anyhow.

We spent many hours formulating possible ways of improving the current developments. Dai even went so far as to retrieve a very shy, very young fae from the woodworking group. She didn't have the disposition to join the training with Sarah, but the girl had a recently revealed Gift that let her manipulate wood like playdough. She could only do a little bit at a time before she was swaying, but that ability made her the primary contact for any future bowyer work in the town.

"No sirs, I couldn't possibly," Marie, the fae, said. Her voice barely went above a whisper.

"Marie, you don't have to do things alone, but I want you to know that your ability can make a difference," I said, tapping my finger against the sphere of wood she'd rolled into a hot dog shape. The grains practically jumped at the chance to be molded by her.

"It takes me so long…" she said.

"Sure does," I said, causing her eyes to jump to mine and the beginnings of tears to form. "But do you know how long it would take for me to do that?"

She shook her head, unsure.

"Infinitely longer!" I called. "Probably impossible to do it as smoothly as you."

Dai gave me an appreciative nod from over the girl's shoulder as he moved on to provide his own form of encouragement. A woodworking book from before the Fall. Just where exactly he'd pulled it from I wasn't sure, but there it was nonetheless. Its pages were quite yellowed and the cover had a number of water stains, but the picture of a young boy hitting a chisel was clear enough.

After that, Marie was practically ecstatic. She was still shy with me and reserved with Rommel, but she gave the large lizardman a big hug. Some would take Dai's tooth-filled grin as a threat, but Marie smiled along with him before shuffling off back to the woodworkers.

When I gave the man a look, all he said was that he had books to spare for those willing to learn. *Maybe I can get Elias and some of the others over here to catalog and preserve his collection. Alan and Ava already broke the ice on meeting other Bunkerites, so to speak.*

Unfortunately, my bibliophilic thoughts were disturbed by the groans of the elf we'd stuffed in the corner of the room. Devon had a large purple bruise coloring his jaw and he rubbed it absently with a grimace.

"I was sure our rock juggling crafter had put you in a coma, Devon," Dai said, adjusting his position on a stone bench I'd crafted for us while discussing weapon development.

"What happened?"he said, blinking and taking in the broken cannon as well as the dozen or so sheets with half-drawn schematics.

Rommel was kind enough to provide a breakdown of what happened, how he'd been an idiot, the degree to which he'd been an idiot, and how he needed to stop being such 'an airhead,' as Daniela called him. The orc delivered this with a perfectly even rumble of a voice, getting an internal thumbs up from me. Reprimands from the quiet guy in the group probably stung more than from the guy you already didn't quite like.

Cannon mishap aside, the day had been an unparalleled success. Alan was on track to cook up a solution for the Dreg, weapons development had more ideas than time and good sense, and the Bunker was as secure as it was going to get.

# CHAPTER TWENTY-TWO

## Harsh Reminder

Over the next few days, I split my time between the testing room, meeting with the council of Wildwood—now including Sarah—and Alan's on-the-spot laboratory. The first two I had somewhat expected when returning to the town, but the last was an exercise in patience.

Somehow, the researcher had gotten Tim and Arnold to collaborate on a wonderful little building just on the edge of the Blessing of Magic. Inside the rock column, wooden walled structure, the man had set up all the measuring equipment he had available. To top it off, he also placed a Metier Crystal modified solar panel on top of the lab to provide for his equipment's electrical needs.

Many of the survivors of the Fall still clung to their electronic devices for one reason or another, but Alan quickly made it clear that his system was A) not for public use, and B) incompatible with regular electronics. The shielding and transformers, his words, were specifically designed to *not explode* in a mana-permeated environment. To the chagrin of the pre-Fallen, it seemed the internet was not yet to make a comeback.

Aside from being the acting public liaison for Alan, I spent as much time as I could trying to keep up with his Metier Radiation theory, which was quickly expanding to include the resonance of the Attunements, the concentrated nodules of infusions, and a number of other factors that I struggled to comprehend, dealing with the way mana actually interacted with our physical reality.

What I *was* able to understand was the foundation of what he called the Attunement purge pulse. Its intent was to create a field where an opposing Attunement would struggle to affect reality. He explained that each time a skill was forming, a similar effect was taking place; it was just in the opposite direction. The spell chain facilitated changes to reality, fed by our internal mana. There was something…meaty about that bit of information, but with everything else going on, I couldn't quite focus on it.

Apart from gaining a headache, I worked with Alan on using his <Infusion> miscellaneous skill. It was a curious process, since it was the first time a non-Fallen had tried the skill, as far as I knew. Ben's enthusiasm to join the effort had still come short back in the Bunker. However, as I watched, the process worked more or less the same. From the plethora of notes Alan took, however, I was able to see that channeling and manipulating the thread took some of his *physical* energy as opposed to using his mana pool like with the Fallen. The behavior of that, plus the ability to gain traits, continued to put the older survivors in a weird place as far as managing the town's needs. At the very least, Alan didn't need my direct help with the circuit-like etching practice he worked with after each of his meetings with Tec.

If Alan was the only person I dealt with, that would have been plenty. However, the Bunker Busters were highly sought after to mediate discussions with the council of Wildwood. The other council leaders for the different trades wanted an undiluted line to the people who'd essentially turned their mundane fields into magically juiced ones. Samuel spent a lot of time with Irwin and William dealing with food production, even going so far as cataloging the effects of various attuned foods. Daniela flipped back and forth with me and Dylan on defensive intelligence while at the same time working with Sarah and Ava.

The two women had taken it upon themselves to turn the training regimen on its head. Ava started from the ground up with the kids and parents not even directly involved with the Guard, getting records built of everyone in the town to better assess its growth. She didn't stop there. The old trainer got Sarah to cut back on her chaotic training sessions by almost an hour out of the day... Just to replace it with some of her own.

Ava had taken the time to formulate general, but individualized, training plans for all of the Wild Guard in the town and was working her way through the prospective trainees. I wasn't rightly sure how they were still getting up in the morning and returning to training, but if they stuck with it, I was optimistic they would have a much stronger starting point than me and my friends ever had when coming to the surface.

To supplement all of the practical efforts of the training queens of doom, the testing room of the crafting hall got a new nickname. The Research and Destruction Department. While each of the different trades worked to improve their understanding of infusions and how their products could benefit, the R&D department was focused on bringing them *all* together into as many deadly devices as possible.

My own role in the new department was helping manufacture the weapons at the final step. Rommel was a huge help in getting the chitin plates we had infused and shaped, while I created various sized <Stone Spikes> for the purposes of testing. With my new level, my base cost skill produced an eight foot behemoth of rock that was not at all practical but totally worth testing. One of the Q4 chitin plates would make its way to that one eventually.

While the cannons were the most time consuming bit of work, the bow projects got a fair bit of love. Marie really seemed to come into her own as she shaped various designs based on what she saw in the woodworking book. Dai used his knowledge of the area's creatures to acquire a few types of sinew for testing. The odd pair worked together, planning to get bows for Eric and Oliver to test. They didn't approach me for the final infusion, instead wanting to test the process at the mundane level until they could get it right.

Even with the influx of resources from the daily runs of the spider dungeon the trainee squads were running, the town was gobbling up resources almost as fast as they could gather them. Thankfully, I was able to pass on my blueprints without any memory episodes, which let the smiths and tailors of the town cut their teeth on making infused armor in bulk. Slow bulk, but more than I would have been able to manage alone.

As I got swept deeper into the administration of the town, I spent less time crafting. The lack of a weapon and shield upgrades for me, even with a variety of materials at my disposal, burned a metaphorical hole in my pocket. I did, however, insist to be present at all new rounds of testing. Not only did it let me act as my nickname, the Vanguard, but it also let me see how each material interacted with infusions, forces, temperatures, manipulation, and a number of other parameters. One overeager demon teen with a caustic cloud similar to Clara's also hoped to replicate gunpowder explosions with his Gift. The first round of tests were promising if extremely dangerous, as evidenced by the broken rib I sported that day. Regardless of the injury, it brought a plethora of new options to mind.

What if I replaced the wooden cannonballs with my <Mineral Strike>? Can a fire-attuned crank the heat up inside the tube before striking the plates to increase the expulsion force? Are the life-attuned able to manifest ammunition directly into weapons instead of relying on pre-carved balls? Arrows?

It was during one of those drifting, daydreaming contemplation sessions when the original reason for all our weapons testing slapped me straight in the face...

"Cover!" The call went wide through the comm-plants. From my relaxed perch on one of the infusion crates, I zeroed in on the source. Clara. The LPS was already open as I adjusted my helm and snagged my naginata from the wall where it rested.

"Moving!" That and various other calls responded through the implants as the Guard mobilized to action with a level of coordination not seen since before the Fall.

Devon and Daniela called out as they zipped towards the north of town where her location blip originated. I'd kept my two friends in my party at all times, and rotated through whoever I was supposed to be working with the rest of the day in my other party slots. It helped get me used to having the field of view markers from other people in my minimap and now it was paying dividends. The two of them, especially the elf, cut through the town and made a mad dash towards the bridge across Lake Sumter. Dai, myself, and a half-dozen other Wild Guard were close on their heels.

"Got regular people with me!" Clara panted through the connection, and I saw Daniela spawn a blip of her own. Her fire wisp cut through the air even faster than the two scouts, reaching Clara and the growing crowd of blips in seconds.

With Daniela engaged, I dismissed the minimap and poured on the speed. Dai easily kept pace with me, having reached Q5 during our last absence from the town, but the rest of the guard struggled to various degrees. The lizardman and I ate up the distance and I cast <Earthen Barrier> ahead of us to provide steps to circumvent climbing the rusted car wall to the north of the town.

Flames immediately greeted me as they revealed a smattering of creatures lurking in the trees. Daniela's wisp shot small <Flame Blasts>, keeping the creatures at bay. Lilly and Clara were back to back, slowly making their way towards the bridge. Ophelia was letting her passive magic wash over several injured people lagging behind the group as Devon and Daniela carried them to the wall.

One of the braver creatures, what looked like a fire-attuned coyote, shrugged off the flames and tried to pounce on Clara. A shard of ice met its charge halfway, stopping it in its tracks, but the blood of the engagement seemed to call the other creatures to the fore.

"<Earth Wall>!" I focused on my helm as I let the amplified skill take shape. The new wall my increased level let me form easily blunted the charge of the creatures as they found stone instead of the two squishy Wild Guard.

Dai wasn't to be outdone as his obscuring mist materialized, followed by a veritable hail of ice nails for anything that circumvented my wall. Lilly visibly sagged, but Clara held her up. Then we were there.

"What happened!?" I asked, pivoting to the flanks of my wall. Out of the corner of my eye, I saw the civilians being helped up the car wall.

"Chased, then more and more came," Clara said. I noticed her eyes were red, thin streaks of blood running down her face.

"I've got a twenty-three count, Ron! Most are Q3 predators," Devon said, interrupting through the comm-plant.

"Dai, get them back. Help me hold them back while we wait for the rest of the Guard," I shouted, channeling <Mineral Strike> into my hands. The amplified wall had cost me almost half of my mana, but it was already recuperating. Like a pitching machine, I lobbed my crystal grenades over the wall and at anything Dai's ice hail missed.

The lizardman practically had to manhandle the two overtaxed women to get them to retreat. When my mana hit twenty percent, I started my own retreat.

"<Lightning Strike>!" The bolt of lightning zipped from somewhere behind me to cauterize a hole in a death-attuned panther moving to flank me. Passing Devon a silent thanks, I finally made it back to the rust wall. A pair of vines plucked me.

"Health?"

"I'm good, quarter tank on mana," I told Sam without turning away from the treeline. Dai's hail was dispersing and Daniela's wisp had long ago stopped laying down cover fire.

"Status?" I asked, eyes roving on the shapes I could see.

Most were lupine and a few odd lizard-looking things, but I did spot another one of those death jaguars. Something about their attunement was making them harder to spot than regular camouflage should have allowed.

"One dead, two out of the fight, and various levels of injury. Cavalry is a minute out," Devon spat out, perching on the wall beside me. The elf was floating on his heels, and I saw Daniela crouched some distance away, holding the creatures in her sight. Knowing her skills, it was probably the equivalent of looking at them down a gun barrel.

"Anything gets close, dust it. If they rush us, I'll make them sink in the ground. Devon, make sure they aren't flanking us," I rattled through the comm-plant. Daniela tensed in anticipation and the elf was gone with the wind.

"I'll work with the injured," Sam said flatly. I watched him call forth his <Vine Whip> to touch on multiple people at once before channeling <Health Bump>. His club was in hand, but he wasn't amplifying anything yet.

Another beast got brave only to get blasted by Daniela. The seconds ticked by and I felt the rumble of feet before I heard them. The Wild Guard and trainees parkoured over the wall and formed up loosely on the other side. As if sensing the sharp decline in their odds of survival, the creatures started to flee.

"Hunt me down those cats!" Sarah howled through the comm-plant and out loud. "I don't want a single one of those sneaking into town."

She wasn't even done yelling the command when the groups split off into squads. I noticed at least one Q4 person took off with them. One of the death cats tried to fight right away, leading to it getting rolled over by two of the squads, but the rest vanished into the woods.

"One mile radius!"the orc council woman called, getting affirmatives through the comm-plant.

After that initial blitz, the wall was left in eerie silence other than the whimpers and groans of some of the injured. Instead of addressing the obvious questions on everyone's minds, we held steady until the squads returned. The Big Guns had remained at the base of the wall, and I watched the rock twins gathering Pith from the few dead beasts while Sarah stared off into space. Clearly, she was coordinating the mile search with her map.

The two of them moved with brutal efficiency through the battle, finishing off anything our attacks hadn't. They only hesitated and called Tim over when they found two humans amidst the beasts. They were dead and mauled beyond recognition.

The world spun a bit as I tried to wrap my brain around what we'd seen. The whole engagement had hardly been five minutes, ten if you counted the first call for help, yet people were dead. I glanced over my shoulder to see one of the survivors that hadn't made it despite the tending of both Sam and Ophelia. *How many more would have died if we had been slower?* That thought echoed in my mind, but a much more painful one seared itself into me. *How many would have lived if we had been faster?*

Unsure of either answer, I watched the clouds of Pith spread through to those present from outside the wall and beyond in the trees. Unlike usual, the warm energy didn't revitalize me but instead felt like another reminder of the brutality of the surface.

The squads made their returns and Sarah set up a doubled rotation for the car wall for the next few days right on the spot. When that was done, Sam fashioned a number of stretchers we used to help move the worst injured and the unconscious Lilly and Clara. The two squads that remained were grave-faced as they looked out towards the trees and started their patrol.

Even with the lives we'd secured, the engagement felt like a loss. The effect was clearly muted for the Wildwoodians, but the mess of feelings only seemed to grow. Just like the questions of what happened and where these people came from.

# CHAPTER TWENTY-THREE

## Ripples

"Do we have a clear answer?" Dylan said, slumping in his chair.

"Last thing we got was that they were attacked in Summer-field. Based on the injuries, I would guess it was those birds again, but they mentioned humanoids," Sarah said, reading from a report.

Everyone in the room tensed at the implication. Our enemy hadn't been idle. Samuel was still working with the injured while Daniela had split a wider patrol of the area with Devon. Dai was doing a sweep to the south to prevent any potential flanking there. All of them were staying at the edge of implant percep-tion, in case they ran into some kind of funny business.

Dylan continued speaking with his daughter, getting caught up with the situation and the engagement. Seeking some space to process what had happened without the peanut gallery, I headed deeper into the council building. Most of the rooms were dark, only lightly illuminated by small windows, but that worked just fine for me. Unfortunately, my attempt to seclude myself in one of the smaller unused offices failed, because Irwin approached me a few minutes later.

"It wasn't your fault, you know," he said. The man crossed

his arms, tucking the talons at the end of his fingers into his armpits. He'd elected to linger by the door.

"But we could have done *more*," I snapped, immediately regretting it.

"Yeah? What would that have been? Less sleep so that one of your experiments kills you? More time on guard so that one of our 'cutting edge' crafters is put out of commission doing a job someone else could do just as well? Or perhaps you thought you should be out there working your little spider dungeon, grinding this 'Pith' stuff?" Irwin barely paused to take a breath and I was distinctly aware of the silence from further down the hall. "I have seen you run ragged and then blast carried to the infirmary more times than I can count, and I've hardly known you three months, Mr. Terrigan. We do what we can, to the best of our ability, but we all lose something at some point. If you waste time questioning what you did, then you are neither working towards your future nor enjoying the present you fought to attain!"

The silence lingered between us as the councilman's words echoed in my mind. It was calloused, but I couldn't deny that I'd already made some assertions of that kind to deal with life on the surface.

I'd struggled past my issues with my uncle, and even forgiven the Bunker's leadership for lying to us our whole lives, because I knew they'd done it out of love. If I had made much more of a fuss, or fought to eke out as much retribution for their actions as I knew I could have, then we would have squandered our time on the surface. We would have let the fear and indig-nation towards our deception dictate the future we'd been hoping to unlock.

Things hadn't gone well on our first outing. They went terrible by almost all metrics, except the one that counts in the end: survival. Just because they didn't go well didn't mean we gave up, but instead rushed to grasp all the opportunities that Bec managed to give us. What would have happened to Wild-wood if we'd opted never to risk ourselves against the wilderness? A slow decline was the best case scenario I could think of.

"Didn't know I was walking into a wake," Clara said from down the hall, snapping me out of my self-reflective reverie. Irwin and I made eye contact. With a subtle nod, the man turned and the two of us rejoined the others in the front room. We arrived in time to see the demoness thank a trainee for having helped her get there, and the youth scampered out of sight when the whole room turned their way.

"Clara!" Sarah forewent any sort of decorum her new station had and crushed the woman with a hug. The demoness let out a single grunt before the normally serious Sarah backed off. "Oh Lord, I'm sorry!"

"I'll be fine." The woman didn't *look* fine, but I wasn't going to point it out. While her eyes weren't bleeding, they were still severely bloodshot, and her gray skin looked clammy and paler than usual.

"Can you tell us what's going on?" Dylan said, pulling out a chair for the demoness.

The woman sat down deliberately slowly. Her whole body swayed and I worried she was going to keel over right there. Thankfully, she took a few deep breaths before looking at all of us. "They were attacking Summerfield when we arrived. They had the whole town pinned in, so we were forced to engage."

"The civilians?" Irwin asked.

"They are from Summerfield, yeah." Clara paled but kept herself together to continue. "We had just enough time to get them running back to Lake Weir, but they chased us. Weir doesn't have enough resources to take on the sixty people, much less while warding off the Tendrils."

"What about Stonecrest?" Sarah asked, arms crossed; the scowl was back on her face. "Their two teams were just as good as the Big Guns."

"Stonecrest didn't have enough resources either. Their teams have been fighting almost non-stop. If my timeline is right, it coincides with us putting the spiders on the defensive by farming the dungeon territory."

"The spiders were hunting north of town?" I asked.

"Seems like. Their main issues were always to the east, but now they are fighting on two fronts. They have been eating their kills mostly, because their farms are a bust thanks to all the fighting. They have a smattering of Q4s in their squads, but they can't afford to take the Pith if they want to keep eating. They hosted us for a few days, dealing with the worst of the wounded, but they couldn't help with the long stretch back to Wildwood," she said wearily.

"How many did we lose? You didn't come back with all the trainees," Sarah said quietly. I hadn't even remembered that she left with a much larger group.

"One of the trainees. Geoffrey and Dennis are holding Lake Weir with the bulk of the trainees. The Tendrils were sending probing attacks, so my guess is that they are trying to take the towns out one at a time," Clara said.

The room fell silent as we worked through the new information. In my mind, the only thing I kept going around to was that we weren't ready. Even with all the progress we'd made, the town wasn't ready to face off against the mind-warped forces of the Dreg. It was almost a guarantee that the Tendrils had been people at some point based on what we'd seen of the afflicted trainees, but there didn't seem to be much of anything human left in them other than a certain level of intelligence.

Fighting creatures like the ants and the spiders in droves like we'd been doing was 'easy' since they followed animalistic tendencies, but each battle with the Tendrils had required us to react constantly just to stay ahead. If numerical advantage was added into the mix, we were well and truly borked, as Danny would say.

"Can the crystals help with anything?" Clara asked, turning to me.

"I… I don't know," I said, shaking my head slowly. "But it is definitely worth it to ask."

Taking a look around the room told me that everyone present had an implant. Since we were going to be asking for help anyhow, I opted to shift the meeting to the whitespace so that Tec could interact more directly. Sarah lent Clara a hand, while the rest of the council waged internal wars with their thoughts. For the life of me, I tried to remain optimistic that there was another option.

Once we got to the Blessing of Magic, Tec instantly snatched us up into its crystalline depths. Instead of just the usual featureless expanse marked by the glowing orb presence of the Entity Cluster, there was now a round table with enough chairs for everyone.

—Accommodations. Discussion does not appear to trend towards brevity.—

With the monotonous and even greeting out of the crystal's way, everyone took a seat. We spent a few minutes getting the Entity Cluster caught up on the status of the other towns, as well as some of the movements the Guard had observed from the enemy. As if not wanting to directly interact in the meeting, a dull ringing echoed through the meeting until a familiar voice joined the hovering orb in the whitespace.

<Tec?>

—Dreg Warriors seek assistance. Combined analysis would be optimal.—

"Hey Bec. We've got a bit of a pickle," I said, addressing the other Entity. Before I had a chance to give the abridged version of what we'd *just* told Tec, the Entity in question affirmed that he'd conferred the information at a speed beyond thought. *Impressive. Maybe I'll get that as a side effect of <Memory Canal>?* I didn't think it was likely, but it was a nice thought to have that the skill would have a further benefit other than interrogation and giving me nightmares.

<That does bring up a number of issues...> Bec droned.

"It all comes down to a simple decision, really," Trey, the fishermen's representative, started. "Are we going to intervene or not?"

"Of course we are going to intervene," Dylan said, rising to his feet. When no one jumped up at his proclamation, the fire-headed man looked to his daughter. "Right?"

"Not easy to say," Sarah said. Her frown deepened further, even if I wasn't sure that was possible. Her tusks were fully visible, giving the woman's face an intimidating edge that seemed to make Arnold, Trey, and William uncomfortable. The rest of the group had seen her face like that enough to not be bothered, it seemed.

"I thought you were making good progress with the trainees. I can imagine that, despite everything, if Clara left some trainees behind then they were worth promoting to Wild Guards," I said, trying to prompt the woman to elaborate.

"As far as I am concerned, those kids proved themselves several times over. Now, I wouldn't say they are necessarily ready to get sent out alone quite yet, but they aren't going to let us down," Clara said.

"That's part of the issue," Sarah said, sighing.

The orc woman broke down the statistics on the trainees. All of them were at least Q3, roughly thirty percent were Q4, and there was one stellar Q5 amongst them. As for the actual Wild Guard, all of them were at least Q4 and battle-hardened in one way or another. She mentioned that the New Hopers were close to having all Q5 members, as Clara mentioned that Godfrey, Lilly, and Dennis had all bumped up to Q5 with her. Other than the Bunker Busters and New Hoper freaks, the other squads were still trying to catch up from being limited in their absorption of Pith. In summary, the Guard were still short of their goal of engaging with a plethora of Q5s.

"We have some really experienced people. Why can't we use them to fight back?" William asked. The older farmer was stroking some kind of scar on his arm absently, but his eyes were sharply focused on the discussion.

"It's not enough. With the qualitative change that happens with each Quotient Level, the beasts we fight are stronger. Not only that, even if we can easily deal with lower Quotient creatures, it doesn't mean we can just ignore them. My team barely made it through a fight with a bunch of fire ants, and that was only because we were pretty familiar with their behavior to begin with," I said.

"The things that could close that gap aren't ready yet," Arnold huffed. "The crafters have been pulling extra shifts just to arm up our boys and girls, but there is only so much they can do, and only so much material we can afford to burn through for training them at the moment, so production is slower."

"I've got an update on that actually," Irwin said, patting his patchwork pants and finding them empty. Instead of saying anything, Tec materialized a sheet of paper in the air above Irwin. The man looked at the sheet with a quirked eyebrow before shrugging and grabbing it. "We've acquired close to seven hundred Q0 infusions, two hundred Q1 infusions, between fifty to sixty of Q2 and Q3s, and just under ten of the Q4s for the various attunements. What that has translated to is having about half of the Guard equipped with weapons and a third armored, including the pieces you've already donated, Ronan."

I gave the man a nod of appreciation, but I could already feel the headache building behind my eyes. Exhaustion wasn't the problem, but the weight of the Dreg was ramping up its invisible pressure on my psyche. Tuning out my own thoughts, I focused on Dylan who brought out a list of his own.

"Short of having daily feasts for the next month, I don't see us starving through the winter. If we keep this pace up, we won't even have to ration. Our food situation is steady and climbing," the councilman said.

"Can we offer that?" Clara asked, some of the anxious energy she'd been holding on to surged as food was mentioned.

"If we divert some of the new refugees to help the farms, we can probably turn up our production," William added, giving Dylan a pointed look. I watched the interplay closely, but all it seemed to indicate was a 'we'll talk later' look.

—It is imminent that the afflicted trainees awaken. They should be of significant support on the field of battle.—

"Tec, we can't just throw people that were essentially just cursed into the deep end. Even if it was at the people that did it," I added.

—Social convention cues speak that the Wildwood Dreg Warrior council disagrees with the Dreg Warrior Leader.—

Sure enough, there were gentle nods from the faces on the table, even the noncombatants. When he seemed to sense the confusion, Dylan affirmed to me that it was most likely that the afflicted would seek swift and savage retribution for how the Dreg Entity played a part in changing their bodies. I tried to think about it from their perspective and it made a bit more sense, but I was still hesitant to let them out to fight. If they appeared unaffected by their conditions, then it was something we could bring up again so I conceded the point.

<The Bunker should be able to provide minimal technical expertise. Unfortunately, the Bunkerites are more on the older side and not properly equipped for combat initiatives outside of a defensive situation,> Bec added.

"Where does that leave us, then?" Clara asked, leaning forward and meeting everyone's eyes. "Do we attack or do we do nothing?"

"It's too soon," Sarah said gravely, and I could see Clara deflate.

"Unfortunately, that is also my consensus. We aren't quite there with our agricultural reserves to sustain a jump in population if we tried to take in the population of the other towns in their entirety," William said, addressing the possibility of evacuating the group.

"They are going to be defenseless!" Clara yelled. "They are coming in droves, and I am pretty sure it's the work of those Tendril bastards. They are using the wildlife against the other towns. They've only made it this long by remaining under the radar and under our protection. We can't abandon them now that a tangible threat is actually present!"

The council devolved into mayhem. Many argued that they'd already stuck their heads out more than they should. Not only did they lose some of their own people in the exchange, but they were still stuck fighting for the sake of the other towns. Clara complained about the council's continued negligence in actually helping the other towns, which was true even if Dylan countered the point. Had the New Hopers not continued to insist on risking the trip to the other towns, they would have all remained disconnected. Adrift in a sea of monsters with no real way of consolidating their strength, regardless of the 'protection' the Dreg Tendrils had offered until we uncovered their corruption.

I wanted to say something—*needed* to say something—but the words failed me every time. I was struggling with a handful of deaths, while the Wildwoodians and the survivors of the surface had lost many times more in their three decade struggle. Anything I could contribute to the discussion felt flat and callous to the actual lives being discussed and weighed. It was a burden of leadership I hadn't even contemplated, and put my bravado in leading the Wild Guard against the Dreg into a light I wasn't exactly sure I wanted to examine.

Thankfully, before the council devolved into accusations, name calling, and words that couldn't be taken back, our silent supporters joined the discussion.

<We have come up with a proposition.>

Bec's voice wasn't overpowering, like the yelling humans, but the entire council paused. Its tone was unmissable. Sarah was actually holding her father as he stabbed a finger at Clara accusingly. The Entity Clusters remained silent for several seconds, and the humans in their varied levels of distress settled back into their seats. The grave atmosphere was somewhat sobered, and I was fairly sure it was because everyone realized the two Entities had watched the humans devolve into anger before them. It wasn't a good impression, even if I knew the two of them didn't sit on propriety like those before the Fall did.

<Tec has been kind enough to run some predictions while you all... discussed.>

*He's really leaning on that sarcasm.* After a moment of consideration, I was surprised it hadn't come up more since Danny, Sam, and I were all part of its personality. My mind didn't have much longer to drift as what he said next snatched up my attention.

<Tec would like to suggest to expand itself to one of these further towns.>

"Expand? Like its influence?" I asked, referring to the area in which the crystal could deter creatures from approaching.

<Yes, but not quite. Tec, if you would?>

—Town Entity responds with an intermediary plan to attack and abstain options. Influence expansion is one potential way of alleviating the struggles of those aspiring to join the Dreg Warrior program.—

—Influence expansion will entail partial fragmentation of crystalline matrix. Fragment will retain a Category Level 2, matching Bunker Entity's earlier processing power and limitations. Installation of this fragment will allow for real time communication between said location and Wildwood. While unconfirmed, proximity between two repulsive areas of influence is expected to reduce the likelihood of creatures attacking. While not directly under the effect of an Entity Cluster's influence, this would expand the human territory boundaries.—

"That sounds fantastic!" Dylan exclaimed, rising to his feet. The man's hair had returned to its warm red glow after the blaze to blue while arguing with Clara.

"What's the catch?" Trey the fisherman asked, crossing his scaly arms. "Sounds too good to be true."

"As much as I hate to agree with our fish friend here, I have to agree. Why hasn't this been an option until now?" Arnold said, earning himself a glare from the other council member.

<I can expand on that a bit. Essentially, it would be the same reason why Tec doesn't just splinter enough pieces to push me up in category. It would dilute him, in a sense. The crystal

here in Wildwood would be slightly, but notably, weaker and would therefore be reliant on gathered Dreg to get back its strength. Additionally, just like how I am still reliant on Dreg to grow, so would the Category 2 crystal that is removed. Its communication and repulsion properties would be costly. However, with the near constant rate of fighting the Guard has kept up, feeding Tec and this new crystal shouldn't be outside the realm of possibility, especially if there are more humans that will be gathering Dreg.>

Running some rough, highly speculative numbers through my head made the decision much more palatable. The appearance of the Reproductor ant, even with the torturous strain it had put on the Bunkerites, had managed to push Bec closer to the next category. If the other towns were in as much of a desperate need, then it would be worth it to turn their struggle into a growing opportunity. Victory from the jaws of defeat, in a sense.

"Do you think the town of Lake Weir will be receptive to joining our group more permanently, Clara? We would have to check with the Entities, but maybe it would be possible to implant the leader of the town to help coordinate with the other Dreg Warriors," I said, redirecting my question to the closest thing we had to a diplomat.

—It would increase the mass needed to be transported, but it will not burden this vessel overly much.—

"Thanks, Tec. And as far as LW? Almost certainly. After seeing our new skills in action, many of them wanted to come back with us right away just for the opportunity. Of course, everyone already knows we just took the ones in most need," the demoness said, nodding the whole time. Her expression tightened, as if she'd eaten something sour. "Stonecrest…Well, they might take a bit more convincing."

Installing a crystal would then effectively create a small network for the survivors to really dig into their territory. If they only had to focus on fighting with the occasional high level creature that ignored the repulsion areas, then trade would be possible between the towns. Not to mention that it would allow the Guard and other Dreg Warriors like us more time to range further without the danger of their friends and families getting killed in their absence. Obviously, being able to launch the attack on the Dreg Entity from Lake Weir would be much more effective, so that wasn't something that we could dismiss as an additional benefit if their leaders okayed it.

Since I personally didn't have any issues with the plan, I tried to think of what Sam and Danny would add to the meeting if they were here. Samuel would want to make sure that everyone was safe as much as possible, and Danny would be clamoring for them to use the crystals offensively somehow.

"It's entirely possible that some of the Wild Guard would need to be stationed there for a while," I added. "I don't know if I feel okay leaving this new Cat 2 Metier Crystal undefended, even if we are able to deal with the Dreg."

"It can be done," Sarah said. Dylan almost immediately moved to protest, but the death glares he received from Clara and the orc woman had him withering back into his seat. "We'll need to help out with their food situation regardless."

—Warning should be given prior to assent.—

"I knew it was still too good to be true," Trey complained.

"Go ahead, Tec. Just lay it on us," I said, bracing for whatever downside we would have to deal with.

—This fragment will be unstable. While the shard is unable to emplace an area of influence, the energy contained within will be released steadily.—

"Can I get a translation on that?" Dylan asked.

<While transporting the crystal, it will instead *attract* creatures until it has enough time to settle. Creatures will seek to claim it in order to generate their own dungeons and territories.>

"Ha! So, we just have to transport a giant magic rock through a beast-infested forest while it throws up a flare telling all the critters where it is? Not only that, but an evil magic rock is trying to sabotage us at every turn. Do I about have it?" Arnold chuckled without humor.

—References to unstable energy status and Dreg Entity identified.—

—Dreg Warrior Arnold, your assessment is correct.—

"Why I ought to—"

"Do nothing. Are you going to argue with a rock that is *actually* smarter than you, Arnold?" Irwin said, cutting the man off. The council let out huffs or short laughs at the word play. With the tension broken somewhat, even if the dwarf in question grumbled his displeasure, the group discussed how the revelation actually affected the plan moving forward.

While the actual logistics would have to be modified, and fighters rallied, the council had already made their decision. Within two days, a force of Wild Guard would head on a tour of the towns to the north, hoping to assist Stonecrest and dig in at Lake Weir with the help of their first crystal expansion.

# CHAPTER TWENTY-FOUR

## The Weight of Living

The energy of the town went from urgent to somewhat manic within the first day of the new arrivals. News of the fall of Summerfield sent ripples of fear and uncertainty throughout the population of Wildwood. Thankfully, the Wild Guard and the council were swift in their propagation of the expansion plan. One of those proactive response things. It really was presented masterfully by Dylan during the evening meal gathering.

Instead of just sending more bodies to fight, which would have been the equivalent of bailing water from the ocean with the town's level of readiness, they would be setting up a connecting branch to Wildwood. The councilman painted a picture of the efforts the people of the town had already made, and how they would be able to help their fellow man simply by holding steady in their work. The Wild Guard would defend, and the town would support them. Dylan stepped off his metaphorical soap box to much cheering and the dour mood took a huge turn.

While the few survivors of Summerfield didn't share in the jump in morale, they seemed just as determined to bring vengeance to the Dreg. Those not recovering were already in search of jobs where they could use their expertise, and the various trades of Wildwood swallowed the help up as quickly as it appeared.

Both Sam and Danny were completely on board with the plan. Daniela grumbled about having to continue using her daggers because, 'You aren't going to have time to get your head stuck up your rear deep enough.' When I just stood there confused, she clarified that that was what she thought I did every time I spent several sleepless days crafting items. While true, it didn't mean that I was idle.

The logistics of splintering the multi-story Metier Crystal had Alan in a frenzy. He wanted to be directly involved, while simultaneously as far from the action without missing a beat from his measuring devices. Just keeping the man from blowing a gasket took my full concentration. Ava stopped by to help, since she was more experienced with his eccentricities, but even she was rebuffed on some things.

"Let him wind down himself," she said, frowning in the direction of his little lab. "Considering how stable things were back in the Bunker, I am surprised he is doing as well as he is."

"Sorry to pull you into this," I said, combing out my beard with my fingers. *I really should have brought a trimmer from the Bunker.*

"Do I need to give you another reminder not to put everything on your shoulders again?" Ava said, quirking an eyebrow.

"Nope. I'm good."

"Great. Now, tell me the plan. Sarah has been running team composition permutations for the squads all day and *that* isn't something I have the brain for," Ava said.

The woman started leading me back towards the training building. The late afternoon sun was splashing everything in orange, but the people of Wildwood didn't seem to notice. I spotted more than a few demons getting ready for their night shifts. Even from the other side of the town center, I could hear Arnold shouting obscenities to the workers about putting things in their place for those coming in behind them. The shadow of a lanky blond and a young teen working on a massive wooden contraption drew the eyes of everyone passing through.

"Samuel is building the cart for the Metier Crystal right now. He and Marie are the epitome of creative introverts; neither of them says a word, but they are working more in sync than I've ever seen *us* work," I said, chuckling. "He's already cooked up another two carts for us to use to supply Stonecrest and Lake Weir. Since the first stretch of the trip is the longest, we are going to be ready to race forward as fast as possible. Leading a wagon train is going to be rough, even with the few dirt roads. Attuned Earth slapped down the vegetation revolution while we focused on surviving."

"I have noticed a bit more greenery than before," Ava replied flatly.

"The hope is that we can clear a straight shot to the towns for the future. Tec 2.0 will implant the leader of Stonecrest while we reorganize the train and show off the perks of joining Wildwood in a more permanent capacity. Then, we'll head to Lake Weir, give the leader an implant, and install the crystal."

"Offensively speaking?"

"You probably know the capabilities of the trainees individually more than I do, but Sarah said that we should have three squads. Plus the New Hopers that are currently in town. The trainees are going to be the frontliners, though, while the more experienced of us will be a reaction force of sorts. Well, except for me, because I am always at the front and will be reacting anyhow."

"You don't always have to be…" Ava said quietly.

"I've come to terms with the fact that if my friends are going to die, it will be after me," I said. Ava seemed a bit taken aback by the edge in my voice.

"Marcus might have been absent from your life, Ronan, but you are as immovable as he was." It was *my* turn to be taken aback. With everything going on, the last thing I expected to hear about was my father. She chuckled sadly. "I wish I could have told you before, but he was the reason Juan and I ever got together."

"H-how close were you to him?" While my uncle had told me about my family, we still hadn't had the time to *really* talk. Most of our time together had been spent coming to grips with the secrets he'd had to keep and our survival on the surface.

"Him and I butted heads on just about everything." The sadness left her laughter for a moment as she stared off into the sunset. "Carla and Dale broke up more than a few of our arguments, in fact. Him and Juan though? Inseparable. I think it had something to do with both of them loving to cook. Anyhow, when he shoved one of Juan's little tarts in my mouth as a way of ending one of my more eloquently erudite points, I just knew I had to trap that cook."

While uncomfortable and wildly personal, I hung on every word. It wasn't that Ava hadn't ever been candid with us. As a matter of fact, many of the Bunkerites found Juan and Ava's relationship sickeningly sweet. The information, the real human connection to my father was something I didn't even know I craved. Ava spent the rest of our walk to the training area talking about other memorable times with my father and I soaked up every bit of it. With each story, I felt some of my stress lift for some reason. It wasn't that the burden of responsibility had grown smaller—the New Hopers and us would still be leading a bunch of teens to what amounted to a battlefield—but it was as if I was just a bit more whole. More put together to handle things. The entire experience left me lost in thought and I barely noticed the arrival of my friends from their own tasks.

One of the trainees brought the meat ration for dinner, and Danny set herself to the task of tossing up fresh salads for all of us. Samuel churned the ingredients right before us from his plethora of potted plants. The evening fell and Daniela summoned her wisp to act as light for us. At some point, Blobby had snuck in and was acting as the mobile dishwasher for our plates. Leftovers went into the slime, clean plates exited. I tried not to think about what sort of residue was on the tableware after passing through the creature.

Since Ava had already been on a roll talking about my father, the evening ran long as she told us all a bit more about our hidden youths and the pasts of our parents. The stories had distinct effects on all of us. Samuel was an endless fount of questions, while Daniela and I turned contemplative. Being able to connect more closely with my friends once again relieved the strain I didn't even know I had been feeling. The only thing I could relate it to was those old military movies I'd watched growing up where the soldiers partied hard before being sent out to fight. They were eking as much life out of the peace they had. There had been a number of those serious and funny military movies available growing up, and having learned about some of the original members of the Bunker, the fact that they were in the terminals made a whole lot more sense.

When Daniela eventually started to run out of mana from maintaining her wisp, static as it was, the group called it a night. Ava and Daniela retreated to the bunks set up in the kitchen while Sam and I threw ourselves onto the bunk and couch respectively. The poor piece of furniture creaked under my weight, but it held.

"How did we get here, Ron?" Sam asked from across the dark room. The gentle glow of his passive magic illuminated a little circle around the blond.

"With our feet?" I asked.

"I'm serious, man. I… We aren't ready for this. The fights up until now were one thing, but this…"He gestured around himself, throwing shadows everywhere as the source of light shifted. "We are just kids."

*I've been so lost in my own thoughts I haven't checked in with Sam and Danny.* My realization felt like a shot of guilt right through the heart. They had always been supportive and I hadn't even talked to them about all that was going on before dropping us into a *whole new mess.* Instead of deflecting like I would have usually, I turned to talk with Samuel directly. "I don't know, Sammy."

The friend I'd shared my whole life with seemed to grow older right before me—magic, attributes, and actual age be damned. "Those... those people are dead. We are sure now that the Tendrils we fought—will fight—are people too. Now we are leading people to kill them too!"

"I can't say I know what we are doing, but I do know that if we do not fight, things will be a lot worse, Sam. You saw the people of Wildwood. Whether we were here or not, they were fighting to live. Sarah against the beasts threatening her home. Clara for the basic decency of helping her fellow humans. Hell, even Kirby with his twisted delusions thought he was doing the right thing." At some point, my head had started shaking slowly. *Perhaps if the Dreg were not actively sabotaging our every move, things could have been different...*

A spell chain flickered to life around my wrist with almost as much ease as moving my fingers. The mana trickled out of me, shaping the unreadable glyphs. "This power, the Gifts the Wildwoodians unlocked long before we came into the picture, demands that we take our dream to the logical conclusion."

"You know that was youthful optimism. Ron, we were *really* kids when we clamored for a life on the surface. To maybe one day see the skyscrapers of big cities, or the wide open fields full of farms, or even the ocean. Even back then, we knew those things wouldn't be possible," Sam countered.

"That's true. And maybe we won't ever get to do some of those things, but what would be the alternative? Roll over and die? Join the ranks of the Dreg, just so that we can torture the existence of others for however long we live? Or maybe go back to the Bunker? Back to the blank walls, and the fake simulations, and the comfortable lies." My voice rose to a harsh whisper, and I hoped that Ava and Daniela had fallen asleep already.

Samuel didn't have a response. He seemed surprised that I had such vehemence built up inside, but I'd chosen to be honest with him. When I could see the wheels spinning in his head, my entire body deflated. The couch groaned as if responding in the absence of Samuel's answer to my questions.

"You are right. We can't go back, and *that* is why we are here." I turned to look at my friend. "You always have a choice, and you always choose to face the problem head on. Daniela always has a choice, and she chooses to let everyone know what she decides. I… I want to give people those choices. That's what I want to choose. If I question why we are here… that is the moment those choices start to dry up."

"So we should keep going, because we are here and we might as well make a mess of it?" I asked, huffing at his moment of introspection.

"No, you asshole, I mean that the choice is no longer one we are making. It has been made. If we aren't fighting for the future, then we are doing ourselves a disservice," Samuel snapped. He marked his words by having a vine grow down from the ceiling to whack me on the head. "We chose to fight, because it gave us freedom. Now, in order to keep that freedom, and give it to others, we need to fight. Attuned Earth or mundane Earth, you fight for the tomorrow you want to see."

Even if Samuel was waxing poetic, he wasn't wrong. I thought back to the joy of sharing the new things we experienced on the surface with my friends and family. I thought back to the joy I found building, crafting, experimenting, and just generally causing mayhem in the name of magic science. I thought back to the joy I'd seen in the faces of the people of Wildwood, even with the pain of their afflicted children fresh on their minds, when they saw us return with the trainees. Each of those had a cost.

"You're right, Sammy." I said, dropping heavily against the arm rest. "Giving up doesn't help anyone."

"Good, because it's your fault we are in this mess. *But,* you should know me and Danny are behind you all the way," Sam said. He dropped onto his back and rolled over in his covers.

"What!? You are just going to go achieve enlightenment or

something and then take a snooze?" I asked, somewhat outraged that he'd disengaged from our conversation.

"If you two don't stop talking, I am going to *enlighten* both of your behinds!" Ava thundered from the other room. For someone without a means of magically amplifying her voice, she sure was loud.

There wasn't a single peep the rest of the night, but the thoughts swirling through my head kept me up well into the night. From the restless tossing in the other room and the night long rustle of the blankets across from me, I knew that I wasn't alone. For some reason, that thought let me finally fall asleep. Despite all the terrible things I was hoping to avoid in our future that would surely still happen, having people around me made that burden just a bit easier to handle.

# CHAPTER TWENTY-FIVE

## The Escort Mission

The final day of preparations went by in a flash. I hardly got a chance to breathe as I worked on armor set after armor set to equip the squad of trainees. None of them were necessarily my best work, but the Q1 force dispersal traits would serve them well.

Outside of my monotonous session of crafting, Samuel completed the carts and Daniela ran through all the logistics necessary to lead our group towards the towns. She ensured that our 'boon' of being present didn't become a huge demerit by cutting into their food supplies simply because we didn't pack enough food. Clara finished recovering, mostly, from her overuse of her abilities and spent her time prepping the trainees to follow directions in the heat of battle. Quite literally.

She spent the entire afternoon burning through the trainees' nervous energy by having Daniela and Sarah use their fire skills to try to catch the trainees if they hesitated when given a direction. It wasn't a perfect substitute for field training, but it still put the youths through their paces. Even Ava approved, which just guaranteed it was a hellish method of training.

That night, there was an impromptu feast by the people of

Wildwood. A pair of the mundane cows they kept had been slaughtered just for the occasion, and we had fresh meat for the first time in our lives; definitely a juicy, medium-rare plus to having traveled to the surface. To everyone's surprise, William brought out a trio casks filled with potato liquor that fed the life of the party. Some of the newly christened Wild Guard hadn't ever tasted alcohol before, and each first timer got howls of laughter as their face puckered up from the high proof drinks. It became a sort of contest to see who could stand the liquid burn without reacting.

Thankfully, amidst the party were competent sober people that replaced the day watch, Sarah made sure of that. She did have a soft spot for them and sent an extra serving of the evening meal for them.

That night's sleep was only a bit elusive, but I was fairly certain it had to do with the dilution of my slurry blood with cheap booze. To everyone's surprise, the life-attuned were almost entirely immune to the inebriation effects of the alcohol so they became chaperones, escorting everyone to their homes when the bonfire started to die down. Samuel was *not* thrilled about having to carry my bulk up the stairs.

When the sun shone through the windows of the training building, a hangover made itself known. Regardless, compared to getting rocked multiple times in all the fights I'd had on the surface, it was only a minor impediment. That is to say, I only complained about it until Daniela's cooking lured me off the couch and into the kitchen. *Crystals bless Juan for teaching his daughter the culinary arts…*

Breakfast was a sober affair. We said our goodbyes to Ava and Alan, who had managed to peel himself away from his lab long enough for a meal, in the privacy of our lodgings before we all left for Tec. I had a rucksack with supplies strapped across my chest, my helm, shield, and the spider naginata while my friends equipped their own gear. The moment it went on our person, the sober atmosphere was traded for razor sharp focus.

The ever-present glimmer of the Metier Crystal seemed brighter than ever as we joined the growing crowd of Wildwoodians hoping to see the fragmenting. Before long, we arrived where the members of the Wild Guard staying behind, and the youngest trainees were keeping the crowd back. Arranged in neat groups behind them were the three squads selected to come with us. At the head of each was the squad leader and the healer of the group.

Outside of the few people I recognized as the squad leaders, it was almost all trainees. The squads were somewhat irregular in size, one was only four people while the other two were five-person teams. The five-member teams were made up of one Q4 leader and healer along with three peak Q3 trainees. The four person group had the breakout Q5 elf trainee in its ranks. Standing at the head of one of the groups was the one-armed orc that had saved me while fighting Kirby. The hulking gray-green man cut an impressive figure next to the dainty fae healer, but if he was in the position to lead even after losing a limb, I was more than happy to have someone as willing to charge into danger as him in the group. I made an internal note to approach them once we were safe in one of the other towns.

If we added the four New Hopers and our three Bunker Busters, it was actually a sizable force at twenty one people. Plus animal companions. *I damn sure hope this is enough.* I couldn't help the thought from surfacing, but I buried it deep. Doubting our abilities just because we didn't have *more* people would be what killed us first.

Being tended by the New Hopers and the Big Guns were a pair of oxen. They were already hitched up to Samuel's carts and a group of the farmers were loading up various supplies onto the back. One would be meant for Stonecrest and Lake Weir, while the other would carry the expedition's supplies as well as the armor they hoped to give the trainees currently fighting. The final, highest quality cart was reserved for our magic rock companion.

I hadn't had a chance to see Samuel's and Marie's masterpiece, but it was truly a wonder of magical engineering. The first of its kind that I was aware of, really. Instead of the slap-stick planks the people of Wildwood used, or God forbid the rough cut logs we used back in the Bunker, the two had coaxed the trees into shape.Unlike his first iteration, this one was almost as tall as me with three axles holding four thick wooden wheels each, rounded perfectly by Marie's Gift. The bark remained, giving a sort of hardened armor for the exterior of the cart and a rough grip surface on the inside. The front was a mess of straps and hooks so that the cart could be attached to any number of creatures. The creature in this case was poor Anthony.

Since our fight with the inferno ant, he'd recovered signifi-cantly. Over the course of the days we'd been back in town, I had also missed his growth. The once human-sized ant now easily matched Samuel's bull, Raymond. *Now that I think about it, I haven't really checked in on Raymond either. That big boy might be even larger now.*

The most surprising thing about Anthony's recovery was the regrown limbs. They looked a bit... *soft* for lack of a better word, but they didn't seem to be an impediment to the large ant. It was probably something the healers were studying in the hopes of helping people like Igor, the orc who'd lost his arm helping the trainees, amongst others who'd suffered to various degrees since the loss of modern medicine. It certainly seemed that Fallen, non-Fallen and the attuned beasts of Earth healed in different ways and with different parameters.

Anthony stood next to the cart, probing it with his antenna before chittering at Daniela in what I could only assume was indignation. I put the interaction on display out of mind as I walked towards the Blessing of Magic. My friends gave me a nod as I walked towards the council of Wildwood.

"Great of you to join us," Sarah huffed.

"Not everyone can handle their drink," Arnold said, wagging his finger in my direction.

"I was more than fine, thank you very much," I replied defensively.

The group let out a nervous chuckle before Clara broached the subject. "Is Tec ready?"

"Ready." The voice of the Entity Cluster reverberated the ground around us. The wisps of elemental mana all around us shivered in the air before resuming their chaotic dance. I heard more than one scream from the general population of the town. It *had* been the first time that Tec addressed them directly. Considering the strength of its voice, which I supposed was a result of the Entity's size, it made sense. Bec had explained that until a crystal was able to imprint a language, it wouldn't be able to communicate. It was the crux of what had led our implants to put us on the path of Dreg Warriors.

Without much warning, a sound between shattering glass and Ava's high caliber rifle echoed through Wildwood. A slab off the top of Tec slid slowly down the side and a crystal tentacle lowered it to the ground gingerly. It looked like a minia-ture version of Tec, even having matching facets in its hexag-onal formation. The same earth quaking voice spoke. "Entity successfully fragmented."

There was stunned silence across the crowd. Even the chil-dren that had picked up crying after the 'ready' were silent after Tec's display. Reliable as always, it was Daniela who broke the tension of the display. "Well? It's not gonna load itself!"

The orcs, dwarves, and myself moved over to the hunk of iridescent crystal. It had sunk a few inches into the soft soil around Lake Sumter, but our combined effort made the trip to the wagon a breeze. I *did* notice red glows coming from several of the bearers channeling mana into their fire-infused items to help with the load. We slid the crystal into place, watching the wheels take the weight better than I thought they would. Samuel stepped up and wrapped the crystal up in vines to secure it to the cart.

The blond gave us a thumbs up as he placed his hand on Anthony's thorax. His decentralized nervous system trait folded out of his palms, contacting the ant. It helped him communicate directions better than any trained animal had any right to understand.

The crystal made its way towards the bridge over Lake Sumter, and the other life-attuned jumped to guide their ox carts up behind Sam. The crowd cheered as the group passed in front of them and onto the aged bridge. Sarah, the rest of the Big Guns, and the council parted with us there, holding back the crowd as we all zeroed in on our task. The trip to the old rusted car wall was the shortest and longest walk I'd ever had and I could see the tension building in everyone's posture. Tec had warned that the crystal would be stable while within its area of influence, but the moment it exited, it would start to attract creatures. How many and how often was something even the Entities could not compute.

Everyone stopped at the wall, suddenly realizing that they didn't know how they were going to get through it. Going around it wasn't feasible, since the cars at the ends partially submerged as they circumvented almost the entirety of Lake Sumter. Just as the group was getting ready to start discussing this first perceived obstacle, Clara shot me a look over her shoulder. I couldn't help but laugh, since only the leaders of the expedition had been given the torturous details of the procession.

I walked up next to Anthony and focused on my helm. <Earth Wall> sprouted from the ground, surging an almost twenty full feet at my standard casting cost to form a ramp to the top of the cars. The top vehicle groaned under the resting weight of my manifested earth for a few seconds until it settled down. Not bothering to wait for my mana to regen, I walked up the ramp I'd created and pulled up another from the earth on the other side. At the point where the two <Earth Walls> met, I used my passive skill to bond the sections of soil together.

Once I gave Sam the thumbs up, he started to make his way up the steep ramp. I was fairly sure if Anthony hadn't 'roided up since the last time I saw him, the ant would have struggled.

As it was, the insect gripped the ramp with ease and only slowed as he pulled the Metier Crystal to the other side. The other squads, other than the four New Hopers who were shaking their heads at my antics, were stunned at my casual construction effort. I didn't tell them that the two walls had taken almost the entirety of my mana pool, but they didn't need to know that.

A few well-placed shouts from Clara and Daniela and the whole group had made it to the other side. I contemplated what to do about the new access ramp for a second until I realized it was the perfect opportunity to finally try something for the first time.

Thinking back to when I first used the skill, I dialed it back to a tenth of the power. The spell chain struggled to form as I mentally only pressed the button for the skill *slightly* in order to reduce the power it drew from my mana pool. Thankfully, Ava's original training of regulating our mana consumption had been quite thorough and the task was manageable even for my brand new skill. <Mudpit> formed right on the surface of my earth wall, turning the once-hard material into a soupy slush that splashed down onto the road and the rusted car wall. It hadn't been perfectly lined up, instead there was roughly a ten foot hole cookie-cut in the wall as the effect transferred into the soil below. More than a few gasps sounded off behind me, but I paid them no mind. Casting <Mudpit> two more times, I cut down my wall to remove the ramp's access completely.

"We are good!" I called, turning to the group. I did my best to hide the ache in my abdomen that came with overtaxing my mana pool in quick succession. It made it very evident that I needed to train with <Mudpit> as much as possible. The skill was already showcasing its power when dealing with defenses. Manipulating the cost of the skill was something I *needed* to be done at almost the speed of thought to be effective during a fight.

Once the group got over their surprise at my abilities, we trudged away from the rusted car wall. When Sam and the crystal's cart got just twenty feet from it, an almost imperceptible whine echoed around us. As we pushed forward, the whine got louder and louder until it popped. A ripple of sensations, both familiar and unfamiliar, assaulted me and everyone present, even the least perceptive in the group. It was the ripple of an Entity Cluster's influence, except this time it felt like it was being sucked back away from us instead of enveloping our group with its reassuring protection.

The second was a slight buzz in the air that drew my attention towards the crystal. It was the buzz that had first drawn me to Bec all those months ago. The fact that I picked up on it meant the clock had started. We were going to have unfortunate travel companions soon.

"Clara, we are up!" I called to the demoness at the head of the column.

"Hustle up, everyone! You know the formation!" she called. The trainees nervously shuffled behind their squad leaders, putting them on the outside of a semicircular formation around the back of the caravan. The healers hugged the inside, leading the oxen. It was going to be the longest short ride of their lives. I walked up to Samuel and Clara who were at the lead. Devon and Daniela blurred out of view as the two ranged out to our flanks, scouting for incoming threats. Rommel and Lilly were posted in the middle, ready to leap out and support any of the sides that got attacked.

"Ready?" Clara asked, glancing over to me.

"As ready as we are going to get," I said, giving my half-regenerated mana pool a look.

"Head out!"

The entire expedition slowly picked up speed until everyone was moving at a steady jog, the pace set at the maximum the ox could keep up. My eyes roved from tree to tree, from the old-road-turned-game-trail to my LPS, where I could see Devon's and Daniela's markers staying just within communication range. They would take turns exiting range, checking the surrounding area, before doubling back and rejoining my and Clara's party.

With the capacity of my party near topped up by including

all of the New Hopers, I could definitely feel the strain as a low grade headache formed the further into the woods we traveled. It wasn't clear if whoever 'created' the party took the brunt of the mental strain, but I had a sneaking suspicion that was the case. Either that, or Clara and Sam were flawlessly ignoring the throbs in their heads.

"Quick contact!"came the call from Devon. A red dot blipped in the LPS and I called for the expedition to halt. A few others quickly joined the first, but disappeared as I heard the telltale crackle of Devon's <Lightning Strike> connecting with targets. "Clear."

"We haven't even gone a quarter mile," Sam whispered.

"This is going to be tough," Clara said, a frown pulling the pale skin on her forehead taut around her horns.

"You can say that again," I chuckled dryly.

—This is going to be tough,—the crystal in the back of the wagon echoed.

"Oh no." Everyone at the head of the expedition almost simultaneously facepalmed.

They were going to have a peanut gallery on the trip, and it had to be from the most literal of the Entity Cluster pair they'd found. As if the first statement had meant to open the flood-gates, Tec 2.0 started to blab about the obvious status of the space in his new, constantly changing, influence. Some of the information was marginally relevant, such as a play by play update of the distance traveled and the extent of its attraction field as affected by the organic density nearby. Some were just random bits of information that Entity was collecting and reciting as if it was dictating an encyclopedia of all the things around it.

By the third scientific species breakdown, the group was begging for more than an isolated contact with the beasts of the wild.

# CHAPTER TWENTY-SIX

## Renown

"<Crystal Cascade>!" I called, releasing the half-powered, augmented skill to our left.

I didn't have time to do much else but bring up my shield to block a leg-thick tongue from sticking to one of the healers in the group behind me. The next moment, I was playing tug-of-war. One of the chameleons hiding in the woods tried to tug me off balance, but I stabbed my naginata into the ground. The soil started to give way, but the move gave me enough time to cast a quarter-power <Earthen Barrier> right at my feet to lock me in place. The creature was *not* expecting that.

When it wasn't able to pull me, the force of its own attack caused the branch it was using for support to snap. Not waiting for an invitation, I used the slight moment of weightlessness to reel it in. Its mouth bulged as I wrapped its tongue around and around my arm and its strange ever-shifting eyes tried to lock on to me. Its tornasol skin flickered as it tried to adapt its camouflage, but it was too late. A shard of ice from somewhere behind me impaled the creature, sending it into a twitching frenzy. When it finally crashed to the ground, I released a <Stone Spike> in anticipation. The compressed earth punched through its head, pinning it and killing it at once. I finally used my nagi-nata's edge to free myself from the sticky tongue and refocus on the rest of the expedition.

The one-armed orc was doing a similar match up with the other chameleon that had ambushed us. Unfortunately, he didn't have my earth manipulation skills, but that didn't seem to stop him as he turned into a comet of fire mid-air. He shoulder-checked the chameleon right in the mouth, toppling it to the ground where it got a haymaker to the eyeball from a familiar dwarf woman. The ocular organ exploded all over her, but it was enough of a distraction that the rest of their squad joined in on the pugilistic assault. Unorthodox, as far as I knew of the newer trainees, but the occasional flares of spell chains told me that the impacts were enhanced by mana one way or another. With their fighting style, it made sense that they would get slotted together in a squad.

Samuel was aglow with green-gold light, channeling it through his femur club and into the nature around us. A number of softball-sized rocks pelted the treeline and I watched as the trees themselves betrayed their charges. Caught in the suddenly mobile branches, half a dozen life-attuned anoles struggled for freedom. Their tails flopped to the ground one after the other, forming a writhing carpet of flesh that was quickly built up as the anoles regrew and re-dropped their barbed tails with a speed only possible thanks to some kind of trait or Gift. A pair of dwarfs caught the tail end of the desperate attack, getting slapped to the ground for their troubles.

"<Earthen Barrier>, <Earthen Barrier>!" I called, keeping my eyes locked on the squirming tails. A Vof raised earth pushed them back, separating the trainees from a dozen other easy injuries. The next thing the tree-wrapped lizards saw was either a wolf fang dagger or a point-blank shot of Freeform <Flame Blast> from Daniela's wisp.

My breath came heavy as I tried to get my bearings again in the battlefield. The other chameleon was dead, both of its eyes now burst. The small horde of death-attuned rodents that had come in from behind us were in various states of smolder and thawing as the fire- and water-attuned of the group laid slumped on the ground. The healers had struggled to keep the oxen from bolting, but now that the pyrotechnics were over, they turned from their animal charges to the wounded.

"Report!" called Clara from atop of the Metier Crystal. A few of the people present uttered grumbles of protest as a way of marking their presence. Tec 2.0, already being called Wec by the trainees for his future post in Lake Weir, gave a more comprehensive report.

—Two and a half dozen death-attuned rodents due south. Primary life-attuned reptile threat neutralized. Five members of the expedition are unharmed, remaining members have injuries ranging from light to severe. Dreg Warrior Squad Leader Igor has sustained the most life threatening injuries.—

"Thanks, Wec. Healers! Rotating triage like we practiced!" The demoness slumped onto the crystal with a sigh, while the life-attuned trainees scurried about like ants. The less injured fighters took up a defensive circle around the carts.

"I'll..." Sam swayed into view from around the cart. "Check on Igor."

"Eye on your mana," I warned, squinting as he waved me off and headed to the squad of arcane boxers. I turned down to look at my still-locked legs and cast a diminutively powered version of <Mudpit>. The cast was more strenuous than any other before it, even the expenditure while fighting the chameleon and providing crowd control. I wasn't sure if it was because I was making the usually-thirty-foot-radius standard cast the size of my palm instead. Nevertheless, it worked and I pulled my legs out of the sucking mud with ease.

"Handy," a voice called from less than a foot away. I jumped clear onto the cart and turned to see Daniela smirking up at me.

"Gah, since when are you so dang sneaky?" *When* did *she get this sneaky? Neither my perception nor my vibration sense picked up on her at all.*

"Pays that I spend most of my time moving around like a dang shadow," she said, pointing over her shoulder to the tree-line. "I've been playing with <Heat Touch> and <Freeform> to mimic the haze wolf. It's not the best, but I think once I unlock the defensive imbue skill, I will have my foot in the door of being even harder to detect. Those googly eyed lizards gave me a few ideas."

"Glad to see you are one of the unscathed," Clara said, rolling her bloodshot eyes. If it hadn't been for her <Scorched Terror>, the fire augmented version of her <Fear>, the backline would have taken even more damage. Dog-sized rats and mice were not exactly pleasant combatants.

"We're going to have to keep a tighter circle. It took Devon and I way too long to make it back," Danny said, eyes dropping to the ground.

"I'm just kidding. We all pulled through," Clara said, putting her hand on Daniela's shoulder. "We should be less than a mile away."

—Approximately 4,902 feet.—

"Thanks Wec," Daniela said, rolling her eyes at the crystal. She checked to make sure I was actually fine instead of just ribbing me about it and went to meet up with tall and broody Devon. The elf smiled as she approached, and I couldn't help but notice the twitch at the corner of Daniela's mouth. As much as it pained me that she enjoyed the company of such an insufferable individual, I knew Devon was good people. If he didn't turn out to be for her, then he might find himself taking a mud bath he did *not* sign up for.

"Form up! We move out as soon as the healers give the clear!" Clara yelled, her voice cracking a bit at the end. She didn't necessarily need to do that since all the trainees had implants, but there was something about getting yelled at in person that really put a pep in your step. "We are almost at the first stop, and then we can hopefully call it a day."

Thankfully, the rest of the trip *didn't* take long. Only a pair of angry asphalt refined tortoises that ambled over to us, and then a small swarm of spiders. I wasn't entirely sure if the creatures had just moved into the area—not according to the New Hopers—or if the crystal was pulling from really far. The spiders were a long way from home. Unless there was another spider territory somewhere to the east, but that didn't warrant much more consideration with the pressing issues of the Dreg.

Nevertheless, we finally made it to the clearing around another car-reinforced defensive wall. A number of churned up fields surrounded the car wall and I could see a pair of trucks with tires that had somehow made it through the apocalypse only to be used as a makeshift gate. A number of people walked the length of the parapet that had been created atop the vehicles. When someone finally spotted the small horde of travelers, a shout for assistance went up. Clara took the lead, preparing to make introductions.

"Angel!" she yelled.

One of the men on the wall seemed to come to the realization that the people gathered were actually friendly people they knew. Angel, a bulky man in his thirties with the beard equivalent of Dylan's fire hair, dropped straight down the outside of the wall without bothering with the gate. The people behind him didn't look particularly thrilled about the development. Even from a distance, I could see them produce a number of pre-Fall bows and nock arrows. They weren't drawn, but I knew you didn't necessarily need that much time to shoot a compound or longbow. The fact they had them was the most surprising bit, considering how much Wildwood struggled to prototype their own. *Though I suppose we are trying to make them infused items instead of just standard tools*—

"Clarita! Friend, you don't know how happy I am to see you. When you said you were going to bring backup, I didn't quite expect this!" the man said, pulling the demoness into a rough hug. "And Mistress Liliana. Rommel and Devon, even? Why, Stonecrest is more than safe now!"

The hugger worked his way through the New Hopers until he reached me and my friends, pausing. I almost missed it, but his face hardened as he gave us a look that could have killed. A moment later, he left me wondering if I'd seen the expression at all. "New friends?"

"Yes, actually. These are the Bunker born we mentioned," she said, gesturing to each of us and introducing us. It was a bit awkward since the rest of the squads, who were busy keeping a good eye on all the surroundings instead of on the conversation, didn't get an introduction.

"Ah yes. The pot stirrers." The man's expression once again became strained, but he reached out his hand to shake with Danny and Sam. The two smiled politely and thanked the man for welcoming them to the town. When he got to me, I felt his grip tighten. "Pleasure to meet you, Mr. Ronan."

"Just Ronan, or Ron, is fine," I said, smiling and clamping down on his hand. He was able to hold off for a few seconds before breaking the too-long handshake. Clara was giving us a weird look, but Angel swept the conversation away.

"Please, come in. It's actually been nice to have a reprieve from the fighting. Not a single peep from the scouts today!"

"Actually, that is part of why we are here," Clara said.

The woman let Angel escort us to the edge of the gate, but we didn't actually head inside. However, through the gaps of the vehicles I was able to see that there was a secondary wall built not far from the cars. It was entirely made of stone. The magically created type, not some one-off section of pre-Fall architecture that had somehow survived. While I assessed every-thing around us, including the distinct amount of Q1 people intermingled with Q3s up on the wall, Clara broke down the plan. When she mentioned that the thing covered in vines and strapped to the wagon with the ant at the head was a hunk of a Metier Crystal, it got more looks than poor Anthony the pack ant did at first.

"Is that for us?" Angel asked, his breath caught in his throat. Clara had shared bits of knowledge with the towns, particularly some of the reasons why Wildwood was so much safer.

"No," I said. Based on Angel's expression, he did not appreciate me entering the conversation. "That is for Lake Weir. If they break, then your town will follow not long after."

Angel seemed to debate within himself for several seconds before coming to some kind of internal decision. He motioned inside with his head, turning without comment.

"Rommel, Samuel. Can you two make sure that we get a resting rotation, please?" Clara said, addressing some of the silent elements that had been in our group.

"It can be done," Rommel huffed. He was already walking away, keeping his meaty arms crossed across his chest.

"I've got to check on Igor again anyhow. You sure you guys will be alright?" Sam asked, looking more at me than at Clara. I could read his tone even without his expression changing. *Don't start a fight.*

"We'll be fiiine," I said, exaggerating while waving a hand in front of my face.

"True. Hardly the first time he's botched a first impression so hard and yet still got the people to help us," Daniela noted. Her smirk split her face as she followed after Rommel without giving me time to come up with a comeback.

"Stonecrest has a thing about power," Clara started. "They know about you and your friends. I wasn't the only one to blab about how much of a difference three little Bunker people made in Wildwood."

"Things have really gone downhill if you are reassuring me," I sighed.

"Not really, but I would say you should expect some…friction with the leader of Stonecrest," Clara said, letting out a sigh of her own.

"I simply cannot wait." There was enough sarcasm dripping off that statement that I was surprised Clara didn't think I started drooling.

"Come on, tough guy," she said. "We'll see how much you keep your cool when you meet the female version of Devon."

"Hey!"the elf in question called from all the way on the other side of the carts.

"That ought to teach you to snoop on people when you aren't scouting, *Devon*," Clara said at the same volume. Somehow she'd figured out the elf hadn't been able to stay out of the juicy, possibly contentious, conversation with Angel even after he was helping organize a watch. I had to fight to keep from busting out laughing.

With the discussion outside done, the two trucks at the front of the town rolled forward and we followed Angel in. Unlike the rough exterior the rusted cars gave the town, the almost seamless stretch of stone that was their inner wall was reminiscent of the time before the Fall. Just over the fifteen foot lip of the wall, I could see the outline of a large building. Angel led us down a well-worn path past the three-car deep wall and to a small opening that barely fit me through it.

A guard on the other side slid a wedge of almost the same shape as the door back into place to close the gap. *Interesting security measures*. Considering the town didn't contend with bordering water like Wildwood, it made sense that they would be able to keep out even small critters if they locked down their entire perimeter.

After going around a choke point formed by cars piled on their sides, I got to give Stonecrest a proper look.

Instead of the slapdash job done on the surviving houses of Wildwood, everything in Stonecrest was made from...well, stone. Several squat houses, thin windows included, flanked a main road from the entrance all the way to the large building we saw earlier. Like a giant billboard, *Stonecrest Walmart* stood emblazoned on the side of the building. Somehow the giant, gaudy lettering for the store itself had survived the end of the world. There was no power to the lights, but there was a fair bit of sprayed paint being used to make sure it remained visible along with the addition of the town name next to it.

As we walked towards the Walmart, I could see a population not dissimilar to Wildwood's. All the Attunements, sans the occasional demon, walking the streets intermingled with older pre-Fall humans. While not surprising since Clara had mentioned the level deficit that both Stonecrest and Lake Weir suffered from, it was a bit jarring to see the uneven spread of levels. Unlike the seemingly minimum of Q2 for the people of Wildwood, there were Q0s amidst the population of Stonecrest. The sheer difference all but confirmed that the Entity Cluster was playing a part in their growth.

I focused on one of the gawking children as we passed. They couldn't have been older than four or five.

<Human>

<Attunement: Mundane>

<Refinement: Mundane>

<Perceived Metier Quotient: Mundane>

Everyone but the children were attuned, but even the ones that appeared as mundane with the implant showed some early traits of their future attuned features. My evaluation of the people of Stonecrest didn't go unnoticed as Angel turned back to look at me.

"What are you staring at?" You couldn't call the man's tone anything but a growl, but the intensity behind his eyes as they met mine was something I recognized: care and concern.

So, instead of rising to meet the response he expected from me, I answered honestly. "I was getting an overview of the people of Stonecrest. Everyone seems healthy, if under-leveled, but considering how you've been faring, I'd say that is more than impressive."

Angel seemed to have the words caught in his throat, taken aback. Instead of figuring out a way of letting them out, he turned and picked up the pace. The power walk wasn't strenuous, especially when compared to the stress riddled hike to get to Stonecrest, but it didn't give me time to take in more of the town. Before long, we arrived at the wide open entry to the superstore, though no automatic doors opened and the greeter was armed with a rifle and a vicious-looking machete.

The guard pressed his fist to his chest and moved out of the way for Angel. I could practically feel the guard drill holes into my back as we passed rows and rows of varied supplies. Unfortunately, very little of it was food. Set up in rows were work-shops not dissimilar to the pavilions that had existed on Wildwood before the Dreg crow attacks. Now I could see them banging out panels of metal and running forges to cast who knew what.

We walked past those too, once again being ogled, before arriving at an inside training area. It didn't look anything like the one me and my friends had built next to the Bunker, or the one Sarah had slapped together in Wildwood. This was a box reinforced with countless shipping palettes of both wood and metal stacked up to the ceiling.

In the center of the strange training area was a woman, tall for a dwarf, with a martial-looking posture. If those old Kung Fu movies I watched were to be believed, it was a horse stance. In front of her were three preteens, two other dwarves and a merman. Each was holding a spell chain in the air between them as beads of sweat rolled down their heads.

The woman leading the training seemed to notice the company and she quickly dismissed the group. Her black hair hung long and her eyes felt like they would cut me if I stared at them too long. They only softened when they landed on Clara, before a scowl returned to her face as they landed on Angel.

"Well?" she said by way of introduction.

"Rachael Barron, leader of Stonecrest," Clara said, seeing that neither the dwarf nor ol' fire beard planned to introduce anyone. "This is Ronan Terrigan."

"Ah! The lauded *Vanguard*, is it?" Rachael teased.

"Suppose that's me," I said, shrugging at the strange atmosphere. *Definitely different than when I met with Sarah and the council of Wildwood.*

"I heard you had a proposition for me?" she said, smirking. *Elf whisper spies? How did she get the information so quickly?*

"Something like that. We were hoping to discuss some of the things going on with the—"

"Dreg. Yes, I've been informed. However, what I want to

know is why I shouldn't just take the crystal and keep it for myself," she said easily.

"Lady, I wouldn't try that if I was you," I said, suddenly *very* done with the whole political dance I'd kept up with since arriving at the town.

"How dare—"

"Now Rachael—"

Both Angel and Clara were cut off by the sound of clapping stone. The entire back wall of the training area had collapsed back to reveal a much more ample training field, this one marred by more than one rock feature I recognized as belonging to my or another dwarf's magical skill arsenal.

"I don't think you two understand the weight of the decisions I make. Until I can be sure of that, this *kid's* renown means nothing to me. If we want to agree to anything, he'll need to Gift Wrestle me impressed," Rachael said. She walked out of the room and into the outside with perfect confidence, even turning her back to us. Angel rushed after her and I could see a rapid fire exchange of information between them.

"This is going the worst case scenario route," Clara said, rubbing her temples right below her horns.

"Care to illuminate?" I said, my earlier frustration replaced with confusion.

"This is going to take a minute," she sighed, leading the way towards the outside training area. As much as I trusted Clara, I couldn't help but think things had gone in a completely wild direction. Most important of all…*What the heck is Gift Wrestling!?*

# CHAPTER TWENTY-SEVEN

## Gift Wrestling

"Okay, let's take it back a second," I said, now the one rubbing his temples. "This is a training, game, gambling thing for the other towns?"

"Yes," Clara responded.

"And you don't do this in Wildwood because…"

"Because Kirby convinced Councilman Dylan that it was a waste of time, even with evidence to the contrary. Part of the reason why me and the New Hopers were the cutting edge as far as Gifts was concerned was *because* of Gift Wrestling. We did more than our fair share of it while we traveled. Some kid named Carlisle figured it out when he was tinkering with his Gift and then it just sort of spread. Devon is particularly good, actually. It's how he got his lightning Gift, before what I assume was his transition to more air mobility skills."

There was a lot to unpack right there, but it made a sort of unfortunate sense. I could almost see Kirby coming up with some nonsense argument in order to kneecap the growing Wild Guard for the sake of relying on the Dreg Tendrils. However, as much as that was an issue I would have to address in my, and everyone's training, there was the current match up to deal with.

"So I just... what? Hold my spell chain against hers?" It wasn't something I'd done before, but I was starting to get excited to try it. While it was a bit bold of me to think it, I didn't believe the elites of Stonecrest could hold out against the implanted and equipped squads. So, humoring Rachel's power play while practicing a new ability was a two-birds-one-skill type situation.

"The trick is to try to get your Gift—skills in your case—to trigger while the other is interfering with it." When I gave her a weird look, Clara added. "Trust me, it will interfere."

Shrugging, we exited the superstore and joined Rachael and Angel where they stood waiting. Even from a distance, I could see the man speaking to her, but she remained unperturbed by whatever had him agitated. When we were less than ten feet from each other, she finally spoke again.

"He ready for this?" she said, addressing Clara and not even looking my way.

"Would it matter?" the demoness shot back, quirking an eyebrow. "He's a big boy. He can handle his own political engagements."

"It's like Daniela didn't stay behind," I grumbled under my breath before locking on to Rachael's emerald green eyes. They were striking. "I got a crash course."

For the first time in the conversation, Rachel looked a bit confused, but before I got a chance to clarify, she had her spell chain up. It took less than a second for a small spray of boulders to eject out of her hand in our direction. Even if I'd wanted to raise my shield to interpose it between the sudden attack, we were just too close. Thankfully, I had a silent but squishy protector close by.

A partial Blobby rolled out from behind a pillar. Its body glowed a deep brown as the rocks veered towards it, like a planet attracting meteors, instead of right into my exposed chest. The smaller rocks barely penetrated the slime, but one of the larger ones nicked his Metier Crystal core. The entire creature jiggled and softened, nearly losing cohesion entirely. Everyone present yelped in alarm as the attack going off actually registered.

To Rachael's relief, Clara interposed herself between us before I blasted her in the face with an empowered <Mineral Strike>. The attack would have also probably clipped Angel, so I would have counted it as a plus. As it was, Clara strained to counteract my strength as a growl escaped my lips. "What the hell was that?"

The town leader seemed taken aback by my reaction, actually taking a step back before Angel could intervene for her. "You didn't call your Gift, you idiot!"

"What? She barely had that spell chain out for a second before it blasted me!"

"Ronan, that's not unusual. Their abilities trigger that quickly," Clara said. It finally registered that she was bodily holding me back so I huffed, apologized to her, and refocused on Rachael.

I wasn't thrilled, some of the excitement of learning and practicing a new ability waning. Seeing she hadn't backed down, or apologized herself, I could practically hear her voice telling me she hadn't done anything wrong. At the very least, she seemed somewhat impressed with my reaction so that was a start.

"Are we good to go in three?" I asked, raising a twitching eyebrow in question.

"Best of three. As a courtesy, I won't count that one as my win to your inept performance," she said, evenly, but from the same spot she'd retreated to after my outburst.

"One," I said, hovering my mental hand over the button for my most practiced skill. My eyes narrowed on her as her information manifested in the edge of my vision.

<Rachael (Human)>
<Attunement: Earth>
<Refinement: N/A>

&lt;Perceived Metier Quotient: 4&gt;

"Two," Rachael said, and I could almost feel the energy coalescing around her. A strange warbling tingle crawled up my toes as she focused, but I didn't think about it much more as I slammed the trigger for &lt;Stone Spike&gt;.

"Three!"

The brown light of two very distinct spell chains formed between us. Hers was like a smooth rolling hill of beige, while mine was a stark umbra of glyphs. Instead of mine remaining tight around my wrist, it drifted in the air between the dwarf and I to clash against the opposing spell chain. An invisible edge formed along the spell chains as they tried to push into the space of the others.

The tight script seemed to throw Rachel off, but I saw her eyes squint in concentration. As for me, a plethora of strange sensational feedback rushed through my mind. It wasn't quite like &lt;Memory Canal&gt; triggering, but it was close. Instead of memories, it was like the connection was to a boulder trying to roll over me to crush me. My first reaction was to crash into the mental boulder and press all my energy against it. It certainly seemed to do the trick.

My spell chain nearly doubled in size and I was able to connect the sensation to when I empowered &lt;Stone Spike&gt; past its usual cost. Rachael gasped as the spell chain expanded, but she didn't back down. Her own swelled in size and I was wholly unprepared for the ease with which she matched then superseded my own at the drop of a hat. My band of glyphs cracked like a fragile piece of glass, the mana quickly turning into the brown elemental wisps we saw in Tec's Blessing of Magic, before dissipating completely. Her own spell chain triggered, empowered to almost triple its size, blasting the ground beneath us with her rock throw Gift. Dents ranging from palm-sized to beach balls appeared on the earth. None were aimed where I'd expected this time, and I had to admit that getting hit by that empowered bit of magic would have definitely hurt.

The world came into focus in a blur. My abdomen twitched

and I would have doubled over had I been new at the whole 'magical side effects' thing. Rachael herself was panting, but her eyes didn't leave mine as she held up her index finger. *One.*

Without waiting, and snarling at the prospect of the little show forcing us into a bad position for negotiating, I held up my hand again. Rachael grit her teeth and swatted Angel away when he tried to approach. "Got another round to win."

The count came much quicker this time, the both of us having gotten a hang for our start timing. Just like before, the spell chains formed and drifted towards one another. Instead of waiting for Rachael to do anything, I dumped half my mana into the spell chain in one go. It was something I'd never really paid attention to, but I watched as the glyphs became more defined the larger the band of mana grew. With my focus on the ring of mana, I almost missed Rachael's counter. Instead of making her ring bigger, she added *another* ring to the mix.

While sharing the same smooth waving pattern, this one was a bit closer to my own umber and instead of meeting my large band head on, struck it sideways. In my mind, the button for <Stone Spike> seemed to sink out of sight from the metaphorical table that I pressed when I used the skill. The combined onslaught of the head on and perpendicular rings was messing with the source of my magic somehow. Nevertheless, I'd invested enough in the spell chain that it ground away the smooth surface of the two rings. Even when some of the glyphs fractured like stained glass in the cold, the dwarf's poofed out of existence. The particles of mana hung in the air for a moment like a choking cloud of cement. I was sure I saw some of them drift towards my own spell chain before the skill triggered and terraformed the center of the training space.

A monstrosity of a <Stone Spike> materialized between the both of us even as I collapsed to the ground. The last thing my eyes saw before I shut them in protest of the pain was the ground heaving down before defying gravity to stab at the heavens. Nearly twenty feet tall and four feet in diameter. If I hadn't been gasping from the pain in my midsection, I would have been gasping in surprise. *So that's what empowered Q5 <Stone Spike> looks like?*

Clara was at my side in an instant, with an unsteady Blobby not far behind. They both prodded me, trying to make sure I was okay. I managed the weakest of replies. "S-side...e-e-effects..."

Several minutes later, when I didn't feel like my muscles were going to rip themselves just from existing, I finally laid eyes on the two Stonecrestians. Rachael was similarly coiled into herself on the other side, while Angel had a grimace on his face. He was passing his hand gently through her hair and I would have had to be an idiot not to notice the significance of that gesture. There was something more than a leader-assistant relationship there.

A few minutes after I was finally able to take in my surroundings, I rested heavily on my elbows until Clara helped me to my feet. She seemed concerned still, but a pained smile from me did the trick in getting her to let go. With some effort, I walked over to Rachael, who'd made it to a knee.

"Let's just say I don't think I want to waste more energy on another bout like that," I said, crouching down to her level. Angel moved to probably scream something in my face, but the dwarf pulled up a hand to wave him off. He didn't look pleased.

"I can... agree to a draw," she panted.

I couldn't help but smirk at the woman. Even if I'd won, it didn't escape me that it was because of my overwhelming advantage in mana pool. The other silent contributor was my Q5 level to her Q4; the qualitative change *had* to have some sort of effect on the actual wrestling part of the process. However, even with that, she'd won the first match and almost the second by having better manipulation of her Gifts. The easy excuse was that she'd had her whole life to train it up, but that didn't detract from the fact that she had more experience to offer.

"We want to work together. There is half a cart's worth of foodstuff that we brought for Stonecrest, and I don't think the healers of the squads would mind helping alleviate some of the food concerns." Just to make sure, I looked over my shoulder at Clara. The demoness nodded once, agreeing with my suggestion. "All I need to do is tell my friend that your people don't have a whole lot of farms and he's liable to turn your town from stone to tomatoes."

Rachael met my eyes with the same intensity despite still working to recover from her own side effects. She didn't answer right away, nor did she rebut the plan. One could almost see the wheels turning in her head.

"Very well. I assume this doesn't come for free, though?" she answered a minute later. "'Too good to be true' is no lie."

"That's a yes and no, Rachael," Clara said, stepping up beside me as the woman finally found her feet with help from a glaring Angel. "All we want the people of Stonecrest to do is join more closely with Wildwood. If you agree, then we would need you to become the first Dreg Warrior of the town for now."

"Dreg… Warrior?" she asked, tilting her head for the first time.

"What I am," I said by way of clarification. With no shame, I turned around and lifted my untrimmed hair off my nape. I hardly noticed it anymore, but the fingernail-sized blend of human technology and Metier Crystals that was the implant caught a glimmer in the sun as I ran my fingers over it. Both Rachael and Angel gasped at the sight, and when Clara matched the demonstration with her own Entity-created implant, the two were left just shy of speechless.

"How…?" Angel managed.

"As I know you are aware, I was born in one of the Bunkers built before the Fall. One of the people living in the Bunker developed this handy bit of technology to protect us from the radiation. Turns out, it let us interface with the Metier Crystals instead. At a certain size, they begin to acquire an intelligence of their own. That is what we hope to use to help defend Lake Weir as the front line of our fight with the antithesis of the crystals: the Dregs," I explained.

"And you want me to get one of those things?" Rachael asked skeptically.

"The benefits are immeasurable," Clara cut in. "Almost all of the squads have one now, and the only reason the rest of Wildwood doesn't have one is because the Entity Cluster is weakened by each one it provides. It was immensely weakened for us to be able to get the piece we are escorting to Lake Weir."

Revealing the fact that the Tec was not running at one hundred percent wasn't my favorite thing, but I could see where Clara was going with her argument. She wanted to pump up the value of what we were offering by showcasing that it was worth it even if it left Wildwood in a weaker position. While I was pretty sure Rachael had caught on to that, she didn't comment on it and instead nodded her head. The dwarf asked a few more questions about what the implant actually did, and when Clara mentioned the fact that it was capable of giving non-Gifted the ability to use skills, she practically pounced on it. Before I needed to explain the limitations of acquiring skills, Quotient, and everything else we'd discovered as fledgling Warriors, Clara smoothly filled Rachael in.

Angel, Blobby, and I were left to lag behind as the two of them spoke animatedly about how allying with Wildwood and the Bunker would bring unprecedented security and prosperity to Stonecrest. As much as I wanted to punch the fire-bearded man beside me for being a hard-headed individual, I couldn't necessarily blame them. If some random person I'd only heard about in passing came and offered to throw everything I knew on its head with a pseudo-takeover, I would have been suspicious too.

Thankfully, I had the best icebreaker to have the two of us start to work past our rough first impressions.

"For the record, I can't say I am a fan of the whole situation. However, if Rachael is okay with this, then I will try to be okay with it. *But*, before we go any further, can you tell me what the *heck* is going on with that living piece of green congealed animal fat?" Angel asked, pointing at Blobby's rolling form besides me. It had the audacity to form a finger-sized appendage to wave in our direction before resuming its roll.

"Let me tell you, I honestly have no idea," I said, letting out a chuckle.

Relief flowed through me, and even if it still felt like someone had taken my stomach for a punching bag, I was able to relax a bit on the walk towards the carts. Getting Rachael on board was a huge first step and after finding out about Gift Wrestling, I could only see our strength growing. All we needed to do was survive our ordeal against the Tendrils and the damn Corrupted Entity.

# CHAPTER TWENTY-EIGHT

## Fledgling Alliance

Getting Rachael the implant took less than half an hour. The process was a bit more involved than when Tec went all gung-ho on the Big Guns, since Wec *couldn't* really swallow her whole. Instead, to Angel's horror, it merely swallowed her head partway down to her chest. I had to bodily restrain the man as Rachael slid into the usually hard surface like a hot knife in butter. Less than twenty seconds later, she was back and blinking. Her eyes remained unfocused for several minutes after, but it was a familiar look; she was looking over her status and possibly the statuses of everyone around her.

From there, Clara and Angel took her to get acclimated and speak with the other influential figures of Stonecrest. The demoness insisted that they were more for management than actual leadership. When things needed a decision, the town came to Rachael, so our 'deal' was as good as secured.

I watched partial Blobby join up with its other half which had been watching over the expedition group. It was a notion I could definitely get behind, even if I rarely understood the slime —or even knew where it was, for that matter.

Daniela and Samuel finished off their conversations with the squads and moved to join me.

"Well? I can appreciate the whole light show, but where does that leave us?" Daniela said, cutting right to the point.

"Clara says we are good. Have one of the squads unload the town's rations and hunker down. I'm gonna need to borrow your healers, Sam," I said.

"Are there injured?" My friend's relaxed pose tensed, but I waved him down.

"No, everyone is fine. Well, Blobby took a hit, but I don't really know how it heals other than with food." I shook my head to get back on the right train of thought. "They are hurting in the food department. If we can build up and leave them with some of that infrastructure behind—"

"Then they might be able to build themselves back up," the blond finished for me. While I'd hoped to get him to relax, he seemed even more tense and eager to go after the clarification. "Point and shoot, Ron."

"Great. Get all but one healer to go with you and meet Clara by the gate in, say, ten minutes? I'll reach out to her since she is probably the one most likely to know who to talk to." Samuel hit me with a thumbs up and rushed off to talk to the squads. I didn't point out that he could have done it all in one single call from the comm-plant, but who was I to decide how he managed his people? And they were very much *his* people. The fae and satyr practically snapped to attention when he approached them, eager to please the strongest healer in the area just for one more minute of instruction or tips. It was an awkward situation, since Samuel was usually extremely flattered but also extremely nervous when he noticed the attention.

"You got a job for me too, rock brain?" Daniela asked, smirking in my direction while I let Clara know Sam was on his way to help with farming.

"Actually, I do. Only if you feel up to it," I replied, looking away like I didn't think she would be.

"Oy! Spill!" she said, breaking her smirk to turn me by the

shoulder. When she saw the grin I was trying to hide, she smacked me in the shoulder. The blow nearly took me off my unprepared feet, but I managed to stay standing. "Jerk. Do you even have anything for me?"

"I do, actually. I need you to start talking to the people of Stonecrest about clearing a road between Wildwood and them. You have some experience with that, and I am sure the town wouldn't mind a pathfinder like you helping out."

"Oh yeah? And what is our mighty leader going to be doing while Sam and I are out there doing the hard work?" she asked, her eyebrows rising in question.

"I'm going to find the town crafters. I don't have enough time to cook up another crafter's hall, but I think they could use a few people with infusion training. Don't you think?" I said, doing my best to hide my grimace.

"Wait, Ron," her voice softened. "That means—"

"Yep. <Memory Canal> is liable to take me on a fun nightmare trip later today. It doesn't matter, though. The town needs it, Wildwood needs the assistance, and *we* need the assistance. The more I keep learning about the surface, the more I realize how out of our depth we are with this whole thing."

"You said Bec didn't give you a solution, though," Daniela prodded. Her face was no longer set in jest, but in concern.

"Yes and no. If I can get better with the skill, then I should be able to control it better. Like what I did with... with Charles," I added. "I also can't ignore that this isn't likely to be the only time I need to extract information from someone. I can live with the nightmares, but not if it's because people lost their life due to my hesitation."

Daniela seemed taken aback by the edge in my voice. Honestly, I was a bit surprised too, but I didn't shy away from it. It was a realization I would have to come to terms with over and over, just to cope with it at the very least. After that engagement, she asked a few more questions about plans for the road before splitting off to do her own thing. There was no doubt in my mind that the first steps to a road between Stonecrest and

Wildwood would be taken before we started on the last stretch of our journey. The Latina hesitated at my side for a second, but quickly left.

"You have any idea where they build stuff around here?" I said, looking down at Blobby. To my utter surprise, the slime actually nodded with its appendages and started to roll back towards the car wall. My feet didn't move until the slime stopped to wave me back in the direction of the town. I sent Rommel a quick message through the comm-plant that he was in charge of the watch before following my unexpected tour guide into Stonecrest. It was almost to the point where keeping track of the questions I had about the slime was taxing, so I opted to just *roll* with it. The total lack of hesitation on the creature's part certainly helped as it guided me around the inside wall.

— + —

"Well, not what I was expecting, but still impressive," I said, watching a trio of dwarves shaping stone with their hands like it was clay. A few seconds after their hands lifted, the rock hardened. For several minutes, I watched the three work to shape several pieces of furniture. One of them seemed to specialize in stone-made household utensils, even. Eventually, they noticed my presence and practically jumped out of their roughspun aprons.

I waved, giving a small smile in greeting as one of them finally got the courage to approach me and my gelatinous companion. "Sir? Do you happen to come with the group from Wildwood?"

"That's right. We've just recently come into an agreement with Rachael to help your town," I said. "My name is Ronan."

"Pleasure. I'm Patrick Patrick," he said, shaking my hand in an equally rough one. *Don't comment on his name. Don't comment on his name.* "Yes, I am aware it is an odd name, sir."

I scratched the back of my head awkwardly. "I guess it showed on my face, huh?"

"Clear as day, sir. What can we do for you?" the man said, pushing past the faux pas seamlessly.

"Actually, I was hoping to help *you*." I rifled around in my cargo pockets until I plucked one of the death infusions we'd gotten from the rats and mice. "Are you familiar with these?"

"That's one of the beads the hunters collect, are they not?" the dwarf said, squinting at the Q2 infusion in my hand.

"Correct, but do you know what they do?" I asked, placing the infusion in his own palm while fishing out another.

"Not rightly. The hunters use them as trophies and some-times to barter, but never seen anything done with them, sir." The other two dwarves had long halted their own work and were now glancing from me to the infusion like I was ready to unlock some sort of secret for them. Which, if I was honest, was sort of exactly what I planned to do.

Without further explanation, I triggered <Infusion> and let the thread of Pith unspool. Unlike the fire, air and water infusions I was more familiar with, the death thread was more like a pulsing cord of purple-shifting black, like a monochrome oil slick. At the sight, the three dwarves simultaneously took a step back *and* craned their necks to try to get a closer look. It was an expression of wonder I was fairly familiar with, and was excited to share. As much as transferring miscellaneous skills and trig-gering <Memory Canal> sucked the big one, teaching and feeding off of other's curiosity was a big plus for me.

"Can I take this?" I asked, pointing to a rough stone cup inside a bin of scraps. I wasn't sure if their Gifts could even produce a failure, but judging from the amount, I was more inclined to think the town was recycling their stoneware. The three gave an eager nod.

The chipped mug was light in my hands. Making sure to set it on the ground since I didn't want to test what the death thread would do to my hands directly, I fed it the infusion. Veins of dark sludge flowed through the cup and it crumbled right before our eyes. When the last of the thread had entered the cup, there was nothing but the very base of it left.

I spent several minutes calming down the dwarves after seeing the display of magic. When I eventually managed to explain what had happened, their eagerness was back in full. Questions bombarded me, particularly about what would have happened if it had been different infusions or different materials. Unfortunately, as far as the death attunement was concerned, I wasn't an expert; I wasn't really an expert on any of them, but I shared what I knew about fire, air, and water, and the few earth and life infusions I'd completed.

After the general explanation, I showcased my H-shield, the naginata and my amplification helm. With each, I gave a bit of a primer on what an infused item was, how it differed from an infused material and how the materials dropped alongside the infusions themselves were the best components to be able to create one of these items in the first place. Following that, I broke down the implant and how it provided the information to accurately work with different materials and infusions. Through this, I made sure to emphasize that there could be catastrophic failures from infusing, showing a few of the burns I had on me as well as the pinprick scars from when that plastic insta-meal tray had exploded in my face what felt like a lifetime ago.

All this information had the three in a frenzy and I could feel their energy lifting my mood just by proximity. At one point, they almost ignored me entirely to ramble to each other about this theory or another they'd held but never confirmed. They were more than a bit dejected when I told them it would be a while before implants were commonplace, but that I *did* have something that could assist them in the meantime.

"I am able to pass on the Gift, or in this case skill, that lets me infuse. It's imperative that the rest of humanity get a hold of this if we are to keep surviving when a nearby cricket could try to kill us all," I said, finally broaching the subject that prompted our meeting. The two men and woman turned serious as I explained the process and that, even without the implant, they would be able to work on their manipulation of the threads of Pith. If I had more time in the future, I would try to give them more detailed instruction and demonstrations. Turned out they didn't need nearly that much convincing to let a stranger give them access to more magic.

The female dwarf put it the simplest way when I expressed my surprise. "You'd be dead if Rachael hadn't trusted you. Either by her hand, Angel's, or any of the other hunters. What you've shown us so far, it's no fiction. It's a key and we just need to put it to use."

After that, the engagement went much like the previous times I'd passed on a skill. Palm to the forehead, stay just shy of triggering the skill and let it work its way forward. For the woman and the other dwarf I got lucky; <Memory Canal> remained as dormant as ever, and I was starting to feel optimistic about the fact that tuning every fiber of my mind towards *not* triggering it would work right off the bat. Unfortunately, there was no such luck when it came to Patrick Patrick.

The world swirled as I caught the expression of a young lizardwoman. She'd not had her face elongated, or frills formed, but the extensive mesh of emerald scales was a dead giveaway. She was mine and I was hers. Her voice was a bit harsh, like all the lizard changed. Nonetheless, as she said my name in sing song, I couldn't help but smile. "Patrick Patrick, you are all kinds of sappy!"

"You say my name like that so much I might have to change it," I joked, squeezing her hand. The mirth in my voice fell as my mind brought up the part of the conversation we'd been dancing around all afternoon. "Do you have to?"

"Father says Lake Weir will be better for us," she whispered, not singing this time.

"They could go! You could stay here. Mr. Barron put me in charge of the Stoneshapers, and I could build us somewhere more comfortable. Somewhere away from your mother!"

"Patty, you know I can't do that. He needs me and I…"She

looked down at her clawed feet. "If you can, try to come find me, alright?"

"I—"

"Don't promise. I know you keep them, and I don't want to hold you to that. Please?"

"Y-yeah…" I said, face dropping. "Sure thing, Lydia."

"Good. That beard of yours isn't quite as dashing when you are pouting," she said, running her fingers through it. I let it happen and the two of us fell into silence as we watched the way pass, savoring the time we had together before everything got tossed on its head.

I blinked to feel Patrick poking me in the ribs. "I think I got it, sir."

"Right, sorry. Sometimes the energy transfer distracts me," I said, blundering through an apology as I retracted my sweaty palm from his forehead. *Yet another story of heartbreak. Yet another separated from the one they love.* Perhaps if the glimpses of the people <Memory Canal> deemed to show me didn't echo my own loss so much, they would be easier to digest. *What does that say about me?*

Considering I had a small audience, I pushed those thoughts to the side and gave the three dwarves another run through of their new skill. They picked it up marvelously, running me out of infusions testing on their broken bits of tableware. One of them even managed *not* to turn the whole thing into a pile of dust, but when I checked, the plate said there was insufficient Pith. Explaining this, and watching the purple-veined piece of stone somewhat warily, I left the group to their own devices. Time had passed unbidden and when I finally looked up at the sky, it was nearing sunset. While my impact was limited, I hoped that the group, who thanks to my unwilling invasion of Patrick's memories I knew was the aptly named Stoneshapers, would be able to give the whole of Stonecrest a leg up.

The rest of the evening went by in a flash. I returned to the rough camp set up outside of Stonecrest. The carts were arranged in a semicircle with the car wall at the back of it. The guards of the town still patrolled up on the crushed vehicles and when I inquired as to any attacks, Rommel told me only a few spiders and two more Q3 lizards. The combined force of the squads stomped it down before the guards could even shoot an arrow. By his assessment, it went a long way to gaining their trust.

The lizards were eaten, instead of dissociated, in the hopes of preserving resources while the healers still worked the inner fields. Just as we were settling in for a lizard stew, courtesy of Daniela's fine culinary skills, said healers wobbled back to camp. The last remaining healer, a satyr woman named Diana, rushed over, thinking they were injured in some way. When the slurred calls for food and sleep came, I knew that Samuel had just worked the group to the bone instead.

There was a little merrymaking around the bonfire. Nothing crazy, but the spirits of the trainees were definitely lifted. Many had never even left Wildwood, and seeing another human town seemed to fulfill some social part of their nature their situation back home had locked away. With my back to Wec's cart and facing out towards the woods, I kept watch along with Devon. One of the squads was always ready to respond while the others were in various states of rest.

And so the night went, with us rotating with Clara and Daniela before rising for the day. It was time to do the final trek to Lake Weir.

# CHAPTER TWENTY-NINE

## Masterful Diplomacy

As it turned out, just leaving wasn't really an option. The moment the expedition started to pack up, the guards went and snitched on us. Rachael, trailed by Angel and the rest of her advisory team, rushed out to formally bid us goodbye.

"You have given us much to think about and much to do," she led with. In her hand was the purple-veined plate one of the Stoneshapers had infused the day before. "You didn't think they wouldn't let me know what you gave them, right?"

"Honestly, I was hoping they would. Just *after* we'd left," I said, shrugging. My friends and Clara were sighing and rubbing their foreheads at the exchange. "We aren't here to be recognized."

"Hmmm. I may just come to not regret trusting you lot," the dwarf woman said, crossing her arms.

"We aim to please," I said, smirking.

While I wasn't a fan of the welcome we'd had in Stonecrest, I'd come to realize I preferred it to the politics I had to skirt in Wildwood. Rachael restated her support for us in front of her staff, and gave a brief update on their resources. They now had enough food to actually turn towards levels at least briefly, and their chief healer, a girl barely in her teens, said they would be able to keep up some of the farms boosted after being shown how by Samuel. It was impressive how much difference cooperating could make, even in just one day.

After some more pleasantries, we finally managed to peel away and rejoin the expedition. The group didn't hesitate to start back up, heading through the woods towards US 441. The road would help speed up our progress north, even if it left us a bit exposed.

Along the way, we passed many more buildings than around Wildwood. While most of the ones in the town proper had been homes that suffered the worst from the elements and enhanced growth of plant and animal life, their few stone block built stores and offices had endured the apocalypse admirably. In contrast, the ones just off Stonecrest looked to be either intact but overgrown, or turned to rubble. As soon as we made it to the old state road, we could see the evidence of countless battles all around the area. Trees turned nursing logs, segments of asphalt churned up like jelly, and scorch marks all up and down the buildings and older trees. In order to make single file progress, I was actually required to liquify the road several times with <Mudpit> before the mess of destruction let our carts through. It was during one of these stops that our expedition was attacked.

A maw of fangs snapped from the edge of the treeline. Like an uncoiled rope, a snake the length of a semi-truck chomped down to nearly encase one of the oxen whole. The fae trainee screamed in alarm as a palm-sized eyeball narrowed on the further prey.

My implant highlighted the creature as it retracted, hauling the oxen back with ease. The vine tack holding it to the cart snapped as our supplies spilled to the ground.

<Cottonmouth Snake>

<Attunement: Death>

<Refinement: Venom>

<Perceived Metier Quotient: 4>

"Form up! Healers, back up!" I said, raising two half-powered <Earth Walls> as I moved to the gap between them. Igor, the one-armed orc, and Rommel were at my side in a moment. Igor now sported one of the tanker armors, additional binding preventing it from slipping where his stump was.

"Venomous," Igor hissed, scanning the treeline. My senses strained to pick up anything, but I swore I could feel a gentle, consistent rumble flowing through the soles of my feet.

"It's flanking!" Devon called through the comm-plant. Sure enough, an oblong blip on my minimap showed where the elf scout had spotted the death snake from his perch on a tree. At the same time, the creature seemed to notice its observer because it snapped towards Devon even faster than it had done for the ox.

Had Devon not been the fastest person in the expedition, I was sure he would have been swallowed. As it were, the snake got a mouthful of lightning and bark for its trouble.

"Hit it at range!" Clara called over my shoulder.

A spray of magic from all the attunements fell over the area where the snake had snapped at Devon. Igor looked to want to rush out there and add his melee-ranged Gifts and skills, but Rommel kept a firm grip on the man.

To the surprise of everyone, the snake slithered away. Patches of scales were gone, smoldering, or cracked. One of its eyes bled purple, almost black, ichor down to the ground as it reared back. Its tongue flicked and its whole body tensed.

<Earth Wall>!

I reacted fast enough to throw up another wall on the side the creature attacked from. It was a testament to its strength that it toppled my unsupported wall and nearly snapped up one of the trainees. Thankfully, crashing head first into a rock wall left it stunned, because the trainees had enough time to backpedal and rain down retribution on it.

A particularly nasty ice facsimile of my <Stone Spike> put an end to the creature. When the snake tried to bite down again, it killed itself with the worst brain freeze to date. A collective sigh left all of us. The trainees that had been raining skills on the snake slumped to the ground in various states of mana deprivation. Thankfully, it didn't seem like any of them had pushed themselves too far. Rommel walked around all the down trainees with ease before laying his hand on the snake. Fire seemed to flow out from under the creature's scales before the entire thing got consumed by them. As the corpse turned to ash, Pith split off and raced towards each of the expedition members.

I did notice a few of the trainees jump back up almost immediately, and when I looked at their information, it showed them now at Q4. *Must have pushed them over the edge then.* Clara sent Daniela and Devon back out to scout and actively shake up the area, just in case anything else was lurking in hiding. While the Q4 creature wasn't necessarily hard for a group our size to deal with, especially alone, ambush predators like it put us at a distinct disadvantage of losing people. Considering how close we were to our objective, stealth could take a back seat for the moment.

When Devon gave the all clear, and even mentioned he could already see the walls of Lake Weir, the group rushed back into formation. Whatever goods could be salvaged from the damaged cart were moved to the other, half-loaded one before being passed to the rucksacks and roughspun bags all the trainees carried. I heard Samuel grumble the rest of the way, both about the dead ox and the broken cart. At the very least, he hadn't named the two beasts of burden, so he was only moderately affected.

The group veered slightly right towards a much more worn street and everyone felt the anticipation climb when Clara verified we were close. Less than twenty minutes later, a pockmarked mess of structures and defenses greeted them. Everyone faltered a step, unsure of what to make of the many craters of smoldering bile, the large cracks running up and down the length of a wall made of both cars and magically formed stone, and the dozens of dead crows arrayed around them.

"Hail!" a voice broke the expedition out of their reverie. As soon as everyone's perceptions picked up on the defenders, blue- and gray-colored blips manifested in my minimap. The hailing voice in question was Dennis, the satyr looking much the worse for wear as his fur was matted and caked with blood. Some patches were missing altogether, or in various states of regrowth that spoke of healed burn injuries.

The group redoubled their efforts to reach the town with no discernible gate and I released my mana without abandon to liquify a smooth-ish path through the bird death zone. The closer we got to the wall, the *less* pleasant the smell got.

"How's everyone?" Samuel asked before we'd even made it to the wall.

"All injuries are dealt with, but we are wearing a bit thin," the satyr said as he lowered a ladder over the side of the wall. I gave the field a quick look before pulling another breaching ramp out of the ground with <Earth Wall>. Dennis sort of just stood there in shock, as did the two recently inducted trainees with him, and the people I didn't recognize that surely belonged to the town of Lake Weir. He eventually had the sense to panic. "They will break through! Why would you put that there!?"

"Dennis, he can take it down," Clara said as she reached the top of the wall. She placed a calming hand on the man's shoulder and I could see tears welling up in his eyes as his whole body shook. He threw his arms around Clara and clung on like a man drowning. The demoness clearly wasn't expecting the response and a glance over at the other New Hopers told me this was clearly not common behavior.

*They are holding on by a string...*

"Hustle up!" I called, snapping the group out of the strange trance the reunion had put them in. "I want one squad swapping out with these folk right now. Healers, I want to see some greenery by the time I come back over this wall. The rest of you are going into town and making yourselves useful."

The expedition hopped to it. I didn't miss the hard set faces as they looked at the haggard defenders, before youths escorted them down the opposite side of the wall. When my mana was recovered enough, I snapped another wall down towards the ground on the other side of the wall for the carts. That was when I finally took in the town of Lake Weir.

Similarly to Stonecrest, the town was built around a large building towards the center. Various hodgepodge buildings lined a main road off to our left that cut through them to get to the larger structure. Between the walls and the main building was a sprawling field of moderately successful farmland. By the look of the oblong path around the farmland, and the two posts with hanging garbs, I was fairly sure they'd built their farm on a sports field of some kind.

People milled about, a few tending to segmented fields and domestic animals confined to pens. Following the rows of fields, I finally noticed two squat watchtowers facing east and west atop the larger building. Unlike the building, those were made of rough wood and even rougher metal, but held one person each.

It was an impressive layout, if almost every surface wasn't pockmarked by the corrosive bile of the crows. A pair of lizard-folk were using a firehose-like Gift to wash the acrid substance off one of the nearby buildings, working with tired efficiency. Through their efforts, I noticed one of the buildings close to our section of wall looked almost intact, and I realized it was definitely magically made.

"The west barrack," Dennis added, spotting my gaze. "Godfrey took a page from your book and built that with help of the town's other earth-attuned. Boy, are we glad he did or we would have lost the town already…"

"We're here, Dennis," I said, adding my reassurance to Clara's. The satyr gave me a tight-lipped smile before rejoining his squad leader.

The moment the Anthony-led cart crossed the threshold of the mismatched wall, Wec perked up . "Living status: 176. Injured: 11. Current skill-wielding individuals excluding Wec installation expedition: 32."

"Is that what I think it is?"one of the trainees that had stayed behind asked.

"If what you think it is is a shard of the thing that's been keeping your town safe for a long while, then yes. It is a Metier Crystal. More colloquially referred to as Wec, the Weir Entity Crystal," I said, projecting my voice out over the other guards who still eyed the cart suspiciously.

"It has a name?" the same trainee asked, tilting her head. I wasn't sure if it was in confusion or exhaustion based on how smudged and worn her... everything was, along with everyone else.

"Yes, I have been given a designation," Wec stated.

"Right, it can talk..." the trainee whispered, trailing off. She turned on the spot and walked toward her spot on the wall. "I'm good. You all deal with the talking rock please. Come get me if more birds show up."

The entire group stopped to watch the orc walk all the way back before plopping into a seated position, eyes facing out towards the wilderness. When the shock seemed to remain on *just* the Lake Weir natives, we resumed following Dennis. It was a short walk, really, from the main road to the large building, but I quickly realized it was more like three tightly spaced long buildings. A faded sign read *Lake Weir Middle School* on one of the buildings, solidifying my earlier theory for the farmland.

As we got closer, I also spotted markings on the face of each of the buildings: a large spray painted fork and knife, a bed, and a book with a hammer. The intentions of the symbols were clear, and Dennis led us to the building with the book and hammer. Immediately, a sight that would have left Dai quivering in his scales greeted us. Thousands of books lined dozens of bookshelves and they looked to still be categorized somewhat properly, if George Washington was still in the history section and the *Eragon* books were in the fantasy section.

An elderly woman fussed at a pair of kids as they argued over a book, but before long they noticed the presence of our armored group. Samuel and Daniela had once again remained with Wec in the center of town outside of the building, leaving me in the very capable hands of the New Hopers.

"Ian and Maurice are back in the furnace room. They are trying to test if different alloys will work better against the bile spit than what the town currently has. Honestly, I say it is just a way of working out their frustrations, since they know as well as we do that the mana formed or infused materials are what make a difference," Dennis said, shrugging one shoulder.

"Have we… lost anyone else, Dennis?" Clara asked, voice shaking for the first time on the trip.

"No, not since Pauly," the satyr sighed heavily. "The town is running low on manpower, even if they are bigger than Stonecrest. Are you sure this will work?"

"Not entirely, but it will at the very least provide some reprieve and options to advance for the implanted. Also, considering we are fighting Dreg Tendrils, I am surprised I haven't seen any afflicted," I said.

"Those eleven injured the crystal mentioned… well, there are exactly eleven people that have been afflicted since we started getting attacked," Dennis answered quietly.

*They are really struggling.*

"What happened to them?" I asked, concerned. The trainees hadn't woken up yet, and it wasn't that I wanted the people of Lake Weir to be test dummies for Dreg poisoning, but any bit of information would be invaluable.

"They are mostly catatonic and their bodies are in various states of… well, of change. It seems to be a bit more uniform for them than the trainees were when we pulled them from that ritual, though. At least they can be directed. Otherwise, I don't think we would be able to tend to them like Tec is helping with the others," Dennis said, leading the group down another hallway lined with classrooms. Each had a small peep window and I spotted several people working on clothes and a handful of woodcrafts. Most looked to have been converted into bedrooms, however. Before long, a slight ringing reached our ears. It was steady and growing louder the further we went down the dimly lit hallway.

"Do you think these two will agree to our help?" I asked, already preparing myself for another political back and forth. With the frequency that had happened since I came to the surface, I was sure I would one day return home and be greeted by political meetings in my dreams even with <Memory Canal> muddling *those* up.

"Ian will grumble, and Maurice will put up a fuss, but they will agree fast enough. Which is for the best; I want to help replace those on watch," Clara said, voice sharp. Dennis seemed to agree.

Less than a minute later, we walked into what had to have been an old storage or loading room. Dennis held the double doors open as I followed Clara inside, ducking my antler helm to avoid hitting some cables dangling from the ceiling. The heat immediately picked up, and the source of the clanging was evident. Two men, one significantly older than the other, were holding a metal plate on an anvil. The younger one struck with steady precision, throwing up sparks to illuminate a myriad of thorn brambles lining his head instead of hair.

The three of us remained by the door as the pair worked the metal, partly to be respectful and partly because they were making an impressive display of coordination. Even the occasional peeks I gave the smiths of Wildwood, sans Arnold himself, looked rudimentary by comparison. The two men could go toe to toe in the metal flexing department. When the metal in their hands cooled enough that they had to put it back in the furnace, they noticed our presence. They didn't appear surprised, so perhaps they *had* known we were watching them.

"Ms. Clara. You are a sight for sore eyes," the older gentleman said, approaching and taking the demoness' hands. To my utter surprise, I realized that beneath the gloves he wore, the smith was nothing but animated bones. His eyes looked sunken beneath a shag of salt and pepper hair, unnaturally so.

He very obviously caught me staring. "Yes, and you must be the Vanguard, Ronan Terrigan."

"Yes, sir," I replied, stretching out my hand in greeting. Instead of him shaking it, his son stepped forward so much in my face that the information snapped to the corner of my vision.

<Maurice Clark(Human)>

<Attunement: Life>

<Refinement: Hardy>

<Perceived Metier Quotient: 4>

"That's *Mr. Clark* to you, outsider," he led with. It really took all I had not to deck the man, hardy refinement or not. I was getting just a little tired of being confronted each time I met a person.

"Maurice, please, don't embarrass us. You know your hands are made for working, not for fighting. You can hardly look this young man in the eye and, if I had to take a guess, he might be twice as wide as you!"the old man said, followed by a raspy chuckle. "My name is Ian. What that crass mop of vines was trying to avoid was you noticing that I am not quite all there, anymore."

To really make his point, Ian removed his work gloves to reveal that, in fact, his hands *were* skeletal. Everything from just before the wrist was a crisp white interwoven by purple veins that seemed to be what kept it all together and gave him movement. His toes wiggled under his rough work boots. "Feet are looking a bit famished too."

"Can't say it's *not* my first time seeing a skeleton trait, but I also can't say it's the strangest thing I've seen. One of my friends can breathe fire, and the other can more or less talk to animals, so…" I said, shrugging and feeling my frustration ebb away. The old man had spunk, and the kind that I could get behind.

"Heh, I like this one, Maury," Ian said, pointing a thumb at me while looking at his son over his shoulder.

"Yes, yes. I suppose if you aren't shaken by traveling from

Wildwood all the way here, then we aren't going to do any better on short notice," Maurice said, rubbing at his temples. As if the strange welcome hadn't happened, the plant-haired individual reached out to shake my hand. "We really appreciate the back up. Most of the town has been running ragged since Summerfield bit it."

"About that, we are hoping to do more than just back you guys up," I said, causing both men to quirk up an eyebrow simultaneously. *Nope. You aren't jealous of their relationship. Nope. You and Dale have something similar.*

"Is he holding back for suspense?" Maurice asked Clara when I didn't follow up with an explanation right away.

"It would be best if you just follow us back outside," the demoness sighed.

I finally snapped out of my thoughts and moved out of the way so Clara could lead the way back out. When I turned to look for Dennis, the goat man had actually taken a seat and just straight up knocked out. It was uncomfortably hot in the forge, even with the large bay door opened, and the man was covered in fur, so I tried to stir him up. All that earned me were some weak slaps to the face. I removed my helm and attached it to my belt. Then I tossed the man over my shoulder with ease before rejoining the group waiting in the hallway. They gave me weird looks as I ducked to avoid my charge smacking his head.

"What? Don't want him to get heat stroke or something," I said, mentally shrugging but not doing so for the satyr's sake. Clara chuckled and something seemed to glimmer in the eyes of the Clarks, but they said nothing. Without further delay, we retraced our steps back through the wonderful library and out into the much cooler outside.

# CHAPTER THIRTY

## Chomping at the Bits

"You... brought us a piece of your crystal?" Ian asked, stuttering at the end.

While we'd been inside negotiating, the blond had retracted most of the bindings on the crystal that were obscuring it. As such, when our group returned to the outside and the Weirdians started to gape at the Entity, I took the opportunity to deposit Dennis on top of the cart with supplies. Rommel spotted the weary man, and stayed by his side just in case he decided to wake up and roll off the cart for some reason.

"That's the short of it," I said, finally moving to slap a hand on the crystal. "This is Wec. Currently we've been dealing with some beast issues while it is in transit, but once it is settled into the town, it should be able to give almost all the benefits of Wildwood. Plus it will grow stronger over time, but that will require more of a detailed explanation."

"But...Wait. How did you...? The distance? The creatures?" Ian seemed to be struggling with words, but Maurice stepped in. He placed a firm hand on his father's shoulder before stepping forward.

"Dennis and Godfrey got me up to speed with the whole

'skill' situation. I may not be a fighter, but there isn't a damn thing that happens in this town without me hearing it. People getting juiced up on Gifts is not hard to cause a stir in the gossip train in town," the man said, pointing to the snoring satyr and far over his shoulder as if to indicate that was where Godfrey was. After a quick check of my minimap, my suspicions were confirmed, but I focused back on the conversation.

"Great, then this will make things easier. We want you to receive one of the implants for the sake of communicating and starting to acclimate people, Ian. We aren't at the level of making them widespread, but the more they become familiar, the faster the transition can be and the stronger the town grows for it."

"Me?" Ian asked in surprise. "I'm just an old man too stubborn to keep his head out of people's business. You'll have to make do with Maury."

"Uh," I said with a bit of uncertainty. It wasn't that that didn't sound like the right idea, but Clara had explained that Ian was the leader of Lake Weir. Not giving the leader the implant would present some possibly awkward optics to the future of the Dreg Warriors.

"Son, I can read you like a book," Ian said, shaking his head and leveling his gaze at me. "You don't worry yourself none about this town while the Clarks still breathe. My daddy and his daddy ran around in this dirt, and now it's my son's turn to run around in this dirt."

"Maybe I can just walk? Running doesn't serve much purpose if you aren't going anywhere," Maurice said, looking sidelong at his father.

"Now, am I going to have to whoop your butt? You know damn well what I was talking about, Maurice!" The bony-handed old man wagged a fleshless finger in his face.

"To clarify, Ian is the leader of the town, but Maurice has been running it the last few years that his father has been getting up there in age," Clara said, unperturbed by the antics before us.

"She's always business, isn't she?" Maurice said, turning to his father.

"You'd do well to take a page from her book from time to time." The old man whacked his son in the back of the head, hard enough to send him reeling, but not to the ground. The group let out a chuckle before Ian zeroed back in on me. "Clara, and by extension, you fine folk have our full support. Already your presence is making a difference, and all you've done is give the people a spectacle."

"I also made a giant ramp over your wall," I said, causing the eyes of the two men to widen. "But I'll fix it, no problem."

Once Clara was able to get them calmed down enough, she explained the process for the implant and formally introduced Wec, who practically gave the two men heart attacks when it spoke. Maurice got the spiel on the benefits of the implant, even for a pre-Fall person, and a promise of a brief orientation at the hands of Clara once the process was complete.

In went the thorny head, and out came a new Dreg Warrior. It was a little frightening how quick the process was becoming. *Considering all that time Alan spent in research down in the Bunker, I suppose I can't complain about it being replicated by our sapient alien rock friends.*

"I have triangulated a position optimal for future and current access," Wec said when Maurice was off with Clara. Ian lingered curiously as I spoke with the 'IT magic department.'

"Isn't your influence going to be too small at this category? How are you going to cover the whole town?" I asked.

"I will be able to cover the north, north-northwest and north-northeast areas of the town. By my calculations, if I am able to absorb the current Dreg of the hunters, I should be able to expand to cover a bit further south as well."

"Very well. Ian, any objections to placing down the crystal… wherever it is it says it's a good spot?" I worried his head would come off with how fast the old man shook it.

"Whatever you need. We've been dealing with any number

of issues thanks to the waves, but having a Metier Crystal to help is an amazing improvement. If it wants to go on top of the school, I'll carry it up the stairs myself!"

"Unnecessary. Between the dormitory and academic building will suffice," Wec said simply.

Without further delay, Anthony plodded towards the designated spot. As infinite as the poor ant's stamina seemed, I could practically see its relief when Samuel released it from its bindings. Like a dog getting comfortable, it spun in a circle before flopping to the ground. We all stood by, petting the creature, as Wec lifted itself off the cart. If moving the crystal, implanting Maurice, and just generally throwing the town into disorder hadn't brought a crowd, the walking Entity Cluster certainly did.

Just like Bec had done many months ago, Wec turned into a crystalline spider to clamber right onto a wide crack in the concrete between the two buildings. Instead of remaining in its hexagonal prism shape, the crystal solidified its limbs to form a hollow pyramid-like shape with a thick section of the iridescent crystal running up the center. We held our breath collectively as Wec reshaped itself slowly. When the last of its body stopped moving, a familiar membrane of pressure enveloped me. Its influence was set.

The moment, however, was quickly broken.

"Hmm. It appears there are a number of creatures flanking to the east," Wec remarked. "Two appear to be of sufficient Quotient to ignore my influence and push the rest towards the town."

"What!?" Ian yelled alarmed. "There was already an attack earlier today."

The man wasn't a fighter, so I took the initiative with the information. "Wec, keep me posted. Current time frame?"

"Current speed suggests one minute, fifty three seconds... fifty two secon—"

"Got it." I cut off the Entity before it could literally count aloud to our demise. Instead, I pulled up my comm-plant and screamed the announcement wide. "Full scale attack on the east side. Retain a single implantee for communication on the west wall. Wild Guard, *move out!*"

The stomp of feet, the flash of a few movement skills, and over a dozen bodies hurling towards the east marked the start of the battle. I snapped my helm back over my head and checked that my friends were ready. Sam's femur club was held loosely in his palm, and Daniela was twirling her daggers, having mounted a suddenly-spry Anthony. "Go ahead, I'll pull up the rear!"

The two didn't even turn as they flashed towards the wall. Sam clambered onto Anthony behind Daniela and I just barely saw his decentralized nervous system connect to the ant's thorax.

"What do you need from me?" Ian asked. His voice was steady, the sign of his initial surprise vanished for practiced efficiency.

"We aren't going to run the town, or take over anything. All we want is for humanity to crawl out of the mud the Fall threw us back into. Strengthen your people, and we'll deal with breaking the waves that crash against the walls," I said, cracking my knuckles before jogging in the opposite direction of my friends. If we were going to be fighting, we couldn't leave an easy in like an <Earth Wall> ramp at our back.

— + —

"Three days... How are there even things for us to kill still!?" Daniela whispered from her slumped position on the wall.

"Feels like a month," Sam followed up.

"Not as bad as that time we found that old shooter game in Teach's terminal," I said, wiping the latest spray of blood off my face.

Even removed, there was an uncomfortable tingling as the crow Tendril's blood tried to burn through me. *Thank the Entities for Limestone Skin.* Not everyone was quite as lucky. The healers moved deliberately from person to person, running glowing hands over wounds, strapping bandages made from leaves that sped up healing, and one even lanced an eerie blood-red light right into people to heal their injuries.

For his part, Samuel was just a wet noodle, except for his eyes. With each twitch of his eyes, a finger-thin vine wrapped around an ankle or wrist before healing energy pulsed into the person. He focused his efforts on the tankers, whose injuries were most severe *and* whose physical stamina was most depleted. It had been almost a day since the tankers received the <Over-healed> affliction, which was followed by the <Physical Exhaustion> one not long after. It was a dangerous place to be in, since it had led to further injuries, but it was a necessity.

The only saving grace for the lower-leveled people was the reprieves level ups gave them. Considering the fervor with which the Tendrils and their trains of monsters had been assaulting Lake Weir, I was fairly sure it was the only reason we hadn't caved. Nevertheless, the fighting was taking its toll. A slight message popped up in the periphery of my vision and I let my eyes drift over towards it. Even with the comm-plant, written messages were the purview of the Entities.

—Influence stabilized.—

—Full effect of dissuasion field is in effect.—

"Can I get the layman translation, Wec?" I sighed, directing my thoughts via my comm-plant at the Entity. This still drew the attention of my friends, since I'd opted to say the question out loud.

—Creature attraction field has been removed.—

—Remaining incursions should contain only the members of the Tendrils.—

"No more beast trains, then… About time."

"Good news?" Sam asked, quirking an eyebrow without actually turning his head.

"Seems Wec has made himself cozy enough to push out all these weaker creatures," I explained.

"Heck yes!" Daniela shouted, thumping the ground with her fist and getting an annoyed chit from Anthony, who was laying down beside her. "Sorry, buddy."

"I'm just glad the bulk is over for now. I think I've had my arm broken at least three times since we started this whole endeavor," I groaned, flexing the fingers on my left hand.

Thanks to the stream of vile crows, even those at Q0 and Q1 that seemed to flock the town, my H-shield had been taking a heavy toll. When another gaggle of anoles and chameleons rushed up from the southeast, I had attempted to pull the same tongue-sticking move from our first encounter, only for the whole thing to explode into scorching hot chitin shrapnel. Had I not been covered in <Earth Shell>, the item's critical failure would have left me worse off than the chameleon that attacked me. Thankfully, the explosion did enough of a number on the creature by cauterizing its tongue *very* painfully. That gave me the chance to close the distance with an X of <Stone Spikes>.

Less fortunate was my need to rely on <Earth Shell> to cover the huge gap in defense my shield filled. Lacking a medieval defense trainer, I had probably been using my shield poorly. Even with that being the case, I'd developed an effective system of countering and charging that fit well with the force dispersal trait. When I was trying to disperse the force with a quarter-inch-thick stone plate, the whole effort was a whole lot more jarring. No matter how much mana I empowered <Earth Shell> with, the skill only formed *faster* instead of *thicker*. When I finally took the time to amplify it using my helm, the skill had the audacity to only thicken another quarter inch, but instead get passed on to one of my nearby allies. <Rock Cocoons>, the skill had changed to. While that addition had been a game changer for reducing the damage the frontline tanks and I received, it didn't solve the issue and habit I had of blocking with my left arm.

It was during those rambling, exhausted thoughts that every hair on my body jumped to attention. Without even needing to look around, my eyes and the eyes of every defender in Lake

Weir spotted the black shadow enshrouded in purple that flew far in the distance. The Appendage made a slow, arcing pass before heading back northwest. Back towards where the Corrupted Entity had gone and where the death zone was.

*There is still work to be done.*

"Why is it taunting us like that?" Samuel asked, finally gathering enough strength to rise to his feet with a hand from one of his own <Vine Whips>.

"I think it knows it can't take us alone," Daniela answered. "It's not the first time it's passed us by, remember?"

"Yes, how could I forget it?" Sam said, shuddering. "That makes it five since we saw it over Wildwood."

"It's smart, or at least whoever directs it is. This means that it is scouting us out and these attacks are either meant to probe our strength or wear us out," I said, sighing.

"I don't think I like either of those options, Ron," Sam said, helping Danny to her feet.

All I could do was nod my head as I ran through a few plans in my head. With Wec stabilized, we would have to move the developments of the towns into high gear—at the very least Stonecrest and Wildwood. If Lake Weir remained the battleground, I didn't think the town would be able to make many strides outside of subsisting. I didn't want to leave the town hanging, but if we didn't build up the rest of our resources, then all three towns would fall like Summerfield.

"Danny, I need you to do me a favor."

"I'm not gonna like this, but go ahead," Daniela said, standing straight, cracking her back and retying her brunette waves into a tight bun. The fire gills and the lines of red that spiderwebbed away from them stood out against the grime and mess that we were all caked in.

"We need eyes on Summerfield. I don't know what we should expect from the town, but a fortified position in the hands of Tendrils is pretty close to a nightmare situation. Once that is done, we'll head back to Wildwood. Hopefully Alan will have something for us, because I am not keen on having a repeat of the bold escape that Dreg Corrupted bastard pebble pulled." My head was already throbbing, and the headache sent needles through my eyes. "That's all I've got. Maybe wait until dawn to leave, we could all use a break…"

"Don't have to tell me twice," she said, sheathing her daggers at her lower back. It was a rough thing that Sam had weaved, and it had to be replaced regularly due to the sharpness of her weapons, but it was an easier carry. "I'll get Devon up to speed."

The slightest of grimaces flashed on my face. Apparently, I could be read like a book. Well, at least by my friends.

"Any kind of business I have with tall and broody is none of yours, *Ronan*. I didn't criticize all the time you've spent with Clara, or that merlady Jolene for that matter. He's good people, good backup, and *great* at making an escape. If what you are suggesting is the case for Summerfield, then him and I will be walking straight out of the pan, through the fire, and into the damn coals. So, I will see you before I leave, but you best keep your face in the mud until I don't feel like smacking it down a peg," Daniela hissed. She hissed *all* of that, and for the entire duration of the exchange, I watched her gills flare so that she didn't even need to take a breath. It was an impressive talkin' to and left me properly mollified.

The Latina shoved her way past me. Samuel sighed heavily and placed a hand on my shoulder. "Worst time, Ron. Worst time. He finally got the…What did she call it…? *Cojones*, to ask her out."

"What? Why am I just hearing about this now!?" I asked, turning around to go after Daniela. Not only was she gone from sight, the last of her armor disappearing over the crapshoot that was Lake Weir's wall, but Sam's grip on my shoulder held me firmly in place.

"Because you like to clash."

"Clash? What is that supposed to mean?" I asked, feeling my exhaustion and confusion mixing dangerously with my frustration.

"Devon? That Rachael lady? The entire council back in Wildwood?" Sam rattled off, counting on his fingers.

"Deserved!" I growled, my voice slipping and drawing looks from the other Wild Guard, trainees, and the few hunters from the town. Upon feeling their looks, I returned them and they all scurried away like roaches in the light.

"This. Stop, Ronan."

"Sto—" My friend's palm found my cheek perfectly. The smoothness of the strike actually drew me up short as my head rattled and the force was slowly distributed thanks to my traits. The shock was more at Samuel hitting me than from the blow's damage.

"You are pulled too tight, Ron," Sam said more gently once my eyes finally landed on his. The glisten of tears on his blue eyes strangled the retort my lizard brain was getting ready to shout at him. "I understand things have been hard. Harder than any slog living in the Bunker might have put us through. But snapping at your friends just as you finally start to rely on us is no way for us to move forward."

I worked my jaw, trying to come up with something to say but my blabbering mouth failed me. There were no snide retorts, or anger in his voice, which meant it would be wrong for mine to carry those. When my brain couldn't work something out after several seconds, Samuel sighed. A much gentler palm met my face and his <Health Bump> coursed through me, removing the slight sting of his slap and relieving any number of minor injuries I'd been carrying around since the last fight.

The blond didn't say anything after that, making his way over to the group of healers. Thanks to my perception, I could hear them discussing how they'd each gone about using their skills to heal, and how they might be able to benefit from each other's techniques and focus. Samuel mentioned that talking with any old doctors in the town could be a good direction. The rest of the life-attuned agreed quickly, their group scattering back into Lake Weir.

Sam's eyes and mine met one last time before he was over

the side, leaving me alone but for the sentry posted on the wall who made a deliberate effort *not* to look at me. A small gelatinous appendage nudged my leg and I petted Blobby's uncloaked form.

"What am I doing, bud? Just because I'm not a fan of someone, I push all my friends away in one fell swoop?" The slime didn't have an answer, of course, but at least it remained at my side. My thoughts were stormy as I made my own way over the wall and Blobby filtered itself through the rusted cars. A pair of Weirdians would be out to collect what meat they could from the mess of low Quotient creatures left beyond the walls. They didn't need my help, and I was sure my mind could use a break for more than one reason.

# CHAPTER THIRTY-ONE

## Intertown Run

The following day after Wec stabilized was a flurry of activity that could *barely* be called restful. Weirdians flipped positions with the Wild Guard, freshened up from their time off the wall. In the town proper, however, we rushed from one preparation to the next. The abilities of the life-attuned were used to the utmost, supplementing the town's food supplies so that the hunters manning the walls could focus on bringing the town from their scattered spread of Quotients to a more respectable force. Thanks to the efforts of the Wild Guard, that was exactly what they were turning into: a force.

Using all the methods tested by Sarah, and enhanced by Ava, back in Wildwood, the demoness laid out a proper training regimen for the hunters of Lake Weir. The few earth-attuned got a crash course at the hands of Godfrey, myself, and one of the Guard trainee dwarves named Craig. With our collective help, and many, many breaks to avoid relapsing into the exhaustion afflictions we'd cleared with the sleep from the night before, the inner portion of the car wall was much reinforced. Godfrey focused on making huge dune bunkers to protect the defenders atop the wall from any spray from the bile crows. The rest of the attunements focused on cleaning up the town with a combination of wind, fire, and water when they weren't supplementing our other efforts.

While everyone still clung to some of their exhaustion, many were happy with the improvements, and morale in Lake Weir was at an all-time high. One of the biggest contributors to this was the nearly tripled-in-size pyramid near the school building. Wec had grown in size to be on the cusp of Category 3, albeit the low end. The sheer amount of Dregs that had been accumulated by the town, not to mention those dancing dangerously close to Dreg poisoning, had provided the Entity Cluster with almost non-stop energy.

It was at the base of the twelve foot structure that the New Hopers, squad leaders, and Weirdian leadership gathered. A trio of old, surviving cafeteria folding tables had been brought out to simplify the gathering, all facing towards Wec.

"This isn't awkward at all," Dennis said, pulling at his goatee and adjusting his rear on the small plastic circles that acted as chairs.

"Not really an official meeting place in town, and Wec isn't really big enough for an audience like with Tec, Dennis. No need to point it out," Godfrey whispered from beside him.

The whispering would have been effective had the group not been seated so close together. Lilly was sitting with Rommel, both quiet and attentive of the gathering crowd, while Clara shook her head, and Devon whittled at a hunk of wood. The creation in his hands looked remarkably like one of the cannons we were developing back in Wildwood. As much as I found the man grating, I would have asked since it was something we both actually worked more or less well on. This particular time, however, I didn't ask because seated between us was a still deadpan Daniela, and an attempting-mediator Samuel. Of course, we were seated on the far right table, while the New Hopers took the middle, and the Weirdians took the other table closest to Wec.

"This is awkward," Maurice said from his side of the table

the moment he walked up. That got Godfrey a slap to the shoulder and a pointed gesture that said 'I told you so' before the stand-in leader of the town got the meeting started. "But it will have to do."

Ian, always moving in to smooth out his son's rough edges, stepped up beside him. "We want to extend a thanks to the people of Wildwood, and to the Bunker folk, who have aided us in this very difficult time. Already Wec has made a difference for our defenders, and none have fallen to the changes with his overwatch.

"I know there is yet more to do. Even before this protection, there was an endless number of tasks," Ian said, producing a round of light chuckles from the gathered group. "However, I asked for this meeting to formalize our joining of your effort. Clara and Ronan have explained, at length, what these creatures attacking us represent. *Who* they represent. I will not say that we can stand up to the strength of Wildwood, or the craftiness of Stonecrest, but I hope to add our perseverance to the fight."

The man made a gentle nod in the direction of Clara and then towards us three Bunkerites. The four other leaders of the town smiled and nodded behind the old man, making a show of their standing. Maurice threw a pair of thumbs up, which was in character.

"You wanna slog through this, or you want me to take it?" Clara sent me through the comm-plant as Ian took back his seat.

"Floor is yours, miss," I sent back, wiggling in my chair and trying not to look at either of my friends. After the way our last encounter had gone, I opted to keep my mouth shut. Intermingling my frustrations with an important meeting just sounded like a recipe for disaster.

"Our current plan is to send out our best scouts to Summerfield. If all goes well, they should be back by end-of-day and we will be better informed about the state of things there after the people evacuated. Part of the New Hopers will remain here, strengthening our position and helping to relieve the strain of the Weirdians. As many of you know, except for our Bunker allies, monster waves like this aren't uncommon. The brutality and consistency with which they are crashing against a fortified position is the issue," Clara explained.

The demoness went on to explain some of the most prominent instances of monster waves, which happened to correspond with the spring season. It was almost surprising, until I realized that if spring was the best time for animals to give birth *before* the Fall, why wouldn't it be *after*? Said animals—enhanced by the mana now integrated into their bodies and augmented by collected Pith—would produce *more* or *stronger* offspring. The image of a swarm of magically enhanced rabbits almost sent shivers down my spine.

"—Ronan will work to pass on his knowledge, along with Rommel, while we are in town." I blinked back to attention at the mention of my name. Sam almost got a message asking why I was being brought up, but all I needed to do was keep listening. "With access to <Infusion>, the people of Lake Weir can start to produce their own enhanced equipment. Unfortunately, transporting stuff from Wildwood will still be limited, even without the press of creatures Wec attracted."

"Current energy expenditures have Category 3 growth projected to within two weeks. Three, if the rate of encounters continues to decrease as we've seen since my stabilizing," the Entity added.

"Right. Once that happens, Wec should be able to initiate communication with Tec. With that, coordination between Lake Weir and Stonecrest should jump up significantly, and Wildwood will do its best to support you all," Clara finished.

Ian let out a breath he'd apparently been holding. Even Maurice looked particularly serious. The other advisors looked distinctly out of their depths. It was time for me to step in.

"Ian, I told you before, all we want for you all is to survive and thrive. Meeting these goals? That's just the first step. Once we can get the Dreg off our backs, the infrastructure we are laying down will let *trade* happen between the towns. Families and friends made across distances often thought insurmountable by any but the bravest!" My voice tinged with fervor as the memories of Patrick Patrick and his departing love flitted through my mind. If the world hadn't gone to crap the moment we arrived at Lake Weir, I might have tried to ask around about her, but I'd hardly seen anything but a bunk and the pock-marked fields around the old school.

The brief speech seemed to do the trick of bringing the Weirdians back. Maurice met my eyes and nodded. "It is like you said. I'll be happy not to have those Tendril bastards looming over us like they have for so many years. Plus, it's not like we haven't already thrown our lot in with you guys."

"Ha! We could always leave," I said, lightly. The flash of horror in the Weirdian's eyes was a tad more than I expected, so I quickly reassured them I was kidding. Sighs of relief abounded and I hid my embarrassment behind a crooked grin.

The rest of the meeting went quickly. Status of resources—food, materials and infusions—was at an all-time high, even with the jump in population the combined squads of Wild Guard gave Lake Weir. We agreed to take most of the creature drops back with us to turn into equipment or weapons to outfit our growing alliance. Plans were made, and smaller meetings were arranged for the farmers with Samuel, the crafters with me, and the hunters with Clara.

While everyone made small talk upon being dismissed, Daniela excused herself to prepare for the scouting mission. Devon left his half-whittled cannon right on the table as he followed after her. She didn't look back at me, or say anything. Not wanting to leave things like that between us, I opted to ping her via the comm-plant.

"Please stay safe," I said quietly.

"I will. Be back in a flash," she replied a few minutes later. It was more than I expected, but it was a first step. Once I grew a big enough pair of pants, I would have to apologize to her about the whole Devon situation. While the man and I got along much better, especially after the pendulum cannon project began, I knew Daniela was one to hold a grudge.

For the rest of the afternoon, I spoke with Maurice and a handful of other people in town. They acted more as handymen than the Stoneshapers or the various tradesmen in Wildwood, but they picked up the knack for infusions quicker than any of the other townsmen; I even managed to *only* add two mildly unpleasant memories to the growing catalog <Memory Canal> was making in my brain. All in all, it was an extremely productive way of burning off the nervous energy coursing through my body as we waited for news from Daniela.

The minutes quickly turned into hours and when the sun started to turn orange in the sky, I was once again ready to rush north into the wilds. Just before Samuel had to bodily restrain me, a ping showed up in the minimap I'd been looking at incessantly. The call on the comm-plant came in only a few seconds later.

"It's not great," Danny said in a weary whisper. "We need to talk."

— + —

"The whole town?" Clara asked, barely keeping to a whisper.

"Far as we can tell," Devon said, flexing his fingers in a gesture I recognized as manipulating his air-whisper Gift. "The Tendrils are digging in. There weren't as many as we've seen before, but none of the ones we were able to identify were lower than Q3 and most were at Q4, not to mention the critters they got as muscle."

"Bunch of fodder, and what seems to be creature leaders. Like 'boss' monsters from those old RPGs, but much more terrifying because they are *actually* trying to eat your face," Daniela added, unhelpfully.

"Does this change anything?" Samuel asked. "I've been observing the wildlife for a while, and I think the Tendrils are running out of gas. Why would they need to dig in? Why don't they just *attack us* with the Appendage and get it out of the way?"

"What do you mean?" Dennis asked. "Sure, the waves have eased off, but Lake Weir isn't what I would call safe."

"Think of it like this," Sam started. "The creatures here hold a tenuous number of territories. They only have so many creatures they can afford to send out without compromising the base of their power. If they don't have hunters to bring them food, they will starve just the same as us. The Tendrils have to keep all of their corrupted creatures fed *and* retain their hold over their territory. This is where their weakness lies."

"That's why they needed tribute from the towns," Clara said, snapping her fingers.

"They were subsidizing their population," I finished, nodding as the pieces fell into place.

"So… What? We've been cleaning out their surplus, is that it?" Daniela asked with a frown. It was quickly matched by the others around.

"I don't think we should view it like that. Each fight we've had with the Tendrils has been hard won. The relentless assault against the town was just another aspect of that. Wec's presence probably drove them into a panic. They overreacted and they had a costly exchange of resources," I said.

"A dangerous assumption," Rommel rumbled.

"Nothing we can do about them. We can only work on us," Devon said, waving his hands through the air.

"Tenderly," Clara added. "If we let our attention drift too much, we will get surprised. During our whole time defending Lake Weir, there weren't any humanoid Tendrils. Something intelligent is still directing them."

We fell into silence at the reminder of the Corrupted Entity. It was impossible to know just what extent of control it had and just how far the support network of the Tendrils reached. Those two questions put any future plans in a tenuous light at best. However, as much as it pained me to agree with the elf, Devon was right. Stagnating was a surefire way of just losing to the Dreg. The slow, choking death Kirby had subjected Wildwood to was proof enough of that.

With the scouting report done, the group spent several minutes discussing how it affected our original plans. Other than deciding to leave a larger presence of the Guard in Lake Weir, nothing really changed. Even the people of the town or the implanted Wild Guard remaining who were climbing up in Dregs wouldn't have to worry about afflictions now that Wec could purge and process the traits. The only detriment to being in Lake Weir was the type of creatures they encountered, which for many of the recent trainees were brand new compared to the more uniform threat of the ants, spiders, and occasional predator that ambled near Wildwood.

We decided on the assignments before calling it a night. Samuel and I would take the lead on the return, taking Dennis with us. Devon and Daniela would act as rotating scouts, spending time across all of the towns as information relays via the comm-plants. It was an imperfect system, but it saved the energy of the Entities and provided a sort of roving patrol in the tenuous territory between the human-controlled towns. Clara promised to supplement their efforts with people from Lake Weir as soon as she could get them trained up. The rest of the New Hopers would remain in Lake Weir, helping to solidify their gains and doing their own 'digging in' like the Dregs.

Since the situation was uncertain, timewise, the group remaining in Lake Weir would pass messages to Wildwood every other day at the latest. The pressure to act was higher than ever and I couldn't shake the feeling that time was running out. It was entirely possible that the Tendrils wouldn't remain content to just fortify and launch an attack on Lake Weir. If that happened, even with the New Hopers remaining in their ranks, it would be an exercise in futility to hold the town.

That particular thought gave my and Samuel's dream of interconnected travel much more weight. A straight shot road from town to town would make it safer and faster to travel. So, when we set out back to Wildwood the next morning, we let the ox set the pace. Igor, the intense one-armed orc, was left in charge of the fledgling squads as Sam and I led the way. With amplified skills, we near-singlehandedly cleared a path south to US 441 and right into the north of Stonecrest.

It had only taken a brief, but still tense, discussion between Sam and I to get up to date on how our skills operated after adding the amplitude items. For the first time, I used a quarter-powered <Mudpit> in conjunction with his amplified <Vine Whip>. My augmented skill transformed into <Landslide>, which seemed like a marginally stronger but directional version of <Mudpit>. The first cast cleared a twenty by twenty swath of land by pushing it away from me like a crashing wave of soil. The utility, even accounting for the fact that it took a literal half of my mana, felt more immediately useful than <Mudpit>. I was the first to admit, however, that I was still very much unfamiliar with the skill other than its soil 'melting' capabilities.

I'd never asked what Sam's augmented skill was called, and all I could do was nod at the impressive name: <Arboreal Grasp>. The skill worked like a souped-up version of his vines, manipulating bark-covered lengths of wood instead of the more generic plant matter his vines seemed to be made from. The key point of the augment, however, had been the fact that it let Samuel take control of existing trees and bend them to his will. Literally.

He mentioned it was a mana hog when it came to *creating* the reinforced vines, but taking over a new lifeform was slightly more efficient. It made clearing a path easy as the blond *walked* the trees out of the way with his amplified skill. A nudge of the roots to get them to rise out of the earth meant that all Igor and I had to do was push against them to topple the trees.

Even with the synergy between our skills, it was an incredible slog, but the ease of travel the wagon experienced on the return trip couldn't be compared—lack of nonstop attacks notwithstanding. While we took breaks to recover our mana, Igor and the others resorted to more explosive and violent ways of clearing the straight-shot road. By late afternoon, we'd arrived in Stonecrest to a much warmer welcome. I'd taken the time in between working on the road to update Rachael through the comm-plant. Even if the woman wasn't much of a talker through the implant, she'd somehow coordinated a small feast for our returning expedition.

The squads ate heartily, morale high as we were closer to home and the mission as a whole had gone well. The mood was somber between Sam and I, but we were at least able to exchange some lighthearted jokes. His mostly about me having 'constipation face' and mine about him being a raging alcoholic as a result of the regular expenditures of our mana pools.

The younger members of the squads looked at our interactions with a funny face, but they always seemed to want to engage us in conversation. It was a good way of passing the time, keeping our thoughts on the small positive changes we'd already made instead of the looming threat.

Thanks to a surprise infusion lesson when Patrick Patrick and his Stoneshaper goons assaulted me, we decided it was best to delay our trip back to Wildwood slightly. It was likely we'd make it to Wildwood before complete nightfall, but the risk was unnecessary. The squads didn't complain about the extended leave, and the people of Stonecrest cheered having experienced fighters in their midst. I saw more than one Gift Wrestle light up the night, but I didn't partake. My thoughts were set on the Dreg, even as I drifted to sleep in the building we'd been provided to stay at.

The next morning went swiftly, especially after having been delayed. Instead of trying to clear cut our way south like from Lake Weir, we assisted the small team of lumberjacks working towards Wildwood by focusing on the thickest stretches of wood. The demoness in charge raised her axe in thanks when we shoved a four foot thick live oak out of the projected path they'd been working. After that, we only cleared the path where it was roughest, making sure to keep over half our mana pools available.

The trip once again went much faster, and the walls of Wildwood came into view just before lunch. A weight dropped off my shoulders and a small cheer went up amidst the expedition. Dennis was particularly enthused to be back. While we still had a long way to go, at least the gears had been put in motion for something bigger than just our Bunker.

# CHAPTER THIRTY-TWO

## The Dreg State

"They are back!" a voice called from the car wall to the north of town. It didn't take but a minute for a long wooden ramp to get dropped on the other side of the wall.

*Apparently I left an impression,* I mused to myself.

Trainees and Wild Guards greeted each other as equals, more than one hug going around as the youths chattered with their older counterparts. Family members lingered near the bridge, and as soon as the trainees noticed, they rushed to embrace them. Parents, siblings, lovers. The trip had barely taken a week, but for people used to losing family to the wild, it might as well have been an eternity.

Amidst the welcoming committee was Sarah. If it was possible, the orc woman looked even more imposing than she had before. My quick guess was it had something to do with the Q5 my implant was telling me she had reached. There was an emblem of rough-worked metal pinned to her chest high on the sleeve of the rough shirt she wore under her tanker armor. A hexagon, notched with six small symbols, and a stylized shield in the center. The woman caught my eye and approached Dennis, Sam, and I. Out of the arriving expedition, ours was composed of cheers and fist bumps instead of more personal engagements, so she had an easy time cutting through the mob.

"Happy to have you back," she said, a thin smile on her face. From what I could tell, it was genuine, but there was definitely something pulling at her.

"No need for a grandiose welcome for us. I'm ready to work," I said, gesturing behind her towards Wildwood proper. She hesitated, but gave a nod in return. Once we were a ways away from the rest of the trainees and the north wall guards, she once again addressed us.

"The afflicted trainees are awake," she said, cutting right to the point.

"Huh?" the three of us said, snapping out of our surprise. It was easy for me to forget how straightforward Sarah could be when I'd seen her interacting with Daniela and Clara in a more relaxed setting.

"They woke up all throughout the day yesterday. The last one woke up just this morning. Billy, Eric's son."

"Does...Does Eric know?" I asked, looking over towards Tec's looming form.

"He was the first I told," Sarah said. "He hasn't left his side. The weird change to Billy's lower body caused a bit of trouble outside of Tec, and he is currently strapped down. Billy isn't the only one, unfortunately. Most of the others are in various states of...*reaction*, for lack of a better word. We've had to house the fire and water trainees in your crafter's hall thanks to the effects of their bodies. Tec estimates they should stabilize over time, just like they did coming out of their coma, but it has no idea how long that could take. Alan has lost any semblance of coordinated communication, even with Ava's help, and is holed up working on something. We have almost a dozen kids catatonic while suffering supernatural transformations without a single clue of what to do..."

The words had left the woman so quickly I almost wasn't able to follow. With every other thing she said, I could see her stiff shoulders sag. Dennis moved to support her, and Sam and I shared a concerned look. We quickly asked her to take us to where Billy was staying, and she agreed without any hesitation.

"What are we going to do?" I asked Samuel via the comm-plant, not bothering to hide my grimace as I communicated silently with him.

"I don't know… If Alan doesn't have anything for us, and Tec says we need to wait, then maybe that's all we need to do?" It wasn't hard to tell that Samuel barely believed himself as he said that.

"We can't just leave them. Maybe if we hadn't pushed Kirby—"

"Don't. Kirby had been doing that and worse to the people of Wildwood for a long time. If we hadn't interfered, then who knows how much worse the Dreg would have squeezed them."

"Do you think he could tell us something?" I asked as we walked off the bridge.

"Kirby? No clue. You said it yourself that he spilled it when we were there. Let's give the trainees a look and we can try to figure out what to do from there," Sam said, giving me a small strained smile. Even with a few doctors and nurses in the mix of Wildwood's survivors and even Lake Weir's, the blond had become something of a medical expert. Much time spent haranguing Alexis and June had given him a keen sense for small injuries and general anatomy, then his attunement gave him the means to address that, amplified yet again by the assort-ment of traits he'd manifested.

We fell into silence as we approached one of the buildings not far from Tec. I could have sworn I saw the crystal glimmer specifically when I looked at it, but my attention was drawn away by the quiet sobs in the room Sarah pulled us into. Beds inspired by Sam's woven designs lined either wall. Upon them were the earth-, life-, and death-attuned trainees that had survived the Dreg ritual several weeks back. They all shifted gently, rocking in place or trembling as they twitched trans-formed features. One of the two life-attuned almost seemed to blend into the bed, as the entwined roots that made up almost fifty percent of her body settled into the bed. Her one remaining eye drifted in lazy figure eights, stopping to focus on something for a brief second before resuming its trackless path.

A gut-wrenching feeling stronger than any mana side effect took hold of me. It was deeper, a sort of primal guilt that argued their state was my fault, just like the death of the other trainees and the Summerfield refugees were also my fault. I don't know how long I stood there, frozen in shock, but when my eyes were able to focus, I could see that Eric was shaking me by the shoulders. His gray eyes burned and swirled with the disguised trait that I knew made him and the other air-attuned pre-Fall Wild Guard deadly with their ranged weaponry.

"Ronan. *Ronan!*" the man managed through clenched teeth. I saw the redness on his face and the bloodshot behind the mystical swirl of his eyes. The distraught father. "Please, you have to help him. I listened to *you*, damn it! I could have been by his side!"

The man thumped me in the chest with the flat of his fist, but I barely felt it. A woman, not much younger than Eric himself and sporting equal marks of grief, moved to pull him away from me. For the first time since walking into the room, I was able to see the scattered family and friends of the other trainees. They shared the undertone of grief and worry that Eric, and who I presumed was his wife, exhibited. The only difference was that I had essentially ordered Eric to wait to rescue his child. The tactical benefits of the engagement didn't matter here, not when it came to the price we paid for them, but I tried to form a response.

It didn't work. My jaw muscles refused to work and once again I was reminded that I couldn't do everything. I'd already failed several times on the surface. Maybe not in the sense of the fights we'd survived, but in the impressions I'd left with people. *Just because you can come up with a good plan doesn't mean you are a true leader, Ronan.* That reminder stung more than I realized. Even when I tried to convince myself that not everyone was going to agree with me, it still came to mind that the origin point for most of the conflicts were my own fault.

Instead of trying to work through my tied tongue, I approached Billy. The youth was condensed mist from the ribs down. Ephemeral outlines of his legs coalesced from the mist every few seconds, but it wasn't long before they dissolved into the chaotic disarray of eddy currents I expected from a visible gas cloud. I saw what Sarah had been hinting at as far as why he'd had to be restrained. His whole body refused to lay flat, and instead hovered an inch above it thanks to a number of ropes across the still solid part of his chest. Billy himself was one of the ones twitching restlessly, eyes open and unable to focus on anything. He was clearly not in a coma anymore, but the boy wasn't all there either.

My own shaky fingers found the boy's arm and I could feel something familiar in the youth's movements. It was the subtly growing vibrations that happened when I infused materials with air. It wasn't the incrementally growing mess of a failing infusion, like with the insta-meal plastic, but the thrum that preceded the solidification of an item in its own right. The growing thrum as I added infusions until the item was sated and changed enough according to its nature.

As the thought crossed my mind, every muscle on my body pulled taut like a bowstring ready to fire. Or like how I'd felt moments before my body attuned to earth. That was the moment before <Infusion> and <Memory Canal> triggered almost on their own. A swirl of colors and a searing pain in my head brought me to a pitch black space. For a second, I was scared I'd somehow killed myself by overusing my more mentally-straining skills, but the blackness slowly settled into a gray-tinged black space.

My eyes naturally followed the gray to where it was most prominent. The color lightened with each foot I tracked until I came upon a small fragmented bubble of white. The center was a tenuous sphere of light while the rest seemed to actively shift and fade to gray as if keeping the darkness away. In the middle of that mess was Billy. The youth looked a bit less catatonic than he did floating above his bed, but the deer-in-headlights look was hard to miss.

When I tried to approach him, my body didn't move at all. Instead of trying to force my body to move, I tried to *think* of it moving. The similarities between the strange white bubble and the whitespace that the Entities conjured up wasn't hard to miss. So, as if I was a thread of Pith being manipulated, I hovered over the seeming void of darkness to Billy's side.

Now closer, I could see that the darkness was more like a thick oily substance—more than *just* the antithesis of the white-space. There was a hunger to the darkness that became different from the apathetic void further away from Billy. The gray was a warzone, and the darkness was trying to breach the barrier around the youth.

*Dreg.*

The thought echoed around me and I saw the white sphere grow slightly before shrinking again. The youth within didn't seem to take notice of my presence, instead playing with the sleeves of his shirt and mumbling to himself. I screamed, yelled, and positively made a fool of myself trying to draw Billy's attention to no avail. *He's trapped by the Dreg.*

Once again, the whitespace swelled, pushing out against the oily black. I wasn't sure what triggered the change, but since nothing else seemed to have done the trick, I concentrated on the thought that seemed to get a reaction out of the world around me. *Dreg. Stop the Dreg! DREG!*

My thoughts intensified and the white sphere started to grow larger and larger, but the black weighed it down, tainting the edges gray once again the moment my mental shouts faded. However, the slight recession had let something click in my mind, particularly because of a dull ache in my abdomen. The telltale ache of mana usage. *This place is affected by my mana some-how...* Once I was on that train of thought, I was able to ride it to remind myself *how* I'd somehow entered the youth's mental space in the first place. Some strange blend of <Infusion> and

<Memory Canal>. One handled manipulating Pith with my mana, and the other connecting with the pathways in the mind. More curious to me was the overlap of both, which was the skill nature of them.

There was no sense trying to apply logic to the fact that I was hovering inside Billy's mind, but I remembered the other time I'd intentionally invaded someone's mind. Charles had been pitiful compared to the oppressive force I sensed from the black, but I leaned on that experience nonetheless. Since I needed a skill to focus on, I zeroed on <Earth Shell>. Without my antler helm, I couldn't amplify it into <Rock Cocoon>, but the concept behind the skill seemed the most fitting to the situation.

With my eyes focused on Billy's absent gaze, I triggered the skill. A ripple of umber flickered around me, a wispy ghost of what my earth armor usually looked like. The ache manifested in my gut, but that was common. Pain was common. What the poor youth was enduring at the hands of the Dreg...*that* I could barely imagine. My frustrations at my failings, at my shortcomings, became the fuel as I fed <Earth Shell>. A few seconds later, it ran out of body to cover but I kept fueling it. Pushing it out to defend against the black poison of the Dreg.

To my surprise, a manifestation of my helm, a boney white pair of antlers, appeared on my head and the umber mana turned into a laser aimed right at Billy. The stream of brown light struggled to cross the boundary of gray, bowing before my concerted effort of mana punched through and struck the youth in the chest. Immediately, a much more solid version of my stone protection manifested around the youth. I could sense a will brush against my own. Weak, exhausted. A slowly spinning circle of mana circled Billy and I recognized it for what it was. His Gift, and it was the only thing keeping the black from claiming him whole.

*Billy! You need to fight!* I yelled through my mind. *You need to fight the Dreg!*

The words seemed to snap the boy to attention, as if sensing the slight receding of the gray fragmentation around him. Almost immediately, the circle of gray spun up. It tried to strangle the beam of mana coming from me, but I just kept feeding my skill. As the youth stirred, the gray stopped reclaiming the territory of his whitespace. The Gift snapped at everything, gray and umber alike. The behavior and my effort reminded me of my bouts with Rachael. This was some primal form of Gift Wrestling, but this was the core of Billy fighting for its survival as a whole. *I got you.*

Gritting my teeth for what I was sure would be one of the top most unpleasant things I'd ever done, I fed more mana to my skill. Immediately, the strain was palatable. I had no way to gauge my mana in the mindscape I found myself in, but it didn't matter at the moment. I strengthened Billy's armor to encase him whole and then I focused on his Gift and tried to pick it as a target. My mana flowed out of me like water through a sieve. The weak band of gray gained a helical companion of umber and Billy finally stirred.

I was ejected out of the mindscape explosively. My vision only caught a brief look of Samuel before I curled in on myself like a pretzel. I was half-certain I heard some of my tendons snap under the pressure I exerted on my body. *Am I screaming?* I couldn't be sure, but I knew that it was only a few seconds before the pain overwhelmed me and a blackness of my own surged to protect me from the pain of consciousness.

— + —

The world slowly came into view, but it was an exercise in agony. Every twitch of muscle, even the ones on my face, ached beyond any right they had to hurt.

"Ronan!" a call reached my ears. Turning my eyeballs, which also hurt, I spotted a mop of blond hair blocking the light from a torch set up behind them. Said mop slowly came into focus as a concerned Samuel. "You've been out for a few hours. How are you feeling?"

I worked my aching jaw a few times before I managed to get out a response. "Hurt."

If it wouldn't have hurt to grimace, I would have when I saw Samuel's decentralized nerves unspool from his palms. The freakiest thing about them was that you couldn't feel them. I hadn't paid a whole lot of attention to Alexis' and Ava's hypothesis on the nature of his particular trait, but I knew it creeped me out. Alas, my everything hurt so I wasn't able to squirm away from my friend's probing.

"You have hairline fractures on several of your bones and I don't know *how many* ligaments torn. My anatomy is failing me in that regard here, but it's *a lot.* I've hit you with several <Health Bumps>, even one <Restorative Surge>, so I don't want to risk putting you into Overhealed affliction territo—"

"Is he awake?" another voice interrupted Sam. *Eric.*

"Yes, but he is—"

"Ronan," the man once again interrupted my friend as he came into view. I could see there were tears in his eyes, but none of that frustrated grief seemed to be present anymore. "I... Thank you."

"Huh?" *That's all you are getting. I think I probably tore my vocal chords too.*

"B-Billy... He—" It was Sam's turn to interrupt the man.

"He doesn't know. He just woke up," the blond said, turning to the older man. I couldn't see Sam's face, even if it hadn't hurt to turn my head, but I could practically *hear* the glare from where I laid.

"Oh." Eric looked distinctly uncomfortable as it finally dawned on him that he'd stumbled on what amounted to a medical scan. *I'm not wearing a shirt either, huh.* Just out of the corner of my eye, I could see some of my spider-webbing arteries full of slurry. One of the lovely additions that had blunted the man's own strikes to my chest however long ago I'd arrived at the medical room.

"Is... okay. Billy?" I managed to ask.

Samuel and Eric shared a look before my friend started to

explain what had happened after I touched Billy. Nothing at first, my eyes rolled up into the back of my head, and Sam started to probe me for what had happened. Eric had to be bodily restrained by cords of vines courtesy of Sam himself. A few seconds after, however, I started to glow brown, before it crawled down my hand into the catatonic boy to encase him as well. That was when things kicked up a notch. Sand and pellets of rock swirled around the two of us as if our Attunements were battling it out. Sometime during that engagement, Billy snapped awake and actively took control of a spell chain. When *that* happened, the script spell chain of Entity-granted skills encased it, choked it, and exploded in a spray of sand. Said explosion left me squirming on the floor, and Billy more or less back in control of his faculties.

The youth was more than a bit shaken by the exchange, and was only able to exchange a few words with Sam and his father before he passed out. The youth hadn't even had time to really come to grip with his non-legs before knocking out. Thanks to a follow up scan courtesy of the local human CT, they knew Billy was just asleep and not back into a coma.

Throughout the whole explanation, I struggled to focus as the pain flowed through my body. It had improved noticeably compared to when I'd interacted with Billy, even from when I'd woken up, but it still left me muddled. Nonetheless, I let out a sigh of relief. If all it took was pain, then it was worth it to save the afflicted trainees.

Unfortunately, that was also a source of problems. At some point during the retelling, the other parents and family of the trainees became aware of my return to consciousness. The unfortunate part came in the form of frantic begging for inter-vention. One particularly bulky man with deep azure scales like a band across his forehead shoved Eric out of the way in his rush to demand for my help.

Samuel was quite stunned by the display; he didn't react fast enough to stop the man from grabbing hold of my arm. The offending limb might as well have been jelly held together by my Limestone Skin. The howl of pain that ripped out of me was enough to shock the man into letting go. It also caused all the other petitioners to take several steps back in alarm. The blond bodily interposed himself between me and the masses, slapping the scaled man's hand away from where it lingered near me.

Despite the set to his jaw, Sam struggled to regain some semblance of order after that development. He sought to answer questions and give reassurances, even when the demanding parents spoke over him; I could see my friend wanted to be done with the social engagement entirely. Even with Eric's help, the insistence of the small crowd remained. Like the angry mob they were, they fed on the agitated energy within each other. They were no longer demanding to have their family looked after right away—my handicapped state was more than obvious—so instead they argued about the *order*.

I didn't have the words to spare to even fight back on the absurd situation. It wasn't a matter of me not wanting to help the trainees, but that they were being ridiculous about the whole situation and therefore putting stress on Samuel. I wanted to personally smack them all for their audacity, but just the thought of doing so hurt.

Thankfully, the commotion didn't *just* attract desperate family members. Like an angry cloud, a familiar group of trainees interposed themselves between Samuel, me, and the parents.

"Oy! Last I heard this wasn't the communal bonfire or the afterhours brawls. What in the Fall are you lot screaming about in the medical building for?" said a loud voice in a compact body. I could just barely make out the top of the newcomer's hair. There were a handful of others lingering in the doorway as the short person pushed forward.

I recognized the fae twins and the pugilist dwarf but their names eluded me as I worked through the bout of pain the scaled man had inflicted on me. I *did*, however, have enough presence of mind to hear the crowd of adults get scolded into submission by the boisterous survivors of the Dreg ritual. The dwarven girl practically growled at one of the parents that tried to bring up some baseless counter argument.

When they saw their hopes dashed, the group returned to check on their family members in the other beds while throwing side glances at me.

"Don't worry, boss man." My brain finally attached the proper name to the female dwarf: Hilda. "We've got your back. Just do what you need to do."

The fae twins turned and exchanged some words with Samuel, but with the jump in pain and the stress of the whole situation, I felt my eyes begin to droop once again. Voices turned into droning that practically put me to sleep. The arrival of the trainees had provided the last modicum of security I needed to relax and let the arduous process of healing really begin.

# CHAPTER THIRTY-THREE

## The Cogs

The next two weeks felt like an exercise in futility. While my body had been utterly throttled by helping Billy, I refused to let it keep me down. So, as soon as I was mobile and with a full mana pool, I would hobble over to another of the afflicted trainees to repeat the process of freeing them from their own minds.

To say the effort didn't take everything I had would have been a lie. Even if most of the trainees seemed to have larger white spaces than the one Billy had for whatever reason, each time I wrestled them back to reality, my body clobbered itself like freshly worked dough.

Each cycle of injury took me longer and longer to recover from to the point where Samuel and Sarah agreed to leave someone on guard so I *wouldn't* try to escape to the crafting hall where I knew the orc and mer trainees were being kept due to their more volatile afflictions. While the trainees that received my help weren't totally back to themselves—they seemed like babies trying to relearn how their bodies worked—their progress was the only thing keeping me going.

All the extra time to think while convalescing was driving

me mad and forcing me to really analyze things, my focus sharpened as a distraction from the pain. I wanted to be out there, fighting the Dreg and making them pay for all they'd taken. If I was out there, then losses would be prevented either by my hand or by the things I created.

That driving thought stemmed from the fact I was slowly putting together: the Entity Clusters were meant to help us acclimate to an Attuned Earth, and the Dreg were their intended targets all along. Bec had all but confirmed this, but the more I examined our interactions with the Dreg and the way the Entities assisted us, it became painfully obvious. I knew in part the Entities were responsible for the mutations of Earth wildlife, but if that was the worst that happened, then humans would have already affirmed their grip on at least some areas of the world. It was possible they had in some places, but that was reliant on their resources before the Fall and the chance that a Metier Crystal had landed near enough to purge them from Dreg.

And there it was, the insidious part of the problem. The Dreg were everywhere, not just where the crystal's influence protected. If all it took was enough of the tainted Pith to corrupt a mind like what had almost happened to the trainees, then how many had been lost to the Dreg over the last three decades? What further plans and power were they growing just out of sight of our three little towns?

And yet, my body refused to recover all the way.

Ava, Sam, nor any of the other doctors scrounged up from survivors were able to figure out why I wasn't healing all the way. Not even Alexia, who braved a trip from the Bunker for my sake, was able to provide some additional insight. Obviously, if I had suffered the injuries I had at the hands of my mana back-lash before gaining my Quotients and traits, I would have been dead ten times over, much less be able to walk aided by crutches. That was even after I'd stopped healing the trainees.

Samuel was optimistic that I just needed to give my body a chance to recover. That my traits already made me extremely sturdy and the passive regenerative nature of our attuned bodies would get me there. However, just lying on the sidelines wasn't what I wanted as the cogs of war really started to turn. I couldn't help but think of Igor who, even as the healers scratched their heads at how to treat him for his missing arm, still fought at the frontline.

As a courtesy for my contributions to the town, Sarah made sure to keep me abreast of the developments with our efforts. She even asked for my input, as bedridden as I was, on formations we could use for defense.

In my absence, the town had continued to prepare. Rommel had finalized the original design of the pendulum force cannon, our name for the part-item weapon we'd created. Two of the things had been shipped, at the cost of one of the Wild Guards to another giant cottonmouth, to Lake Weir. That was another death that weighed on my mind. *The last one had been brought to heel and I wasn't there! They could have lived!*My mind repeated that during any opening it had to hate my inability to function.

It had been a necessary risk in the hopes of dealing with the latest rounds of attack by the Dreg. Apparently, when their ground and air assaults had been rebuffed, they had opted to double down on the air ones. The shift went from quality to quantity.

What could only be described as toxic air raids were pummeling the Weirdians. Even with the help of ranged Gift attacks and the new stock of bow items and arrows Wildwood started to produce, it was just too difficult to land a blow on the creatures. At least two more Weirdians had succumbed to the bile, and the defenses we'd worked hard to reinforce during our time there were once again suffering. It was a war of attrition the Weirdians were barely surviving. I was fairly sure all it took the crows to bomb the town with their corrosive entrails was some time regenerating their mana.

With my knowledge of the Stoneshapers' abilities and Arnold's super dense <Stone Anvil>, I drew up a rough design for defensive walkways. A thin layer of the dense stone, shaped into a slanted trapezoid, mounted above columns of earth. Condensed earth ditches would line the covered walkway so that water-attuned could wash off the bile off the surfaces and move it away into decomposition pools. The pools had been there since the Weirdians started being attacked, but due to the frequency of the raids, they had grown from near-fetid puddles into cesspools of disease. Unfortunately, that was a problem for the future, since the people preferred the disgusting pits to having the chemical burns the crows' attacks left behind.

Even with the co-opting of Arnold and one of the Stone-shapers from Stonecrest, the situation at the front only got marginally better. The only benefit to the whole situation was that pretty much everyone playing an active role in the fighting had reached Quotient Level 4 and gained one to two traits beyond their existing attunement-race ones.

And so, that left me propped on an <Earthen Barrier> just outside of the medical building as I watched the final group of ex-trainees get inducted into the Wild Guard and sent to Lake Weir to relieve the defenders for a time. There was one more group of trainees, many being groomed even before they'd unlocked or achieved proficiency with their Gift thanks to the expectation that they would be able to make use of an Entity-given skill.

Everyone in the gathered group wore variations on my armor blueprints with painted emblems of the Guard. Where the paint had come from, I could only guess was Stonecrest's superstore or some other unraided location. The squad leaders each had one of the rough metal broaches I'd seen Sarah wear.

Councilman Dylan spoke some encouraging words to the youths before they marched over to a cart with their supplies and yet another pair of pendulum force cannons. Sarah had been standing off to the side and escorted the expedition up the bridge to the north. My weakness burned like the worst case of heartburn I'd ever experienced, and the pain only added insult to injury.

"You might burn a hole in them if you stare so hard," Dylan said, snapping me out of my reverie.

"I should be out there…" I replied weakly.

"Couldn't agree more," the fire-headed man said, groaning and taking a seat next to me. "Tell me, Ronan, why are you throwing yourself so hard at the meat grinder of reality?"

I quirked an eyebrow at the man. We'd come to have a level of respect for each other since I'd arrived at Wildwood. I recognized him for what he was, a skilled politician who'd been blinded by one of his closest friends and was working to make amends. And he recognized me as a pain in the ass that did whatever was necessary to accomplish his goals without compromising his morality. *Why* he was asking about my motivation was beyond me. "It's the right thing to do."

"Understandable. But is it the right thing for *you* to do?"

I turned to look at him, wincing as my muscles complained against the quick motion. "What does that even mean?"

"You know, Sarah is worried about you. So are your friends, and even the people of Wildwood are concerned. Especially the parents of the afflicted, once they realized the torture they asked you to endure on behalf of their children. Torn, I would call them. There is a distinct reason you haven't seen any more parents snooping around the medical building, prodding you or even helping you escape so you can heal their kids. Your friend Sam has plied quite the guilt trip on their heads."

"I put them in that position," I replied quietly. His smooth non sequitur threw me.

"No, you didn't. You made a decision. A very *hard* one. If my word means anything, I believe it was the right one. Working with my daughter closer to the front than I ever have has highlighted the…brutality that I'd distanced myself from. Even under the threat of the Dreg, Ronan, we are doing much better than those early days after the Fall…" I saw Dylan's eyes look off into the distance and his flame hair seemed to flicker almost into inexistence. It was similar to when someone was looking at their status, but I recognized it as the faraway look of reminiscence well enough.

Instead of breaching the man's reverie, I examined what he'd said. He wasn't the first to talk about those 'early days.' As a matter of fact, I had a very unfortunate memory in the noggin from Dai that told me all about that despair from the point of view of those growing up on the surface. It wasn't the same as actually enduring it, but it put things into perspective. I was definitely not the only one to suffer, nor the only one with a motivation to change the state of things.

"You need to give yourself a chance to come to terms with yourself," Dylan said out of the blue.

"Huh?"*Man, is all this pain scrambling my brain too? It isn't like he stuttered.*

"Ronan, you aren't the same person that first walked into this town."

"Yes I am?" I responded, even if it sounded more like a question, even to my own ears.

"No." Dylan turned to meet my eyes and the flame of his hair darkened. "You are the same at your core. Your values, the things you hold dear, are the same. Your knack for problem solving and—if we are being fair—stubbornness, are one and the same.

"However, the burden of losing people? The burden of responsibility? That's a crucible you don't come out unscathed from. I wasn't much older than you when the Fall happened, you know. Seeing the world come crumbling down around us left many as empty husks. Shells of their former selves. We did what we could, but only those who wanted to live made it and even then, many didn't. *That* was one of those hard decisions. If we'd tried to save everyone, then no one would have been here within these walls to greet you three when you left the Bunker."

Dylan rose to his feet, coughing to clear his throat as it had become husky the more he talked about the past. The councilman took a deep breath before turning back to me again. "Take stock. Once you accept what you are now and *who* you are now, I think things will fall into place. You are needed, and your work is not forgotten. Know that."

Without further ado, the man strode away as if he hadn't been talking to me. I followed him with my eyes as he met up with a group of fishermen returning from Lake Sumter, smiling and patting them on the back as he went. I didn't know what had spurred the councilman to engage me in conversation, but I could almost hear his words resonating in my head still. *Accept what you are.*

The thought tumbled through my head for several more days. Other than for the updates from Sarah, I hardly left my bed as I tried to process that thought. *Turns out I haven't really been much of an introspective person, huh...* The slightly self-deprecating thought actually put what I believed to be one of my core personality aspects into perspective. I was sarcastic by nature, and sometimes that sarcasm let me think outside the box.

Like a rug unrolling before me, the comments Dylan made crystalized in my mind. They were all true. I was a brusque person by necessity, but also by choice. My friends associated with me partly because of our bond from the Bunker, but just like the others in the Bunker, we formed our own clique of shared interests. All that meant, however, was that I had been a true turdwad about the whole Devon situation. Not only that, it had propagated to several of my interactions with the people of Wildwood, Stonecrest, and Lake Weir. I'd turned one of my ways of bonding into a tool. That was definitely *not* who I wanted to be now.

By the end of my days of self-reflection, the alliance was still plodding forward. I came to accept that there wasn't anything I could do on the frontlines, but maybe that was okay. Even a stretched spring had some bounce to it. If I had to remain injured, then I would just find a way. I would find a way to contribute, like I did when I almost drove Elias mad about getting us access to the implants.Like I did by doubling down on helping the Metier Crystals. And, like a knot coming undone, I relaxed for what felt like the first time since leaving the Bunker.

A perfect note strum through my body. A notification flashed on the edge of my vision. *I unlocked a trait?* That was all the time I had before my body twanged like one of the practice bows Marie produced. The vibrations I'd been subtly feeling more and more suddenly tickled my whole body at once. Even with my eyes shut against the strange twitching of my limbs, and the accompanying pain from my injuries, I could see. Not necessarily *see*, per se, but I was distinctly aware of where things in my immediate vicinity were. The wooden logs holding the springy vines of Samuel's custom beds, the thin metal tin full of water for me to drink, the pair of mud-and-gore caked boots resting on the ground, ready for me to head outside. Beyond what I would guess was ten feet around me, everything was hazy blurs that suggested shapes to my new sensory input.

I don't know how long I spent there, panting, before the swell of a whole new sense evened out. I wasn't entirely in control, because as soon as I opened my eyes, the bubble of vibratory feedback around me overlapped with my sight. It was like hearing each step creaking underfoot on a wooden floor, except I was standing on concrete. And the end table was also creaking. As was the water in the cup. Thankfully, the air was blissfully 'silent,' but even just the empty room left me catatonic. *If this is anywhere close to how the afflicted feel, then I can relate with being spaced out.*

For the sake of keeping my sanity, I opened my status so I could focus on something else. *Let my subconscious work on figuring out all this sensory input. Hopefully.* With the world still shivering in my periphery, I clung to the unwavering script of the implant display.

**Subject:** Ronan Terrigan
**Health:** 100% (Unafflicted)
**Mana:** 100%
**Metier Quotient:** 5 (22%)
**Dreg Accumulation:** 0%
**LPS:** Wildwood Bunker, FL

**Communications**
**Party**
**Skills -** *(1) Selections Available*
**Traits -** *(0% Banked)*
**Attributes -** *Growth Quantified*
**Skills:**
Offensive
- <Stone Spike> / **Imbue** / <Mineral Strike>
Defensive
- <Mudpit> / <Earth Shell> / <Earthen Barrier>
- <Freeform>
Misc
- <Pith Mana Lock>
- <Infusion>
- <Memory Canal>
**Traits:**
Limestone Skin
Quake Osseum
Slurry Ichor
Harmonic Sinew
**Attributes:**
Strength: 1.76 > 1.79
Mobility: 1.53 > 1.63
Perception: 1.89 > 2.09
Refinement: 1.42
Containment: 2.28

There were a whole lot of things to unpack. First on the list was the fact that all the banked Dreg I had for my traits had vanished. The source of that, if I had to take a guess, was the new line in my traits.

**<Traits:>**
**<Harmonic Sinew>**
<Your tendons have taken on new seismologically sensitive properties while being nourished by your Ichor and bonded to your Osseum.>

While it wasn't overbanked like my other traits, the fact that it seemed to provide a literal sixth sense seemed trade enough for me. There was something about the description that tickled the back of my mind, but my occipital lobe was already busy enough making room for this new vibrosense, so I put it to the side. The other thing that blew my mind was the ginormous growth to my perception attribute, and the notable increases to strength and mobility. My other attributes had been crawling forward thanks to the abuse, training, and struggle of just living on the surface. The jump from Harmonic Sinews, however, threw me two whole Quotients' worth of growth in perception. *No wonder it feels like I can hear the fibers on this blanket...*

I spent several minutes just reading and rereading the information on my status. It had been a few weeks since I'd bothered to even look, and while my health, mana and attributes were the only things that really changed, it really put things in perspective for me. I wasn't even close to the Ronan that had first stepped gingerly on the surface, nor blasted plastic shrapnel all over his chest from improper precautions, or even killed a monster to save his friends. I was a Dreg Warrior, for better or for worse.

Snapping the status closed with a thought, I took a deep, steadying breath, swung my legs over the side of the bed and stood. I spent several seconds trying not to puke as vertigo overwhelmed me. That got pushed back down, and I steeled myself for a step.

Two very surprising things happened. First, there was actually *not a hint* of the pain I'd been suffering from for close to three weeks. Second, my face struck the ground so hard that if my head wasn't almost as hard as the concrete it was made of, I wouldn't have had to worry about much more after that.

# CHAPTER THIRTY-FOUR

## One Step at a Time

As embarrassing as that first step had been, at least there hadn't been anyone around to see it happen. One interesting discovery of slamming my face on the ground was that everything around me snapped into clear detail for a brief second before returning to the outlined nature I'd experienced while more comfortably on my bed. The fuzzy outer range of my sense also receded, as if the impact had pushed against the unknown materials. Thinking about it logically, that was exactly what it must have done.

Instead of bothering to get up and risk another groan-worthy, concussion-worrying fall, I stayed on the ground. It was closer to what would now be providing me sensory data. Hoping to test my earlier theory, I flicked my finger into the concrete. Sure enough, even if on a smaller scale to my face plant, a ripple of clarity originating from where my finger struck appeared around me.

Several minutes passed while I distracted myself testing the range of my new vibrosense. A flick of a toe here, a knock of knuckles here. Even if the sensory input was a little overwhelming, I just couldn't stop. It was like finding a hobby you never knew you wanted and then getting fully submerged in it. After tapping my knuckles against the particle board end table, I was also able to notice that different things seemed to 'buzz,' for lack of a better term, a particular way when my senses picked them up. *Maybe I can sense some of the density proper—*

"Ah! Mr. Ronan!" The young guard, Glen, that had been assigned to keep me from wandering stepped into the building. I'd been aware of a shifting pattern in my vibrosense, but my focus had been entirely on the particle board-concrete floor dilemma.

"Oh, ah—"

"Are you hurt? Do you need me to get Mr. Sam? Can I help with—"

"I'm alright, thanks," I said, coughing to try to politely interrupt the man's panic. Keeping my eyes shut, I pulled myself up to my hands and knees. The outline for the elf lit up with each shifting motion, but curiously only his feet and boots lit up clearly. Unfortunately, I didn't have much time to dwell on that as the eager youth yanked me to my feet.

*Impressive strength for an air-attuned.* I had to shake my head to stop myself from going off on a train of thought about the possibilities and tendencies of attunements as well as their corresponding attributes.

"Sir, you are standing upright!" Glen exclaimed.

"I've…had a development," I said, taking note that he was, in fact, right. Along with that and the utter lack of pain, I almost felt whole. *If only I could walk at all…*

Crushing that hesitation, I took a step forward. If my eyes plus my vibrosense were going to leave me bedridden, I would put one of them on hold. Since I didn't know *how* to put the vibrosense on hold, sight would just have to take a back seat.

The flat of my foot cushioned much of the force, but the ripple of clarity told me where everything nearby was roughly. If I had taken a longer step, I would have had to endure something worse than faceplanting on concrete. Stubbing a toe.

"Sir, are you sure you are okay? Why are you holding your

eyes closed? Oh my God, are you blind!? Ms. Ava is going to have my head. She told me to keep an eye on you and if your eyes aren't working, then she's going to take mine and maybe give them to you and then *I'll* be blind and—"

"Deep breath, Glen. Deep breath. I really *am* alright. I'm just dealing with…a strange trait, that's all."

Instead of a deep breath, the elf let out more air than his lungs had any right to hold before plunking down into one of the empty beds. The gesture was as clear as day to my new senses. "I thought I was a goner."

"I could use some help getting to the other afflicted, though," I said casually.

"Oh, sure let me—Wait a second. I'm supposed to keep you from doing that!"

"Yes, but that was before I was healed up. Now I'm good!" I said, throwing as much enthusiasm into my voice as I could. *How do people even maintain bubbly personalities? I only faked a sentence and I'm exhausted.*

My feelings aside, the burst of energy seemed to be all the confirmation Glen needed. The youth grabbed hold of my forearm and led me out of the door. Over the first few days of my injuries and reinjury, he'd been by my side to help me in all sorts of ways. Even if his mind was a runaway train at all moments of the day, Glen was an honestly nice person. That made me feel a tad bad about stretching the truth, but it wasn't like he would have to endure punishment. I had his back on this.

If my epiphany was accurate and my body was strengthened by my new trait, then helping the last afflicted should only be incredibly painful instead of death-inducing. While I couldn't see the people looking at the strange sight of me in a robe, barefoot, eyes closed, and with Glen leading me forward, it was almost a guarantee they were gawking. The fact that my vibrosense told me the clear ripples of feet around me halted when we got close was telling enough.

A familiar building came into vibro range. The thing that brought me up short was that the whole thing rippled constantly. There were ripples based out of the smithy, the leatherworkers, and even the quiet clothiers with hand-sized circles of clarity, but that wasn't it. It was the parts of the building that had been shaped by my skills that seemed to react to my senses, letting the ripples flow with the most clarity I'd perceived so far. My gaping must have gone on for long enough that Glen got nervous again.

"Sorry. Just taking in the sights," I said, unable to keep the smirk off my face at the play on words.

Glen shrugged, resuming the walk into the test room. Where before there had been a rough work table filled with infusions and various creature bits, there was now a strong table purposefully carved for containing the infusion blobs. There were two people talking quietly at said strong table, both of which pivoted in surprise. Far in the corner, near a pair of slit windows I didn't recall putting in the room, were the five remaining afflicted trainees.

I wasn't sure what exactly I expected to see, or sense, but it wasn't the mess of responses I got. First of all was the temperature mess. It felt like a cold winter day *and* a sauna at the same time in the room. Goosebumps rippled my skin even as sweat poured down my face. A frown creased my face as I tried to interpret the way *fire* came across my new vibrosense. It was like the ripples were more turbulent waves. Something about particle vibrations with changing temperatures must have had to do with it, but I simply didn't have the experience to really interpret the sensation. In contrast to the fire, the two water-attuned trainees had tight bubbles of near flat space around them. At least, I figured that was where the water afflicted were because I could feel the chill on my right side more.

Hesitant, but resigned to the task, I opened my eyes slowly after walking closer. Sure enough, the strange pattern impressions from vibrosense overlapped with my vision. Thankfully, the walk from the medical building had given me a baseline to work through the sensations and I didn't get the immediate urge to puke from vertigo. It was distinctly uncomfortable, and I didn't think I could walk far with both senses warring for control of my mental processes, but it was a good first step.

Not wanting to back down, I placed both of my hands on the two water afflicted. One landed on the turquoise ice that had replaced most of her upper body and the other splashed through the youth's arms. They were water with a strange membrane, similar to Blobby's exterior. Once I was able to get a hold of *something*, I flexed my will. <Infusion> and <Memory Canal> triggered. My mind was tugged to two different black-gray-white spaces. As if it had sensed some kind of discrepancy, the two spaces snapped together like two unfocused images suddenly jumping in resolution.

Thanks to the nature of <Rock Cocoon>, I was able to target both of the afflicted at once. Practicing the mental command was easy, and I pitted myself against both of their gray-space bubbles to get at them. Almost instantly, when their white spaces expanded, they touched. Like a bubble in the bath merging with another and growing in size, the blackspace buckled under the merwoman and lizardman struggling to reclaim their sanities.

Almost as soon as I'd started, I found myself curling into a ball with pain. But, for all that it consumed most of my attention, my body only groaned with displeasure. My vibro went a bit haywire as the pain wracked my muscles, but it soon passed along with the mana side effects.

"Mr. Ronan!" Glen's voice finally reached me through the pain. He was hovering over me, so I reached out my hand for him to help me to my feet. I was sore, but the fact that I'd been able to endure the exchange was already an incredible change.

"It's okay. I just… I just need a few minutes and I should be okay to help the others," I panted, glancing toward the fire-attuned trio. *This is going to be unpleasant for more than just my side effects.* Two of the orcs had parts of their bodies that seemed to smolder without prompting, and the third had the fire equivalent of Billy's misty limbs, if only reaching to his waist.

A quick series of ripples moving away from me told me that the people that had been working silently in the test room had scurried away. "T-they are probably going to get help," Glen said. I didn't need my enormous increase in perception to read the nervousness in his voice.

"Let them. We'll be done by the time they get back, and I certainly don't want to deal with their parents. Or Sam and Ava, because that will probably be a worse scowling than I want. I'd rather just be unconscious for it," I said, cracking my neck.

"Oh, alright. Wait—" Glen snapped to where I was leaning forward. *My mana is back up to over ninety percent and if the collective effect I'd observed to push back the Dreg grew with more bodies, then...* "What do you mean *unconscious*? Mr. Ronan!"

The world fell away as I pressed my forehead against one of the non-smoldering bits of the middle orc and placed my hands on the shoulders of the others. Same as before, three bubbles of whitespace of various sizes appeared around me. Hoping that my plan worked, I focused my skill on the one with the largest of the three. The green-skinned youth stirred, meeting my eyes, before taking in the space around him. I couldn't necessarily communicate, but I tried to gesture with my arms to push even as I focused on pouring mana into them.

Sure enough, two gifts sprouted from within them. One a placid stream of red, while the other a more jerky zig zag of energy. My own umber mana embraced both. The gentle stream slowed even more, but it fed on my mana to grow to enormous proportions around the orc. The other seemed to crystalize, refracting light in hundreds of directions as it continued to zip all over the place around its owner. Without much delay, the zippy gift crashed against the grayspaces, causing it to wobble. The accompanying Gift seemed to stretch, losing some of its thickness but making up for it in total circumference.

The moment the grayspaces of two of the afflicted overlapped, the whitespace seemed to get sucked, initiating that bubble effect I'd witnessed with the others. The legless orc stirred, and their Gift manifested as well. Without needing to be urged, all three of the Gifts spread the tunnel until the bubbles joined together. The boundaries were pushed further to accommodate the two orcs in the center until it crashed into the third and my consciousness got booted out.

The three youths crackled with sightless heat, searing the small hairs on my arms and flash drying the sweat that had been raining down my forehead. An unfortunate side effect of the method I'd discovered to help all three at the same time was that I didn't actually lose consciousness like I expected. My mana pool had only dropped just below thirty percent and the twitching ache in my abdomen actually hurt less than the flash burn the orc kids had given me.

Groaning as I laid there on the ground, Glen was in a panic. I could just barely hear him mumbling about how Ava was going to kill him, or maybe Sarah, and oh God, please not Clara with her caustic gas. He even drew up short as he remembered my other friend, Daniela, then the youth's knees buckled and *he* fainted.

"Well, that's just awkward…" I groaned, working my fingers to try to gauge how badly my burns had affected me. Other than the layer of crispy dead skin, nothing was out of place. There wasn't an ongoing smell of burning flesh, so I was also optimistic about that.

Exhaustion washed through me at the flurry of events that had happened throughout the day. My mind was still passively working through my vibrosense, incorporating it. Laying there on the ground, I was able to sense the gentle thrum of Glen as he fidgeted and even a gentler ripple from the five beds as the youths stirred from their Dreg afflicted states.

*Hey, I didn't pass out but maybe I can just… take a little nap…* I let the quiet frequencies of life lull me to sleep. It was just like falling asleep at a sleepover in the Bunker, except I was sure the vibrosense ripples were less disruptive than Daniela's snoring. For the first time in a long while, my sleep was free of the <Memory Canal> nightmares.

# CHAPTER THIRTY-FIVE

## Get Well Soon Present

My very pleasant bit of sleep was disturbed by the agitated jabbering of three very familiar voices. One of which I was surprised was jabbering at all, considering I couldn't recall the last time Alan had jabbered about… anything.

"Can you all argue *not* where I am sleeping?" I said, rolling over in bed. Unfortunately, the motion sent a ripple of clarity originating from my whole body. It felt like the equivalent of the Bunker's light alarm system flipping all the lights on at once when it was time for me to get up for morning lessons. Truly a whole new exercise in torture for those that weren't morning people and all thanks to my new trait.

"Ronan!" Ava called out, not bothering to be gentle as she gripped my shoulders and flipped me around to face her.

"Ouch?" I said, squinting up at her face.

"Ugh." The older woman released me and I flopped down to the bed, unable to keep the smirk from my face.

"Oh great. He *is* back," Sam said, and I didn't need to have my sight nor my vibrosense trained on him to know he rolled his eyes. He also couldn't hide the hint of relief in his voice.

"Good to see you too, Sammy," I said, squinting in his direction.

"What? Why are you doing that? I thought we established the joke has passed. Har har, very funny. Can we get to the serious part of this greeting, Ron?" Sam said in the closest approximation of a growl the blond could get to.

"Well, you see, that's part of the serious part," I said, lowering myself back down. My mind was still working out the cobwebs of sleep, but I ran them through what had happened —I checked the intensity of the light coming in through the windows of the medical building—the previous day. Leaving out the more introspective parts, I explained the facsimile to the Entity whitespaces that I encountered when I helped the afflicted. Neither commented on the fact that I finally revealed what had happened each time I touched one of the trainees, but I could see the wheels already spinning in their heads. For Alan's part, his eyes were ready to bulge out of his head.

Since he hadn't asked a direct question, I ignored the mumbling as Alan worked through his own complex thoughts and finished the story with my recounting of using consecutive trainees to 'pop' them out of the Dreg's oppressions.

"Of course," Alan said, notably louder. "Psychometrically linked interactions. If the Metier Entities can interface with both cerebellum and cerebrum, then it is entirely possible that those are one of the places where mana makes its primary manifestations. If I can interface with it using an analogous scaffolding, then…"

Without warning, the man dashed away. I was distinctly aware of how *little* his ripples actually were before he vanished, but I didn't know what that meant. Not that I had a handle on the whole *sixth sense* thing.

"I'll… check on him later," Ava said. One of her feet was pointed towards the door, but I watched as she made a deliberate decision to turn back around. Thanks to vibrosense, I could *feel* that her foot didn't change direction, even if she was facing me. "Your recklessness is the current problem."

"I'm fine, really. Well, it's more like I have one of my cylinders clogged, then someone slapped on an external cylinder to compensate," I said, attempting to explain how I felt about my sight plus vibro situation.

"Brain probing is really outside my wheelhouse," Sam said, gesturing towards my slightly singed head of hair. His decentralized nerves curled and uncurled in his hands. Now that I wasn't restrained, I could shiver freely at the sight of them and at the possibility of being touched by them.

"Can you tell us anything else? How are you really feeling, Ron?" Ava asked, turning from sharing a look with Sam.

*Honesty time, is it? I* have *been a huge turd.* "I'm sorry. I *am* fine, better than I have been in a bit. I just... I guess I needed to take a step back. Since *that* wasn't happening, getting sat on my ass by our new reality really did the trick for me."

All I could do was shrug helplessly when neither of them responded. Squinting at them seemed to do part of the trick to reduce my vertigo, so I was amazed they were able to keep such serious expressions through my recounting. After a few seconds of awkward silence, the two of them let out deep sighs.

"Ron... You know what? I'm not gonna do it again. I think you are a big enough boy to recognize your own shortcomings. Just... the next time you feel like gaining a masochistic streak in order to feel better about things you can't control, do it when none of us are around. Please?" Ava said, the woman leveling a pair of gray-glowing eyes at me.

"Noted," I said, tongue tied and unwilling to respond to her level of intensity. It wasn't like she was wrong either.

"I'm going to check on Alan. Samuel, please help him deal with... whatever he's dealing with." After meeting my eyes one last time, she turned and strode out of the medical building.

"Daniela is going to tear you a new one, so I'm not gonna bother," Sam said, plopping onto the bed across from me. "*Buuut...* it's good to have my friend back."

"It's good to be back. I'm not looking forward to *that* conversation," I said, scratching the back of my head. "She's probably still pissed at me."

"Nah, but she will be when she hears about your shenanigans. You know she's been keeping tabs on how you're doing. When she's not blasting fire down the Dreg's throats, of course. Hard to keep track of where she is when she's constantly alternating between Lake Weir, Stonecrest, and here."

That tidbit of information made me feel both better and worse for being a crap friend. There was nothing to do but apologize and try to be more cognizant in the future. I asked Sam for some suggestions on how to deal with my new... sensory situation. If I couldn't fight, I would still help out in town, but already my blood was itching to punch some faces in. Or pick them, or slash them, or generally strike them with stones of some variety. *Man, really discovered a bloodthirsty streak since coming to the surface, huh?*

Samuel spent some time probing me, to my chagrin, and having me better describe what I sensed. After I walked him through my testing and my observations about people, materials, and the like, he pulled out a notepad. His face scrunched as he wrote down several notes, prodded me some more and asked pointed questions about what happened while I kept my eyes open. The whole barrage of questions and testing took most of the morning, and by the end, I almost would have rather helped another afflicted. Nonetheless, Samuel did not disappoint.

"Here is my recommendation," he said, handing me one of his notepad sheets. The writing, in typical medical professional fashion, was barely legible. It might have been a result of vibro lighting it up as it crinkled in my hand, but I was pretty sure it was the writing. The short of it was that I should alternate between relying entirely on vibro, being blind so to speak, and then running simple exercises with both. This included not just physical fitness type training, but small hand eye coordination. He even recommended that I try swimming in the lake, as a means of testing the limits.

Pushing *that* frightening experience for future Ronan, I

agreed to a few more days in the medical building until I could safely traverse without sight. Samuel made the point clear that if he found me attempting anything combat-related before he and Ava did another physical on me, I would be physically forced to remain in bed. The fact that he said that with a perfectly flawless smile definitely got the message across.

With his checkup more or less complete, Sam got me up to date on the state of the afflicted. While most were still struggling, they were already up and about. Many mentioned they had vague memories of when I'd interceded on their behalf, but not all of them. That was fine with me. Being recognized wasn't my goal in their treatment, even if I knew the gossips would already have that information spread through the town. It often made me wonder why we needed our comm-plants if the rumor mill was often more effective for sharing information.

When Sam eventually left, I laid back on the mattress and read through the list of tasks he'd suggested I work my way through. Starting from brushing teeth and toe touches all the way to sprints and cartwheels.

"Did he have to make this so comprehensive? It's like I need to relearn how to live," I sighed. *I suppose I am. Man, this is going to suck...*

While I was completely right about how the vibrosense adjustment process went, it gave me the opportunity to reacclimate myself with the town after my days in recovery. Moving about with vibro certainly slowed me down, but I wasn't locked up like before. Ava still scowled at me every time she saw me, but that wasn't too far from the norm before we'd stepped on the surface.

Compared to before our excursion to the other towns, morale was at an all-time high. Part of it was the return of the afflicted, considering they were related to a not-insignificant portion of the town. Another was that something akin to 'trade' had been established. Every three days, a relief team of Wild Guard would rotate north, bringing some of the armor and weapons the crafters of Wildwood had been able to infuse. Even without the guiding hand of the status the implants provided, the other Fallen had no problem using the attribute boosts of the items. Even those who were born before the Fall could, at the very minimum, benefit from the defensive differ-ence the tanker armor and cowls provided, the former of which was being almost entirely snagged by the people of Stonecrest.

A thrill of excitement filled me as I thought about my proto-type armors spreading far and wide. It wasn't even something I'd considered a possibility, but the more I spoke with the Guard and some of the Wildwoodians brave enough to go along on the squad swaps, the more I realized it was more inevitable than anything.

The final thing that seemed to blow up morale was the fact that people were learning to infuse without a direct memory transfer from me. It started in the forge, more or less as an acci-dent. One person infusing was interrupted by another person holding an uninfused piece. The accidental mishap turned into a collaboration of sorts, wherein the dwarf that had been lugging the sheet of metal to cool touched upon the concept of infusion. It was subsequently repeated until the dwarf in ques-tion was able to unspool Pith from one of the blobs alone, essentially giving him the miscellaneous skill without even having the implant or myself to shove it in his noggin. From there, almost everyone in town wanted to learn it; this explosion of knowledge soon trickled to the other towns, even if their infrastructure lagged behind the Wildwoodian infusion bandwagon.

In my frantic crafting, I'd left a tool to shore up defenses for our people and I couldn't be happier. The uselessness wasn't much diminished, but I at least cloaked myself in the mantle of aiding from the background. It wasn't a mantle I wanted to hold longer than absolutely needed.

So, the first day after my return to ambulatory shenanigans, the crafting hall was an explosion of activity. Many had been reserved about experimenting since the afflicted were being housed there, but almost overnight, the addition I'd seen start to spring up was complete, and twice over. Each of the major crafting professions— smith, woodworker, and tailor —each had a strong room attached to their wings of the hall. It was fairly astounding how quickly the people worked, but I could sympathize.

If you spent your whole life cowering in the dark, unsure if life would mean anything regardless of your struggles, and suddenly there was a shining opportunity to actually gain control over your life, you would grasp it firmly however you could. *I certainly did.*

As I worked on getting acclimated to vibro just by being in proximity to the thriving hive of activity that was the crafting hall, a most unexpected person pulled up beside me.

"Vanguard," Rommel rumbled.

"You can call me by my name, Rommel," I said, chuckling to myself. My eyes were closed, but the man's bass of a voice was hard to forget. His footstep ripples were unfamiliar, but they marked him as a large individual. Putting two and two together from there wasn't hard.

"I believe you are more than just your name. Perhaps you haven't heard it, but the Bunker Busters are all spoken of by their nicknames," he said.

"Oh? Didn't realize we all had one," I said, turning to the man and opening my eyes to a squint. I'd heard *mine* several times on the front while someone in the squads wanted to get my attention quickly.

"That is the point." For the first time I could recall, I heard the large orc laugh from deep in his chest. It was curious to see the force actually manifested as tiny waves flowing through the ground. "No one wants the Torch to know they've been talking about her behind her back."

"Let me guess, that's Daniela?"

"Precisely."

"Honestly? I totally understand. Even if her nickname is pretty cool," I said, snorting at the blush that would creep on her face before she *torch*ed the people responsible. "What's Sam's?"

"The Druid."

"Again, can't really argue with that. Sometimes I think that Sam is better at talking to plants than he is people." That earned me an amused huff from Rommel. *You fall in that same camp, buddy; except maybe not plants, probably little defenseless animals, if the stereotype holds.*

"There is something I've prepared for you," he said, breaking the silence that had fallen after the brief conversation. "Please follow me."

Without bothering to wait for a response, Rommel strode forward towards the original strong room. Focusing on the trailing ripples of clarity his steps left, I tapped the ground with the heavy wooden pole Marie had been kind enough to wood-shape for me. Rommel's footsteps, plus my own tapping, was more than enough for me to get my bearings and walk a normal stride forward. When I stepped into the main hall, some of the people loitering discussing this or that project parted without a word.

*That* was distinctly awkward, but my pseudo-blindness wasn't necessarily a well-kept military secret. I caught a few nods through my squint and offered a genuine smile in return. As much as I wanted to get back to fighting, the act of learning, crafting, and building was what grounded my thoughts. Just as I was ready to make a snide remark about what the orc had 'prepared' for me, I stepped around the bend and *felt* what he was referring to.

In my days after developing my vibrosense, I'd discovered that things affected by mana reacted differently to the sense. It was part of my hypothesis of why I was only able to sense people's feet clearly, even if the vibrations of their motions should have traveled all the way through their bodies. This was especially true from Blobby when he came to visit me and I had absolutely zero warning before I got a chest full of gelatinous slime.

This strange phenomena occurred in the *opposite* way with infused items or materialization byproducts, meaning things conjured into being thanks to a skill. My naginata, for instance, put out long, quiet waves of energy just *existing*. Sam's armor also lit up with the strange eddies of live fire when he took it off at the entrance of the medical building. The entire building that was the crafting hall let out deep steady throbs that lit it up in vibro every so often.

The thing laying on the strong table shimmered with the eddies of a fire infused item, but they were stronger than anything I'd seen. I hadn't had the opportunity to look at the stinger staff Clara carried after gaining vibro, but I couldn't imagine even *that* having a stronger signature.

I opened my eyes all the way, vertigo be damned, just to be able to get a proper look at the piece of armor in front of me. In as few words as possible, it was astounding. Maybe not an artistic masterpiece, but it was beautiful in its practicality. Two of the torso-sized chitin plates had been melded seamlessly together, accented by some of the head-sized plates of a Q1 ant studded all over it. The infusion welds weren't anything fancy, but there wasn't a single skip in them. My fingers itched to grab hold of the tower shield.

"Go ahead. A defender should have a proper shield," Rommel said. I'd forgotten he was in the room.

I took some unsteady steps forward, making sure to keep my eyes open, before my palm landed on the shield. It was reminiscent of an old Roman shield I'd seen before, a flat semicircle beneath the studded exterior. The piece of armor was warm to the touch as I picked it up. I almost dropped it in surprise. It had to be almost fifteen pounds of shield, and the reason was revealed when I flipped it over.

Bands of metal crisscrossed the inside, also welded to the chitin with the power of a fire infusion. There were four enarmes on the inside, so the shield could be worn vertically or horizontally along its length. Lining the path where the arm would go were several entwined bits of wolfhound leather and woodshaped supports to take yet some more of the force.

With the intense once over I gave the piece of armor, it was no wonder its information bloomed in my implant.

<Quotient 4 Chitin Scutum>

<Attribute: Strength>

<Trait: Force Dispersal>

The shield was yet one more level higher than my own helm, lending a massive jump to strength if activated. My body itched to put it to the test, but I was liable to hurt myself more than actually come across as even slightly proficient.

"Take this as thanks for your sacrifices. And, if I know you at all, to use it to protect us," Rommel said, snapping me out of my daze.

"Oh, you are damn right I'll use it!" I slipped my arm through the enarmes and grunted slightly at the weight. If it had been before stacking five Quotients and numerous passive gains, I would have struggled just to hold the thing for long. Now, it felt like I had put on my <Earth Shell> just by picking it up. Only my head and shins down were exposed as I hefted the shield. If I really wanted to bunker down behind it, it wouldn't take much of a crouch. "I'll get—Woah!"

I attempted to spin to look back at Rommel. While holding on to the shield, my vibro picked up the surge of motion as well as the heat ripples and made me miss my step. Like a clumsy fish out of water, I flopped onto the tower shield and bonked my head on the top lip before spilling out on the ground. Once again.

"Perhaps walking is advised before putting the shield to use?" Rommel said, chuckling.

"Touché, orc boy. Touché."

# CHAPTER THIRTY-SIX

## Escalating

The fireball flew true, but my shield easily intercepted it. With it out of the way, a <Mudpit> flowed out of my hand. The liquified earth caught three of my five opponents, causing them to sink two feet into the ground as they struggled to resurface. I used three minutely powered <Stone Spikes> aimed at their chests to mark them as 'out' without feeding the skill enough mana to actually injure them.

A tingle on the back of my neck pushed me to fall into a roll to my left. An elf girl passed by the space I'd occupied like a buzzsaw, pinwheeling with blades of condensed air along her arms. Without waiting for permission, I planted my shield on the ground and used it as support to kick her in the chest. Now spinning out of her control, she slumped to the ground. The steady ripples coming from her downed body told me she wasn't preparing anything, so I turned back to the last remaining fighter.

He'd been keeping his distance, hoping to get an opening, but vibro gave me the advantage in melee range. Seeing that it wasn't going to present itself, Igor gave me a savage grin. The one-armed orc rushed me down.

"<Stone Spike>, <Stone Spike>!" I released two half-powered skills in the path of the orc, but the man displayed the main reason he was still allowed on the squads even missing an arm. Gouts of flame like thrusters sprouted from his shoulders to redirect around the attacks. The third spike I raised right as he dodged, he merely crashed through. A haze of smoke trailed him as he shook off the bits of rock and his eyes locked on mine.

A tiny wave of vertigo threatened to overcome me as I pivoted to put my shield between us. I squashed it. The force of vibro settled down around me and my focus pinned sight as the dominant sense. It was the trick I'd been working on over the last week in order to shortcut my sixth sense's sensitivities. Each motion still registered within my bubble of clarity, but it was hardly obtrusive when it let me see the direction forces were being transmitted. *And right now, they are being transmitted by that punch to my face.*

Since I'd never done it, and I wanted to test just how much improving my strength had affected my sturdiness, I cast an empowered <Earth Shell>. The stone bloomed up from my pores to cover everything from my torso up except for my nostrils and eyeballs. Bracing my feet in a wide stance and flexing my back, I took the punch right on the forehead. The <Earth Shell> there fractured, but held.

The first thing I noticed was that it was the strongest physical hit I'd received since vibro came into my life. The second was that if I hadn't been suppressing vibro, I would have been thoroughly scrambled by the force of the impact dispersing through my body. The third was that when I braced properly to take a blow with my whole body, at least with the strength of a weakened Igor, I barely felt it.

The orc grunted as his fist came back bloody, at least two of his fingers bent the wrong way. Before he was able to use his thruster skill to get back out range, I cracked my arm's shell and delivered a gut punch that doubled him over. As he was folding, I shoved my tower shield in his face and knocked him back to the ground. The heat from force dispersal barely tickled the fire-attuned man, but the impact still carried a fair bit of weight with it, not to mention the rock-encased force of my punch to the abdomen.

"Halt!" Sarah called. A grave Ava and Samuel stood beside her. Even from their spot across the training area, I could see Ava start to discuss something with Sarah and Samuel begin to manipulate his vines. Small bushes bloomed beside Igor and the air blade elf I'd kicked, dousing them in healing energy. Three smaller vines helped the trainees trapped in my <Mudpit> by breaking up the soil around their legs.

I offered Igor my hand as soon as the <Health Bump> had finished its work. "Good work."

The one-armed man huffed. "You were fighting us with one arm tied behind your back the whole time."

*Wow, an arm joke? Talk about dark humor.* "It's not entirely true. I tapped out my mana pool fighting you guys. If I hadn't been able to trap all three of the others right at the beginning, I would have been down to melee only."

"A melee where dealing damage to you is just as hard as at range. I will say, it felt good to go all out and not be worried about dying. Godfrey, Rommel, and Sarah are often too busy for me to spar with them," Igor said, shrugging. "Not many people can take a punch from me anymore."

"Tell me about it," I said, brushing the crumbling rock off my hair.

"Show off," he said, huffing a small gout of flame through his nostrils.

"I wouldn't have gotten a chance to show off if not for you," I said, remembering what I'd hoped to do now months ago. "I've meant to thank you for that."

"Breaking your ribs? No problem. I don't think I'll get many more chances to do that anymore," Igor said, shooting me a tusk wide smile. "Don't mention it. If you hadn't gotten the other kids, we would have both been missing more than just a limb between us."

"Yeah, I'm sor—"

"Nope. None of that pity crap. I got enough of that from my mom and my sister. Just make sure you are available so I can sock you in the jaw a few times during my next training slot and we'll call it even. Deal?" Igor reached out with his hand and we shook. The two of us shot the breeze for a few minutes as the trainees hobbled over to us.

We ran through the scenario verbally, commenting on what they could have done to change the tide of the fight. The lizardman and the dwarf in the group were particularly interested in learning how I was able to control my <Stone Spike>skill so well, since they had similar Gifts. Igor praised the young elf for her initiative to get in there, and asked her to stop by his Wild Fist squad house for more hand-to-hand pointers. Hilda, the boisterous dwarf with the chipped tooth, was going to be off Lake Weir shift for the next week and she could spend some time with the youth. She practically squealed and the three trainees discussed how else they might use their Gifts in hushed voices.

When the councilwoman of New Earth finally joined us, her expression was still grave. *That has nothing to do with my combat readiness assessment.*"What's up, Sarah?"

"Tec just got word that the Appendage attacked Wec," she said, her face set into an even deeper scowl than usual.

My whole body tensed as the image of the giant crow attacking Lake Weir ran through my mind. "Casualties?"

She shook her head. "None. Thankfully, sending Arnold and that Stoneshaper to Lake Weir was the right call. The two of them improved on your shelter design to reinforce the buildings in the town against the bile bomb runs. Unfortunately, the town's food was completely smothered by that strange death aura. The healers have been running ragged dealing with the weird infections the creature left behind, but the next few days are going to be a close thing."

"What can we do?" I asked, stepping closer.

"Get ready," Ava said as she walked around Sarah's imposing orcish form. "Because you are cleared to fight."

A flame that had been lying dormant in my chest ignited. I wasn't sure if it was the fact that this was my *third* combat readiness assessment, or if it was the sudden jump in attacks by the Dreg, but I wasn't going to fight her on the decision. After almost two weeks of near-constant nausea, I'd finally had my efforts recognized. Vibro wasn't completely under my control, but with people risking their lives on the frontline against the Dreg, I wasn't going to wait to join until I was in optimal condition. At the very least, I could be the human meat shield.

— + —

The rest of the morning went by in a blur. The months of strife since first throwing off the chains of the Dreg had turned the people of Wildwood into well-oiled machines of action. Samuel, Marie, and two others who'd awakened Gifts worked to create *and* reinforce the handful of carts the Wild Guard had been using. Each was loaded up with food from the stores in town, Dylan and William relenting on their winter stock. They'd been hesitant to send so much, but Sarah went into the council room then came back out ten minutes later with the approval. No one had seen the two older gentlemen since, but they were sure they were going to show up eventually...

Meanwhile, the rest of the town plugged away. Healers redoubled on the fields while the demons of the town worked the compost piles using a variety of decay, rot, and caustic Gifts. After a field was cleared, Clara was actually called in to cast her fire-augmented caustic cloud to clear away weeds and vegetation to nurture the next round of plants the life-attuned were going to coax into bloom.

I watched the whole procession with a stunned expression. There wasn't even space in the crafting hall for me to attempt to contribute with last minute touches to a pair of pendulum force cannons, or to a new round of shields that had death instead of fire infusions at the base. The whole process was an exercise in anxiety, personally, as I found myself as a courier for the stuff being loaded in the cart. Sarah took stock of all the Guards present, making sure that at least four squads remained to defend the town in addition to the Big Guns. No one commented on the contents of said squads being some of the more *green* members. Once those were selected, she had the rest of the squads line up on the bridge over Lake Sumter.

Occasionally I would catch glimpses of a shaggy mop of blond hair on a lanky frame, but Sam was often gone as soon as I spotted him. He was simply in too much demand. Daniela actually arrived while the town was in a frenzy, bearing the same message in case the Entities had failed to communicate somehow. Her custom armor had burn patches and her curls were shorter than I remembered them, but her expression was as fierce as I'd ever seen her. My staring obviously alerted her and she almost seemed to jump when she saw me sitting almost casually on a log by the bridge. Blobby, being the slime that it was, waved an appendage in greeting. All I could do was hold my head in my hands.

Unfortunately, Daniela didn't approach me but at least she gave me a stiff nod of acknowledgement. It was something, and more than I could ask. Nevertheless, I stood and watched as lunch was passed out for all the Wild Guard assembled. A young boy, one I recognized as one of the most recent to awaken his Gift, placed the bowl of salad in my hands before skedaddling on a trail of fire. Nervous to go, but not wanting to be in the way or rushing, I ate my salad in relative peace. There was something about it that was spicy, but not in a burn-your-mouth kind of way. It sort of set you tingling, and I could see it wasn't just me as the squads shifted more in their spots.

"I'll make it brief!" Councilman Dylan spoke over the crowd. *There he is!* "Things are not going to look great when you get there. Most of you have been to Lake Weir since the first excursion. This is going to be worse. Your goal is to provide relief and to come home safe. The town of Wildwood cannot stand without its people, but neither can we stand by and let others suffer."

His flame hair rose higher with each word, a beacon that focused all of the Guard. Instead of closing out his speech, he stepped back and let Sarah take the fore. "For the future!"

"We guard!" the squads responded, a cacophony of sound that shook the ground and lit the entire bridge with vibro. The stomps of feet that trailed were hard to follow as the Wild Guard marched towards the north. It wasn't a military-grade procession, but everyone in the squads moved with practiced ease and remained clustered with their peers. Clara, Rommel, and Godfrey took up the lead as they headed across the bridge. Lilly rode on top of one of the ox-pulled carts in the middle of the squad groups.

I hopped to my feet only to run into Sarah. With the thrum of footsteps, I hadn't even bothered to actually use my eyes to spot her as she came. Her ripples had been hidden, and I'd had my eyes closed to prevent vibro from leaving me a nauseous mess on the ground. "Oh, Sarah. Sorry, I didn't have Sam and Danny with me, otherwise I would have lined up the Bunker Busters with the others."

She immediately waved it off, instead pulling a small wooden box from a satchel at her side. "Daniela is on her way already, and Sam is going to meet you at the car-wall. I just wanted to make sure you got this before you left."

Inside the wooden box was one of the emblems I'd seen on the squad leaders. It mirrored the one on Sarah's own armor, except for one key difference: it was almost perfect. The edges of the metal still looked slightly uneven and there was a hint of rust in the emblems, but it was a *league* above what everyone else in the Wild Guard wore. The circle's six smaller emblems were stamped clearly: a sun, a flame, a stone, a moon, a raindrop, and a swirl of wind. Sitting in the middle of that was the shield with one final addition.

"A... house?" I asked aloud as I held the handcrafted brooch up.

"No, rock brain," Sarah said, channeling her inner Daniela. "A *bunker*."

A smile quirked my face and for some reason, dust chose that moment to assault my eyes. Nevertheless, I met Sarah's eyes and nodded. "Never had jewelry before."

"Don't get used to it. *Something* has to remind people that you actually can differentiate your head from your rear," Sarah said, huffing and crossing her arms. Her voice lowered, and the light amusement was gone with the wind. "You bring them back, Ronan. Bring them back like you brought us back."

A tingle ran down my spine as I remembered our first encounter with the Big Guns. The clench of my mana tensed my whole body, so all I was able to manage was a nod and a vicious smile. Sarah let me and Blobby pull up the rear of the procession. Even from all the way across the bridge, where Sarah and the other members of Wildwood were no bigger than my thumb, I could feel the weight of responsibility settle across my shoulders. Their stares burned a hole through my back, seeking out their loved ones.

"Hmmm. Heavy is the head indeed," I said, recalling one particularly animated session of literature at the hands of Elias himself.

# CHAPTER THIRTY-SEVEN

## Foothold

The squads were well on their way down the fresh and new intertown road, nicknamed AE-1 as the Attuned Earth's first road. Possibly presumptuous, but I wasn't going to argue with the dozens of people who'd worked to make the trade route happen. Myself included. Not long after the car-wall had left our sight, a quiet spurt of ripples entered the extended range of my vibrosense.

Considering the direction it was coming from, I wasn't particularly concerned it was an enemy, but I settled into a low stance. Samuel quirked an eyebrow, but spun on his heels to draw his femur club. Finger-wide vines curled around his feet, ready to pounce.

The squad closest to the back noticed my shift, and turned to face the possible threat with practiced ease. A bulky lizardman glared at the packed dirt road from over one of the chitin shields while the rest of his group held skills and Gifts at the ready. When the steps drew closer and a fiery outline appeared along with a plume of dust, I almost cast <Stone Spike> right in its path. Thankfully, I recognized the scrunched up face amidst the fire with my much improved perception.

"Is that...?" Samuel started.

"At ease," I called over my shoulder, straightening and glaring at the approaching form. The squad shared a tense look before opting to catch up with the procession. It had stopped not long after the squad had formed up, but with the number of people, it still took a minute for everyone to respond. *We'll need to work on that for sure.*

A gangly middle-aged man slowed his pace as we came into view. Steam was rising from his body and I could see the flush on his face extended at least down his neck and to his arms. Smoke continued to trail out of his ears for several seconds as Alan gathered himself. "Need. Field. Tests."

"Alan, you know it will be exceedingly dangerous in Lake Weir, right?" Samuel said, releasing a <Health Bump> into the man that set his breathing to a less frantic pace.

"Danger is irrelevant. The purge protocol will require me to finetune the frequency and amplitude to match the energy signature of the most recently—"

"The thing you were working to deal with the Dreg Entity?" I said, cutting Samuel off before he could protest. We both shared the biggest concern for the man: his unpredictable nature and poor social interactions could lead to him getting in a less-than-ideal pickle. However, if the researcher was close to developing the weapon they needed...

"Yes. With the Categorical increment to the Weirdian Entity, research should continue unabated," Alan said, standing up straight and adjusting his white lab coat and duffle bag. I had no idea what was in the bag, but I was sure it wasn't camping or survival equipment.

Samuel turned me around, giving Alan our back. Our eyes met and a rapid fire conversation took place. Even the power of the comm-plant couldn't compare with the pseudo-mind reading close family could develop. It was mostly in the eyebrows.

*He can't stay,* his eyes said.

*We need him.*

*Are you going to keep tabs on him?*

*If I have to. We need this, and if being in Lake Weir will put him closer, it's a chance we need to take.*

"Gah! Fine. But you better put a squad in charge of checking up on him. We both know you are liable to go down a rabbit hole of your own. That's *if* you don't spend the whole time getting knocked on the head beyond the wall, you brute," Sam snapped, disengaging from the conversation entirely.

Alan hadn't reacted at all to our dialogue, but the moment I turned around, he just picked up his bag and headed after the caravan of Wild Guards. My eyes landed on the lizardman of the squad that had turned around, the squad leader based on the brooch on his upper back, and a smile crept on my face. I was almost certain that I saw a shiver run down his spine before the green-scaled man looked my way.

Having Alan tacked on to the procession was as much an exercise in patience as I expected it to be. Thankfully, the man only asked inane questions of the poor Wild Guards I assigned as his overwatch. The elf girl in the squad had explicit instructions to find me or contact me with the comm-plant if Alan started to amble or act erratically. No small part of me felt bad for thinking of Alan as a troublesome resource, rather than the brilliant mind that he was, but needs must. It was one of the many hard decisions I'd come to realize were just a part of living on the surface.

Everything was going well on the trip, and our stop at Stonecrest was brief. One of the Stoneshapers was reinforcing the one assigned up north and would ride with us. To my surprise, I saw that Patrick Patrick outright refused to go as the small party of Stonecrest's leadership greeted the Wild Guards. He insisted that he had responsibilities to maintain in Stonecrest. Rachael didn't look happy by the public forum the man employed when the towns had been cooperating so well, but the other Stoneshaper, Tara, jumped to Patrick's defense and into the wagon. Due to the pressing nature of our deployment, the arguing was minimal from that point on.

On the shorter stretch from Stonecrest, our group wasn't really concerned about encountering any enemies. Not only did we *not* have the attraction aura of Wec, but the sheer size of the group made all the creatures wary of approaching us. Many watched us from deep in the woods and pre-Fall ruins. The only thing that made me keep vibro running on full was the possibility of encountering another cottonmouth. The ambush snake was the only creature that seemed to be able to avoid detection until the caravans were right on top of it.

Just as I was getting ready to relax, we entered the implant range for the defenders of Lake Weir.

"Support to the east!" a voice called, wide to all people in range of comms.

"There's a deer building a ramp!" a feminine voice called back.

"Got it," another, more familiar, voice rumbled as Maurice cut through the panicked chatter.

"All forward!" Clara called out and the squads whirled into action.

One of the squads was left behind with the four wagons as the rest of us charged forward. Very quickly, the variances in attributes were made apparent as Sam and I, as well as the half-squad of the New Hopers, took the lead. However, the months fighting and defending, even with the increased requirements of higher Quotients and more participants, had pushed the majority of the Guard to Q5, if not the cusp of it. Finally being able to dissociate their kills also made an enormous difference for their power leveling.

Clara quickly took control of the larger scale direction. The most mobile squads, the Dervishes and the Night Whistles, split off to round the wall from southeast and southwest. Tara the Stoneshaper and Igor's Wild Fist cut a hole into the side of the wall and allowed the rest of the group into the town without slowing down. Before we were even through, Clara shot me a meaningful glance that said it all.

As soon as the last person was through, I turned and slapped an <Earth Wall> to cover the opening. My fine tuning with my amplified skills was still rough, so when the rock pinched upward, it pushed a bit *too* much. The top of the wall cracked, and I grimaced. *I'll fix that later.*

When I turned around, I made a mental note of the various changes that had taken place since my last visit to Lake Weir. Several towers now rose up along the town's perimeter and evenly throughout the town's territory. Even from the south side, I could see flashes of red, blue, and purple coming from the towers built right onto the top of the old school. Connecting those towers and the main building were souped up versions of my covered pathways. Metal glistened, polished smooth by bile, but holding strong. The rest of everything visible in the town was covered in muck and the stench of rot permeated the air.

"Clara, send a squad east and the rest straight north!" Daniela's voice chimed through the comm-plant.

Surely directed by the demoness, Igor and his Wild Fists split off and vanished around one of the school's exterior buildings that hadn't been reinforced by mana-created stone.

Vibro swelled around me, throwing all sorts of ripples from the rushing group around me. It all blended with the signature of the different materials I hadn't familiarized myself with and I missed a step as vertigo tipped me forward.

"Woah there, cowboy," Sam said, pulling me back by my vest before I could tip forward.

A <Health Bump>, quickly followed by his <Adrenal Surge>, flowed into me to clear the sensation. Doing my best to remain in the fight, I suppressed the feedback from vibro as much as I could by focusing on the smell around me. It was a distinctly unpleasant choice, and it almost made me nauseous by itself, but it honed my focus enough to dull vibro.

"I'm good. Just... adjusting," I huffed as we turned to stay under one of the covered pathways.

"Good, because we need some ramps," the blond said, turning to point to where we approached the stairs up the wall. At the speed the group was going, we would just crash into it. *Except for the air-attuned. They might be able to clear the new twenty foot walls around the town.*

Instead of dealing with all that, it was my turn to act once again.

"Everyone in two lines!" I yelled. The group looked distinctly confused, but the squads of four and five quickly oriented themselves in front of me and Sam, Clara at the lead.

Bracing for the pain that would follow the manipulation, I cast <Earth Wall>, at half power, focusing on height versus width. Just forcing the slight modification caused me a headache, and my abdomen twitched as mana flowed into my antler helm before the amplified skill triggered. Thankfully, my aim was good. The slab of stone rose up from the ground unbidden, crashing onto the top of the wall for support thanks to the angle at which I'd released it.

The squads didn't slow down at all as they clambered up it, spreading to reinforce the Weirdians on the wall. Already spurts of magic were splashing down against whatever creatures were on the other side. My feet took me to the top of the wall, <Crystal Cascade> already taking shape over my palm.

— + —

"This intensity... Something's changed," Clara said, rubbing her shoulder where a Tendril deer had impaled her. The creature had died not long after thanks to inhaling a lungful of her scorching death cloud, but the wound had still knocked her out of the engagement fairly early. It was healed now, but there was only so much the life-attuned could do about the phantom discomfort that followed severe injuries. I was no stranger to it.

"Damn right something's changed," Daniela said, slamming

her hand down on the table. "They finally grew a pair and sent that *beast* after the town!"

"What Ms. Eloquence here is getting at," Devon said, cutting Daniela off before she could go on one of her tirades. *He's not being unreasonable. It's an important discussion and we need to stay on topic. Why do I just want to punch him in his chiseled jawline?* "Is that Summerfield is now as hunkered down as it's going to get."

"Confirmed?" Ian asked. Maurice stood behind his seat to the right, also nursing a nasty broken arm. It had been healed until he'd crashed from the Overhealed affliction, so he had to ride it out before finishing the treatment.

"Oh, Summerfield is Dreg-ed up, alright. It's got some strange plant walls just shy of the ones we've got here," Daniela said, throwing a glare at Devon before it softened on the old man. "No new watchtowers other than the two originally in town, but they've got crows posted up there. Getting close is rough. By our count, there are at least twenty of the humanoids at Q3 and a handful at Q4. We are fairly confident that their Tendril beast horde has been culled severely, outside of a few notable exceptions in the form of those damn birds and their big daddy."

"That's what they are throwing at us?" I asked. The fact that I was squinting at the gathered group had already been addressed, thankfully, but the Weirdians still gave me strange looks. I couldn't care less. After fighting for the majority of the day, my head was throbbing and I'd already puked twice out on the battlefield.

Daniela didn't say anything, but she nodded in response. The tension in the classroom-turned-war-room could have been cut with a knife as everyone processed the information. Maurice and Ian started speaking quietly between each other, even if it was perfectly audible for everyone in the room. Five Quotients worth of perception would do that. Instead of letting the heavy silence and quiet-not-quiet conversation continue, Clara cut right to the point.

"Options?"

"We hold out?" Sam said.

"How are we going to keep feeding Lake Weir?" Daniela countered. "It's only a matter of time before some of the bigger beasts to the west join the Dreg attacks, or just decide that one of the Wild Guard caravans are easy pickings. That's a surefire way of getting whittled down."

"The town is already getting whittled down." Maurice grimaced. "After that Appendage thing swooped by, not even the life mages have been able to grow anything edible. Ration projections put us at one month, and by then, we'll be right in the middle of fall. If we can't get situated before winter…"

"We might as well be shooting ourselves in the foot," Clara finished, getting nods of agreement from Devon, Ian, and Maurice. We'd yet to experience a winter on the surface, but everyone we talked to spoke of how harsh they were. We didn't have any specifics, so I opted to trust them on that.

"I could maybe work with the Stoneshapers and create that prototype vertical garden I…" Samuel added weakly. The tired looks he got from around the table had him tapering off, slouching deeper into his chair. "Never mind."

"It could very well be some kind of side effect from the Appendage's Gift," I said, placing a hand on his shoulder. "If we haven't been able to grow anything on the ground, I don't think building up will give us the solution. It would also high-light it as a target for the crows, which will make it harder to protect even if it did work."

Samuel wanted to drop lower in his seat, probably completely out of sight if I knew him, but I held him firm. "We'll still need you to figure something out. Daniela is right; we can't just rely on Wildwood for this."

The man gave me a solemn nod and turned from the start of his downward spiral into a pensive brooding. Not the optimal situation, but a working Sam was better than a shut-down Sam. Once again, the twinge of guilt for pushing my family and friends burned in my gut.

"What does that leave us with?" Devon asked, leaning forward on his borrowed desk.

"Evacuation?" Clara suggested.

"Fight," Maurice said.

"That's what we *are* doing! They are just going to keep collecting creatures from the surrounding area to drown us in a sea of bile when we are resting!" Daniela said, heat rippling out of her fire gills.

Ian steepled his fingers, looking at everyone present before speaking. "We cannot afford to lose our foothold in the area," he said, his face grave. All the age that had been staved off by his recent rise in Quotient made itself known with just one expression. "Our only redeeming advantage is the distance between Summerfield and the Dreg rot territory. If we fall and these Tendrils fortify *here*, even Stonecrest's walls won't be able to keep back the attacks."

"Whimpering back to Stonecrest or Wildwood will only prolong the issue," Maurice added, placing his hand on his father's shoulder. "If we run now, we'll be forced to keep running."

*Damn. He's right.* The truth of the two Weirdians' words settled on us. It was more like a slap in the face, but deep down I was fairly sure everyone present already knew that we couldn't afford to lose. We might save lives, but we would only be delaying. None of the scouts had ever been able to go far to the west, due to the intense insect territories there, or to the east, thanks to wildly dangerous swamps creatures. The north was just as much of an enigma and according to any of the survivors, the south portion of the state was just straight up underwater. We were in a tiny pocket of safety that we'd slightly expanded, only for the Dreg to clamp their greedy hands on.

"Can we... stop the bleeding, so to speak?" Clara asked, leveling her eyes on me. The question was implied.

"Alan isn't done. He's already working, but I have no idea how long it will take him to isolate whatever variables he says he needs to isolate to get *that* plan to work," I said, sighing.

"*Isolate*," Devon said, more to himself than as a response.

"Devon?" Clara asked, nudging the elf with her staff to bring him to the present.

"Sorry. Wait, I'm working through something. Ronan, you and Samuel managed to keep that dirty Metier Crystal contained, right?"

Both of us nodded.

"Sure, but the moment we looked away, it called for a taxi," Daniela butted in. I did notice her use of *we* even if the only ones able to somewhat keep the Entity contained were me and Sam. In my case, I was fairly sure it was just because the thing *liked* that I'd defeated Kirby for some perverse reason. She wasn't at all responsible for the prison break, yet she'd still thrown her lot in with us. *Way to make me feel even worse for being an ass, Danny.*

"That's not the problem. That thing could probably fly from the death territory down to Wildwood in, what, a few hours? If that? That twisted piece of junk crystal needed to call it. It also had to risk being present when Kirby was going *cultleader* on the trainees. If we can snag the crystal, call the bird and kill it, then put the rock in a deep dark hole where no one will find it, then the problem will be solved! No murderous flybys and no more Tendril-creating juice."

"There are so many 'ifs' in there, I don't even know where to start," I said, slicing my hand through the air. Even through the glower Devon threw at me, he deflated. "But I don't know if we can afford *not* to gamble on 'ifs.'"

"Come again?" The elf seemed shocked that I'd agreed with him.

"I don't think throwing the Corrupted Entity in a hole will deal with the problem, but if we can make a better prison for it, then it should be manageable. At least until winter passes and we can figure something out, or Alan cracks the purge technology. Whichever comes first," I said.

The looks around the table were still grim, but there was a palpable lift in the overall mood. Just saying we were going to fight was one thing; driving everyone to survive was the basis of all of our struggle. But fighting with a goal in mind, however unattainable it seemed? That gave purpose.

It was one of the things my uncle had always emphasized. Many people, even before the Fall, just went through the day in a monotonous doldrum. Being confined in the Bunker made that about a thousand times worse, but my uncle made sure that I looked at the big picture. We were still alive, and we could work to be better for the next day. *Man, was he smug when Elias agreed to the implant program.* I chuckled to myself as I pictured what he'd be doing were he in this meeting with us. Probably something profoundly silly to lift the mood, followed up by some speech about thinking outside the box. Then, he'd immediately go into one of his retellings of the numerous times he had to pseudo-engineer a fix for the water treatment system.

*Purpose. You sure know what you are doing, huh, Dad?* I didn't even recoil from the fact I'd thought of Dale as my father. For all intents and purposes, he was. Even if I wanted to call him what he *actually* was to me now, his lessons and support wouldn't leave me.

The odds were still stacked so high against us, I couldn't see the top of them. *But if I can't see how high they are, why should I worry any more about it?* Gears positively shifted, ideas and plans started to sprout like mana-fueled weeds.

# CHAPTER THIRTY-EIGHT

## Two Prongs

After several more hours of discussion and arguing, our makeshift war council was able to come to a decision: a two-pronged counterattack.

We did our best to keep the plan simple, even if a few contingencies were mixed in. The main goal would be to draw as many of the forces of the Dreg towards Summerfield as we could. The objective there wasn't victory, unless a truly golden opportunity presented itself somehow, but to cause as much damage as possible. Without the Dreg Entity, the strength of the Tendrils in the area should drop and enduring the winter or routing them should be more than possible. With how close the death territory was to Summerfield, we hoped that the Appendage would be inclined to intervene in the defense.

Meanwhile, the second prong would be zeroing in on the death territory, looking to extract an unwilling Dreg Entity. The details of the squad breakdown were still up in the air, pending additional information. Said additional information was the thing leaving me most nervous.

Daniela, Devon, and Dai were gearing up to comb the death territory more thoroughly than before. With the ability to shortcut from Lake Weir, they hoped to avoid much of the predator territory to the west. The triple D scouting team was assembled at the wall just the next day, after two more smaller scale attacks by the Dreg.

I hadn't seen Dai in a minute, and the lizardman had somehow grown even more lithe, if that was possible. His scales had darkened considerably, but were dull to the usually reflective sheen of the other water-attuned. Small ridges had grown down the sides of his head, outlining more of his elongated head than any of the other lizardfolk I'd seen.

It reminded me that while the pre-Fall humans, and for us Bunker Born, traits molded us more severely in a shorter span of time. They were part of a kaleidoscope of features that seemed close to skills in many cases, like Irwin's claws or Dylan's flame head, and as far from them in others, like my own defensive traits or Ian's partial undead-ness. The whole thing was just a poignant reminder that there were still many, many mysteries to uncover about our new home on the surface.

Awkwardly, I didn't realize that I'd been burning a hole in Dai's back. The man seemed to detect my staring, since he approached with a measured stride directly towards me. "Like what you see?"

"Sorry, got... caught in a train of thought. Inspired by the new ridges, for the record," waving one hand absently towards his head.

Thankfully, the usually ostracized lizardman took the fumbled complement in stride. "Lets me handle changes in temperature better."

"That would do it," I said, as if it made the most sense in the world. It might have; I was just on my back foot and chose to go ahead and agree blindly.

"Ronan, we are the ones going out into the Wild. There's no need to be so nervous," the large lizardman reassured me, placing a clawed hand on my shoulder and flashing a too-teethy grin.

I was able to restrain my shudder at the gesture, but just

barely. The lizardfolk, and the mer to a certain extent, were some of the most changed by their attunements. Where the other attunements seemed to just change colors or *add* features to a human canvas, the water-attuned *redefined it*. The whole thing was somewhat refreshing, if still unsettling at first.

"Right, sorry. That's precisely the problem, I think. I'm just not as good at the sneaky-sneaky, stabby-stabby stuff as you are."*And Daniela being more or less alone as you try to cover for each other practically gives me hypertension for the whole duration.* Each time I knew she was delving on a scouting mission, all I could see was her, wrapped up in black spider silk, ready to get slurped up by the core members of the spider dungeon.

"She's got good backup. I may not be as fast as either of them, but I've been working as a bodyguard for the trainees for months now. She won't leave my senses, I promise."

Filing away where he'd been through most of the defenses of Lake Weir and also that he'd said *senses* and not sight, I gave him the strongest smile I could muster. Admittedly, it was quite weak, but the man rejoined the other scouts. Daniela glanced at me the moment Dai rejoined them and then excused herself.

The Latina approached with confidence and unfaltering steps. Her eyes seemed to burn with an inner intensity that probably would have sent someone that hadn't grown up seeing her wet the bed and pitch a fit over her oatmeal packing. A few seconds later, she slapped me right across the cheek. Vibro went haywire for a moment but the force just tickled my toes as it left my body.

"I suppose this is where you ask me to forgive you, huh, rock brain?" Daniela sneered.

"You don't have to, if you don't want," I said, having already practiced what I was going to say to her a million different ways. "Your affairs will only be my business if they involve your safety or that of others."

Daniela sputtered for almost a minute before squinting into my squint. "Took the high road on this, did you? Fine, I can live with it. Next time you pull some crap like that, just be prepared to lose a finger or two."

Her even delivery of the threat made it weigh just a tad more somehow. With the tension broken between us, we discussed a handful of nonsense topics and got each other updated on the comings and goings to the town. She was particularly interested in how I'd been handling my vibrosense, going so far as to point out that she was starting to develop something extra to her eyesight. It wasn't fully fleshed out, but after gaining her fire breathing trait, heat was temporarily visible when she released it. She wasn't sure if it was something like the darkvision natural to the demons, but infrared instead. That left my thoughts spinning for several minutes as I contemplated, fighting the urge to start up a proper census of all the survivors, implant or not, to project possible traits.

Regardless of what I *wanted* to do, the time for the scouts to leave came. Maurice produced three bags of supplies for three days. It came from their long term stores, composed of dried meats and a camelback for water. Instead of tents, there were fold out hammocks that the three could hopefully use to camp outside of range of ground-prowling predators. Daniela shared one last meaningful look before throwing an arm over my shoulder in a half-hug. "You take care of them, Ron. Take care of them like you have Sammy and I."

Without saying anything else, she turned and dropped over the side of the wall. Dai followed silently behind, adjusting the tank of water he always carried on his person to more comfortably rest next to the bag of supplies. Devon hesitated as the two walked towards the treeline that would cut northwest. My eyes locked on his and my face scrunched into a frown. He blinked, then a gust of wind carried him even more silently to land beside the other two.

His voice drifted to me, not through the comm-plant, but from an impressive distance using his air-whisper Gift. "I will die before she does."

I barely suppressed the chill that crawled down my spine. It was true that Devon and I clashed for reasons that I honestly couldn't put my finger on, beyond his growing relationship with one of my best friends. However, the fact that the elf had echoed the sentiment I held deep in my heart almost exactly… It lifted a small weight off my shoulders. With that weight somewhat alleviated, I could sharpen my focus. The allied towns were going to war, and I needed to be ready to be the frontline. No one else would get more satisfaction from cracking that Dreg bastard than me.

— + —

Once again, the wait for news from the scouts was torturous. The unrelenting cogs of war, however, waited for no one. So much so, that it was during these preparation days that two major war effort changes occurred. These, I thought, would change the way the fight would go. Of those, the first was the most 'clever.'

One of the particularly entrepreneurial Stoneshapers had the audacity to burn through a large stock of spider-acquired air infusions to determine their critical point when used on mundane stone and mana-created stone. The results, and the data gathering, were extraordinarily painful, which was how I found out about it. Apparently, Sam had been called so many times that he'd opted to just leave a <Bush> there to channel healing for the Stoneshaper. It was mana intensive, but mana wasn't the limiting factor for the people of Lake Weir, it was time. The result and cost was more than worth it.

The numbers were rough, but a stone projectile the size of one of our wooden cannonballs would reach the critical explode-in-your-face state after about half a Q1 infusion. Mundane rocks would last less than a quarter of that. Said entrepreneur also provided the timeframes it took for that change to happen, highlighting that the fragmenting explosion happened much, much faster the more of the infusion was applied.

The barely sixteen year old dwarf had brought an effective way of creating shrapnel grenades back into the fight for the surface. However, not only were they limited to the impressive throwing power of some of the more strength-inclined defenders, but they could be loaded into the force pendulums to deliver a small explosive ordinance. Their effective range was small, but the future was bright for that particular individual and his methods.

The second wild thing that came out of those restless days was a dang Sam-spurned, metal-covered, double-ox-powered *tank* for lack of a better description. The mad combination of vehicular engineering from Sam, weaponry from Rommel, and armor from the recently transported Stoneshaper Tara produced something truly terrifying. The Stoneshaper had gotten some mild success in shaping thin metal by encasing it in rock to *then* shape it, and she'd immediately turned that application to help Samuel with his project. The result was a beast with magipunk proportions.

A semicircular wedge like one of those Volkswagen beetles from before the Fall housed the two oxen and a 'gunner' seat. Alternating slits in the wood provided vision for the gunner, allowing them to orient the oxen to reposition the tank. Mounted above the wedge was an honest to goodness rotating platform where the two force pendulum cannons sat. The metal plates provided a low-ish friction area to act as a platform, but Samuel and Tara were already discussing ways of improving the system. Thanks to the magical nature of the force dispersal trait, recoil wasn't a huge problem and Rommel actually mounted the largest versions of the cannons I'd seen to date.

When the weapon was tested on one of the creature hordes, its effects were clear. Combined with the critically infused cannonballs, it became a truly deadly weapon for the fodder we were sure to encounter at Summerfield.

I couldn't be happier for every bit of development. However, they did leave my own accomplishments, as far as getting vibro better under control, seeming small. Since I'd been a constant presence on the frequent attacks on the Weirdian walls, my flipping and ambient control of the new sense was quickly becoming accustomed to the chaos of a monster swarm. It bode well for my survival, but did nothing to relieve the stress that Lake Weir was under.

The attacks came from the north, east, west, and even a few from the south. The Tendrils were getting bolder in their tactics, and I spotted humanoids far behind their beasts on more than one occasion. The moment anyone moved to engage, they would vanish, not bothering to fight back. The fact that their attacks were centered on the animal Tendrils instead of the previous humanoid patrols spoke of their relative scarcity. I didn't want to think that it was the opposite, a ploy to get us overconfident, because that would not bode well for any of our plans.

It was during one of these particularly fruitless pursuits that the tables were turned on one of the Tendrils and its earth deer mount. A mist rolled out from the woods in the direction it was running in, followed by a gust of wind. Like a horizontal tornado, the gust accelerated a fireball right into the creature's chest. The explosion threw it off the deer's back and its body ragdolled even as the flames clung to it. A moment later, a pair of bone knuckles crushed the creature's head into the ground. The mist cleared, revealing an ice-pin-cushioned version of the earth deer. Dai nodded grimly as a greeting even as Devon wiped off his knuckles on his pant legs.

"Good to know we are needed for something other than scouting here. How did you expect to catch this thing with turtle speed, Ron?" Daniela asked as she dropped from a tree.

I let out a huff, smirking up at the trio. "I could have caught it eventually."

"Maybe, but I guess we'll never know," Devon said, turning around and giving me a grin that instantly made me want to remove it from his face.

"I hope you all came back with something more than

jokes," I said, the knot of worry in my chest having evaporated the moment I saw their attacks.

The mood sobered instantly, and I felt a tad bad about my comment. As much as they irked me, the three had been doing what they were, in fact, the best at: scouting.

"We found it, Ronan. It has to be."

— + —

I gave the scouts a few hours to get settled down and rest while I gathered the other leaders. Wec would have joined us in the outside meeting area, but ever since the Appendage's attack, the Entity Cluster had been struggling to maintain its area of influence against the creatures at its borders. Even with its jump to Category 3, it wasn't able to restrain everything, especially when the humanoid Tendrils acted as commanders.

Once Maurice, Ian, Clara, Samuel, and the scouts were arrayed in the war room, Dai opted to start. The man asked to join a party with all of us with implants, quickly sharing a minimal marker of a location towards the center of the death territory just south of the wildly verdant zone.

"This," he said, gesturing roughly to the location on the physical map on the table. It was more accurately portrayed in the minimap, but easier to communicate using the physical map, especially with Ian not having an implant. "Is where we believe the Dreg Entity is located. There is a cave mouth that isn't filled with water and has absolutely no business being anything but muck, rotting plants, and clay. The area adjacent to the healthy plant seems much sturdier than the rest of the death territory, but we couldn't get much closer without being swarmed."

"That's not all. Summerfield isn't the only place with humanoid Tendrils now," Devon added.

"Could they have recalled creatures from afar?" Clara asked. "I know we've seen dozens since the Fall, but not quite so many since they agreed to give us protection. Only a representative or those collection patrols."

"Unfortunately, it is entirely possible," Daniela said, grimacing. She didn't even take the opportunity to crack a joke or act superfluous; she looked bone weary.

"Is there anything we can do about that?" I asked.

"Reconsider holing up instead of going on the offensive?" Ian replied, his bone hands rubbing his temples as he worked the option through his mind. He shook his head after less than a second of consideration. "No... we can't do that or we will be running even harder once they consolidate."

"Double down?" Maurice asked, turning to his father.

"Double down. We are going to have to trim the composition we were hoping to have for the direct offensive," Ian said. He didn't seem to like what he was suggesting and, if I got his meaning, I wouldn't either.

"What do you mean?" Sam asked, leaning forward. As the head of the healers, the composition was already a big concern for him. While the squads had their three-to-four members to healer ratios, neither the Weirdian hunters nor the hunters from Stonecrest had such formal arrangements. There *were* healers amidst their ranks, and time spent under the gauntlet of waves the Dreg threw certainly improved their skills, but Samuel wasn't confident they would be able to handle much larger clusters of people.

"I think we need to zero in on a strike team. Nothing superfluous, and only well-oiled machines of Dreg killing potential. Unfortunately, said strike team should include most of the people here in this room," Ian said, gesturing to our side of the table. Even though Maurice was excluded from his father's arm sweep, he didn't appear bothered by it. The thorn-haired man could be particularly agreeable sometimes.

"If we do that, then who is going to take command of the force going to Summerfield?" Sam asked, his frown deepening. It wasn't hard to imagine the flit of scenarios, none of which would be good, that were passing through the blond's head.

"You are, Samuel," Clara said, cutting through the silence as Sam worked through his thoughts.

"Oh, sur—*Wait*! I can't lead the attack. It should be one of the squad leaders. Igor! He can do it, right? He's been in the Wild Guard for a while," Sam said, spinning from side to side. He met my eyes, Daniela's, and then Clara's.

"Ha! As if we could get that meathead to do anything but charge in a straight line," Devon said with a snort. "I second the motion for Samuel's lead."

"Come on, guys, you know how much I struggle here in this setting!" Samuel pleaded to me and Danny. The Latina and I shared a look that said *You tell him, or I tell him*. It wasn't like options were growing on trees, unlike his healing abilities.

"Sammy, you've already been taking the lead in a lot of things. Not only that, considering the group size difference you *have* to go with them. None of the healers have as much reach and flexibility as you do on a wide field," I said, placing my hand on his shoulder. The life-attuned slumped, eyes vacant. It wasn't a situation I wanted to put him in, but I was almost certain the allied fighters would listen to the Druid. I was pretty sure Sam by himself had patched up at least everyone in Lake Weir once or twice, and everyone knew that you didn't mess with the healer.

"Okay…" Sam said weakly.

"Oy! None of that weak sauce crap!" Daniela said, gills flaring as she jabbed a finger into his chest. Samuel flinched, causing Daniela to reel it back a bit. With softer eyes, she tipped Sam's head so he would look at her. "Just because you don't like interacting with people doesn't mean you can't do this. Delegate. It's apparently the true art of leadership. Haven't you seen how much Ronan has been bossing the two of us around as of late?"

"You've been doing a good job, Sam. If you hadn't been around, Bunker knows how things would have gone while I was out of commission with the trainees and the whole vibro situation," I added.

"I would have probably blown up on a bunch of people. Three, minimum," Danny said, twirling her hand as if it was an obvious conclusion.

The tension dispersed like so much smoke. Light chuckles left the people in the war room, slowly climbing until they were almost hysterical levels of laughter. It hadn't been particularly funny, but with everyone high strung, it was a good way to shift perspective. Daniela shot some more jokes at Sam, who quickly retorted with some targeted lizard jokes for her own growing number of non-human-looking bits.

Even through all this, I could see Clara pass notes to Ian every few minutes. It was obvious they were keeping the discussion of the squads silent, happy now to have commanders of sorts for both parts of the attack. Instead of bringing the discussion back on track, I added my own touch of rambunctiousness to the mix, hoping to distract Samuel from his upcoming task. Whatever Clara put together, I would trust. Ultimately, the composition didn't matter until we were executing our plan, and by that point it would be do or die. Possibly worse, if the Dreg Entity was able to capture us.

In the wake of those dark thoughts, the night flew by and dawn rose up as we prepared to strike back against the Dreg in force.

# CHAPTER THIRTY-NINE

## Rush the Bog

There was one final surprise prior to the deployment. Samuel revealed a secret project that he and Ava had been developing in Wildwood: rot taters. Regardless of the tension all of the squads were under, they all unanimously flinched when my friend plucked one from the back of one of the carts where they'd been stashed. It didn't look too dissimilar to the other potatoes we'd grown... aside from the strange tentacle-esque protrusions of deep purple blooming from the plain brown skin. The name didn't do it any favors either.

Nonetheless, Samuel wanted everyone to take at least one of the infused tubers with them on the excursion. It wouldn't negate death attacks, but it *did* make a difference. In order to get the buy-in that he believed the food deserved, he called Clara forward the moment the squads had lined up. He then proceeded to inhale the potato, probably to avoid the taste as much as possible even if he still grimaced, before asking her to release her caustic cloud. The demoness actually looked hesitant, but when Samuel didn't flinch, she acquiesced.

The purple-black cloud was only about half of its usual size, but it was still enough for Sam to walk through and be completely out of sight for a second. On the other side, there was a slight irritation to his skin but that was quickly dealt with by his passive regeneration right before everyone's eyes. The squads exploded with any number of questions and specula- tions. I even heard one particularly intrepid demon amidst the recent trainees ask if it could be cooked into a meal.

Seeing that the situation was getting out of control, Clara clapped her hands and her <Fear> blanketed the unruly bunch. The effect washed over me also, but it was much more muted. A moment of consideration made me realize it was probably due to trying to affect so many people at once. Something had to give. The demoness released the Gift, having now gotten every- one's attention.

"I know these are exciting times." She placed her hand on Samuel's shoulder. I wasn't sure if it was a sign of solidarity and support, or just to help her keep steady after the <Fear> display. "However, this excitement needs to be tempered with the possi- bility that not everyone here will make it back."

That certainly sobered the mood. There was not a single sound other than the whistle of wind and the creak of boots on the wall where the people of Lake Weir and one squad remained to guard them.

"We aren't going out there just to collect materials. Heck, we aren't even going out there to collect meat so that our fami- lies can make it through the winter. We are going to fight to protect our home, and make sure that invaders are *not* welcome. Now you will be going out to meet these invaders, backed by our strongest healer. Survive, struggle, and the future may yet smile on us. For the future…"

"We guard!" The voices were deafening as they called out in unison.

Now much closer, I could see how vibro reacted to the soundwave without it hitting quite as hard as the previous time. My improvements in dealing with vibro since we left Wildwood were noticeable.

Following the call and response, Clara had all the Guard

and the two handfuls of defenders from Lake Weir pass by the cart with the rot taters before posting up by the gate.Out of the corner of my eye, I watched Alan shuffle out amongst the fighters being deployed and snag a handful of the infused spuds. The man vanished around a building, clearly rushing back towards Wec based on the direction of his ripples.

Snapping my focus back to the departing soldiers, I saw something slightly amusing. My ramp was still there after our explosive arrival, and the more agile squads had no qualms about using it to top the wall. Not everyone seemed as willing, but I overheard more than one prodding dare to follow up the ramp.

Shaking my head at the nervous antics of the other fighters, I walked up to the demoness commander and lifted my eyebrows in question.

"Our team is already decided, Ronan," Clara confirmed.

"Oh?"

"They are right here," she said, pointing to the people that had been loosely gathered around her. All of the New Hopers, with us Bunker Busters and two life-attuned. Of the two, I recognized the fae Ophelia and she gave me a meek wave before turning to her satyr companion. Of course, included in that count was Anthony the fire ant and Blobby...wherever it was stealthed at. Even with vibro, I'd only been able to sense the slime when it was in motion.

Samuel was obviously standing to the side, talking with Daniela in a hurried voice. I opted not to interrupt, but I did turn when he strode over to me. When I'd seen him depart from Danny with a rough hug, something in my chest clenched and I had to swallow to clear my throat.

"Hey, Ron. I'm gonna need a hand with the wall so I can get the Arbor Turtle out there," the blond said, pointing over his shoulder towards the force pendulum tank. Another life-attuned was leading the two oxen into the door flaps built into the back of the contraption so they could get loaded up.

"Sure, Sammy." I glanced over my shoulder, but I could see

that Daniela was making a concerted effort *not* to turn around. The slight shaking of her shoulders was mark enough of her internal emotions.

The two of us walked forward, and the other life-attuned gave a quick bow before scurrying into the Arbor Turtle. I quirked an eyebrow in Sam's direction, but all he could do was shrug. "Not impossible to operate solo, but much harder. Maurice figured giving me a second would be a good idea."

"You are taking this surprisingly well," I said, trying to keep my voice even and free of the guilt. There was a healthy dose of second-guessing thrown in there also.

"Ronan. I'm introverted, not unreasonable," Sam said as we stood before the small gate that acted as the northern entrance to the town. It wasn't even half the size of the Arbor Turtle. "I know you well enough to know that if you had an alternative, you would have spilled it."

The last bit came out strangled, but all Sam did was gesture at the wall. With a flex of my will, <Mudpit> formed. The stone sloughed down slowly. Unlike mundane stone and earth, mana-created stone resisted the magic of my skill. By the time <Mudpit> ran out, I had to cast it again for the last of the opening to muddle on the ground. The life-attuned inside the tank was cursing up a storm, surprised by the display of my Quotient 5 dispositions.

"Stay safe, please?" I managed to say. The Arbor Turtle was trundling forward towards where the squads waited beyond. A handful of stragglers, or perhaps those not confident on making it down the wall, snuck out of the opening I created.

"I should be telling *you* that," Sam said, putting his hand on my shoulder and gripping it. "I'm not the one walking into the beast's mouth."

"True, *but* I am definitely sending a death bird right to you, plus a dozen humanoids."

"Quite rude of you, if I might say," Sam finished.

I turned our half-hug into a full one, and we crushed each other with our embrace. It wasn't pretty, nor quiet, but I couldn't care less. However, when we separated, there was barely a hint of those turbulent emotions. All I could see was the Druid and I did my best to project the Vanguard. Samuel clambered onto the top of the Arbor Turtle and I stared after him as the bulk of our forces rushed towards a fight they weren't likely to win. On purpose.

"We need to be heading out too, Ronan," Clara said. The demoness walked up beside me, stinger staff in hand. "Dai will be running the communication chain between the death territory and Summerfield. We want to make sure to be in position before… Before they make contact."

Taking a deep breath, I focused on the gap I'd created. Those brief minutes with my friend that I distinctly hoped would not be the last. Then, I raised an <Earth Wall> to fill the gap. The strain of the cast was minor, even as it channeled through my helm, but the pain dialed me in. The faster we put that rock out of commission, the better.

The first stretch of the trip was easy. After all the waves of Tendrils trying to overrun the Weirdians, the local wildlife had opted to migrate somewhere less chaotic. A handful of birds took to the sky with our passage, but all I could do was focus on our advance. Clara made sure to keep regular contact as we relayed between our shared parties. While our group had been kept to ten, the maximum extent that anyone present could sustain in a party, we kept them split. Daniela, Lilly, Ophelia, and me, while Clara kept contact with Dennis, Rommel, Devon, Godfrey, and Diana. It was a slightly uneven split, but the demoness seemed better at dealing with the input than me, especially after I'd started to deal with my vibrosense.

The first bit of trouble came in the form of a nostalgic foe.

A pack of haze wolves interposed itself between us and the rough path the scouts had plotted out to lead us to the death territory. The lead wolf bared its teeth at us with a growl, the air rippling around it as it eyed us. Its information rippled across my vision, telling me that the leader was a Q4, while the other larger beasts were Q3, and the two cubs at the back were just Q1s. It wouldn't be hard for us to defeat them, considering everyone in the group except for the satyr, Diana, was Quotient 5. The only concern was any injuries the creatures could inflict, hampering our advance.

To my surprise, Daniela stepped forward and mimicked the wolf. I watched as her fire gills shuddered and sparks illuminated her throat from within before a short gout of fire lashed out at the air between our two groups. That certainly seemed to throw the haze wolves off, but it also marked the start of our fight.

The beasts rushed forward, the Q3s blurring further as the temperature in our patch of woods picked up. My perception highlighted several of the leaves wilting before my eyes as the combined heat index surged past one hundred degrees in the span of a breath. A breath that would have been robbed, had our group not had experience fighting the beasts.

"<Mudpit>," I whispered, focusing on the ground just ahead of the creatures. Instantly, the liquified earth started to bake under the heat the beasts put out, but it was enough of a distraction for our team to strike back. A short crackle of lightning stopped the lead Q3 short, before it was speared by an ice dagger to the face. Godfrey and Rommel unleashed boulder tosses and fire disks at the other two creatures. The boulder took one of them in the snout and the snap of bone announced its death as it ate its own jaw. The other took two disks to the mane, which surprisingly only sheared the top of its pelt off, but *did* cause it to stumble. The <Mineral Strike> I'd casually held in my hand bloomed over its head mid-throw, pelting it with fragments of amethyst.

Dennis had his flute to his mouth and the two Q1s swayed on their legs. Every few seconds, they took a step forward, gnashing their teeth at the satyr even as he was joined by Diana and Ophelia in suppressing the creatures non-lethally.

As for Daniela and Clara, the women were handling the Q4 just fine. The lead wolf seemed stunned that Daniela practically ignored its heat waves, dancing around a snapping jaw to score a number of gashes on its body courtesy of her wolf fang daggers. The creature was just one step behind and with each cut lagged yet more on top of it. However, that was probably a result of the <Fear> Clara was pummeling it with. It flinched when no attack was coming, letting Daniela plow through the openings of the SUV-sized beast. When the wolf yipped at the air, it practically garroted itself just by virtue of where Daniela was positioned. She didn't let the opportunity go by and her hands blurred as she cut an X under its jaw.

Daniela snapped out with <Flame Blast>, making space out of the haze and throwing debris up in the air to distract the wolf as it bled out. A few seconds later, it slumped to the ground, and then stilled. The Latina ripped another <Flame Blast> as a double tap, confirming the creature was truly dead.

*Never mind. For this particular group, that was a bit of a joke.* That was one way of putting your mind into perspective about how much we'd changed since acquiring the status. It had taken all Sam, Danny, and I had just to take down one of the Q3 beasties. Now, Daniela had almost singlehandedly taken down one a whole Quotient higher.

There was a bit of commotion next to the two Q1 wolves. Rommel tried to approach them gently, but each time they snapped back. Even if their heat was barely bothersome for me, and even less so for the large orc, the fangs weren't for show. Dennis' song intensified and the two creatures swayed visibly before plopping to the ground.

"They are too old to imprint, Rommy," the satyr said, patting Rommel on the back. "Best put them out quickly."

The man nodded, retrieving a hunting knife from his ankle before repeating a similar motion to Daniela's with the smaller wolves. It didn't even look like their bodies were completely bled before they started to dissociate and simmer into ash piles. Two pristine pelts and their Q1 infusions remained in their place.

*Samuel could have done it.* Regardless of their level of aggression, I was almost sure that my friend would have been able to cut through the creature's baser instincts. *There's no time for taming things. That will have to come later.*

The party gathered all the loot in a bag to be collected later. I watched my level progress climb a solid two percent. Compared to the widespread fighting at the wall, smaller squads were the way to go for leveling. Instead of receiving that much after a week of fights, it came from just one engagement. Nonetheless, I still had a ways to go before my next level. Grinding to that degree would have been optimal for this engagement, but again, we didn't have the luxury.

**Subject:** Ronan Terrigan
**Health:** 100% (Unafflicted)
**Mana:** 100%
**Metier Quotient:** 5 (41%)
**Dreg Accumulation:** 3%
**LPS:** Wildwood Bunker, FL
**Communications**
**Party**
**Skills -** *(1) Selections Available*
**Traits -** *(16% Banked)*
**Attributes -** *Growth Quantified*
**Skills:**
Offensive
- <Stone Spike> / **Imbue** / <Mineral Strike>
Defensive
- <Mudpit> / <Earth Shell> / <Earthen Barrier>
- <Freeform>
Misc
- <Pith Mana Lock>
- <Infusion>
- <Memory Canal>
**Traits:**
Limestone Skin

Quake Osseum
Slurry Ichor
Harmonic Sinew
**Attributes:**
Strength: 1.79
Mobility: 1.63
Perception: 2.09
Refinement: 1.42
Containment: 2.28

After the brief intermission and a well-timed snack, we crossed the last bit of distance to the death territory. Considering we barely skirted the predator territory, I was glad we'd risked sending people to scout ahead. If the pack of haze wolves were the dangers at the edges, I was hesitant to head deeper into that territory.

When the vegetation started to die out, changing from towering pines and wide-reaching oaks to low brush and cypress trees, Daniela took the lead directly. She veered left and right with ease, maneuvering the woods with practiced ease until we arrived at a small cluster of trees. Upon closer inspection, however, I realized it wasn't just a cluster of trees but a super-sized cypress tree. The vertical growing roots of the tree had reached a truly immense scale and soon the reason became obvious.

<Bald Cypress Tree>
<Attunement: Water>
<Refinement: Oxygenation>
<Perceived Metier Quotient: 2>

The organism served like a superstructure of sorts, providing a small garden of verdant plants and vines. Other than the occasional pulse from a blue-colored piece of bark, the cypress tree looked harmless. Considering Daniela brought us right to it, it must have been verified by her and the others.

Unfortunately, the wonder of finding our third attuned tree specimen was muted by what lay just beyond it. Past its influence was the death territory, and the difference was notable. Seeing it for the first time brought me up short. The biggest clearing I'd seen since coming to the surface, but it was deceptive. I could see the shine of water and liquified mud in the distance. As I focused on vibro, this was confirmed once again as I encountered the ripple signature of water, solid earth, and muck in a haphazard pattern within the range of my senses.

I was able to penetrate a bit further thanks to the varied, yet darkly shaded wildlife. Over a dozen creatures—frogs, crows, vultures, and even a handful of gators—were in various states of conflict all throughout the bog. Other than the huge propensity for black amidst their coloration, there were shock flashes of purple and gray among them as they utilized some of their death Gifts. That was it, because every single creature was death-attuned.

Near where Daniela pointed out the cavern, I could make out the only splash of color amidst the low bushes that marred the bog like fuzzy mops of beige hair. The humanoid Tendrils the scouts had reported. They seemed to only amble, interacting with each other with vague hand gestures but otherwise standing unbothered by the clash of nature not a hundred feet from them. As I watched them not even bother to keep a proper watch, my low, simmering hatred for the Dreg was stoked.

"Daniela," I hissed, barely keeping it at a whisper. My knuckles went white around my spider naginata as I tried to bore a hole into the closest orange-red humanoid. "Get ready, and give Dai the signal."

The brunette tried to catch my eyes, but I kept them zeroed in on our target. Daniela gripped my shoulder for a second, but turned to let the group know she was going to rush to the transmitting range. As Daniela faded from view, Clara and Ophelia appeared beside me. Each had a variation on a grimace as they scanned the bog for themselves.

"How long do the rot taters work?" Ophelia asked.

"We aren't quite sure what the factors are, but probably something like ten minutes of extra protection," I said, doing my best to breathe and answer without the maelstrom of emotions in my chest. It was important information that I'd forgotten to make sure the group had before we practically waded into the swampland head first.

"Understood. I would recommend waiting until we are in the thick of it to eat them. Sure, we will miss the effect on our initial charge, but hopefully our element of surprise can compensate for that," Ophelia said, pulling out one of the potatoes and giving it a look over.

I turned enough to get the fae in my peripheral and nodded. No sense being so entrenched in my own thoughts to ignore a good plan shift.

"Message relayed." Daniela's voice came through the comm-plant wide.

The New Hopers and us freelance squad members all tensed. Weapons were drawn and armor adjusted. Thanks to the efforts of Wildwood, all the defenders had some form of armor. Either the tanker armor, like what Rommel was wearing, the cowl like Daniela, or a small vest with a wider panel on the back that seemed to be aimed at healers. This last armor piece was what Ophelia and Diana were wearing. Dennis, like myself, had opted to remain free of armor other than our funny headwear. My antler helm might be a bit excessive in look, due to the rack on it, but the satyr seemed to be wearing a flytrap for a hat. It was odd, but considering all the things I'd seen on the surface, if he thought that was what he needed to wear, I wasn't going to judge.

We stayed crouched within the cypress tree's embrace for almost half an hour. Daniela returned, posted up beside me, and yet there was still no reaction from the creatures of the death territory. Just as I was getting ready to ask Daniela to check in, a pair of injured crows half-flew, half-crashed into a hill not far from the cavern mouth. We watched them spiral down with bated breaths before they started to screech a horrible tune.

Like a macabre orchestra, those two creatures caused the

swamp to still. The humanoids rushed over, the most active I'd seen them since we arrived at the death territory. After somehow communicating with the creatures, one of the golden life-attuned Tendrils started to blast the hill with zaps of yellow energy. On the third, a wing three times the size of its body slapped it away like a cheap toy. Then the hill rumbled and sickly purple light rippled along the surface.

"T-That's not a mound, is it...?" Diana said, voice quaking.

As if to confirm our suspicions, a second wing exploded in a spray of mud and water, releasing a cawing crow. The Appendage's information instantly flitted across my vision before the creature took to the sky in a blur of purple. We watched the beast do a single loop of the death territory while the Tendrils gathered themselves up and shot towards the east. The Appendage was not far behind, all heading for Summerfield no doubt.

*Show time*, I affirmed to myself, channeling some of my mana to tense my muscles against the shiver that passed through me at the sight of that creature. *Stay safe, Sammy...*

# CHAPTER FORTY

## Appendages

"We need to move as soon as those things are out of the woods. There is a risk that the Appendage will circle back, but we are going to have to take it," I said, choking up my grip on the naginata.

"That stuff is going to be like soup," Daniela said, pointing to the bog. The ruddy tracks and furrows the Tendril creatures had carved on their way east all but confirmed that.

"I'll take care of it," I said, taking a deep breath. "Just step where I step."

The group nodded and we crept down the small island of integrity the cypress had carved out for itself. When my boots sank four inches into the ground, I stepped back and focused on the straight path to the cavern. I didn't pay attention to the creatures that were already turning to eye the interlopers, but instead focused solely on vibro. It wasn't a straight path that would serve us the best, but it should let me save enough mana that we actually made it across.

<Earthen Barrier>. I slapped the skill into action in my mind. I kept it to a quarter power, dipping five percent of my mana pool with each cast, but creating a three by three platform out

of the garbage terrain. Then I rushed forward. The New Hopers and the others followed one platform behind as I raised platform after platform, veering us to the left to one of the sturdier islands amidst the swamp. The moment my foot touched down, vibro practically screamed at me.

The stuttered warning was enough for me to miss putting my foot right in the gullet of a Q3 death alligator that had been lurking just out of sight and hadn't moved until we arrived at his doorstep. The snapping of its jaw closed actually set my ears ringing. Vibro was scrambled slightly, but not enough to put me out of commission as I shunted the sense for my eyesight. Thankfully, I wasn't the only one able to navigate the environment to cover up my blunder.

Frost sprung up as a wall, punching up on the creature's mouth before it formed a rough band around it. With its jaw clenched shut, it threw itself into a wild roll, cracking the ice and flopping its way onto land, where it was swiftly decapitated by a triple dose of Rommel's fire disks. Its information flitted across my vision for the briefest second before the life winked out of the gator.

<Dreg Tendril (Florida Alligator)>

<Attunement: Death>

<Refinement: Rot>

<Perceived Metier Quotient: 3>

Unfortunately, the delay of dealing with the creature was enough for the beasties to lock in. A handful of crows had risen from some of the nearby shrubs to circle above us. These were swiftly handled by Devon as he used gusts of wind to rebuff the bile raining down on us, and snips of lightning to cause the creatures to crash down. Godfrey hoofed it to the front, covering for me as I got my bearings and we alternated using our earth skills to make progress. He materialized boulders far ahead where I pointed while I cut the distance between the islands.

Daniela snapped out her wisp, a constant presence over our shoulder that sent out tracing fireballs against any creatures trying to approach us. Dennis, Diana, and Ophelia hit the party with the occasional heal, doing their best to stay in the middle of the formation as Clara and Anthony brought up the rear.

Three frogs were waiting at the next island. Sticky tongues that dripped with acid flew towards us. Grunting, I smacked them aside using my tower shield. The chitin hissed, but was mostly unaffected as the force of the impacts, plus my arm swing, evaporated the frog saliva. A small snake tried to pounce on me from the side, but I had a sneaky companion also watching my back. Blobby intercepted the creature with its body, almost instantly drowning it as it swallowed a mouthful of slime.

Rebuffed by my defense, the creatures weren't expecting the <Mineral Strike> that landed in their midst. Just like with the alligator, my eyes locked on their bodies long enough for my implant to trigger.

<Dreg Tendril (Water Frog)>
<Attunement: Death>
<Refinement: Mucus>
<Perceived Metier Quotient: 2>

<American Water Frog>
<Attunement: Death>
<Refinement: Mucus>
<Perceived Metier Quotient: 3>

It was somewhat surprising that Tendril and non-Tendril creatures were interacting, but it wasn't the first time. The apparent disparity in power was also interesting, but I didn't have the time to contemplate why that was the case. As more creatures started to spring up around us, I started to ignore the implant callouts. Nothing drew my attention, power wise, but I knew their numbers could easily overwhelm us. Pushing through to that cavern was our only option now that we were in the middle of the bog.

Burning through a bit more mana than I wanted, I skipped pointing out the next low spot for Godfrey and rushed the last fifty feet to the edge of the cavern. Instantly upon arriving, I set about casting size adjusted <Earth Walls>. My mana flowed like a river, and the discomfort in my abdomen climbed with each skill I channeled through my helm, but we needed to be able to defend. With four walls, two short and two tall, lining the perimeter, our team dug in.

Dennis immediately set about reinforcing my walls. Growths of the same bushy grass lined the entire space, a series of them making a point of growing overtop the cavern mouth in the direction of the overly fertile land around the Metier Crystal. Almost immediately, he straightened and his playing picked up tempo.

"Three. West," he panted between breaths into his flute. Godfrey didn't need more direction and clambered up the side of the cavern more deftly than I would have expected from a dwarf.

"Anthony, back him up. Burn anything that tries to splash him," Daniela said, concentrating on maneuvering her wisp to keep tagging targets approaching the group.

"Ron, what's your mana at?" Clara asked, tearing her eyes away from the tide of creatures heading towards them.

A flick to the display in the corner of my vision flashed the number twenty-seven as I focused on it. I relayed as much. Even as she grimaced, the demoness started rambling, a plan clearly forming in her head. "Keep watch on the cavern; we want to make sure that nothing is going to jump out of there to attack us. Unlikely, considering it hasn't already, but I am not going to bet on anything. When you hit eighty percent, take Daniela and Ophelia down there. We'll hold the line, but if at all possible don't take too long. I'm not liking what I see…"

On cue, a bombardment of bile rained down on us, but was met by yet another gust of wind from Devon. Instead of just spraying it wildly, the elf redirected the attack towards the vulture that was sweeping down on one of their earlier kills.

The bird thrashed wildly as the corrosive contents of the crows' stomach burned its wings. An opportunistic gator snapped up the bird, even as a handful of frogs harassed it.

The offensive against the group wasn't organized in the least, but they had the numbers advantage. Not only that, even if it wasn't intentional like the fire ants, a mid-fight feast would cause some of the small threats to possibly jump a Quotient.

After letting her know about that possibility and receiving a stern nod in return, I set into the frustrating task of recovering. While my time spent as an invalid had improved my patience by a noticeable degree, the sounds of the fight behind me set me on edge. In the hopes of being somewhat useful, I extended vibro as far as it could go while keeping my eyes closed. The fight on the bog side was relentless as Devon and Lilly released skills regularly, but with a steady pace.

A number of creatures, large and small, rushed towards the walls I'd created and through their strange resonance, I could see that they'd already been weakened by a variety of acidic, basic and generally caustic substances. Thankfully, we had our own erosions expert as Blobby intercepted the smaller creatures attempting to circumvent our defenses. The slime split and rejoined its two bodies with a smoothness that beguiled its gelatinous body. With each successful creature eaten, however, I could see it slowing even as its bulk continued to grow. Even while attacking, the slime made a distinct effort to protect Ophelia and Diana whenever they were threatened as the women released heals sparingly.

The thing that really disturbed me wasn't the controlled chaos of the fight behind me, but the utter silence from the cavern. As if it was a black hole, the constant ripples of battle penetrated a few feet before the force was dispersed almost immediately. *This cavern is made from mana-created rock. The densest rock I've encountered so far...* I certainly didn't like where that thought led, but I did my best to use my 2+ Perception Attribute to pierce into the murky darkness of the cavern. The black spread deep, much like the blackspace inside the afflicted...

As if it had heard the earlier pronouncement, a notification flashed, announcing my mana was at eighty percent. The battle had died down some behind me, but I could see Rommel clambering up the cavern's side to swap with Godfrey as the healers went to work on the dwarf. It was going to be a rough defense.

"I'm ready," I said through the comm-plant. *Hopefully that's the least disruptive way of communicating right now.*

"Danny, Ophelia—with him. Godfrey, back up and at 'em. You can sleep when you are dead," Clara responded. As I watched, the woman's eyes once more burned with purple and red. A screech pierced the air before she turned and puked on the ground just over one of my short walls. She added quietly, "Don't take too long."

Grim faced, I stood and adjusted my straps on my shield so it was vertical to the ground. My grip on my naginata loosened as I popped half the rot tater in my mouth. Instantly, a combination of sour, bitter, and ashy rattled my tongue but I swallowed anyway. It was quickly followed by a gag-inducing second half. My affliction popped up, stating I had the Boon of Death. The timer showed eight minutes and twenty seconds, already counting down. As Daniela and Ophelia copied my actions, we headed into the cavern.

Daniela kept her wisp right overhead as we power walked down an increasing slope. A strange muted light started to suffuse the vibro-dead rock around us. After the straight minute walk, I risked a look at my minimap.

"We are almost at the—" My whisper cut off as the slope flattened completely and we found ourselves inside an impossibly hollowed out space.

The source of the muted light became readily apparent. Instead of the vibro-dead rock around us, the back wall of the cavern was made up of the iridescent kaleidoscope of what had to be the Metier Crystal hidden within the fertile territory. The things that truly threw me off were what was standing at the foot of the truly massive crystal.

Galloway. The humanoid Tendril we'd encountered, the first to actually communicate and negotiate with Wildwood, stood with its arms tucked behind its back. Its palm frond wings were spread wide over his shoulders as the creature regarded us with a flat expression. Just over its head, attached so much like an engorged tick to the Metier Crystal, was the Dreg Entity. Thick veins of black spread over the surface of the untainted crystal, suppressing its rainbow glow in many areas of its exposed facet.

"It appears the children have come to play," Galloway said, his mouth splitting to reveal its needle teeth. A warning flashed on the edge of my vision, and I took an involuntary step back.

"Oh, shi—" Daniela's voice fell on deaf ears as I reread the words. My implant even deemed it pertinent enough to highlight the concerning bits of information revealed.

&lt;Dreg ***Appendage*** (Human)&gt;

&lt;Attunement: Life&gt;

&lt;Refinement: Growth&gt;

&lt;Perceived Metier Quotient: *7*&gt;

# CHAPTER FORTY-ONE

## A Little Squeeze

All I had time to see was the flex of the wings on Galloway's back. Some of the instincts I'd been building after fighting hundreds of monsters on the surface had me raise up my shield. Thankfully, I'd been intelligent enough to listen to said instincts because a pair of leaves sharpened to a ridiculous degree impacted my tower shield. A plume of vision-distorting heat was released as the force dispersal took the brunt of the blow, but I still felt all of my traits kick in to handle the force of the impact. Even with all of that, one of the frond blades sliced a gash on my shoulder, laughing in the face of my Limestone Skin trait even as Slurry Ichor moved in to help.

"Impressive. You are beyond the capabilities of what the Aberrant predicted," Galloway said, tilting his head almost in wonder. Then the man snapped two more fronds from his wings, both clearly not aimed at me. It didn't take a tactical genius to realize what was happening, so I sent a silent prayer that Daniela's perception was enough to dodge the attack and interposed myself between the Appendage and Ophelia.

Sure enough, the blow came less than a fraction of a second

after I was in position. This one came in high, skidding up over us but putting my shield out of line with me.

"Suppressing fire!" I yelled to Daniela through the commplant.

The woman didn't need to be told anything else as <Flame Blasts> ripped forth from her wisp to strike the Appendage. Unfortunately, it was putting its Q7 attributes on perfect display. Barely winded by the display, Galloway actually started to speak even as it dodged the splashes of fire that remained on the ground for a few seconds.

"Did you perhaps believe you could defeat me?" Galloway said. "I will warn you that the Fall has been most kind to people like me."

"Unscrupulous assholes, you mean?" Daniela said as she did a cartwheel to dodge a leaf blade Galloway sent in response to her words.

>The Sullied, fleshbag.<

*Great, now the crystal is also involved.* I grimaced as I remembered the incessant berating from the tainted rock. The Appendage released another spray of leaves and even as I hunkered down, I was able to see that they had to regrow on his wings. The man had plenty to spare, but it would be a marked improvement if he didn't have a half-dozen to let loose at any one time.

"The Aberrant is correct. You have merely expedited your doom. Perhaps you would reconsider? Beings of your caliber —" Galloway was cut off as a second wisp materialized in the air above his head. The creature glanced at the thing even as a steady stream of fire rained down. Instead of faltering, Galloway ate the fire full on in the face, moving his wings like a pair of hands to slap them together onto the wisp. Its flame sputtered and I watched Daniela falter in her constant dodging.

The opening was not missed by our opponent, and I had just enough time to raise an <Earth Wall> in front of Daniela as the wings repositioned. The moment the frond impacted the stone, it sank a good two inches before stopping.

"We need assistance!" Ophelia called through the comm-plant, wide to the New Hopers posted up above us.

"Neg-negative! The creatures have gone into a frenzy! Something is burning its way to us from across the bog," Clara replied back before the line went dead.

I grit my teeth and threw up a second wall before leaving Ophelia behind. *This stalemate isn't going to get us anywhere. Kinda wish we had more varied infused foods right about now!* Even if we did, I was fairly sure they wouldn't have done much against the pure physical damage of the frond daggers. The frustration of the fight was already getting to me.

Every few seconds, even as Galloway continued to dodge Daniela's attacks, the Appendage sent a leaf blade at me. Testing. Some went high, others low, others purposefully aimed at my companions in a bid to distract me, but I knew they were safe at least for the moment. The closer I got, the more I was able to read through vibro. To my utter surprise, the entirety of Galloway's body was highlighted. Unlike regular humans, the Appendage was just a pulsing mass of *life*. And that life *pulsed* right before it released a frond to attack.

While my attempt to close the distance with the Appendage led to a number of minor scratches and a *very* sore arm, the advantage vibro gave me let me stay just ahead of Galloway. A small frown was marring the smooth golden features of the creature when a new message went wide through the comms.

"That Alan guy, the one from your Bunker, is here!" Clara half-panted, half-shouted.

I missed a step. Galloway capitalized. <Earth Shell> bloomed as I drowned it in empowering mana, but it wasn't enough. The frond hit me high in the chest and I was fairly sure I heard one of my ribs crack from the force that punched through my rock armor and actually managed to damage my Quake Osseum. If the follow up message hadn't come so soon after, I might have lost some of my drive in the fight. Just one hit had almost laid me out completely.

"Says some sort of ritual is done!?" Clara asked with more than a fair bit of confusion.

*He's... Oh crap!*

"Danny! Go get him!" I gurgled, dribbling blood. I ripped the frond out of my armored chest and ducked behind my tower shield as more daggers flew forward. My health flashed a warning at seventy-five percent, but I ignored it. This fight would be touch and go the whole time, the notifications would just distract me.

The scent of lavender flooded my nose and the pain in my chest lessened, sharpening my focus on the Appendage. *Thank you, Ophelia.* With that silent support, I felt some of my confidence return. Since it was already there, I smeared some of my Slurry Ichor on my chest, hardening in seconds, while patching my <Earth Shell>. *I have a sneaking suspicion I am going to need every bit of my mana.*

Galloway easily spotted Daniela turning to run, so I burned mana to create an <Earth Wall> to cover her back. Just in time, because the life Appendage didn't delay in sending a spray of leaf blades after her that fit snugly into my wall. The impact cracks of a half-dozen targeted leaf blades rendered it pretty much useless, but all that was left of Daniela was her wisp. Thankfully, it was still tossing fireballs at the Dreg creature. I didn't want to imagine what kind of pain Galloway would rain down while unimpeded.

"You cannot defeat a true Sullied, earth boy," Galloway said, the first hint of frustration leaking into his voice. "How would you expect to defeat the Aberrant?"

"Well, I have a plucky personality. Maybe that will do it?" I said, hoping to stall for time as the cocky Appendage drilled into me with its featureless eyes. Unfortunately, the stalling worked both ways, because the fronds were visibly regrowing on the creature's back.

— + —

"I'm sending speed your way!" Daniela shouted through the comm-plant. I didn't have time to process the nonsense coming from her before I ducked another attack from Galloway.

Another wave of lavender whiffed by my nose as a frond blade sliced my calf. It hadn't been but thirty seconds since Daniela had escaped, but her wisp was almost out of juice. Without it putting pressure on Galloway, the man's accuracy and speed of attack was forcing me on the backfoot. As I cast another <Earth Wall> to protect Ophelia from one of the Appendage's probing attacks, a gust of wind ruffled my hair. Danny's words clicked. *Devon.*

"What the hell do I do with this!?"his voice snapped through the comm-plant. In the elf's hand was an amalgamated contraption glowing with the internal iridescent light of a pure Metier Crystal. A band of metal encircled the whole thing, and I was fairly sure I spotted the strange glyphs that formed spell chains for skills. Perpendicular to the metal band was a halo of visible golden light.

>STOP HIM!<

The Dreg Entity's immediate hiss seemed to snap everyone from the surprised pause following Devon's arrival. Galloway moved directly, physically, to intercept. Thankfully, vibro had lit up like a candle as the Appendage stomped his foot in the elf's direction. A half-dozen half-powered <Mineral Strikes> streaked to the space between Devon and Galloway. It was a costly attack, but worth every bit of mana. The Appendage backpedaled to redirect his approach, and I watched Devon dodge with practiced ease. It wasn't the first time the elf had seen my skill, but it *was* Galloway's. Unfortunately, the small bits of aquamarine and malachite that pelted the Appendage weren't enough to dissuade it from still chasing Devon.

"Put it on the Dreg rock!" I shouted, gritting my teeth for the next part of the fight. I tapped the comm-plant, sending a message to Ophelia directly. "This is going to hurt!"

For the first time in the fight, Galloway jumped back in surprise. I'd charged at it, shield leading the way, in the wake of my <Mineral Strikes>. Each step I focused *behind* the Appendage, putting spurts of <Earthen Barriers> and <Stone Spikes> as low-powered as I could, staying just above five percent mana in my pool. The pain in my abdomen was climbing steadily, but I caught sight of a gray blur practically walking on the cavern's ceiling. I wasn't the only one to notice.

"Insolent fo—" Galloway didn't get to finish because I'd started channeling the last bit of my mana into the spider naginata. My body practically *breathed* in the speed as I closed in on the Appendage with a sweeping slash of the weapon. The blade just nicked the creature, but I watched as its eyes widened in surprise. First blood. *Well, on our side. I've been bleeding since the beginning...*

I knew the simple attack wouldn't be enough to keep the Appendage engaged, so I continued to flow into a series of blows fueled by my three extra levels in mobility. The attribute boost did wonders for my balance, even with vibro going at full blast, but I knew I was on a timer; my body didn't regenerate mana fast enough to keep the item fueled indefinitely. But Galloway didn't know that, and I certainly wasn't going to tell him.

When he saw the attacks weren't stopping, and I was just fast enough to deflect his thrown fronds, he switched up the tactic on me. The Dreg creature charged *me* instead. Our collision left me reeling, showcasing that the Appendage had a higher strength than me. Not surprising, considering the two level lead it had on me, but what it did next was what really complicated things. The fronds on its back snapped forward like hungry snakes.

I whirled my naginata to deflect the first, but its other one slashed down onto my helm. The force sent my brain scrambling as the vibro went wild, but I managed to keep my feet. A healing wash from Ophelia reached me and I swallowed the bile rising in my throat. The creature and I exchanged blows faster and faster, pitting my marginally superior mobility against its overwhelming strength and flexible natural weapons. Each impact, slash, and punch I caught on my shield washed us in heat, but Galloway didn't seem to care. Madness burned in its eyes as I continued to land small blows that spilled its golden sap blood all around us, mixing it with my Slurry Ichor.

The only thing keeping me standing was the steady stream of healing from Ophelia. Unfortunately, we only had so much mana between the two of us. The moment my channeling on the naginata sputtered, wounds started to pile up. My <Earth Shell> started to crumble as more and more impacts cracked the defensive layer. When Ophelia yelped, I sensed her fall to the ground through vibro and the healing stream stopped abruptly.

"You. Cannot. Win!" Galloway spat in my face as one of its fronds took me high in the shoulder. The bladed leaves easily punched through my Limestone Skin, coming out the other side. Not bothering to stop its charge, Galloway slammed me right into the closest wall, digging the fronds deeper into my shoulder. My shield arm went limp.

"Ronan! This... the display says there isn't sufficient Pith!" Devon air-whispered to me. The elf was holding the glowing contraption against the Dreg Entity, but bands of black smog lashed out against him. Already, I could see mounting wounds on his body as he used his free hand to spark <Lightning Strike>, barely keeping his hold on Alan's tech. His breath came in ragged through the whisper, marking his own rapidly declining mana pool.

"I heard that!" Galloway said, smiling cruelly. Its needle teeth stretched unnaturally wide on its face. An overwhelming scent of vanilla assaulted my nose as he spoke. "Your meager strength is insufficient! I've had about enough of you *pests.*"

Something in its words tickled my pain-addled brain. Something that would cause me even more pain. *But... if it lets us live, what does it matter?* Life *is all about pain.*

I dug deep. I zeroed in on the memory of my fight with the spider that had been turned into the very weapon I held in my hand. I overdrew my mana. An empowered <Mineral Strike>

hit Galloway point blank. The explosion peppered me with shards of cinnabar, but it did a much bigger number on the life-attuned ex-human. Furrows had been carved in its chest as it stumbled back several feet, removing the fronds pinning me to the wall.

*Twenty feet.* Vibro practically screamed the information, the spacing and trajectory of the Appendage, even as I felt my body start to harden from the influx of Dreg. Refusing to let it end at just that, I tapped into the tower shield. My tendons screeched in protest and I could practically hear the hairline fractures blooming on my Quake Osseum, but my body held for the scant few seconds I needed it.

There were multiple factors that led to *speed*. While the mobility attribute determined how fast your body could move, it was still hard capped by how much force you could exert on the world. Being able to jump ten feet in the air was different from being able to jump five, twice, in the same span of time. At that moment, what I needed wasn't dexterity. It was burst power.

Like a rusted engine, my legs protested the motion, but the four extra Quotients worth of strength was enough to push me straight into a football tackle. Even as Galloway's feet left the floor, its frond wings snapped forward to stab me in the back. I didn't try to avoid them more than taking the frantic blows on my crumbling <Earth Shell>. The distance was eaten up so quickly I actually crushed Galloway against the larger Metier Crystal, stealing its breath long enough for me to disengage.

But then that was all, a sickening pop announced when my knees fell out of place and I crashed to the ground. Every muscle fiber felt on the cusp of snapping, so all I could do was twitch on the ground as Galloway gathered itself. Its face truly twisted, furrows forming on its bald head and a primal hiss exited its mouth. Until one of the wildly flaying bands of death coming from the Dreg Entity cut a groove into its side. The Appendage yowled and turned towards the source of the offense only to see the chaotic bands floating all around it.

Even as my shoulder muscles tore in half, I dug one last

action from my overdrawn mana and wrecked body. I lobbed my naginata like the worst javelin known to humanity pre *and* post end of the world.

Thankfully, I had a nudge of help. Even as Devon took a skin blistering death band that scalped him, lightning-infused gusts sucked up the naginata and plowed it into Galloway's torso. The spider limb wasn't able to pierce the Metier Crystal, but it did send the Appendage back towards the Dreg Entity.

The momentum of my throw, plus the lightning, plus the wind made any attempt to protect itself against the death bands worthless. The smog sizzled as it tried to cleave through Galloway's limbs and its prodigious regenerative capabilities fought back. It was hard for my mind to wrap around the inhuman screams that followed.

>Inept! Exit the area of influence before—<

The Dreg Entity didn't get to finish before the strange contraption let out a gong of power. The halo of light expanded until it enclosed the Appendage, then the crystal contraption started to swell, hiding the metal band from sight. The bits of healing that Galloway had been using to combat the death bands seemed to disappear, getting absorbed by the ring and then the Crystal. Galloway's scream of pain jumped from preternatural agony to a silent thing that contorted its features even more. For good measure, Devon slapped his palm onto the Appendage's skull.

"<Lightning Strike>!"

The sparks caused the Appendage to spasm and then start to dissociate right in front of us. Pith swirled like a small typhoon, most of the flakes funneling into the growing crystal, but the others loomed ominously around the ceiling of the cavern. It was the single largest cloud of Pith I'd seen, even when harvesting all the creatures after our skirmish with Kirby. When the Pith quivered in the air and the halo of golden light winked out, I turned to see the contraption expand to encase the Dreg Entity like a cancerous growth.

>The Aberrant will rule your world, fleshbag! You cannot withstand the will of Absco—<

The Dreg Entity's ranting winked out. Silence hung in the air for a full second before a familiar tingling rippled over my skin. An expanding area of influence. Considering, *hopefully*, that the Dreg Entity was neutralized by the still growing mass of Alan's contraption, the only source was the giant Metier Crystal that made up the entire back wall of the cavern. As if it was reading my thoughts, the crystal wall glimmered and *flowed* to encase the walls of the cavern just as they started to crumble.

As the giant Entity moved to protect us from the cave in, the floating Pith finally decided what it wanted to do with its life. Most relevant, it branched five ways and one of those struck me right in the chest. Every single one of my injuries reasserted itself before my eyes rolled up into the back of my head and consciousness was washed away in a torrent of burning, cool energy.

# EPILOGUE

## TWO WEEKS LATER

The incessant blinking in my eye snapped me out of sleep. Considering it was the first time it had happened, I immediately jumped to alert, scanning the empty room around me. My eyes pierced only partly through the fog of sleep and darkness, but vibro called out every piece of furniture in painstaking detail. The intensity brought out the headaches I thought I'd gotten rid of from the early days of my vibrosense. When I finally confirmed that there wasn't anything actively trying to murder me, my eyes unfocused to look at the notification that had manifested in my vision.

—Need to speak.—

It was bolded and in red font. Considering how far out of range I was to Bec, the only Entity responsible could be Tec. Groaning all the while, I stretched out my body. A lingering stiffness had plagued me ever since that fight with Galloway. It wasn't surprising, but even the intervention of Gec hadn't been enough to deal with *all* of my overdrawn mana.

*I have nothing to complain about. Everyone had it a lot harder.* The grim thought crossed my mind as I strode out of the training building. I considered taking my gear, but the spider naginata was just a charred piece of history now and I doubted anyone was going to attack me in the middle of the night. It wouldn't end well for them.

My steps were slow and steady as I did my best to keep the ripples from vibro contained. I could sense a few people stirring in their homes as I passed them, and I even sensed someone training in the open yard down the road from the dojo we stayed at, but no one stumbled into me.

Before I knew it, I had crossed the town square where the crafting areas had once been and then past the few surviving brick and mortar structures that served the leadership of Wildwood. All but one window was dark, but it didn't surprise me that Irwin was up counting money. The trade between the towns had boomed after the Dreg Entity had been neutralized and the remaining Tendrils scattered.

Like pushing into an invisible bubble with my whole body, I entered the Blessing of Magic that clung tight to Tec. Even after months exposed to the magic wisps of energy that radiated from everything, it still gave me pause. Unfortunately, the Entity Cluster didn't like delays on its house calls because a crystal tentacle snapped me up the moment I was in range. The world became a swirl of colors as Tec pulled me into its body and subsequently into its whitespace.

—Greetings, Dreg Warrior Leader Ronan.—

"We really need to make away with the title stuff." I sighed.

—Current population suggests there is a positive reception to the usage of titles to place stand-out individuals within a hierarchy easily understood by the layman.—

"Right. We can deal with *all that* some other time. Why did you call me up, Tec?" The thing I really appreciated about Tec and its fragmented progeny, Wec, was their ability to cut through social niceties. Sometimes aggravating, but when one wasn't in the mood, it was appreciated.

—Humanity traitor Kirby has requested your presence.—

"You woke me up… in the middle of the night… so I could talk to Kirby," I said slowly, almost doubting what I'd heard.

—Affirmative.—

"You know what," I said, throwing my hands up in the air. "Sure. Why the hell not? It's not like I have anything better to do."

—Wonderful.—

"I was being sarcastic, Tec," I replied flatly. "*Why* does he want to talk to me, and why *now*?"

The Entity hesitated for several seconds before it spoke again in its monotone drone. —He has been requesting an audience since your success against the Dreg-affiliated Entity Cluster.—

"Two weeks. Two weeks, and you tell me now in the middle of the night!" I said, unable to keep the irritation out of my voice.

—I believe he will… expire. Soon.—

"E-expire?" *That's not a good word to use to describe a person.* Tec didn't elaborate, so I rubbed my temples and agreed for real to the meeting. There had to be a reason. As much of a narcissistic, marginally sociopathic, and selfish person as I thought Kirby was, he didn't strike me as the type to be superfluous and call me out to his… death bed… for no reason.

The world swirled again and I found myself in a short hallway made of Metier Crystal. The slight pressure, or closeness, I'd come to associate with the whitespace was nowhere to be found. I was physically present in the jail cells Tec had formed to hold the traitors of Wildwood. A pulse of light flowed along the ground like a golden trail from a video game, guiding me straight and to the left. As I followed Tec's direction, I passed by the squad that had been complicit in Kirby's scheme. None of them looked to be doing well, even if I knew that Dylan and Irwin had been interacting with them almost daily for their meals.

I didn't give their glassy-eyed looks much more than a glance, instead focusing on following the golden path and entering a doorway that formed out of the crystal. Shackled to the wall was a sack of skin and scales that approximated who Kirby had been. All but the last wisps of the man's hair remained even as his face was framed by more wrinkles than even Elias before becoming attuned.

"Marvelous. Marvelous. They weren't lying. Not lying," Kirby stammered as his eyes wavered until they landed on me. The shackles flowed down from where they were holding the man up and let him sag down low without their support. His bare feet attempted to find purchase on the crystal, but after the first attempt failed, he just gave up and laid half-propped on the walls of the crystal cell.

"Kirby… what is going on?" I couldn't necessarily say I felt bad for what he was going through, but it was still shaking something in me to see a person reduced to such a clobbered mess.

"Perhaps I should have heeded his veiled warnings…" Kirby started, staring through me. "All those unwilling meetings in the dark. He knew it, but I thought it was a trap. I was so blinded I couldn't even see the poison I was drinking with my own two hands."

"Who is 'he'? What poison are you talking about?" I said, taking a step forward and drawing his eyes once more. My muscles were tight and it had nothing to do with the backlash from overdrawing my mana.

"What poison? You know damn well what poison!" Kirby snapped. His teeth snapped at me, but his feeble frame barely lifted a couple of inches before he slumped even lower. "The Dreg, you fool. It sustained us, gave us the edge that we needed. Without it… we are just husks of what we once were."

"That makes no sense," I said, shaking my head. Dreg came from Pith. How could they be poisoned to this degree without being afflicted? My thoughts went to the other men in the cells, each showing some lesser version of what was happening to Kirby. "What am I missing, Kirby? Tell me!"

"Your little 'status'… Your advantage… It is not original.

The Aberrant laid claim to that when they started meddling. Meddling, yes. That's what you could call it…" Kirby trailed off, but some of the intensity of his past returned.

With a surprised tug of his arm, his wrist let out a definite crack and the limb came free. Snakes of crystal sprouted from the ground, binding the man's limp arm as it attempted to grab at my collar. I hadn't realized I'd been crouched, moving closer and closer. I'd seen the move coming from a mile away, and I doubted Kirby would be able to injure me in this state, but the sheer madness in his eyes was what caused me to freeze.

*The status existed before? The Aberrant had access to something like it? Was it feeding levels to people using Dreg somehow? Is that why Kirby and the others…?*

"I see the gears turning," Kirby sputtered. "Perhaps… you can still correct my mistakes. Seek the Sand Courier where the Dreg is strong and the humans are stronger. Look for him beyond the influence of the crystals, where their gaze doesn't pierce and their grasp is weak. Shine above others and he will seek *you*."

As he said this, Kirby's scales rippled before falling to the ground with quiet tinks. Each let out a tiny ripple under the gaze of vibro. When the last fell, so too did the man. His last breath fogged the crystal at my feet.

# ABOUT FRANK G. ALBELO

Frank is a Civil Engineer graduate who rediscovered his passion for writing. The twenty-something year old is happily married and has a toddler who is a cute, but huge, troublemaker. Originally born in Cuba, Frank moved to Costa Rica at a young age and then to Miami, Florida giving him a wonderfully diverse view of the world to draw on for the worlds he creates.

He has been writing stories since he was young and reading them way before that. He hopes to continue to write tales and create wondrous systems to share them with readers. Some of Frank's other hobbies include Magic the Gathering, video gaming, and bugging his wife about buying new bookshelves to accommodate the books that seem to magically appear in their home.

Connect with Frank G. Albelo:
Patreon.com/Falbelo
Facebook.com/FAlbeloWriter
Discord.gg/A6srSxk

# ABOUT MOUNTAINDALE PRESS

Dakota and Danielle Krout, a husband and wife team, strive to create as well as publish excellent fantasy and science fiction novels. Self-publishing *The Divine Dungeon: Dungeon Born* in 2016 transformed their careers from Dakota's military and programming background and Danielle's Ph.D. in pharmacology to President and CEO, respectively, of a small press. Their goal is to share their success with other authors and provide captivating fiction to readers with the purpose of solidifying Mountaindale Press as the place 'Where Fantasy Transforms Reality.'

Connect with Mountaindale Press:
MountaindalePress.com
Facebook.com/MountaindalePress
Twitter.com/_Mountaindale
Instagram.com/MountaindalePress

# MOUNTAINDALE PRESS TITLES

## GameLit and LitRPG

The Completionist Chronicles,
The Divine Dungeon,
Full Murderhobo, and
Year of the Sword by Dakota Krout

Metier Apocalypse by Frank G. Albelo

Arcana Unlocked by Gregory Blackburn

A Touch of Power by Jay Boyce

Red Mage and
Farming Livia by Xander Boyce

Space Seasons by Dawn Chapman

Ether Collapse and
Ether Flows by Ryan DeBruyn

Dr. Druid by Maxwell Farmer

Bloodgames by Christian J. Gilliland

Unbound by Nicoli Gonnella

Threads of Fate by Michael Head

Lion's Lineage by Rohan Hublikar and Dakota Krout

Wolfman Warlock by James Hunter and Dakota Krout

Axe Druid,
Mephisto's Magic Online, and
High Table Hijinks by Christopher Johns

Skeleton in Space by Andries Louws

Dragon Core Chronicles by Lars Machmüller

Chronicles of Ethan by John L. Monk

Pixel Dust and
Necrotic Apocalypse by David Petrie

Viceroy's Pride by Cale Plamann

Henchman by Carl Stubblefield

Artorian's Archives by Dennis Vanderkerken and Dakota Krout

Vaudevillain by Alex Wolf

www.ingramcontent.com/pod-product-compliance
Lightning Source LLC
Chambersburg PA
CBHW051512250626
47156CB00001B/63